Mia Emilie

UNHISTORIC ACTS

Book 2 The Watchers Trilogy

with best wishes Mia Emilie

Excerpt from *Middlemarch – out of copyright, and used with grateful acknowledgement to George Eliot.*

ISBN: 978-1-9161399-1-6

Book design: The Art of Communication book-design.co.uk

Images: Shutterstock

DEDICATION

In loving memory of my best friend,
protector and adventure buddy.

Orsen

Forever running free.
Never forgotten. Always missed.

"For the growing good of the world
is partly dependent on unhistoric acts;
and that things are not so ill with you
and me as they might have been,
is half owing to the number who lived
faithfully a hidden life,
and rest in unvisited tombs."

George Eliot, *Middlemarch*, 1871

PROLOGUE

Edinburgh, November 1839

In his study, Doctor Gordon McCraken woke with a start, instantly alert and listening. On hearing nothing, he yawned and stretched. Smiling, he pulled a large leather tome across his desk, thinking of Amy Dudley and his plans for her.

Soon, I'll have everything.

Still smiling, he slipped the book into a drawer and locked it away. From the hallway the clock struck midnight and he hoped his wife, restless in her final months of pregnancy, was finally asleep. Putting the desk key in his pocket, he rose, thinking of his bed. Climbing the stairs, he noted the butler tray attached to the bannister still held his wife's empty plate, knife and fork. He frowned, pondering Iona's appetite that rose and fell to no pattern. He paused, hearing a scrabbling noise.

Rats, in the walls?

A woman's scream, high and terrified, ripped through the house and he raced up the final stairs. Pounding along the landing it came again, shatteringly close, and he threw open the bathroom door. The stench of blood smacked him.

'Iona? Iona!'

His wife was naked, on all fours, pregnant belly purpled and white. She convulsed and more blood spilled down her thighs. She screamed again, deafeningly loud in the tiled room.

'Help me,' she wailed.

Gordon raced out again, cursing at his medical bag downstairs. Instead he grabbed the knife from the tray and rushed back. His wife was panting, groaning and pawing at her distended belly. He fell to his knees next to her.

'Iona, please! I must cut you, carefully.' He wiped the knife, trying to see through the blood. 'Please, we have to.'

'Get it *out*!'

More blood and shit gushed out. Gordon tried to stem the flow, but his knife, hands and arms were instantly rinsed with clots. Abruptly Iona vomited and collapsed, head smacking the tiles. He cried out, dropping the knife, and turned her over, cradling his wife.

'Iona, Iona?' he sobbed.

But her dark blue eyes, like cornflowers and twilight, were blank. Their baby silently slipped from her, adding a bloody river to the already pooled floor. Gordon howled, clutching at skin and hair. He heard a splintering, and not recognising smashing wood, gripped Iona, scared she had broken in half. Sudden shouting and footsteps thundered up the stairs, but he was barely aware of the men grabbing him and one crying out:

'Mercy me, they're deid! He's murdered his wife and bairn!'

PART ONE

CHAPTER ONE

Edinburgh Prison, January 1840

Gordon broached consciousness with lungs afire and chest like stone. His thoughts were tissued and tatty, like so much flotsam.

Shite! I should be deid.

Then, like a bubble bursting, sound splattered him. Moans, metal on metal, and sudden steps came closer and then worse: voices.

'This is Gordon McCraken, Doctor.'

'Christ fend us, nurse! I know who he is. Proceed.'

'Aye, Doctor. Tuesday last the prisoner refused all food and water. During the night he stripped to his skin and, standing on his bed, reached the bars of his cell. He stood there, in the freezing weather, naked as the day he was born.'

'Mercy me, did no one attend the man?'

'They discovered him on the midnight rounds, but he refused any who spoke to him.' She sounded defensive. 'They tried to talk him into coming away, but he wouldnae listen. He had to be prised from the bars, then he collapsed and was carried here.'

'Damn eejit, what could've possessed him?'

'He wanted to sicken to death, he said as much.'

Paper rustled and the doctor stepped closer. He must have bent as the man's breath was suddenly warm and smokey on Gordon's face.

'Puir fellow, such a waste,' he muttered and moved away. 'Well, small mercy as it is, we'll no add to the man's arrest charge by recording his effort at suicide. Better enter mad, there's no law against that as yet, and daft in the heid he must've been.'

The rest of their conversation receded as Gordon fled to blackness. Iona's voice echoed in his head, cutting through his darkness.

Gordon, just pretend to be deid, then m'be they'll string you up quicker. Or just bury you, alive. Either would serve.

He silently agreed, but his lungs crackled, and a groan scraped his throat, forcing his eyes open.

'You're awake,' a nurse said.

He started when she touched his forehead, sleeve brushing his arm. Pain bloomed everywhere and a cough splintered out. Gordon gasped and sucked down water the nurse presented.

'Where?' he managed.

'Prison hospital.' She pursed her lips. 'You surely should be deid by now.'

He nodded, pleased to have been right. The nurse smoothed her apron and its white hurt his eyes.

'But the pneumonia has broken,' she continued, 'and our doctor thinks you'll recover, maybe enough for your trial. Set for two weeks' time, I hear?'

He hated them then, for saving him, the doctor he once knew and the kind nurse. She moved away and yet he remained still, desperate to return to the senseless pit he had been in. Memories rose, making his jaw clench. He welcomed the pain, trying to sink away into it, but it wasn't the same and his senses remained clear. He lived in a tiled darkness awash with Iona's blood, until mercifully exhaustion and pain took him.

When next Gordon opened his eyes, gaslight picked out faces and stone walls. Everything smelt worse, tainted by opium and gas. His ward mate's snores and breaths were too close, too warm. He rubbed his face, feeling his tangled beard and slack skin. Coughing, hurting, he fumbled for water, trembling elbows barely holding him up.

It didnae work. I'm still alive.

AYE, IT SEEMS YOU CAN NO OUTWIT GOD WITH ILLNESS AS SELF-SLAUGHTER. SUICIDE IS ALL THE SAME IN HIS EYES.

Iona's voice was matter of fact and filled with certainty. He drank the water and managed to refill his cup from the jug. He sat back, propped up on the pillows, and listened to his breaths; gauging the weight of his bones and limbs against all his agony. He wondered how he could have failed to die from the pneumonia. The suffering it had taken to contract seemed little more than a nuisance now the illness had been robbed of its purpose. Gordon groaned, abruptly understanding. Despite having lost God, he was unable to take his own life with more direct means, such as knife or gun, for fear of the consequences.

It seems I've no choice but to recover, so the hangman can finish me. It'll be a quicker, more merciful death than I'd planned.

BEGGARS CAN NO BE CHOOSERS.

Gordon nodded and drained the cup. He slid down, covering his chest, and did his best to sleep.

From then on Gordon's mind flailed. Every night he struggled to save Iona and their child, thrashing in blood. Daily his soul would be afire. He would silently scream, cursing the hospital, prisoners, staff; willing them to burn to ash from his pain. Then he would shake and tip to blackness. His whole being becoming a stale void that sucked in every word or gesture making those around him mere shades, silently mouthing. He barely noticed being fed and watered, medicated and exercised. His once wide frame diminished, skin turning grey with the fragility of old newspaper. Although six foot tall, he seemed to shrink inside himself while his fox-red beard and hair became patchy and silvered. Reeling from mute agony to exhaustion, he would drop to sleep. Floundering in bloodied nightmares, he would wake to his burning soul.

Then after two weeks Gordon could stand and move about unaided, and was thus deemed well enough for trial. He scarcely noticed the proceedings, shutting out the public gallery. He tried not to taste the sweat and perfume of so many, tinged with the chamber's leather and old wood. Black-coated lawyers spoke in dull tones and were harder to ignore. He closed his eyes and focused on his impending death, engineering a serenity about being with Iona once more. Abruptly a man's voice cut through his calm, sparking recognition and flicking his eyes open. His neighbour, Malcolm Blair, finished taking the oath and settled on the stand. A lawyer stood.

'Mister Blair, you found Missus McCraken and the defendant. Please tell us what happened that night.'

Malcolm nodded, his face set in serious lines.

'I was passing Doctor McCraken's house, on the way to my own, you ken? I'd been to a wee gathering for my nephew.' He glanced at Gordon, then away. 'Well now, I heard the screaming and it fair tore my heart out. So I banged on the door, and it wasnae but a moment before there were two or three of us a-hollering and banging.

But it did no good and the screaming got worse. Afearin' something frightful, we broke in the door and ran up the stairs.' He shook his head. 'We found them in the bathroom and a more horrid sight I've never seen.'

'Mister Blair, can you explain what you saw on reaching the McCrakens' bathroom?'

Malcolm took a deep breath, his ruddy face greying.

'Missus McCraken was awash in blood, I never thought a body could hold so much. There was a bairn,' his voice cracked, 'a bairn deid on the floor. Doctor McCraken was covered in blood, clinging to his wife and howling fit to crack ma skull, wi a knife there at his side. For the longest time he would no leave off her, though we tried. He kept shaking the puir woman and calling her name.' Malcolm's breaths were loud in the hushed courtroom. 'All the while Doctor McCraken looked wild and queer, saying over and over how it was his fault she wouldnae wake. Then the constables came.'

Gordon bowed his head, tears falling to his hands. He retreated inside his skin, listening only to his heartbeat, wishing it would falter and stop. The courtroom faded until he dwelt only in black numbness. He managed it so well that it came as a surprise when he was asked to stand for the verdict. He got to his feet, blinking as if seeing the courtroom for the first time and stood, head down, to hear his fate.

I'll be with you soon, my love.

Gordon pressed his palms to his eyes, seeking to stem relieved tears.

'Not proven,' came the announcement. 'Therefore, the accused is acquitted.'

Gordon staggered as the judgment registered. Time stopped. His guts heaved, bile souring his mouth. The sound of the gavel seemed to vibrate through him. Someone was shaking his hand; Gordon stared, belatedly recognising his lawyer. The man's long face was alight with pleasure. He was curiously shaped with a chest that ran into his stomach, so his body resembled half a pear.

'Congratulations, Doctor McCraken, you're a free man.'

Gordon looked away, his hand falling limply from the other's grip. The courtroom was emptying. The jury leaving and Iona's parents pushed past him. His mother-in-law's eyes were tear bright and his father-in-law held her arm, leading his wife out, both looked as if exhaustion held them upright. Neither met his gaze. Gordon felt newly raw, and looked to his lawyer; *McDougall?*

'Acquitted, how?' Gordon asked.

Beneath his moustache McDougall looked confused and slightly hurt, tweaking his glasses with a habitual movement.

'The jury, quite rightly, found nothing factual to prove you a murderer, Doctor McCraken. You're free to go.'

Go where? Home?

Gordon imagined the grey house on Heriot Row, and suddenly laughed, tasting it as bitter as it sounded. McDougall's shocked expression stoppered his noise. Gordon abruptly sat, fingernails digging through his beard to his chin.

'I killed them,' he said. 'I should be hanged for it.'

The lawyer sighed.

'We've been through this.' McDougall's voice was quiet, even sympathetic, making Gordon despise him. 'Their deaths were no your fault, anyone with sense sees that. Why else would your sister-in-law hire me? Missus McCraken died so unexpectedly and the child she carried had no chance of survival. The jury had the wit to recognise the accusation of murder to be naught but hearsay from the neighbours who found you and your wife.'

The lawyer's hand warmed his shoulder and Gordon resisted the urge to jerk away. Iona's voice was soft, but implacable.

The lawyer's wrong, naturally. It is your fault.

You could've saved us.

I ken that. I'm sorry.

That's no enough. Make amends. Try again.

He groaned, uncaring it was out loud.

Dinnae ask me that, Iona. Suicide would mean I never see you again.

Face it, you're a coward, Gordon McCraken.

Filthy murderer.

He stood, suddenly, recoiling from McDougall's hand, and stumbled outside to find a grey sky capping Parliament Square. Before him was a crowd of reporters. In every hand a notebook waved and the storm of questions echoed off the buildings. At the centre, Iona's parents clutched each other. His father-in-law looked bewildered and held his wife close, her face buried in his coat. Gordon stepped back, hiding in the shadows. He moved from shade to shade, away from the crowd, and headed for High Street. In the grey light the reporters grew dark in his gaze. The bustle of High Street drew him like lodestone.

'McCraken!'

The call came from ahead. Gordon leapt away, across the square, without seeing who it was. Every breath hurt and he knew his ill body stood no chance of a sustained getaway. He cleaved to the next building, grateful of its shadowy renovations, and staggered inside. He hid in a stone arch, struggling to hear over his own breaths. There were no following footsteps or voices. Gordon leant back, letting the cool stone ease his head. Staring up he flinched at the glory of St Giles cathedral towering all around him.

The vengeful Lord, his angels and saints, picked out in coloured glass, peered and pointed at him. Gordon moaned and bent forward, unable to bear their scrutiny. He shut them out with hands over ears and eyes screwed tight; but still they thundered in his body and soul.

'My son, are you unwell?'

The voice broke through the riot and Gordon managed to look. A white-haired priest stood before him, cassock midnight and dusty against the stonework. Gordon sagged against the arch.

'I'm sickened to my very soul, Father.'

'Well, staying there won't cure a thing. I'm Father John, come bide with me a wee while, there's a brew in the presbytery I'm willing to share.'

The kindness pierced something in Gordon. As if in a dream he averted his gaze from the accusing angels and stumbled after the priest.

Chapter Two

In the presbytery Gordon retreated to a fireside chair and rested his chin to his chest, his head too heavy a burden. He roused enough to take the offered cup, wondering at such old man's hands before realising they were his own. He tried to concentrate on what the priest was saying.

'It's an odd day for an outing with such thin attire, Doctor. You'll catch your death.'

Gordon frowned and looked down at his shirt.

Did I have a coat earlier?

He looked at Father John, thinking to explain, but couldn't find words that made sense.

'It disnae matter,' he muttered.

'Your attire or your death?'

Gordon shrugged, wishing he hadn't come, and tried to find somewhere to put the cup and saucer. John lifted a pot and filled Gordon's cup with sweet-scented tea. Saliva sprang warm and sickening on his tongue and he sipped, letting the liquid scald while he stared at the priest. John's slender face was restful and easy to see in the room's light.

'Doctor, are you warm enough?' John asked.

'How do you ken I'm a doctor?'

'You treated my sister for a broken wrist, two years gone. Without you she would've lost her hand to a claw.'

Pressure throbbed behind Gordon's eyes.

'I killed my wife.'

John's calm expression didn't change. He sipped some tea before answering.

'I heard some reporters say you were acquitted today.'

Gordon shook his aching head, hurting his teeth. The sense of unreality returned and with it an urgency to be somewhere else, somewhere safe. Panic welled.

But I've nowhere safe to stand.

John was speaking again, and Gordon struggled to listen.

'You should no blame yourself for what happened, my son. It was God's will.'

So much blood.

MY BLOOD. YOUR CHILD'S BLOOD.

'Father, please stop. I've naught left, no even faith.'

Abruptly the weight of divine abandonment was too much and he shook with sobs. John took his cup and saucer, stemming the spillage. Gordon's chest hurt like ripped meat and he fought to regain control. Finally, his heaving lessened.

'You've been ill in spirit and body,' the priest said. 'So I see your faith has been tested. But there's always a way back. Absolution may be a divine right, but I think if you tried to forgive yourself, it would be a beginning. Is there no way you can manage that, Doctor?'

Gordon hiccupped snot and took the extended handkerchief. Wiping his face and blowing his nose, he stared at John. The man's kind expression never altered and for a moment Gordon let himself believe he might find salvation.

'How?'

John proffered the refilled cup, smiling when Gordon took it.

'Each man must find his own way,' the priest said. 'I believe that utterly. I feel if you look deep inside, you'll discover a strength of purpose and the path to forgiveness.'

The cup shook at Gordon's lip, but he managed a sip. The sliding warmth eased his chest and tiredness dragged at his bones, urging him to curl up and sleep.

Dream of blood.

So. Much. Blood. It wasnae God's will, but yours.

There came a knock at the door. Gordon's cup slid about its saucer. He stared as the opening provided another priest, who slipped in and spoke quietly in John's ear before exiting. The door opened wider and a man in a top hat and emerald green frock coat and trousers stood on the threshold. His arms were full of a coat and hat.

'There you are,' he said. 'I've been looking everywhere for you. I'm sorry, Father, I'm Iain McDougall, Gordon's lawyer. Come on, Gordon, I've a cab waiting to take you home.'

McDougall, that's right.

John stood, smiling and introducing himself. Gordon rose and let himself be bundled into coat and hat. Abruptly they were outside the cathedral, on High Street, the rain unpleasant on his face. He stood by the cab watching the horse fidget against its shafts. Warm skin on skin made Gordon start and he found John's hand shaking his and didn't hate it.

'Come back whenever you've a mind, Doctor. There's always tea brewing and a warm chair.'

Gordon's lips felt tight with an unused smile. He managed a nod before climbing into the hansom cab, feeling it sway; bringing bile to his throat as he sat. McDougall darkened the door and settled next to him. The driver gave cry to his horse and they lurched into the Edinburgh traffic while Gordon hunched in the dark interior, terrified of going home.

CHAPTER THREE

On the edge of Edinburgh's New Town, the hansom cab halted in front of Heriot Row. Gordon alighted when told to and stood next to McDougall, blinking in the light. He became aware of the lawyer's inertia and with an effort followed the man's gaze. A large cart, pulled by two huge horses, stood tethered near his newly installed, and strangely open, front door. A knot of neighbours and bystanders were gathered at a respectful distance, watching the house and chattering like magpies.

'What new torment is this?' Gordon murmured.

By unspoken agreement the two men walked toward the house. The small crowd grew quiet, watching them. McDougall, a little ahead, frowned at the cart, peering as if seeking an owner's sign. Gordon eyed the horses.

'Samson, Goliath?'

The horse's heads turned at the sound of Gordon's voice. On reaching them he stroked their noses and let soft, equine lips nudge his coat pockets. He moved past and into his house, McDougall in his wake. With each footstep, heat flushed through Gordon; it grew harder and hotter, burning like fire in his blood. His weakened state slid from him like water off glass and a force built under his skin, straining his ribs. Inside, the doors to the study and drawing room were shut and silent. He moved on, abruptly stopping at the bottom of the stairs, and clenched the newel post, legs unable to move upward. Shaking from memories, he was relieved when only silence resounded from above. A sudden noise came along the hall, from the dining room. Gordon reached the door and shoved it open.

A bull-like man in his late fifties turned from inspecting the dining table. He had a long, black beard with two grey streaks running down that gleamed like old pewter. Standing square, the man stared challengingly with deep-set eyes that were seemingly black. But Gordon knew them to be the dark brown of otter pelt, a mirror of his own.

'What the fuck are you doing here?'

'Such low cursin', boy!' The man chuckled. 'They should hang you for that, along with the murdering of wife and bairn. Justice in this country is a shambles.'

Gordon desperately wanted to lie down, just fall to the floor, but knew any weakness would be pounced upon. He gripped the door frame, letting it and his anger hold him upright.

'Get out of my house.'

The man's eyes narrowed, and he covered the distance between them, halting inches away.

'Aye well,' he drawled. 'It seems I'm m'be a touch untimely, but seeing as I'm here an all, why no be a good wee fellow and let me take what I want?'

Gordon could find no words, anger tightening his throat. Suddenly McDougall stepped forward, his bulbous stomach almost touching the newcomer.

'It *seems* that you've broken into my client's house, Mister…?'

'McCraken. Angus McCraken. And it's no breaking when you've a key.'

The lawyer looked sharply at Gordon, who managed a nod.

'Mister McDougall, meet my father. Who seems to have a stolen key to my house.' He looked at Angus. 'Now, get out, before I send for the constables.'

His father laughed and shook his head.

'Och, on your way then, laddie, for I'm certain those in charge of the law will be happy to rush to your aid.'

Gordon's gaze blurred and he struggled to breathe.

'Gordon?'

He turned to see a willowy woman whose sharp green gaze matched her tone. His mother's long red hair was shot through with silvery thread and tied simply at the nape of her neck. She held his large leather book and a covered wicker cage whose inhabitant cawed softly.

'What the hell do you think you're doing?' Gordon demanded. 'Put those down and dinnae touch them again.'

His mother sniffed but complied, placing the items on the floor; she never took her eyes from Gordon.

'We thought you'd be elsewhere, son,' she said.

Gordon fought to control his temper and stepped away, so his back rested on the door frame; he kept both his parents in sight. Footsteps approached and a black-haired man in his twenties emerged from the depths of the house, slight frame much like his mother's. He carried what Gordon recognised as bed linen.

'Da, I wondered if we could pad the furniture with these.' Seeing Gordon he stopped, his expression turning sullen. 'Oh, how are *you* here?'

Gordon stared at his younger brother and then rounded on his father.

'You brought Fergus as well?'

His father looked unrepentant and hitched himself onto the dining table. He produced and lit a pipe, the thing small in his hands.

'It's a long journey from Balerno and your brother

wanted to be useful. There's many a good piece of furniture here to take back and I promised him first choice if he helped.'

Gordon stared at his family in disbelief.

'None of this is yours!'

His mother drifted across the hall to rest a hand on Fergus' shoulder.

'Now, Gordon,' she said. 'That's no strictly true. You've no other kin since…'

She trailed off, looking away, and his father smiled around his pipe stem.

'Since you killed Iona and the bairn,' Angus said, as if commenting on the weather. 'You know as well we do, if it wasnae for your Uncle Stewart, God rest his soul, taking such an uncommon interest in you, you would no be in this fine house with all this bonny furniture going to waste.' He nodded to McDougall. 'Lawyer will tell you, being Stewart's half-sister means your mother's more than entitled to what she wants, once you're deid or in the madhouse.'

Gordon cursed and stalked to his study, daring his legs to fail. He retrieved a key from the desk and unlocked a cabinet. Reaching inside, he took his musket from its holder and checked the loading. Returning to the hall, he levelled the weapon at his father.

'You've got less than two minutes to get out of my house, or so help me, I'll take us all to hell.'

McDougall went white and uttered an oath. His mother drew a breath and pulled Fergus to her. Angus's eyes narrowed, calculating. Gordon knew the old man was quicker than his bulk appeared to allow and swift with his fists. More, that Angus would have a gun to hand, but he gambled not close enough to matter. He took a step toward his father, noting the lawyer backing away, nearer his mother and brother.

'Get out, McDougall,' Gordon called. 'Dinnae try and protect those two, for they'll be next, once I've done for this bastard.' His attention fast on Angus. 'You see, Father, I've naught left and I'll be right glad to take youse all with me.'

Angus glanced at his wife, and then the front door. With a shrug he got off the table. Gordon tracked him with the gun and Angus smiled.

'Och, dinnae fash yoursel', son, we can wait. You've the look of a corpse as it is or in need of a good long stay in Bedlam.' He looked to his wife. 'Morag, let's be away for home, I'd like to beat the darkness back. Fergus put those things down and get out to the cart.'

Fergus dropped the linen but didn't move. His gaze flicked between his father and brother.

'Just get out,' Gordon repeated. 'All of you. And Mother, leave the key you stole.'

His brother was gone on the last word, the front door barely swinging with his leaving. Morag was close behind, a key falling to the rug. His father took his time, puffing smoke as he went, as if out for a pleasant stroll. Gordon followed him to the door, gun barrel inches from Angus's back, and when his father turned it levelled over his heart. The man glanced down, smiling again, and called over Gordon's shoulder.

'McDougall, is it? Aye well, be certain and send for us when the laddie's in the earth or living with the witless.' He produced a handwritten business card, letting it flutter to the floor. 'Balerno is a small place. Everything you need to know is on that card. Dinnae fret, we're easy to find.' He looked at Gordon and touched the gun muzzle. 'I'd keep this handy, son, you never know what wee scunners are about.'

Angus tipped his hat and left, shutting the door behind him. Gordon sagged and the gun slipped from his fingers to be caught by McDougall. The lawyer fumbled with it, cursing.

'It's no loaded,' Gordon mumbled, resting his forehead against the door.

From outside a snap of reins sounded and the cart rumbled, fading away. Gordon crumpled and curled against the front door, letting darkness take him.

CHAPTER FOUR

Gordon came to, suffocating in whiteness and gasping for breath. The white abruptly vanished and McDougall stood next to him holding a dampened towel.

'It's all right, Doctor.'

Gordon sat up, easing his legs from their propped position, and it took him a moment to recognise his kitchen.

'How are you feeling?' the lawyer asked.

Gordon took stock of himself.

'Exhausted, in truth.'

McDougall nodded and busied himself at the range; the smell of coffee made Gordon's mouth water.

'How long was I insensible?'

'About half an hour. Apologies, but I could no manage you up the stairs. This was the easiest room to get you to and to warm. I'm surprised you're awake, given all that's happened.'

A soft caw made Gordon turn, muscles protesting, to see the uncovered wicker cage his mother had tried to steal, sitting on the table. A black form with bright eyes peered between the spars.

'Quile.'

He opened the door, letting the crow hop out. She fluffed her feathers, claws tapping the table as she preened. From the range McDougall eyed the bird.

'Your pet's been very quiet,' he said.

At the sound of the lawyer's voice the crow cocked her head, fixing her gaze on him. Gordon stroked Quile with a fingertip.

'She's no really a pet, more of a house guest.'

Memories assailed him, rushing with emotions.

If Quile still loves me, m'be I'm no so terrible?

SHE KNOWS NO BETTER. IF QUILE TRULY UNDERSTOOD WHAT YOU'D DONE, SHE'D PECK YOUR EYES OUT AND EAT YOUR BRAINS. IT WOULD BE NO MORE THAN YOU DESERVE.

McDougall put out cups.

'The coffee is to be black,' he said. 'For there's no a drap of milk to be had.' He gestured to the crow. 'How did you come by your bird?'

'My wife found Quile in the Gardens, abandoned as a chick, and we raised her. We tried to release her more than once, but she'll no leave. I imagine my mother found her loose and coaxed her into the cage, probably hoping to sell her. That woman always had a way with birds and beasts, and cares naught for who owns them, as long as they can be sold for profit.'

His last words sounded bitter even to his own ears and Gordon rubbed his face trying to wipe away the recollection of his family. He suddenly stood, dizziness making him sway, but anxiety pushing him on.

'Steady, man,' McDougall said, looking alarmed. 'What are you looking for?'

'A book, leather, quite large. My mother had it.'

'Ah, would that be it, over there? I carried it down with the cage. You seemed so protective of it I was loath to leave it unattended.'

Gordon followed the man's gesture and with relief found the tome on a pantry shelf. He picked it up, stroking the cover, and sank into the chair. His tight chest lightened a little and he drew a surprisingly easy breath.

The image of Amy Dudley's skull, smooth but for two ragged holes, engineered an abrupt focus and a spark of something he had forgotten; interest. Unbidden his mind provided Amy Dudley's height, calculating it against numbers he knew represented wooden talons and horns, gouging out for her. He looked about, seeking a pencil, some paper, his notebook. With a fingertip he drew the shape of a skull on the table, an urgency possessed him, and frustration bloomed when he could find nothing to write with. He stared at the leather book on his lap.

It helps, possessing her secrets again helps. Maybe a future in this world is still possible?

No. Only death will redeem you. Murderer. Monster.

He imagined wood smacking a skull, splitting it open. Amy Dudley falling, dying amidst bloody splatter. Iona soaked in scarlet clots and broken in his arms.

No redemption for a husband killing his wife. Contemptible. I branded Lord Dudley contemptible.

Aye, and now you're the same, you ken?

Tears smeared his view and he rubbed them away, hoping McDougall wouldn't notice. Quile hopped onto his shoulder, beak busy in his hair. The coffee pot rattled, making Gordon look, to find McDougall watching him.

'Where's your housekeeper?' the lawyer asked.

Gordon closed his eyes, focusing on Quile's fussing. The weight of the tome on his chest was comforting, like a blanket.

'Gone,' he said. 'I paid her off, sent her away. I'm supposed to be in prison, ready for the hangman, so it was ridiculous to keep her. I hoped Quile would leave too. I left a window open for her.'

The dark behind his lids was enticing. Gordon wanted

to fall into it, but the sound of pouring and the coffee aroma roused him. With reluctance he placed the book on the table and took the proffered cup from McDougall. The lawyer settled next to him, sipping his own brew and watching the crow. Quile tucked herself into Gordon's neck.

'The bird does seem very attached to you. What did you call it?'

Gordon's skin weighed him down and he wished the lawyer would leave.

'Her name's Quile,' he muttered.

They drank in an increasingly uncomfortable silence which he hoped would force McDougall to go. The kitchen seemed to sway, aiding his dreamlike state. He tried to form words to make the lawyer leave, but his tongue was numbed like his thoughts. McDougall poured more coffee and glanced at him.

'I hope you dinnae mind, Doctor, but with your lack of a housekeeper, I sent to my wife about sparing some supper. In truth, I'd feel unhappy taking my leave until I'd seen you fed and settled.'

Gordon was unsure what to say, feeling any food would taste like sand and yet too deadened to decline. McDougall seemed to take his silence as assent and gazed about the kitchen. Spying the leather tome, the lawyer bent forward, squinting at the spine.

'Leonardo da Vinci, how interesting,' he said, reaching for it. 'May I?'

With an effort Gordon rested his fingertips on the cover, halting the lawyer's momentum, and met McDougall's gaze.

'It's the most precious thing to me,' Gordon managed. He swallowed, forcing himself to coherence. 'It's something I thought never to see again,' he said, mind sluggish, adrift in wool, and he wished the hangman had him. 'Aye, peruse it then,' he murmured. 'But be mindful of its age and worth to me, else I'll truly have naught left in this world.'

McDougall murmured reassurances and settled the book, opening the cover to reveal the sepia drawings of anatomy that Gordon knew so well. The lawyer made appreciative noises as he turned the sheets and, despite himself, Gordon's mouth twitched in a smile. McDougall handled the pages reverently, turning each with fingertip movements.

'I can see why it's so precious,' the lawyer said. 'How did you come by it?'

'It was a gift. From Iona.'

The candlelight slithered sideways, leaving trails of fire in his gaze. He gave up trying to speak, but focused on the rustling parchment, sinking into the sound until it was all that mattered. The pages continue to turn, recalling to him how the book's secrets had once immersed him. He remembered finding the hidden contents. How they had led him to Doctor Bennett in London and his longed-for destiny.

Soon, I'll have everything. How could I have been so stupid to ever believe that?

STUPID KILLER OF WIFE AND BAIRN. IF AMBITION HAD NO MADE YOU BLIND TO ALL ELSE, YOU COULD HAVE SAVED US. YOU'RE NO DIFFERENT THAN LORD DUDLEY. WIFE MURDERERS.

He closed his eyes, feeling sick at the abrupt similarity between himself and Robert Dudley. The whispering pages took over, lulling his senses and tortured mind. Suddenly, in the susurration of parchment, he heard again whispers from those long dead. Unbidden, the remembered delight and excitement on discovering the tome's concealed documents took him. Shadowy figures flickered behind his lids. A woman running, running in vain for her life. A man, studious and fierce all at once, scribing at his desk, haunted by the dead woman. A fiery queen, watching and waiting.

'He was a genius.'

The lawyer's voice broke Gordon's visions. Heaviness returned to his body and soul; he opened his eyes to the present and the pain.

'Who?'

'Why, Leonardo da Vinci.' McDougall tapped the book. 'The author of your most precious possession.'

'Aye, the author, of course. He was, indeed, a brilliant man.'

A knock on the front door, sounding distant and hollow to Gordon, announced the supper Missus McDougall had provided. The lawyer harrumphed, shutting the book, and left to fetch the food. Gordon closed his eyes again, seeking to re-conjure the distant past.

It's no good, Gordon, to try for refuge in such things. Amy Dudley is as lost to you as I am. It's the here and now you've to make amends for.

He knew she was right. Bleakness settled, bone and soul deep. As the darkness claimed him, the inside of his lids became swamped with bloody memories and Gordon sank drowning into them.

CHAPTER FIVE

After that strained supper Gordon was uncertain how many days had passed before he saw McDougall again. The man's appearance on his doorstep should have been a cause for surprise, but Gordon felt only mild curiosity.

'Why are you here?' he asked.

A breeze caught the lawyer's frock coat. It menaced his hat and caused the leaves in the hallway to dance. McDougall squinted at him.

'It's a snell wind out here, Doctor McCraken. Might I step inside?'

Gordon shuffled away, uncaring if the lawyer followed and heard the other's boot-falls hollow on the floorboards. The front door closed, and Gordon walked away, increasing his pace so McDougall stumbled in his wake. Abruptly the following noise stopped, and muted light spilt about the hall. Gordon blinked and turned. McDougall was gone.

Fucking off so soon, Mister Lawyer?

Using the low curse buoyed Gordon and he moved to the study. McDougall stood inside, amidst the mouldering leaves and newspaper pages. He had his hat in hands, inspecting a broken window and blackened wall. Gordon rested against the door jamb, watching. The lawyer turned in a slow circle, crunchy with glass, boot prints making patterns on the ashy floorboards until he faced Gordon with a troubled expression.

'Doctor McCraken, what happened here?'

Gordon shrugged.

'Children, vagabonds, my neighbours. It disnae matter.'

'Breaking your window and shoving in lit newspaper is a serious business! They could've killed you.'

'Aye, suppose they might have, at that.'

It wasn't the possibility of fire or dying that he minded, but the thought of thieving or prying fingers. It's why he had taken to hiding his treasures. The lawyer was speaking, and with an effort, Gordon listened.

'And where's all your furniture, the rugs and carpets, Doctor?'

The question seemed to get lost in the ceiling, echoing about.

'Sold.'

Gordon could think of no other words. The lawyer moved to the only items in the room, two large trunks, and opened the lids, frowning at the books filling each. He turned to Gordon, questions clear in his expression. Gordon shrugged and left, walking deeper into the house. He kicked at empty whisky and wine bottles as he went, enjoying the skittering sound. Above the noise, he heard McDougall opening and shutting doors and the lawyer's footsteps going up the stairs. Gordon left the kitchen door ajar, settling in the wingback chair he'd dragged there from his study. He pulled the blanket about his shoulders and listened to the lawyer moving above and about. He wondered if they had finally decided to hang him and hoped so. He slugged whisky from a handy bottle, closed his eyes and waited. The door creaked further open.

'Doctor McCraken?'

'Why are you here?' Gordon asked again, without opening his eyes.

'Your sister-in-law sent me. It's been more than a month since the trial, and she's worried about you.'

'Margaret.'

'That's right, Lady Margaret Drummond. She hired me to defend you. Do you remember me, from the trial?'

He thinks I'm daft in the heid.

YOU ARE.

He opened his eyes, staring, unblinking at the lawyer.

'Aye, I remember you, and the trial. It ended badly.'

'I beg to differ, but that's by the by. Pray, why have you sold all your belongings?'

McDougall rested his walking cane against the table, looking stern, cross even and kept twitching his glasses, peering about. Gordon laughed without mirth.

'Why in the hell do you think? No one wants me to treat them. No patients, no money. And here's the rub, if I starve or die of the cold while I've means, then I'd no see Iona again. So, I'm emptying the house before I sell the bricks for a pittance.' He raised his hands. 'For you see, man, suicide is suicide, sayeth the Lord.'

'Now, Doctor McCraken, there's no need.'

But Gordon pushed on, enjoying the lawyer's discomfort.

'It would be so much easier if I were an atheist, do you no think? But sadly, it seems I'm no even that. In which case there must be money for food and fuel, until all means are exhausted. Then I can die of cold and starvation in peace on the streets. Satisfied?'

McDougall looked far from pleased.

'And the servants?'

'I've nothing to pay with and more to the point who would work here, after...'

Gordon shook the blanket off and sat forward. He opened the range door and rattled the poker about the warm inside. The lawyer shook his head and walked around the kitchen while Gordon watched. The man seemed intent on prying, opening cupboard doors, lifting crust-riddled plates, avoiding bird droppings and scaring mice into dark corners. He glanced at Gordon and turned to the long table rammed against the back door, his expression pitying.

He'll lock you in Bedlam. The rest of your life with the screaming mad.

No!

Gordon rose, hand aching on the poker. He stepped toward the lawyer whose touch had reached the Da Vinci tome. Gordon lunged forward and grabbed the book, the poker clattering to the floor. McDougall spun, stumbling, staring as Gordon settled back in his chair, clutching the tome. McDougall unfastened his frock coat to bend and picked up the poker then sat on the table edge.

Fool, now he has a weapon.

No matter. He'll need to kill me before I'll go to Bedlam.

That end to you would be fine, you ken?

McDougall's gaze was understanding, his expression compassionate, and he laid the poker aside.

'Doctor McCraken, Gordon, I've been instructed to offer you a restful stay at a suitable sanatorium, in Europe perhaps. For as long as necessary, for you to regain your health.'

He's lying. It's Bedlam for you.

Gordon fumbled for the whisky bottle. He found it difficult with the book, and was pleased to manage, tipping and sipping from the open neck. He eyed the lawyer over the rim.

'Getting me out the way is she?'

Gordon spat to the floor, enjoying the flicker of distaste on McDougall's face.

'If you're referring to Lady Drummond, then no. Your sister-in-law only wishes to help with this offer.'

'You're lying. If Margaret cares why does she send you and no come herself? Why was she no at court, or visit me in prison?'

'Her husband, Doctor, and his political standing. Lord Drummond has forbidden his wife to see you or support you publicly. Lady Drummond has agreed and promises the continuation of a contented home life if Lord Drummond finances your needs, privately. Until such times that you're fully recovered.'

'Ha! That old bastard never liked me.'

'Doctor McCraken, it's plain that you're, let's say, struggling here. Lady Drummond feared as much. She feels the change in a restful place, helped by doctors who understand your problems, will benefit you greatly.' He looked about with sad countenance. 'And I have to agree.'

'You agree?' Gordon sniggered and then sobbed, fanning the bottle with snot. 'You agree, when my, when this, this is your fault? And hers!'

'I dinnae see how.'

Gordon rose; placing the book on the chair and clutching the bottle, he stepped toward the lawyer.

'I'm guilty of murder and should've hanged! Get. Out.'

McDougall didn't move. Gordon raised the bottle, liquor splashing his beard, so he was unable to see through tears and contorted muscles. He wiped his eyes with a clenched fist. McDougall re-buttoned his frock coat and gathered his cane, his expression sympathetic.

'I, for one, believe you only loved your wife. The offer is there, Doctor, please think about it. For your sanity's sake, man, if naught else. I'm to return at ten o'clock tomorrow, for your answer. Be warned, should you go, I've agreed to accompany you.'

The kitchen door banged shut and the lawyer's boot-falls were loud beyond it, then gone. Once more, but for mice, a crow and dead wife, Gordon was alone.

Later, when next Gordon awoke, the kitchen was chilly and dark, smelling of old ash and neglect. Quile, in her rag nest, was merely a blacker smudge on the pantry shelf, the gleam of an eye all that gave her away. Gordon fumbled the empty whisky bottle to the floor, where it rolled and clinked amongst its brethren. The leather tome was warm in his arms and he patted it, enjoying the feel of something so solid. Balancing the book's weight, he lit a gas lamp. Leaning into the flagstone cubby hole he took coal nuggets from the bucket and added them to the smouldering range, prodding it to red, raging life. He scratched his beard, the movement dislodging old skin and snot to his nails and he rubbed them loose on the chair. Getting stale bread from a cupboard, Gordon used milk in a jug to soften it, before eating with great tearing bites. Then, tugging at the blanket, he studied the dark beyond the kitchen window and gauged midnight to be two hours away.

Time enough.

TONIGHT, COULD BE THE NIGHT.

I hope so.

He felt calmer and opened the book, tracing Leonardo da Vinci's anatomical drawings, turning the old pages carefully, slowly, right to the end. He hesitated, poised over the inside back cover. Sighing, he touched the raised stitches and lifted the vellum that hid the secret pocket. With trembling fingers, he slid a parchment packet and papers out.

WHY HAVE YOU KEPT ALL THAT? YOU'LL NEVER ACHIEVE GREATNESS NOW.

You gave me this book.

THAT'S NO THE REASON.

He wiped at his tears and read an old newspaper

clipping about an anatomical expert, setting up practice in Edinburgh. He barely recognised the description of himself.

Now, you're just shrunken and meaningless.

Waiting to die. No more than you deserve.

I ken that, Iona.

Moving the clippings, he fingered the twelve heavily written pages from Doctor Bennett.

Three letters, it feels like there should be more.

They're as meaningless now as you are.

Using Amy Dudley's secrets to prove her murder, we might've changed the medical world.

Arrogant fools, both of you.

He felt hollow, as if a tiny remaining spark that had somehow survived in his soul had suddenly been snuffed out. Senses deadened and wretched, Gordon traced the sender's name. The bleakness throbbed intensely when he followed the whorls and loops of the man's writing and recited the address.

'Doctor Bennett, Russell Park Square, London.'

Words from the pages caught him. Against judgement and will, he re-read the letters, crying some more. Finally, he moved the pages to one side and came to the packet of tied, brown-spotted silk.

'Hello, Sam,' he murmured.

He eased the ties and peeled the oiled paper away, lifting the first parchment page free. The sepia date of 1560 blurred under more tears. He wiped at them, afraid they might fall to the document. Gordon breathed deeply, letting the caress of old parchment bring a small calm. He then re-read secrets written by the Sheriff of Oxford, Sir Samuel Banks, about the death of Lady Amy Dudley.

After he had read Sam's accounts, as if of their own volition his fingers found his slender calfskin notebook. Inside were his translations of Sam's notes from their mix of Latin and old English alongside drawings of Amy Dudley's skull he had made from Sam's indication of where the wounds had been. He traced the gouges in the skull he had painstakingly measured and drawn with such precision. Sam's sketches of the staircase where she was supposed to have fallen to her death were intricate; the wicked carvings of mad beasts that stuck out with beak and claw, done from different angles. And finally, the candlestick, the weapon used, the sheriff believed, to bludgeon her ladyship. Sam had described it in detail, including its height and weight, but not drawn it. Nearly three hundred years later, Gordon had been able to faithfully reproduce it with pen and ink. His efforts, he knew, were a dull parody of Leonardo da Vinci, yet drawing these things had brought Sam's investigation to life.

In past moments of heady pride, Gordon had believed he had added to the sheriff's conclusions. More importantly, the discovery of Sam's notes on Amy Dudley had brought him to Doctor Bennett and the means to fulfil his all-powerful need to be a pioneer in the medical profession. Now, he remembered with shame the hours he had wasted making his calculations, suppositions and drawings into Amy Dudley's death. The long nights he had pored over his plans with Doctor Bennett. Time he could have been with Iona.

Soon my love, my soul will join yours and beg for forgiveness.

HURRY, THEN. FOR THE NIGHT GROWS LONG WITHOUT YOU.

Gordon replaced all the documents and hid the book, once more set in his purpose. Reaching beneath the table he unhooked his medical bag and set out on the familiar walk to Old Town.

CHAPTER SIX

In the dark of that midnight Gordon left his house and crossed the road into Queen Street Gardens. By keeping to the shadows, he made quick progress to Fredrick Street. While developing his plan Gordon had realised that, due to his former practice and current notoriety, a shadowed route was needed. Even when wearing a black top hat and coat, Gordon worried that the heavy medical bag and his well-known face were too memorable. It had been problematic as Edinburgh's New Town was still newly built and had been laid out in neat squares and straight lines, making his late-night movements conspicuous. Gordon had spent three nights mapping out the darkest and least populated route to the jumble of medieval streets that made up the Old Town. Still, sometimes, on the edge of his senses, he felt someone was there, following him, watching him. He knew, even though he never saw them properly or heard them distinctly, that the darkness held someone who wouldn't leave him be.

Now, three weeks later, he hurried across Prince's Street Gardens toward the Old Town and the night again felt hostile, holding concealed foes. He sensed the lit and black windows sheltered judging, watching figures and hastened his pace, trying to outrun the hidden eyes. Gaining the Old Town, Gordon slipped through back alleys, keeping to pools of dark and so avoiding the many narrow pubs and grog shops still rowdily open.

Less than half an hour after leaving home, Gordon moved down Fleshmarket Close, then to a tiny alley and to the back of the Black Boar pub. The tavern's rear courtyard, lit by a single gas lamp, thrummed with muted music and voices. Avoiding stacked barrels and rubbish Gordon slipped into his hiding place – he knew the skinny pub well, this was his twelfth such vigil. It had been easier than he had imagined, discovering the villainous types he needed. What had taken the time was learning their nasty habits and what inducement he could bring to implement his plan. He gauged his wait had been twenty minutes when Big Man appeared, slightly earlier than expected. Big Man dossed against the pub wall and lit a pipe, so the fleck of red showed his meaty face and sunken eyes with every pull. Shorty was on time. The little dandy sauntered down the alley whistling that irritating ditty he had picked up last week. Gordon's gaze narrowed as the men met and spoke; the usual glint of money passed hands. Big Man said something, and Shorty nodded, disappearing a hand-sized jewel case into his coat. Feeling his heart unexpectedly quicken, Gordon stepped into the light. The two men froze, and Gordon imagined hands gripping hidden weapons. He hefted his bag, comforted by the weight, and moved with false confidence.

'Gentlemen,' he said. 'I've a proposition for you.'

Shorty took two steps right to form a loose wall with Big Man, leaving space for them to close on him together.

'Oh aye,' Big Man said. 'What makes you think you've anything we want?'

His voice was low, and Gordon knew it was meant to draw him closer.

All the better to hear you with.

Do it. Now.

Gordon stopped a good four feet from the men and opened his bag.

'Jewellery. Sold without question, for a fair price.'

'Fair is in the purse of the beholder.' Shorty sounded amused. His thin face was shadowed, but his eyes gleamed as they darted from Gordon to the bag.

'It's understandable,' Gordon said. 'You want to judge what I'm offering, before we arrange a price.'

Gordon lifted his case, pointing the opening toward them, letting the contents catch the meagre light. Shorty took a step, bending forward in eagerness. Big Man raised a hand.

'Be still, man, we've no knowing this cur.'

'True,' Gordon said. 'I say we keep it that way.' He shook the case, causing the contents to clink appealingly. 'I need money and have something of value to sell. Mister MacNair suggested I seek you out.'

The name, overheard three nights ago, eased the two men as Gordon had hoped. Big Man eyed him then gave a nod and gestured Shorty on. The little man's gaze raked Gordon, as if looking for a weapon, before he minced forward. Gordon drew the bag back, feeling inside until his hand closed on a familiar shape. Shorty's gaze was pinned to the case and he was a mere half a step away.

'So, what you got for us?'

Gordon pulled out the ladle and smacked the dandy's cap from his head. Shorty rocked back as if punched.

'Eejits, the pair of you,' Gordon said. 'You think you're so fucking clever.' He advanced and slapped Shorty's cheek with the big spoon. 'Stupid scunners. I can no wait to tell Mister MacNair how I bested you both, with a ladle and bag of cutlery.'

Shorty hissed a curse, a knife springing to his hand. Big

Man came on, keeping low and threatening with a thick cudgel.

Here it is, at last.

Abrupt light spilt from the pub's rear door. A woman tumbled from the Black Boar, laughing and holding her skirts. She stopped, staring at the men.

'What?'

Her voice was too loud in the small space. Big Man turned and lashed out, catching her arm with a sickening crack. The woman gave a gasping cry, falling to the ground.

'Shite!'

Despite his size, Big Man ran like a hare. Shorty spat at Gordon and bolted after Big Man, toward Fleshmarket Close. Gordon didn't notice as he knelt to the woman. She had fainted from the shock and pain. Her eyes were closed and skin pale beneath dirt, but her breathing was strong. Gordon held her and probed the stricken arm.

'Broken ulna,' he muttered.

He dragged his bag toward him, digging inside to shake the cutlery from the wrapping of tablecloth. Pulling the cloth out, he tore it into strips. Then, using fragmented barrel struts as a splint, he bandaged the broken arm. He then folded the other part of the tablecloth in half to form a sling. It was awkward, putting it on the woman, but he managed, binding the arm tightly to her body. Finished, Gordon stood, abruptly aware of the open pub door, and looked inside at a grimy passageway which clearly led to rowdy patrons and more light. He glanced at the woman, who hadn't stirred. In one decisive movement he gathered her up, careful of the injured arm, and went inside. Navigating the corridor, he kicked open an interior door. Fetid warmth, laden with beer, mayhem and sweat, assailed him. A stout man, filling tankards, looked up from the patrons.

'Bess!' He bustled over, expression alarmed and angry. 'What have you done to my wife?'

The noise lessened, piano petering and too many curious faces turned his way.

'The arm is broken and will swell,' Gordon said. 'She needs to lie still.'

'What happened?'

'More damage will manifest if we stay like this.'

The man's frown deepened, but he led Gordon out from the taproom and up a twisty staircase to a bedroom. Below, the hubbub and music rose, seeming to swell the floorboards. Gordon laid the woman on a bed that beat along with the pub din and instructed the man as to his wife's care. The landlord listened intently and nodded, looking wary and worried at the same time.

'She only went to fetch another tun. What happened?'

'A man hit her with a cudgel and ran away.'

'You saved her and doctored her arm, out there?'

'Aye.'

'You've my thanks.'

Gordon tipped his hat and made to leave, but the landlord's hand on his sleeve stopped him.

'I've a wee bit of money,' the man said.

Gordon shook his head, hurrying down the stairs, and barely saw the passageway in his haste to leave. Bursting from the pub he gathered his belongings and fled. By the time he reached Prince's Street Gardens, Gordon's lungs hurt. He sank to the ground, lying prone amidst the dirt and grass. He stared up at the sky, wearing his weariness like a second skin and imagined the ground splitting to let him fall and lie in the ghost of drained Nor Loch, covering him with its mud. He pictured it seeping into skin and every bone, swamping his agony like a balm.

Perhaps then I'd finally die.

His dead wife didn't reply, and he felt bereft. The stars blurred with his tears, tilting in his watery gaze. He gripped the earth and was abruptly reminded of the injured woman's broken bone under his hand. The image of her was suddenly clear in his mind and a kernel of some new, but familiar emotion gave him pause. He sniffed and tried to recall its meaning.

Satisfaction?

He pictured the injured woman's husband, tired face creased with worry and then relief. The man's cracked voice saying he had saved her. A strange feeling grew, breaking him open like an egg. He cried at its intensity, but the feeling soothed him, quietening his breaths and heartbeat. He closed his eyes, yet the shadows didn't drag at his bones in the all too familiar way. Gordon wondered at the new feeling, finally recognising it.

Peace.

He remained very still, as if moving would scare the feeling away, and tentatively explored it. Gordon gave a hiccupping sob.

It's real!

FLEETING AND WORTHLESS, LIKE YOU. IT CHANGES NAUGHT.

For once, Gordon wasn't sure he agreed with her and let himself think of the injured woman. He recalled the feel of the ripping tablecloth and how easy it had been to properly bind her. Again, the husband's face, the words and gratitude boosted the peaceful feeling. It soothed his weary bones and frantic mind.

What if I'm no worthless?

YOU CAUSED THE WOMAN'S INJURIES. YOU'RE A BURDEN ON THE WORLD. A MONSTER.

But I remedied it. I saved her.

A new thought, tentative and wonderful, lifted him.

Suddenly he remembered Father John's words.

What if, by saving others, I can be redeemed? Forgiven, even?

No one will let you save them. You're a murderer.

He recognised the truth of that and hated it. His thoughts spiralled toward blackness, the dead weight of guilt dragging once more. He tried for calm, thinking of the husband and injured woman, but it didn't work. Frantic, disjointed memories of blood and snapping bones stole his new-found peace, engineering panic. He squeezed his eyes shut and tried desperately for calm. Abruptly came the image of the leather tome and he could almost feel the serene old parchment in his fingers, re-reading the puzzle of Amy Dudley's death. The enjoyable hours he had spent on it flooded him with new serenity. Suddenly he sensed how Sam must have felt, the dead woman's champion with his unshakable resolve to save her. Slowly the memories of blood receded, and Gordon breathed deeply. He filled his aching lungs and opened his eyes, feeling a difference in his scorched soul.

There's one I can still save.

She's already deid, murdered like me.

But my plan with Doctor Bennett for Amy Dudley could still work. And it means I can save Amy Dudley's soul from the taint of suicide. Something that never truly left her, something Sam never achieved. My salvation for hers. I can still be a pioneer!

It's pointless. You're a worthless worm.

By saving her, using the plan we had, we can still bring about a way to help others with my work. I might be redeemed, salvaged, forgiven as Father John said I could.

You're shrunken and meaningless. A deid man who has no stopped breathing, yet.

If I save Amy Dudley, I can save myself. I can be all I

wanted to be!

DOCTOR BENNETT WILL NEVER RISK HIS GOOD NAME, HIS PROFESSION, TO HELP A DISGUSTING MURDERER.

He might still, for Amy Dudley. I must try. I must.

CHILD KILLER. COWARD. WORTHLESS MAGGOT.

Iona's voice faded to an unintelligible whisper. Gordon's eyes closed, yet the stars still whirled behind his lids and he watched them until sleep took him.

CHAPTER SEVEN

Gordon woke to the lustre of pre-dawn, clothes and beard unpleasant with dew. He shivered, sat up and put his hat on. In the pale light he glanced about, thankful the gardens appeared deserted. The grass seemed different, greener somehow while all about birdsong silvered the air. Gordon stood and felt strange, lighter, as if he had shed half his body weight. He stared at the ground half expecting to see it like an empty snakeskin. He wiped his beard, seeking to warm his face, and set off for home. While he walked the sun rose to brindle Edinburgh and Gordon admired the towns, old and new, made beautiful by its light. As he strode along Frederick Street, he heard humming and, with a start, realised the sound was his. He halted there, in a patch of white sunlight and listened; birds, hooves from a hansom cab and the bustle of dawn risers, but nothing more. Iona was silent and Gordon wasn't sure how he felt about it. Carefully, fearing Iona's scathing comments, he thought about Amy Dudley.

I must go to Doctor Bennett to enlist his help or naught will be possible. But I need to visit Oxford first.

He waited, lungs aching on a held breath, but there was only silence. He sighed and continued on his way, thinking about money. By the time he reached home, Gordon had a plan and was looking forward to seeing McDougall. He stopped his key at the front door, hand turning the knob; it was already unlocked.

Did I leave it like that?

Thinking back, he couldn't recall his actions when leaving the house last night, but acknowledged it was possible. Stepping forward, Gordon halted just inside the threshold, listening. The house felt empty, smelling of neglect and ash, only rustling leaves as welcome. Gordon went inside, shut and locked the front door. Moving into the house he watched the shadows and noticed the study door.

Was it open when I left?

He pushed inside the room, seeing only the familiar emptiness and the two closed trunks. Shaking his head, he pulled the door closed.

THE LEAVES ARE ALL WRONG.

Iona's comment stayed his hand. He moved back into the study, staring at the littered floor where leaf mould was scattered about. For a moment he didn't understand, and then heeded the crush marks and cleared trail, as if someone had walked about.

Probably McDougall's doing from yesterday.

JUST AS YOU MOST LIKELY LEFT THE FRONT DOOR UNLOCKED?

Gordon tried not to listen but opened his medical case and slipped out the toasting fork, finding comfort even in such a meagre weapon.

Could my father have come back? Is he hiding, waiting somewhere?

Gordon made his way through the house, checking every room, alert for any sound. He found other doors open and things felt odd, as if slightly askew. Yet there was nothing definite. Nothing that couldn't have been McDougall yesterday. Feeling unsettled, but convincing himself it was the lawyer's doing, Gordon hurried to the kitchen. He thrust the door open, halting on unsteady legs, but everything looked as it should. He stumbled inside and sank into his chair, still clutching his bag and the toasting fork. He closed his eyes enjoying the warmth the range had kept and after a few minutes sleep tried to creep in. He groaned and rose, shaking the cutlery onto the table and placed the empty medical bag on his chair. Then, using both hands, he hefted the coal bucket from its cubbyhole, shifting the flagstone that formed the pedestal floor to reveal a dark hole. Reaching inside, Gordon took out the satchel which contained the leather tome, his notebook, medical tools and the few drug filled vials he had kept. He was tempted to sit and go through his treasures again.

SAM WASNAE REAL. IT'S ALL FAKERY AND WRITINGS OF A CRAZED MIND.

That's no true! He was real, I'll prove it.

YOU'RE A SCUNNER. AN EEJIT. YOU'LL NEVER BE ABLE TO PROVE SAM EXISTED, BECAUSE HE DINNAE. YOU'LL NEVER SAVE AMY DUDLEY. LOOK AT YOU, YOU'RE DISGUSTING.

Gordon looked down, suddenly ashamed of his filthy hands. Abruptly his lip curled at his tatty appearance and pungency.

McDougall will never be persuaded by this stinking old heap of a man.

STAY THEN. DIE FROM COLD AND NEGLECT.

He tried but failed to remember the last time he had bathed and the thought of using the bathroom sickened him. Hiding all his treasures once more, Gordon rummaged about the pantry until he found a bar of laundry soap. He draped a tablecloth for a towel over his arm and pushed the table away to get to the back door. Trying to turn the key Gordon paused, frowning, then understood; the door was unlocked. He glanced down and his stomach abruptly clenched, the soap bar slipping through his numb fingers. It skidded across the floor, spun and slowed, before coming to rest near an ashy boot-print which pointed outward, leaving the house.

He stumbled back, breathing hard, and barked his calves on the table, almost sitting on it. Chest tight and muttering obscenities, eyes cutting from the boot-print to the back door, Gordon reached his chair. Sinking into it, his vision blackened, and his head buzzed as Quile's claws scraped his scalp. He let out a shout that sent the crow flapping back to her raggedy nest. He stood, almost tipping the chair over, hands clammy on its leather and took a step toward the kitchen door, wanting nothing more than to flee.

Where can I go? McDougall. McDougall will help me.

NO ONE WILL HELP YOU. NO MCDOUGALL. NO BENNETT. STAY AND FACE YOUR FATE. COWARD. MURDERER.

Gordon sobbed. He thought of Doctor Bennett, of Amy Dudley's salvation, his pioneering work, and it steadied his nerve. With halting steps, he crept toward the back door, alert for any sound or movement from outside.

There's no one in the house. I checked.

LOCK THE DOOR AND RUN. OUT INTO THE COLD. FIND BIG MAN AND SHORTY.

No! What of my tome, my work and Amy Dudley?

AMY DUDLEY.

Iona's voice was contemptuous.

Gordon retraced his steps and hefted the poker, happy to feel its weight. He tried to see into the backyard, but dirt gave no hope of it. With unsteady steps he gained the back door and thrust it open. Issuing a strangled cry and brandishing the poker, he jumped out. Pigeons leapt to the air in a clapping of wings. Nothing else moved. He slumped to the door frame, using the poker to hold himself upright.

SOMEONE WAS HERE. SOMEONE'S COMING TO GET YOU, DOLE OUT WHAT YOU DESERVE. YOU WANT TO DIE.

Gordon shivered and didn't answer, afraid of the deluge he would unleash from her. Instead he lifted the poker and went to search the house. Again, he found nothing overtly amiss. Returning to the kitchen, fearful sweat was an added pungency on him. Gordon retrieved the soap, stepped around the boot-print, trying to ignore it. If he stayed close to the house the grey walls offered privacy from the neighbours. Luckily the water pump was near enough to allow him to bathe away from unwelcome eyes. He scrubbed until his pale, freckled skin was hawthorn red, uncaring of how cold it was.

BLEEDING IS A START. BUT DYING WILFULLY OF COLD IS STILL SELF-SLAUGHTER. BETTER THAT THE INTRUDER RETURNS AND FINISHES YOU OFF.

He wilted under Iona's tone, but splashed water on his genitals, gasping at the frigidness, driving her away.

Amy Dudley needs me. I can save her, save myself and help people. I can continue my work. I can.

His breath hissing and body dripping under the tablecloth, Gordon re-entered the kitchen. He avoided looking at the unknown boot-print and stood by the range. Rubbing himself dry, he muttered about children poking about where they shouldn't. Perhaps it was just the curious, come to see the murderous doctor's house, and for a second he almost believed it.

When he was dry Gordon slipped into his night-shirt. He ate cold chicken and potatoes, swigged down with whisky, feeding Quile some chicken skin. He left the kitchen and went to dress in the only untouched place in the house; his wife's dressing room. Inside he welcomed Iona's ghost, letting her presence fill the space, so her insistence at his death receded and he managed to dress without breaking down. Still his fingers shook as he straightened the cuffs of his wedding shirt. It took him several tries to fasten the silver cufflinks, touching their thistle emblems and the engraved G and I almost broke him. Afterward, breathing hard, he closed his eyes, trying to find a measure of stillness against memories and the now unfriendly house. Feeling calmer, he tugged at the once well-fitting sleeves, wondering how ridiculous the finery looked on his shrunken frame. But apart from the filthy clothes he had taken off to bathe and the nightshirt he had just removed, they were all he had left. Gordon tried very hard not to think of the last time he had worn them. Yet somehow the coat smelt of that summer three years ago and it was as if the day's joy were held in the argent threads. He blinked and pushing memories away moved to the sash window that overlooked Heriot Row and the Gardens. Rubbing a section clear of grime, he wondered how long until the lawyer arrived.

In the glass and dirt his reflection looked back and seemed a bent, twisted thing. It looked older than his thirty-six years, brown eyes wary and pained like an animal in a trap. He barely recognised the face, shadowed as it was with a deep weariness. A sleeplessness now aided by the unfamiliar boot-print downstairs. Gordon glanced across the room, reassured the chair was still wedging the door shut, then stared beyond his reflection, unable to bear the stranger he had become. Below, Heriot Row and Queen Street Gardens were full of a life he had forgotten. Two women, feathered hats and parasol swaying, walked small dogs and ignored a match-seller touting his wares.

Did those women glance up here? Were they in my house, prying, looking for my treasures? Looking for me?

PROBABLY.

A gentleman on a bay horse rode past, tipping his hat to the women before entering the Gardens.

Who is he? Where did he come from? Were they all in here, in my house together, waiting for me?

I EXPECT SO.

He tried to remember the look of the rider's boots.

Were they like the print downstairs?

COULD WELL HAVE BEEN.

Nearby, a newspaper boy called headlines on land clearance and famine, selling a paper to a rotund man as he hailed a hansom cab. Gordon then recognised a neighbour, an elderly chap, ambling toward the Gardens.

Those neighbours found me, found Iona. They wanted to hang me! Hate me, they hate me.

AYE THEY DO. WITH JUST CAUSE. CHILD KILLER.

At the garden gates a stranger stopped Gordon's neighbour and the two stood, talking. Gordon peered, but the smeared glass and distance foiled him. Suddenly the unknown figure turned and looked up. The startling face was grimy, showing a harelip, starkly pink in the beardless face.

SHITE! He sees me!

SENSES YOU. TWISTED MIND TO TWISTED FACE. COMING FOR YOU.

He stepped back, away from the stranger's intense stare that seemed to bore through glass and skin to his bones. His heart hurt, thundering in his chest like a last furlong. Light headed, he glanced toward the blocked door, wanting again to flee. He looked back to the window and the two figures.

Still there. He's still there! He must have been the man in my house. The man who's been following me. Watching me.

COMING FOR YOU. MURDERER.

A hansom cab abruptly cut the view and stopped outside

the house so McDougall could alight. Gordon could see the lawyer was in no hurry and stood, waiting while the cab drove away, fiddling with his cane, covered basket and bag. Gordon tried to scream, but no sound came. He wanted to beat the window, but couldn't move. Still McDougall fussed, unaware the harelipped man watched him. The sight made bile rise in Gordon's throat and he struggled to breathe. The lawyer finally approached the house, passing out of sight. Suddenly Gordon could move; he hurried across the room and pushed the chair away. He took the stairs two at time to throw open the front door, surprising McDougall in the act of knocking, and the flustered lawyer bent to retrieve his bag. Gordon stared toward the Gardens, but the man with the harelip had gone.

CHAPTER EIGHT

Within minutes of the lawyer's arrival the house seemed less hostile, enabling Gordon a modicum of composure. They retreated to the kitchen where Gordon sat on the edge of his chair, fidgeting and watching McDougall. The lawyer became busy, removing hat and coat. He produced a stew pot and coffee from his covered basket, stoking the range and placing the stew to heat. He filled the copper kettle before setting it to boil and opened empty drawers.

'Do you no even have a spoon left, man?'

'Here. In here.'

Gordon opened the table drawer and the contents rattled under his hand. McDougall eyed him and fished out a wooden spoon, stirring what smelt like beef stew. The lawyer found plates and cutlery, cleaning them and clearing the table of detritus. Gordon moved about the kitchen, touching things, unable to settle, keeping his gaze resolutely from the boot-print. His restlessness delivered him to Quile. The crow was in her cloth nest and opened an eye at Gordon's stroking. Her blue/black body shifted in pleasure and her beak clicked softly.

'It will no take long to heat,' the lawyer said.

'You're a surprising specimen of domesticity,' Gordon said.

McDougall raised his eyebrows, his mouth quirking

with a suppressed smile.

'Aye, well, although I've been married these past ten years the old habits of a bachelor die hard it seems. And you, sir?'

'Bachelor for many a year, before. But I never lacked support, not since childhood or in my student days, nor since, thanks to my Uncle Stewart's largesse.'

McDougall stirred the stew, sniffing and tasting with appreciative noises.

'Lord Stewart Kilbride, that would be?'

Gordon nodded and the sudden need to talk, to fill the silence, was forceful, catching him unawares.

'I was ten when we first visited my uncle at Kilbride Castle, just after my brother, Fergus, was born. I remember exploring and finding the library.' He tried to stop the words, but something had unleashed those wonderful days. 'I barely left that room the whole time we were there. Somehow my uncle found me, and we spent hours together one day. After that, he persuaded my mother to leave me there, to be raised with his son and given an education.' He swallowed, trying to drown the abrupt bitterness on his tongue. 'As you witnessed, my father has ever been resentful of my good fortune.'

His father's spectre abruptly squashed the compulsion to talk and Gordon took quick steps to his chair, resuming his perch. The need for redemption burnt in his mind, making his fingers tap across the table and around the plate. The thought of being able to work at what he loved once more lightened his blood and engineered a deep sense of satisfaction. He couldn't contain his need, his drive to press on, to seek answers for Amy Dudley, for himself. McDougall settled on a dining chair that had somehow survived the purge, his gaze on Gordon.

'Doctor, are you feeling quite well? You seem somewhat agitated.'

With an effort Gordon stilled his fingers and settled back in his chair, toes curling and uncurling in his stiff button boots.

'I'm fine.'

'Really. Are you certain you've no been imbibing chemicals? A wee something to liven you up?'

'Opium or the like? I'll admit to using the stuff on occasion but no recently.'

'So, what has you excitable? The prospect of a trip to Europe, perhaps?'

You'll never be better. Never be whole. Suffer as you should. He'll ken you're mad.

Gordon looked away, fingers rubbing his trousers and gaze settling on McDougall's basket.

'What else did your inestimable wife send?'

McDougall gave him a narrow look but delved into the basket. He produced a cooked ham, bread, tea, milk, wine, whisky, and showed off an apple batter pudding ladled with honey. The kettle whistled and McDougall rose, removed it from the range. Minutes later the scent of coffee mingled with the stew and Gordon drew a shuddering breath that ached his lungs.

'There was someone here,' he said.

All movement stopped.

'When?'

'Early hours this morning. I came home at dawn to find the front and back door unlocked.'

'I see.'

McDougall's tone was unimpressed. Heat flushed Gordon's neck and he rose, pulling the table from the back door.

'I was no in drink! Here's a boot-print. Look.'

McDougall did as bid, crouching to see better, and then

rose, staring at it. He raised one leg, measuring the ashy tread, still visible on the grey flagstone, against his own.

'Well, it's no mine.'

'Nor mine,' Gordon said, showing his own, longer sole.

They put the table back.

'So, someone broke in,' McDougall said.

'Nothing was broken. I'm certain they picked the lock as, since my parents visit, I made sure there's no key apart from mine to steal. I'd suspect my father, but he's more the smash sort if there's no key to be had.'

'All right, why would anyone take the effort? Money or food? If so, they were disappointed. There's naught left for anyone to steal, except maybe coal. You rest easy, I doubt they'll be back.'

Gordon didn't reply. In two strides, he reached the cubby and removed the coal bucket. Dragging the flagstone away, he reached in and pulled out the satchel.

'What on earth is that doing in there?'

Gordon ignored the lawyer, discarded the bag and put the book on the table. Turning to the back cover he slipped out the documents and, going through them, he was relieved all were there. Belatedly he noted McDougall at his elbow, staring at the old parchment sheaves.

'What is all that?'

Gordon tried to shuffle the pages away, but his fingers shook too much. McDougall took the sheaves from him, flicking through them with a puzzled look.

'Doctor McCraken, I've no clue as to most of this.' He held the letter packet from Doctor Bennett, reading the first page. 'But you seem to be in contact with a most eminent London physician. Could this person aid your recovery? Would he, for instance, be willing to recommend a suitable sanatorium?'

Something stirred in Gordon, his breath faltered, and he

swallowed rapidly.

'Mister McDougall, I've had something of a revelation.'

He stopped, wondering at his own courage.

You're ridiculous. He'll laugh while sending you to Bedlam. You're to die amongst the mad. Where you belong.

NO!

The force of his reaction drove Gordon deep into his chair, shaking and trembling. McDougall, still holding Doctor Bennett's letters, looked at him with concern.

A little while later Gordon sipped his coffee, studying McDougall, who ladled stew over potatoes. The lawyer handed him a steaming plate and Gordon managed thanks through numbed lips. McDougall settled, fussing with his brew and dinner. Gordon wrestled with his bravery, screwing it so tight that his spine felt rigid with it. Then he blurted out,

'What do you know of medical jurisprudence?'

'So-called forensics?' the lawyer asked. 'Enough to know that it's a crucial part of educating such as yourself, Doctor. It ensures proper medical procedures and processes are used in criminal investigations. I've had to deal with medical witnesses who dinnae have the benefit of such teachings. Such a lack can put a trial in jeopardy.'

Gordon nodded and ate a forkful of stew, barely tasting it.

'It's part of what brought Doctor Bennett and I together,' he said.

Again, Gordon's courage failed, dropping from him until he felt bereft and weak. He pushed his food about, his throat too narrow for it and words. McDougall ate with relish and seemed unconcerned about Gordon's manner, for which he was grateful. His gaze roamed the kitchen, alighting on the back door and his thoughts stunted on the intruder, making panic flutter like moths. Looking down Gordon found his fist clenched around his fork, hurting his palm. With an effort he eased his fingers away. Black rage, like bile, rose to drown the panic.

How dare they come into MY house. Seeking to destroy my only hope of redemption? The only way back to my work. It will no stand!

Gordon waited for Iona to berate him, belittle him, but his wife remained silent. He knew then, without a doubt, that using his knowledge, his medical skills, he had to save Amy Dudley and himself. Needs must, McDougall had to be drawn in to help. The man must be made an ally. All his fear turned to anger, then hardened into determination. Gordon cleared his throat.

'Consider some pity for English lawyers,' he said. 'For in England the teaching of forensic medicine is limited to the apothecary and one professorship at the University of London. It is no taught at all in the Royal College of Physicians.' He stopped, pleased and amazed that his voice was so strong and sure. He swallowed. 'And you see, with Doctor Bennett's help, I was hoping to bring about a change.'

McDougall frowned around his chewing.

'If what you say is true, then I admit the English do seem short sighted. Forgive me, Doctor, I fail to see how, as a Scottish trained practitioner, you could have any hope of influence in London. Unless you were secretly educated at Cambridge or Oxford.'

Gordon grimaced at the old law that made it impossible for him to practice in London.

'That's precisely why I sought Doctor Bennett's help and patronage. He'd agreed to advocate instigating forensic medicine and to support my intention of teaching it at the

Royal College.'

McDougall inclined his head with a shrewd look.

'Clever. A neat way to bypass the law. However, I'm sure you'll need more than a patron to get a new science approved in that institution. Surely, you need proof it works and is viable?'

'Aye, you do. We had barely fashioned a plan to gain means of proof, when…'

Gordon forked stew, suddenly hungry. McDougall continued eating, his eyes speculative. For a while, there was nothing but the scrape of crockery and men satisfying hunger.

'So, how did you and Doctor Bennett intend to prove forensic medicine as worthwhile to the English?' McDougall eventually asked.

Gordon licked his lips and swallowed some coffee.

YOU NO CAN SAY IT, CAN YOU? TERRIFIED, MURDERER.

HE'LL RIDICULE YOU. QUITE RIGHT, TOO.

If I save Amy Dudley, I can save myself. I can work again.

THINKING IT DISNAE MAKE IT SO.

Gordon gripped his fork, but it trembled against the plate and he put it down, clasping his fingers to still them.

'There were recent cases which I did put forward. But there was only one death that Doctor Bennett was interested in using. It so happened that I'm uniquely placed to use forensic medicine to investigate it. In fact, if I'm honest, it was Doctor Bennett's obsession with this particular death that prompted me to seek his help. An obsession that I'm hoping will persuade him to continue with our plan, despite the risk I now pose to his good standing.'

'What is this death, this obsession of Doctor Bennett's?'

Words and feelings tumbled inside Gordon. Taking a long breath, he gained a fragile calm that steadied his voice and nerve.

'The death is centuries old, but still controversial.' He halted, trying to untangle his thoughts and emotions, to pick his words with care. 'At the time it had a huge influence on English politics and royalty. It was ruled accidental, but I was going to prove the death a murder using forensic medicine. Given the death's notoriety and continued mystery, once conclusively solved, no one in the Royal College will doubt the validity of the science. With Doctor Bennett's advocacy I can then teach the pioneering field.'

McDougall looked interested and was plainly considering what Gordon had told him.

'I admit this change in you is encouraging, Doctor, and I see how things are,' the lawyer said. 'The plan will now be doubly beneficial to your Doctor Bennett. Firstly, he will be part of establishing a powerful, new science. Secondly, he gets to investigate a death he finds supremely interesting. You're hoping to lure him with the idea that, should you fail in the endeavour, he can attribute all blame to you with no stain upon his own reputation or standing. Perhaps you'll even conduct the investigation in secret until you can present the murder as an accomplished fact?'

Gordon nodded; the irony of how his unforeseen situation could now help shape his future redemption was not lost on him. He stared at his plate and tried not to think about blood. Looking up he found McDougall watching him. The lawyer sat back, dabbing his mouth with a napkin.

'All right, you've cornered my interest,' he said. 'So, tell me, why is that tome so important to you and whose death are you planning to investigate?'

CHAPTER NINE

Gordon's fingers dallied on the tome's cover and he struggled to speak. McDougall busied himself pouring whisky for them.

'Let's start with something that's been bothering me,' the lawyer said. 'Why is that book important enough to hide when there's no one here and you've sold everything else?'

Gordon consciously loosened his fingers, stroking the warm leather as if it were Quile.

'It was a gift, as I said.' His guilt spiked, making him sigh. 'There's no simple reasoning I can give.' He struggled, trying to fit words to his chaotic feelings. 'It's as if knowing the book and documents are there means a small part of what was, what could've been, is still alive. And because I destroyed, well, everything, I can no bear to have it just lying around mocking me. Nor can I get rid of it, if I'm to somehow succeed and continue my work. So, I hide it, but sometimes, I just…' Gordon wiped his eyes. 'I'm sorry, I'm talking nonsense.'

'You didnae destroy anything, you ken? It was an unfortunate—'

'Please, stop.'

McDougall's expression was sympathetic, and he nodded at the book.

'So, what's its significance to this death, to your

investigation?'

Gordon put the tome on the table and turned to the back. Slipping out the documents he rested a hand atop them.

'You cannae tell anyone.'

'Agreed.'

Gordon sorted the papers and notebook into three piles, pointing to one.

'These, as you know, are letters from Doctor Bennett.' He touched his calfskin notebook. 'These are my translations, notes and calculations.' He placed a hand on the oilskin-wrapped parchments. 'And these, these are the accounts of Sir Samuel Banks, who was a Sheriff of Oxford many years ago.'

'Forgive me, but what has a Sheriff of Oxford to do with your investigation?'

Gordon drew a fire-warmed breath that tasted of coffee and stew. He tried to ignore his clenched stomach and sipped some whisky.

'Sam was the man in charge of the jury's official enquiry. He was also charged to a clandestine mission, to find the truth behind Lady Amy Dudley's death.'

McDougall frowned.

'Amy Dudley, should I know the name?'

'You may have heard of her as Amy Robsart? No? All right, how about the story of an English noblewoman who mysteriously fell down some stairs, breaking her neck in an empty house?'

'Aye, I've heard of that. Was there no something strange about the whole thing?'

Gordon's fingers shook as he unwrapped and unfolded Sam's notes, wondering where to start.

'Strange, indeed.'

He fanned out the pages, putting them into some sort of order, and then proceeded to tell McDougall of the events at

Cumnor Place in 1560. After nearly half an hour McDougall was leaning forward, eagerly viewing the notes and utterly captivated by the story. Gordon felt a surge of triumph and continued.

'The rumours have never subsided as to whether Amy Dudley died from accident, murder or suicide. Many thought her husband, Robert Dudley, had her killed.'

'Hardly surprising given the odd circumstance of the puir woman's death. Was Lord Dudley truly such a man as to be party to murdering his own wife?'

'It seems so. There were whispers of it or divorce, so he could be free and marry the queen. Others are convinced Lady Dudley committed suicide, something Sam strove to disprove above all else.'

'No wonder, it's an evil taint for a soul to lie under especially if untrue.'

'Aye, a dreadful sentence for an innocent. But you see, the coroner's report states that although her neck was broken, there were also two holes in the left side of Amy Dudley's skull. One half an inch deep and the other two inches.'

'That's an awfully difficult thing to do as suicide, surely?'

Gordon held out some pages, which McDougall took. He poured more whisky for them both, passing a glass to the lawyer.

'The coroner was called Pudsey,' Gordon said. 'But it seems his report has been lost or destroyed. Thankfully, Sam detailed everything, as you can see, including Pudsey's findings, along with his investigation and the clues he found that proved murder.'

McDougall was nodding and, his gaze keen using Gordon's translation as well as his own knowledge of Latin to read Sam's notes. Then he pointed at the page, turning to Gordon.

'Here, who were the Watchers?'

'Sam was never sure. He seemed to think they were men either hired by Robert Dudley to kill his wife, or a faction comprised of Dudley's enemies. Sam's primary theory was that the man's enemies banded together and killed Amy Dudley, thus ensuring Lord Dudley was accused, and then forever thought of, as murdering his wife. Sam believed they even murdered others, including a messenger named Daniel Fleet who carried Amy Dudley's warning "Watch for the Watchers".'

'If true, that's horrendous.'

'Indeed. But however the woman died, his wife's death ultimately dashed Dudley's plans to marry the queen. The taint of murderer never left him. Queen Elizabeth could never marry a man thought of as such and expect to keep the throne. Look what it did to her cousin, Mary.'

'Oh aye, terrible mistakes the woman made.'

They fell to silence, both thinking of queens long dead. McDougall returned to Sam's notes and kept reading.

'It says here that your sheriff believed that the Watchers or Lord Dudley were looking for something. That whatever it was may have had something to do with Amy Dudley's murder.'

'Aye, but, as you can see, that part is vague. Sam's writings give only a shadowy sense of the object or document the killer sought. It might have been something that could threaten the queen or threaten the rebels. Sam's ambiguity is strange, at odds with the rest of his recordings, which are incredibly detailed.'

'I can see that.'

McDougall continued reading, tweaking his glasses and muttering to himself. Gordon sipped whisky and tried not to mind the other's fingers on the parchment. Finally, the lawyer set the pages aside, his gaze thoughtful.

'Now, as I understand it,' he said, 'this Sam of yours attributes Amy Dudley's death to being hit on the head with a candlestick, and then her neck broken. How she came to die was then made to look uncertain, perhaps to throw suspicion on Lord Dudley, but perhaps no. The sheriff also theorises that Amy Dudley held something that either her husband or his enemies sought that could threaten the English crown or the rebels, the search for which ended in her murder.' The lawyer smiled slightly and touched the parchment. 'And somehow, you believe you can use the information Sam recorded to conclusively prove Amy Dudley was murdered, using forensic medicine.'

Gordon drained his whisky and strove for an even tone. 'Does it seem so ridiculous?'

McDougall let out a long breath, studying the parchment.

'No exactly ridiculous, but I fail to see how you can conclusively prove murder with just these notes.'

'I've taken measurements from them and done the calculations.' Gordon retrieved his notebook and flicked the pages. 'See here.'

McDougall took the notebook, examining the sketches of candlesticks, staircases and skulls. He studied the dimensions and figures meticulously detailed alongside each version.

'Impressive. Yet, I can no help but wonder if the Royal College will feel the same way. Equally, you must find a way to authenticate Sam's documents, indeed the man's very existence, if you wish to be taken seriously.' Ignoring Gordon's black stare, the lawyer returned the notebook. 'What of the coroner's report – you said it was lost or destroyed?'

Gordon hated his own secret fears being spoken by

another and forced himself to swallow some whisky, easing his tight throat. He shuffled Doctor Bennett's letters, finding a tiny newspaper clipping.

'We have a theory about the coroner's report.' He refused to say how nebulous the notion could prove, instead focusing on explaining the possibility. 'In your business, I assume you know what the assizes were in 1560?'

McDougall removed his spectacles, producing a small cloth and cleaned them.

'A somewhat ponderous form of what they are today. The assizes would have travelled the country back then, gathering information on criminal and civil matters for the crown.' He replaced his glasses and the cloth vanished into a pocket. 'Your coroner's report into Amy Dudley's death would've been entered into the rolls. So, if it still exists, the report would be stored with that date and particular county rolls.'

'What do you mean by rolls?'

McDougall put one fist atop the other and pulled them apart, as if unrolling something.

'Hundreds of years ago records were written on parchment that was stored on long lengths and unrolled, hence being called rolls.'

'I didnae ken that being a lawyer meant they taught you so much pertinent information.'

McDougall's eyebrows climbed.

'Sarcasm? You clearly *are* feeling better, Doctor.'

They shared a smile and Gordon realised with surprise that he had a liking for the man. He handed McDougall the newspaper clipping.

'Doctor Bennett sent me this last year. It's about the opening of the new record office in London with the headquarters and main archive on Chancery Lane. The government has spent years collecting documents from various places, including criminal records. They're now storing them in newly appointed buildings.'

McDougall tipped the tiny paper to the light and read it.

'You believe the coroner's report will be amongst them, if it survived.'

'Aye.'

'And the buildings and contents are open to all?'

Gordon leant back, reaching for the whisky bottle, and topped up his glass.

'Not exactly. Doctor Bennett made inquiries and the records will be available to certain professionals, such as lawyers and doctors, for a price.'

'But if the coroner's report is truly gone, what then?'

Gordon sipped, trying to gauge McDougall's temperament, but his quickened heartbeat was intrusive, scattering his thoughts. He tried to honey his words.

'There's something definitive I'm planning to use,' Gordon said carefully. 'Either alongside the coroner's report, or without it.'

'Sounds intriguing. Does Doctor Bennett have this definitive evidence?'

Gordon turned his glass, staring as the lamplight patterned the whisky with fire.

'No, it's stored in Oxford.'

He glanced up to find McDougall watching him.

'What is it, exactly?' the lawyer asked.

Gordon steadily met the other's gaze.

'Amy Dudley.'

McDougall frowned.

'There's a diary or letters?'

'No. I mean, Amy Dudley. Her bones.'

McDougall's eyebrows drew down and his expression soured.

'You intend to become a resurrection man, Doctor?'

'Hardly. Doctor Bennett can ask for the bones to be disinterred, once we've got the attention of the Royal College. They'll agree to it. Either because they want us to fail or they want us to succeed. With the influence of Doctor Bennett and the Royal College, I'm certain the Church will allow it.'

McDougall shook his head, looking sceptical.

'Do you no realise,' Gordon said, 'it's the only way to accurately account for the head wounds? A candlestick can be improvised or even manufactured. To be definitive, I must use Amy Dudley herself.'

McDougall rose, making the table rattle. He gathered bowls and glasses, muttering while avoiding Gordon's gaze. With sure fingers, Gordon opened the leather book, turning the pages until he found Leonardo da Vinci's anatomical drawing of a human spine and ribs.

'What of these?' He gestured to the drawing, so the lawyer glanced at it, his brow furrowed. 'How do you think Leonardo da Vinci drew so accurately, centuries ago?' Gordon asked. 'He must have had human subjects. Dead ones. You must ken our law now allows the use of cadavers for anatomical study.'

'But *you* are no using a fresh cadaver for anatomical study, Doctor McCraken, you're talking about disturbing the dead. Digging up the puir woman's earthly remains to experiment upon them. It's immoral. You go too far!'

He hates you now and disnae believe Sam exists.

Gordon ignored her.

'Many believe Amy Dudley committed suicide. Suicide victims are legally allowed for medical study.'

'You yourself said the suicide is mere rumour. One you hope to disprove! You cannae elect what's of import or no, to suit your needs.'

Heat flushed through Gordon and his words ground out.

'And I can no save Amy Dudley without her bones!'

The heat abruptly fled, leaving him feeling white and exposed. McDougall turned from the sink with a puzzled expression.

'The woman is deid, what are you trying to save her from?'

'It disnae matter, it's no you I must convince.'

The lawyer inclined his head in acknowledgement, jaw tightening and relaxing. After a small silence his gaze became thoughtful.

'What if I help you?'

'But you just said—'

McDougall raised his hand.

'For the heinous act of exhumation, you must convince Doctor Bennett, then the Royal College and the Church. Something I hope you fail at. But searching for the coroner's report will require meticulous attention.' He adjusted his glasses, peering at the clipping again. 'Equally, if your Doctor Bennett is reluctant to continue your undertaking, a lawyer's authority in this new records archive will be needed. For your standing is no what it was and you've no practice to speak of. I realise the search may be in vain. Yet I'll help, in the hope that, should we find the document, the bones will prove unnecessary. The report may lend enough credence to Sam's existence and spur Doctor Bennett to continue with you.'

Gordon stared at the lawyer, his thoughts shifting from dark to light. Connotations flickered in his mind.

'You would truly help me in this? Come to London with me – why?'

'I've been tasked by Lady Drummond to convince you to seek help and aid your recovery. She's instructed me to set aside all else in this pursuit. Now, I'll no play false that this course you've presented is something I agree with or expected. But, the change in you can no be ignored. I'd be remiss in my duty if I refused to help you achieve it, if it aids your recovery. But I'd need to ensure Lady Drummond's willingness to finance the venture, to help you with this.'

Gordon had almost forgotten his sister-in-law.

'I've some money left from the sale of my possessions,' he said. 'It's no much. Do you think Margaret will help? I'd be reluctant to tell her, or anyone, about our plans, for they might seem strange to them and enough to lose any support.'

McDougall's expression turned thoughtful, his eyes narrowing.

'Aye, well we're to London to see Doctor Bennett. A man in a perfect position to aid your recovery. More than that she needn't ken until we've more solid ground to stand on.'

Suddenly Gordon wasn't sure McDougall was helping him with a view to succeed or merely accompanying him to catch him should he fail. His fingers found the tome and he struggled for a moment, wrestling with his stubborn tongue and unwieldy thoughts.

'I need to go to Oxford first.'

The lawyer stiffened and Gordon shook his head.

'No for Amy Dudley, although I'd like to visit the church where she's buried. I need to find Foxcombe Manor.'

'What's that?'

'Where Sam lived. You're right, I need to prove he existed. That something tangible of the man is left, other than these documents.'

'Surely there'll be records, a grave, something?'

'Aye, possibly. But I ken where the manor is, or what's left of it, and there's plans of Foxcombe Manor with Sam's documents. It will be the easiest and quickest way to prove he lived and died where he says he did. The records can come later, after the coroner's report.'

McDougall looked sceptical.

CHILD KILLER. WIFE MURDERER. SAM'S A MYTH. YOU WILL FAIL.

Gordon stood, rubbing his arms, pacing, trying to think.

'I ken how you believe visiting Oxford is a nonsense. But I need to find Foxcombe. I need…'

Words failed and wetness starred his eyelashes. Gordon stopped and lowered his head, defeat covering him like a cloak. After a moment warm fingers gripped his shoulder.

'Oxford, then London,' McDougall said. 'As soon as word from Doctor Bennett reaches us to come. But if he refuses to help…'

'Then I'll find another way.' Gordon raised his head. 'But Doctor Bennett will no refuse.'

Meeting McDougall's gaze Gordon wondered who he was trying to convince, the lawyer, or himself.

'Finding Foxcombe Manor will no be any easy thing,' Gordon continued. 'It's in the countryside somewhere and will involve hard riding and camping in unfamiliar woods. Would you be willing to tackle such a venture?'

McDougall smiled, his eyes alight.

'My grandfather was a Highlander and loved no better thing than taking me hunting and fishing. I've done the same with my own son. We've spent many a night in old shepherds' huts and ridden in terrible weather. A southern jaunt will no concern me.'

Gordon gripped the man's fingers with his own, again rendered speechless. A small flame warmed his chest, spreading through his body and lessening the shadow on his soul.

CHAPTER TEN

They spent the rest of the day making plans. Finally, Gordon, armed with the poker, closed and locked the front door after McDougall. He stared into the dark hall, willing himself to move. Despite the lantern, the house again seemed a hostile force, ready to fall on him at any time. It took all his nerve to brave the blackness and hurry to the kitchen. Once there, breathing hard, he barricaded the door. Settling into his chair, letting his heart quieten, he gathered the precious letters and documents. Sorting them into their respective piles, his fingers lingered on the plans of Foxcombe Manor.

He poured more whisky before unfolding the parchments, seeing the building come to life once more in pen and ink. Both plans were dated 1560. One was of the manor without a library and one with the new room built. Gordon had often wondered if the library had ever been completed or if the plan was just a theoretical drawing. He placed a thumb over the rectangle of a well in the drawing without a library. Again, wondering if its placement had stopped the building; for in the other, newer plan the library stood over the well site. Although when holding the newer plan up to the light, he knew a faint outline of the well could be seen in a corner of the library. This had happened, Gordon surmised, when at some point the drawings must have been put together while not quite dry. The ink of the well from the one without the library transferred to the other, causing the faint outline on the newer one. With a fingertip he traced the rest of the lines on the library diagram. Just knowing those rooms and walls were where Sam had lived, laughed and loved made the man seem closer. He folded the parchments and opened the tome to the back, absently running a finger along the stitching. He stopped, frowning, feeling a slight rise where the thread met the spine.Slipping his hand inside the secret pocket, he employed his fingernail, testing the edge of whatever was there. Something was trapped in-between the tight edge of the pocket and the back of the tome. With infinite care he plucked at it, worrying for the book's integrity, and managed to work it free. It was a piece of parchment, no more than four inches wide and twice as long. It was filled with tiny written gibberish bar the last line: "Beginning with Caesar then V". He placed it on Sam's notes and saw the penmanship was the same. He sat back, bewildered at the oddity and senselessness of what Sam had written. His gaze was drawn to the only line that he could read, turning it over and over in his mind.

'The only Caesar I know is the Roman general,' he muttered.

Suddenly he was transported back to Kilbride Castle. He recalled his uncle in the sunlit library pulling down books, reading aloud of long-dead leaders, empire's battles and strategies. The heady smell of books like a balm came, along with the fascination and delight of reading the stories with his uncle. His thoughts still full of books, he reluctantly became aware of the kitchen again. His fingers traced Sam's indecipherable writing, trying to make sense of it. He rose and glanced at the back door, where the boot-print lay. Gordon squared his shoulders and picked up the lamp but at the kitchen door he hesitated. Turning back, he retrieved the poker and put a tablecloth over his shoulder. Hefting the poker he headed into the dark house.

Walking the hall, ghostly in his lamplight, he listened over his treads and breathing, trying to hear above the creaking house.

HE'S IN THE HOUSE, WAITING.

Gordon stopped, glancing back toward the kitchen and listening, listening. There was only the rising wind and rain clattering at the windows.

FOOTSTEPS. CREEPING. CREEPING TOWARD YOU.

Gordon's breaths quickened and the study seemed a long way away. Still, he pressed on, the strange parchment dominating his thoughts, even swamping Iona. Gaining the study, he found the room chilled with the broken window letting in cold and damp, despite the newspaper stuffed into the break. Yet his lamplight tamed the chamber so it seemed friendlier and he shut the door, feeling instantly better. Placing the lamp on the floor and the poker against the wall, he dragged one of the trunks in front of the door. He sat on the lid and waited as his heart slowed to normal. Gordon then rose and hauled the other trunk over. Sitting on it, he opened the lid of the first and revealed the wealth of books bequeathed to him on his uncle's death two years previously.

Feeling the loss anew, he ran a hand over the spines. Pausing, he lifted out one about Henry the Seventh. Opening it, he read the first paragraph, then with a sigh replaced the book. Spreading the tablecloth on the floor he began to search, examining and taking out books, placing those he wanted on the tablecloth. Once he'd gone through one trunk, he changed places and rummaged in the second. More books soon piled on the tablecloth. Then, beneath a tome concerning battle strategies, he found an unfamiliar walnut case. The burnished wood glowed in the lamplight and he lifted the box lid to display a revolver. All around it, nestled in specially made compartments, were a round tin of percussion caps, a box of explosive envelopes, cleaning cloth and oil. A folded paper was tucked down the side and turned out to be instructions and a message. He read with interest about this gift from an American named Samuel Colt to his uncle. The message revealed it came as thanks for the substantial Kilbride investment in Colt's new invention – the revolving percussion weapon.

Gordon took the gun out, glinting like mercury, and felt its hard weight. He followed the instructions and loaded the gun, replacing it in the case. Feeling more secure than he had in hours, he finished searching the trunk, taking out one more book. Removing the revolver, he put the case on the tablecloth along with the books and gathered the cloth to form a makeshift sack. He moved the trunks from the door and tucked the revolver into his trouser band. Slotting the poker through as a handle he shouldered the sack. He picked up the lamp and left, closing the study door behind him. The darkness was still barely held back by his light, but now, with the gun in his waistband, the house seemed less hostile and forbidding.

In the kitchen he placed the cloth sack and gun on the table then wedged the dining chair beneath the door handle. Satisfied, he fed coal to the range and settled in his chair. With Sam's strange parchment to hand he picked up the first book and perused its Roman history for Caesar, hoping for some sort of insight into the jumble of letters.

For a time, Gordon was immersed in the rise and fall of the Roman empire, the battles and politics. The fourth book he picked up was entitled *Lives of Caesars LVI* by Suetonius. Of the twelve Caesars contained in the book,

Gordon turned first to Julius Caesar. He read about the first Roman triumvirate formed with Crassus and Pompey, of the stunning strategies and vision in the Gallic Wars that propelled Julius Caesar to become a renowned general and politician. But then, with the next words, his mouth went dry. Suetonius wrote about the Caesar cipher, a secret way of writing invented by the general. Gordon stared at the story and then at the parchment.

'It's cipher,' he breathed. 'Sam wrote a cipher!'

He pulled his notebook from amongst the papers and found a nub of pencil. Staring at the gibberish writing, he knew, from translating the other documents, that Sam's alphabet had been different to his own. Gordon wrote the alphabet as he knew it, the twenty-six letters, A-Z. He then wrote the Elizabethan alphabet, only twenty-four letters and marked the U, V, I and J with their different uses. Then he examined Sam's final line again, alongside Suetonius's description of the Caesar cipher.

'The Caesar cipher is done by a substitution of three letters. Yet, Sam's V is the Roman numeral for five. So, move the alphabet along by five?'

He tried it, moving the Elizabethan alphabet along so the A then became E and so on, but still the message remained a garbled jumble. He rubbed the back of his neck, jaw tense, and tried to think. Quile croaked and he looked up to see her spring from her nest, to fly-hop to the table. Thoughts sluggish, he watched the crow saunter around the books and parchments. Occasionally she cocked her head until she reached Gordon. Then her claws tap-tapped on his notebook, her bright eyes inquisitive, muttering for food.

'I dinnae ken what it says,' he told her. 'M'be its bloody meaningless.'

Quile pecked the page and he rose, getting a dish of scraps for her. She ate cleanly, with quick, stabbing motions while Gordon returned to the message. The knot in his neck felt like a fist, but he fell once again to contemplating that final line, "Beginning with Caesar then V."

'Caesar at the beginning?'

Unused to the work after his months of confinement and decline, his fingers cramped around the pencil. He ignored the pain and doggedly wrote the alphabet again. Under the first six letters he wrote "CAESAR" then shook his head, scoring it through.

'A can no represent two different letters.'

He rewrote it, omitting the second 'a' in Caesar. In this way the plain text alphabet A was represented by C and so on until E was represented by R. He then moved the rest of the alphabet on by five so after the R in "CAESR" came "VWXYZ" and so on. It seemed to him now, staring at Sam's jumbled words and his cipher, that he might make sense of the thing. Laboriously he began to decrypt the message but stopped when the first three words remained nonsense. He threw down the pencil, hissing through his teeth and flexing his pained hand.

'For the love of Mary, will you no just make sense!'

WHY ARE YOU WORRYING OVER IT? IT'LL MAKE NO DIFFERENCE. YOU'RE NAUGHT BUT A FAILURE. GIVE UP AND DIE. IT'S ALL THAT'S LEFT FOR YOU.

Rain rattled the windows and the kitchen seemed to darken, the lamplight fading. Gordon put his head in his hands. Quile's beak nibbled his ear and then ruffled his hair.

'How many times you daft, wee bird, I've no insects living in there,' he muttered.

He raised his head, fingers finding her warm body, and he stroked her while the aching in his hands lessened. Unbidden his gaze wandered over his writings. Tiredness made his bones heavy and he pulled a blanket around him. The table swam in his gaze, sleep trying to take over. He wanted to hide everything but found his limbs immovable as if saturated wood. Closing his eyes, letters swirled in the darkness, vying for attention. An S turned sideways, became a dog barking and rushed around. It chased the B which ran along as if on wheels. Suddenly he was wide awake, pushing the blanket away. His movements startled Quile, complaining, back to her nest.

'I didnae take out the second S and R,' he muttered.

Returning to the pencil he rewrote the cipher alphabet, with "CAESR" at the beginning. He then moved the rest of the letters along five and this time didn't include the S and R further in the cipher alphabet as already represented in "CAESR". He began to decode the message, heartened when the first word emerged as 'Hugh'. He became even more excited when the third word became 'Foxcombe'. Gordon had no idea how much time passed but he didn't stop until the whole message was done and translated into his own, twenty-six letter, alphabet. Dated November 1561, it read;

> Hugh, greetings. Foxcombe is flourishing with Joan safely delivering our second grandchild, named Martin. Mary's wedding is set for May twentieth, to which you and your wife are naturally invited.
>
> The library is near completion including the addition we spoke of. Men have been twice more to Foxcombe and left with as much as they came with, naught. Thankfully it appears our esteemed friend has kept counsel about us, yet we must remain on guard. Be advised, in the event of change in our esteemed friend's silence, Foxcombe's addition will be used for us to gain Cymru. You should know, as no other will, that this exit is all well. In

> six months hence, you will see for yourself. Be sure to write when to expect you, mayhap May tenth would suffice for our reunion.

Gordon let out an explosive breath, all tiredness forgotten. Reading and re-reading the message, it felt as if Sam were sitting before him, speaking of his home life. Despite the centuries that separated them, he felt deeply satisfied that Sam's life had flourished and that the man had been happy after the investigation into Amy Dudley's death. He read the document again, reasoning that the esteemed friend must be Queen Elizabeth and the men who had come to Foxcombe were undoubtedly from Lord Dudley. That the library had been built excited Gordon, feeling as if he and Sam shared a confidence.

'What was the addition?' he wondered aloud. 'And how could it help them escape?'

He again unfolded the plans of Foxcombe and, taking in their fragility, copied them into this notebook. Yet the diagrams yielded no clue to the addition Sam had written about.

'Perhaps it will be clearer when I get there.'

Suddenly exhausted, he hid all the documents in the tome, sliding it into the satchel and replacing it in its secret hole. He drained his whisky and settled in his chair, wrapping the blanket around him. Quile's wings made a soft whirr and she landed on his shoulder, nestling into his neck. Her musty odour was oddly comforting, and he welcomed her warmth. He looked, and seeing the gun was near to hand, the chair wedged firmly beneath the door handle, Gordon fell asleep.

CHAPTER ELEVEN

The following afternoon found Gordon walking across Prince's Street Gardens, into the Old Town, wondering if anyone watched him. He made his way through the narrow streets, eyeing anyone who passed, his mind full of Amy Dudley. Despite the cool day, laundry flapped on poles protruding from windows. High above, seagulls sailed in the bits of sky between roofs. An old woman leading a goat emerged from between dingy houses to eye him suspiciously before moving on. Two grubby children sitting on a spiral staircase watched as Gordon walked beneath an arch and out onto Nicholson Street. He looked back to see if the children followed him, then the crowded street gripped all his attention.

The wide road was busy with hansom cabs, carts and horses. Women carrying baskets and pushing prams chatted and shopped. Pipe-smoking men meandered between the more serious top-hatted gents. Moving amongst them, praying he wouldn't see any familiar faces, sweat prickled Gordon's neck. A barrel of a woman stared at him and Gordon lowered his head, touching his hat rim, and hurried past. His gaze grazed a shadowed doorway, then fixed on a man watching him. But it was only a barber, manhandling a sign. Gordon's breath eased.

Inside the tailors he purchased suits and a Macintosh

coat, paying the shopkeeper with barely a word. He had the items wrapped and addressed, thinking delivery would be better, would cause him less anxiety, than having to carry everything about the crowded streets. The shopkeeper studied his name on the parcel with a puzzled air, gaze flicking to Gordon and back again. Hating the man's prying looks, Gordon suddenly decided against delivery. He hastily gathered the packages and left. Outside the shop he abruptly stopped in the doorway, watching the street, wondering who might recognise him. His skin crawled and he was certain someone was there, watching and waiting for him. The throng slipped and slid past in coloured suits and dresses, amid skipping children and parasols. Unexpectedly it parted, as river around a rock, to reveal a man, face skewed pinkly by a harelip, staring. Gordon stumbled, groping for the shop door, parcels spilling left and right. Glancing back, the man had gone. He almost fell when the shop door opened, and the tailor's gaze found his own. Muttering an apology Gordon hurried next door, into the gloom of the barbers.

Within a few minutes he was seated in the barber's chair with a glimmer of an idea. Thinking of the harelipped man suddenly strengthened the idea into resolve. Gordon tugged his thick beard, peering in a spotted mirror. The barber, a porcine man, watched while stroking his own flowing beard and moustache. Gordon met his gaze in the mirror.

'I want it all gone, please.'

'Are you sure?' the barber asked.

'Aye, all of it.'

'What if we leave some side whiskers? Give your face a wee covering, at least.'

Beneath Gordon's fingers the ruddy bristles were red and gold in the gaslight. He shook his head.

'All of it.'

The barber shrugged, his expression disappointed. Gordon closed his eyes, trying to stay calm but the harelipped man stalked his thoughts.

The brute is coming for you. You should let him.

Why me?

You're a murderer. Is that no reason enough?

Not any more.

Scissors abruptly clicked across his chin and Gordon flinched, making the barber tut.

'Try and be still, sir. We're going to be a wee while, for it's a magnificent beast we're slaying, more's the pity.'

Gordon murmured an apology and settled back. He strove to ignore the clack and clipping of the scissors and the closeness of the barber. Yet it was increasingly difficult as the man's harsh hair oil and slim cigar smoke wafted in his face with each movement. It seemed hours before the scissors stopped, the fallen hairs tickling his nose and fining the air. Gordon stroked his prickly face, touching the cleft in his chin properly for the first time in a decade. Quick movements and whooping sound made him turn. The barber was stropping a cut-throat razor, peering intently at the blade moving along the leather.

He's going to slice you up.

Gordon's hands clenched on the chair arms, shoulders stiffening and sweat prickling against his shirt.

Works with the harelipped man, like as no. In it together. Murder for a murderer.

Gordon screwed his eyes shut, fingernails digging into the chair.

'You all right there, sir?'

He opened his eyes to the barber's gaze and glistening blade. The man looked wary and spoke slowly, as if to a scared animal.

'It'll no take long now, sir. Unless you've a mind to keep the wee bit that's left?'

'It's all to come off. Pray continue.'

'Aye, I will do. But you'll need to ease your jaw, for it's a sharp-edged blade and your jawbone will prove it, unless you keep it soft for my strokes.'

Gordon worked his mouth as if chewing and rubbed his face, easing the tightness. He leant back in the chair and nodded. Forcing himself to stillness, he hardly breathed as the blade slithered across skin, slicing away the remaining whiskers. It seemed to take as long as the scissors and Gordon barely kept his panic at bay, fuelled by Iona's whispering. Afterward he breathed deeply, relief turning his limbs weak. His face felt raw. Despite a warning, he flinched when the hot towel was applied. Muttering, the barber removed the towel with unnecessary force and took Gordon's money without a word. The man retreated to clean up, offering neither a smile nor nod, clearly offended by his customer's reactions.

Gathering his parcels, Gordon stepped out onto Nicolson Street and shivered in the chill of late afternoon. His face felt as if it were being continually slapped. Without the dense beard protection, the cold made his teeth ache. He resisted the urge to rub his face and, instead, lowered his head, joining the tide of people flowing down the street. At first, he just wanted to get away from where he'd seen the harelipped man and so let the crowd's rhythm take him where it would. He fell in step with the hard walkers, rather than the meandering folk, but kept constantly looking around for the harelipped man.

HE'S HERE. HE'S GOING TO STAB YOU. CAREFULLY. QUICKLY. BLEED YOU TO DEATH LIKE A DOG IN THE STREET.

He tried to see everywhere and everyone.

Find you. Murderer. Child killer. Get what you deserve.

He tried to block her out by quickening his pace, but the swirling people kept forcing him to walk slowly. He felt vulnerable, exposed to hostile eyes, stony elbows and muttered oaths. Waiting, just waiting for the harelipped man to slide from them and kill him. The crowd ebbed and flowed around him, but the measure remained steady. Gordon's presence caused no outcry, but he knew there were whispers, secret, pointing fingers and stares. He dipped his chin, the air numbing his naked face. Again, Gordon tried to move faster, but the pressing flow kept him to a walk, until it poured out onto the High Street. On impulse, he turned left toward St Giles', seized by an abrupt need to see Father John.

Gordon, free of the crowds, approached the cathedral, rehearsing explanations of, if not his entire restoration of faith, at least the belief that redemption, however unorthodox, might be possible. But most of all, he wanted to sit in Father John's comforting presence, find a measure of peace in tea and undemanding talk. Still, the cathedral edifice nearly broke his resolve. The soaring glory to God skewering him with guilt and shame. It took an effort of will to cross the threshold and walk the cool corridors to the presbytery.

Gordon went to knock but heard voices beyond the door. Fearing his nerve would break in unknown company he settled on a stone bench tucked away in a shadowed alcove to wait. He rested his head between a column and the curving wall, grateful the natural darkness hid his eyes from the stern, stained glass stares of angels and apostles. He placed his parcels on the bench and took out his pocket-watch, but it was too dim to see the face properly or the beating hands. He wondered how long he could bear to wait.

HARELIPPED MAN WAS WATCHING AND FOLLOWED YOU HERE.

I'd have noticed.

YOU DIDNAE NOTICE I WAS ILL, AND THEN YOU LET IT KILL ME.

That's a burden I'll always bear.

DYING WOULD EASILY RID YOU OF IT.

Leave me alone!

YOU COULD LET THE HARELIPPED MAN FIND YOU, IT'S SIMPLE.

Gordon pictured it, sure the harelipped man would use bare hands to strangle him. He could feel his throat tightening under the imagined fingers and squeezed his eyes shut, willing the pressure away.

No one and nothing there. Nothing and no one there.

He repeated the thought over and over, drowning Iona out, forcing himself to believe it. Suddenly he opened his eyes.

What if the harelipped man is no interested in me at all? What if he's just a man? Can personal darkness do that, succumb the senses to persecution?

In his mind the sightings of the harelipped man ran together and the menace seemed to drain out of them.

I must have left the front door unlocked and it had to have been McDougall, leaving the inside doors open.

THE BOOT-PRINT, IN THE ASH?

Probably the housekeeper on leaving the house for the last time. Or like the lawyer said, maybe someone had been inside and left because there were no goods to steal. Have I been a fool?

He rubbed his bare face.

YOU ARE A FOOL.

I'll tell Father John about the harelipped man and the house. He'll help me understand it all.

YOU'RE PATHETIC. IT'LL MAKE NO DIFFERENCE. YOU'LL FAIL.

I can at least try.

To quieten his dead wife, Gordon once again calculated Amy Dudley's height against the measurements of Cumnor Place staircase. Abruptly the presbytery door opened and Gordon, sitting in the dark place, easily saw the man who emerged. The figure was swathed in a long coat with a flat hat pulled low over his brow but was unmistakable. Gordon's breaths became shallow; nausea swept through him as the wall dug into his spine. The man glanced back into the room and then, peering left and right, hurried away. Gordon tried to rise, but the sight of the harelipped man had destroyed all nerve and thought. Suddenly Father John, cassock askew, stumbled into the presbytery doorway. The priest abruptly dropped, as if his muscles and bones had turned to water, and with a cry Gordon scrambled to him. The man's lips were blue, his breathing harsh and the whites of his eyes rolled wildly, then he shuddered and lay still.

'Father John!'

Gordon put his ear to the man's chest and heard nothing. He placed trembling fingers on the priest's neck and felt the blood stilling, vein failing. Gordon reeled back, away from the awful truth; Father John was dead. Beneath his hat Gordon gripped his hair and stared about, a shout forming, but then:

THERE'S A MURDERER HERE! MCCRAKEN'S HERE!

He swallowed his cry, pressing his lips together, and scuttled back from the body. Footsteps sounded. Pushing his shaking legs to action, Gordon ran for home.

CHAPTER TWELVE

The door to Heriot Row slammed shut. Gordon sank to the leaf-strewn floor, fist to his mouth and tears sharp on his bare face.

I have to leave.

RUN COWARD. RUN AWAY.

The knocker sounded and Gordon froze.

'Doctor McCraken, can you hear me?'

With a sob Gordon struggled upright and let McDougall in. He paused to peer past the man, but there was only drizzle and the darkening day. Gordon shut and locked the door then shambled back, lungs aching, and eyes blurred. Legs abruptly failing again, he fell against the lawyer's supporting arm.

'Doctor McCraken, what's the matter?'

Gordon shook his head. McDougall muttered something and led him to the kitchen, where he settled Gordon in the wingback chair. The lawyer poured a large whisky and forced Gordon's hands around the glass. The tawny liquid sloshed as Gordon managed to take a slug and then another, while McDougall stoked the range.

'I saw you,' the lawyer said, 'racing through the rain as if the hounds of hell were after you. I called out, but you didnae hear.'

'He's deid.'

McDougall straightened, frowning.

'Who's deid?'

'Father John.'

For a moment McDougall looked blank.

'The priest from St Giles?' he said.

Gordon nodded and swallowed more whisky.

'I think he was murdered, poisoned.'

'Why in God's name would you say that?'

'I was there. I saw what happened.'

'I see.'

Gordon struggled to rise.

'I didnae do it!'

McDougall looked alarmed and placed a hand on Gordon's shoulder, pushing him back.

'No one would think so.'

'They would, someone would. They'll come for me. Oh no! No!' He gripped McDougall's arm. 'My parcels, I left them there, on the bench. My name's on them!'

McDougall patted his hand.

'All right. It's all right,' he said. 'I'll go to St Giles' now and fetch them. It'll give me a chance to find out about Father John.'

'You cannae say I was there!'

'I'll no say a word, but you must promise you'll wait for me here and finish your whisky.'

Gordon nodded, letting his hand drop from the lawyer's arm. His body suddenly deflated as if his bones had turned to dust and the blood vanished from his veins. McDougall topped his glass up and left, promising to lock the front door behind him. After the kitchen door closed, Gordon wedged the chair beneath the handle and retreated back to the warmth of the range.

He's gone for the constables.

No.

You'll see. Or he's gone for the harelipped man. Knows all about your treasure.

In a sudden panic Gordon moved the coal bucket and flagstone pedestal. His groping fingers met the bulky satchel and gun metal and relief made him weak so he couldn't move for a moment. Then he took out the bag and revolver, gripping them to him, and settled in the chair to wait for McDougall.

It seemed time fled and yet crawled after McDougall left. After a while the afternoon turned to dusk and Gordon lit all the gas lamps, piling the range with coal, stoking it to a rage. He pretended the house didn't yawn, dark and empty, about and above him.

'There's no one there. No one and nothing. Nothing and no one.'

Only madmen talk to themselves.

Gordon grunted, found another bottle of whisky with an inch or two left. He settled back in his chair, tome to hand and gun on his lap, watching the door. Every utterance of the house seemed too loud, groaning and shuddering like a weather-beaten shack.

You want to die, remember?

That was before.

Before you found redemption in Amy Dudley and your work? Dinnae be absurd. You'll never be forgiven. God hates you.

From above, something thumped. A heavy something, like a person; like a man entering through a window. Gordon rose, hand trembling on the gun, and went to the door. Listening, listening to the moving building that yielded nothing and no one. He moved the chair, letting the door open a crack, and the revolver felt sweaty and solid in his hand. He raised it, following the muzzle out into the dark house, and stole down the hall, hating the leaves and empty bottles that screamed, HERE HE IS! Shadows of people followed him and fled before him, dark on dark. Then came a skittering and scratching of nails on glass. He crouched, breath hurting and catching, staring at thin arms stretched across the study window. Sweat stung his eyes and he almost squeezed the trigger; almost, almost, shooting, swaying, tapping branches. Sudden thumping was louder, closer. He rose, lunging, tripping for the front door, revolver raised at the man beyond.

'I am very sorry, Mister McDougall,' Gordon said.

'Aye, we've established that.' The lawyer fingered the hole in his top hat. 'Still, it might've been worse.'

'I didnae mean to fire. It just went off.'

They were back in the kitchen and McDougall placed his ruined hat on the table alongside Gordon's packages. He took off his frock coat, draping it over the dining chair.

'I've heard those Colts can be tricky,' McDougall said. 'Especially when fired in the dark, by the panic stricken.'

'Again, I'm sorry.' Gordon gripped McDougall's arm. 'What of Father John? Tell me, please!'

'I'm afraid Father John is indeed deid, but from nothing more sinister than a heart attack. It was a weakness he had.'

Gordon sank into the wingback chair, face in his hands, feeling his palms slick against his skin. McDougall moved about. Water poured, the coffee pot gurgled and soon the smell permeated the room. Gordon lifted his head, trying to banish the image of Father John falling, dying. He watched as McDougall rinsed cups, wondering how to explain about the harelipped man.

HE'LL NO BELIEVE YOU. YOU'LL SOUND MAD. OFF TO BEDLAM!

Gordon stifled a groan.

'We have to leave for Oxford, now, today. Tonight.'

McDougall stared at him.

'You're making no sense man. You've had a shock, I'll grant you that, but there's no need for such a drastic course.'

'But Father John…'

'Doctor, no one will think that had anything to do with you.'

Gordon shook his head, his thoughts fleeing like wild hares. He took a deep breath that shuddered in his chest.

'There's a man. Watching. Following me wherever I go.' McDougall's gaze narrowed but Gordon ploughed on. 'I'm certain he was here, in the house. The boot-print must be his.'

'What makes you think that?'

Gordon flung himself up to pace the kitchen.

'Because he's watching me! Following me! Outside in the Gardens, down Nicholson Street and then to St Giles'. He was there.' Gordon gripped McDougall's arm again. 'He murdered Father John!'

McDougall's expression was sympathetic, and he lifted Gordon's hands from his sleeve.

'Come now, Father John died from his puir heart giving out. Sit yourself, Doctor, drink some more whisky. It'll help steady your nerves and we can talk of this man you think you've seen.'

Against his protests, Gordon allowed himself to be seated and handed the whisky. He gulped and his knotted insides loosened slightly from the warming liquid. McDougall sipped his own drink, watching with a concern that made Gordon ashamed of his actions.

'It might help to cheer you to hear of my good news,' the lawyer said. 'Lady Drummond has agreed to finance our trip to London, including board and lodging. So, we can leave as soon as we have an invitation from Doctor Bennett.'

Gordon abruptly stood, drink sloshing on his hands.

'You dinnae understand! The harelipped man is coming to kill me! We have to leave, now. Tonight.'

McDougall stood, carefully placing his glass on the table, and spoke slowly.

'There's no one coming to kill you.'

THINKS YOU'RE MAD. MAD. MAD. MAD.

Gordon saw the truth of her words in the lawyer's expression.

'Get out,' he said. 'Get out. Leave me be!'

'Doctor, I really think—'

The revolver felt lighter than before and Gordon twitched it toward the back door. McDougall gathered his things and made to speak but thought better of it. He backed from Gordon, fumbling with the table and door before pulling it open. With a final look of entreaty, he disappeared into the rain and dark yard. Gordon waited until he could no longer hear the man's footsteps and the squeal of the gate told of the lawyer's complete departure. Gordon closed and locked the back door. He spun back to the kitchen trying to hold on to his thoughts and balance.

I have to get out. I have to leave. Money. I need my money.

He stared at the suddenly unfamiliar kitchen and it seemed like a tomb closing in while the night and rain pressed behind him.

Banks are shut. SHITE!

His chest heaved on a sob and he staggered to the chair, half falling into it, the gun lank in his grip.

HE'S COMING.

Iona's voice was soft, like a whispered promise. Gordon bolted up and stared at the windows and door, but they remained blank and black. He wedged the dining chair under the kitchen door handle and stood, panting, hand clutching the revolver. His gaze fell on the parcels retrieved by McDougall and hope surged. He scrabbled, sobbing and fingers clumsy until they closed on his purse. He emptied the contents onto the table, counting once, twice and a third time.

Please let it be enough to reach Oxford.

No enough time. Never enough distance. He's coming.

He hurriedly packed the satchel containing the Da Vinci tome, his medical bag, now full of his surgical instruments, into one of his new sealskin bags. He piled his recently purchased clothes and supplies into the other and pulled on his new Macintosh coat. He put everything on the table and looked around the kitchen. His gaze fell on Quile, watching bright eyed from her nest. Gordon went to get the cage and stopped, his thoughts going to the days ahead. He stroked her bony head, fingers and voice shaky.

'I'll leave the back door open,' he told her. 'You can go when you please.'

She clicked her beak, black gaze unwavering, and he felt like a traitor. Stifling sobs, he focused on his route to the coach-house in the Old Town, not daring to use one any closer to home. Gordon put out the gas lamps, shouldered his belongings, and tucked the Colt into his pocket. The kitchen was lit only by the ruddy range and now seemed a warm, safe place. Gordon hesitated, his hand on the back door key, rain pattering the glass. Above him the house suddenly creaked, as if the boards flexed under booted feet. Gordon unlocked the door and, pushing it open, stepped out into the rain.

Only to stop on the threshold; the rain on his naked face was cold and unpleasant and the yard black. The only light came from behind, making it impossible to see ahead. A soft touch made him yelp, but it was only Quile settling on his shoulder, nearly dislodging his hat. He silently cursed her, while too pleased of her company to try and force the crow away. In those moments his eyes grew accustomed to the dark and he went to the gate, bracing himself for the squeal, easing the latch. Slowly, slowly he pulled the gate and then he was through, into the narrow alley. Neighbouring windows lit the dark, enough for him to avoid the rubbish. To his left, the alley yawned away into darkness toward the New Town. To his right, toward the Gardens and the Old Town, it spilt out into gaslit rain. Yet shadowy gates dotted the alley route and worried Gordon with their impenetrable blankness. Suddenly a bulbous figure emerged, hastening toward him. Gordon's breath turned to ice and his fingers sought the revolver.

'Doctor?'

It was McDougall. Even in the poor light Gordon could see the lawyer's pale face pinched with cold, glasses spotted with rain.

Waited to take you to Bedlam.

'Just let me be!'

He surged past but the other caught him in a fierce grip, pulling him close.

'No,' McDougall hissed.

They struggled, Gordon fumbling with bags, desperate for the gun. Quile flapped and cawed, wings in his face and claws in his coat. McDougall dragged at him, hissing words lost to Quile's noise. Suddenly the lawyer's face was close to his.

'For the love of Mary, will you quiet the confounded bird or he'll hear us.'

Gordon stopped moving.

'Who?'

'Your godforsaken harelipped man, you raging buffoon!'

The lawyer tugged his sleeve, pulling left, into darkness.

'We're to go this way, to the New Town, if we're to avoid him. Come on.'

Gordon shivered and Quile settled on his shoulder again. Iona's voice shouted about lies and the madhouse.

'You're certain you saw him, the harelipped man?'

'For the love of… I stepped to the Gardens earlier, to think. I wanted to give you time to calm down. There's a bench beneath a yew tree that protects from the worst of the rain and I waited there. In the Gardens, I spotted a match as it lit a cigar and the glow showed a face, the harelip clear as day. Your man is watching the house and if you continue this way, he'll certainly see you.'

'How did you… I mean, did he see you?'

'No, I used the Gardens' far gate and came back this way. Now, we must walk into the New Town and find a cab, if we're to go unseen.'

McDougall moved away, paused, waiting. Gordon glanced at the mouth of the alley wondering if the lawyer lied. The gas lamps sparkled in the rain. He looked back to McDougall, a grey pear shape against the blackness.

'You dinnae think I'm mad?'

McDougall was suddenly close again.

'You should be, after everything you've been through, and could be. Yet I saw the harelipped man and while I dinnae ken what it means, he's real enough and watching you.'

Gordon felt light headed, as if the rain had washed reality away.

'We're to Oxford then?' he managed.

'I suggest we stay at my home tonight and buy camping supplies at first light. Then we leave for Oxford tomorrow, as soon as possible.'

'What of your wife?'

'She kens we're to London, we'll leave it at that. No need for her to worry unduly.'

McDougall moved away and this time kept walking. With a last look at the alley mouth, Gordon turned and followed him.

CHAPTER THIRTEEN

For Gordon, the journey to Oxford was a blur of cold coaching inns and poor sleep. He only felt safe when moving, putting miles between himself and the harelipped man. Each stop, with horses milling, coaches arriving, changing passengers and bustling inns, had him on edge. He constantly checked others' faces and avoided as much contact as possible. He kept to their room, even to eat, with only McDougall for company. Over those solitary meals McDougall theorised on who the harelipped man was and what he wanted with Gordon. Gordon contributed little, unwilling to voice his fears and trying to quiet Iona's insidiousness. Each night he wedged a chair under their shared door handle and checked the revolver was loaded, keeping it to hand. Through each such stop he sat vigil with a bottle of whisky, waiting for the next coach and listening to the lawyer's snoring. Each onward journey was uncomfortable, the jolting coaches affording little sleep. Only the whisky and McDougall sitting close by helped. When they finally arrived in Oxford, Gordon stared at the brightly lit High Street, flinching at sounds and other people. Then clutching his belongings, he stumbled after McDougall to their room, falling almost immediately into a fitful sleep.

He awoke hours later to darkness and McDougall snoring like old thunder. He took out his watch and a lit match showed him 4am. The lawyer's snoring climbed to a whistling crescendo before dying, only to begin rumbling once more. Gordon's thoughts slipped and slid toward the harelipped man only to shy away, and Iona snickered at his cowardice. He rose, knowing rest was over. Turning up the gas light and moving about caused McDougall to wake, blinking.

'Are we leaving?' he asked.

'I'll see to buying horses after I've been to the church. I'll meet you outside in an hour. Be ready then, please.'

McDougall grunted and sat up.

'You're to see Amy Dudley's resting place?'

'Aye. To pay my respects.'

Gordon dressed quickly, shouldered his bags and left the lawyer pondering breakfast.

Against the stars the spire of St Mary's was a dark splinter and he headed toward it.

YOU'RE RIDICULOUS. WHAT DO YOU EXPECT TO HAPPEN?

I just want to be close. To pay my respects.

EVERYTHING WILL BE LOCKED. YOU'LL NO GET IN. NEVER GET CLOSE.

Then I'll just stand outside, for now. I'll see Amy Dudley, eventually.

YOU'LL NEVER GET THE CHURCH'S CONSENT.

Doctor Bennett will, in time.

FOOL. YOU'RE GOING TO FAIL.

The wrought iron gates facing the High Street were indeed locked. Unwilling to leave, Gordon moved alongside the building and next to the church St Mary's Passage was a dark hole. Gordon unhooked the shuttered lantern from his pack. It took a moment to ignite and then the sliver of flame guided him onward. Gordon followed the pitch-black passage as it bent right alongside the church, hoping for a garden or cemetery he could sit in. Abruptly the church wall was broken by a soft finger of light. He stopped and his lantern showed the dim outline of a badly latched door. Gordon pushed, causing it to swing, making the light grow. He listened and, hearing only early morning birds, slipped inside.

St Mary's, quiet and cold, was lit only by a few candles. The shadows made the vaulted arches and soaring roof seem endless and huge. Gordon moved silently between pews, hushed by the emptiness. He studied the shadows, fingers tingling, and each breath fogged the cool air, drying his throat. Reassured there was no one there, he swallowed and put the lantern down. After another look around, he rested his packs on a pew. Still alert to any sound or movement, Gordon extracted the leather tome. He sat next to his bags and, with careful fingers, took out and read Sam's notes on Amy Dudley's funeral. He stood and orientated himself until certain he had the right place. Then, repacking everything, he gathered his belongings and lantern, and made his way to St Mary's west end.

He lifted the light, showing a twisting, wooden staircase which cast everything into shadow. He held the lantern closer to the wall, expecting carved stone squares, and found disarray. Many of the graves were open, black holes and the air was alive with dust and cut wood. Gordon steadied himself on the staircase, his breath punchy. The lantern swung and its light caught the heavy grave markers, stacked like cards on the floor. Next to them, a sign forbade entrance and stated the galleries were under restoration. He looked, following the curve of spiral stairs up until it disappeared, and understood. The graves had been opened and bones removed in case the galleries collapsed and crushed the dead to ash, or if the builders damaged the graves during the works. He imagined that all would be re-consecrated and returned when it was safe. He studied the black holes and wondered which one had held Amy Dudley and where she was now. Abrupt footfalls made him turn, legs trembling and breath held hard. In the glow of a candelabra, a man with protruding eyes appeared.

'What are you doing here?'

Gordon stepped back, blinking, startled into truth.

'I came for Amy Dudley.'

He gathered himself, every muscle ready to shove and run. The church warden lowered the candelabra and grunted.

'You're early. But better that than late.'

Gordon stared, his chest tight and knees failing. The light suddenly shone on him, brutally close. Then the warden moved away, vanishing into the gloom, candlelight trailing weirdly in his wake. Gordon blinked and felt trapped, wanting to run, but needing to stay and understand what the man meant. He moved from the stair, getting a clear line to the door and braced to run. The warden reappeared, carrying only one candle in a holder and a canvas bag. He put the candle down on a stair and motioned Gordon closer.

'Open the lantern some more,' the man said.

Gordon did as bid, and the light illuminated the bag interior. Inside he could see a box, packed around with wool to protect it. The warden lifted the box out and turned it, so the dark wood caught the light.

'It's all been done as instructed,' he said. 'I used a pauper to replace Lady Dudley, boiled the flesh off the neck bones and skull. No one will know it's not her ladyship. This is the box as ordered, all lined properly with lead and that, so she's all safe.' He opened the lid. 'See, she's all content and snug in there. Better than that draughty ol' hole at any rate.'

Amy Dudley stared up at Gordon. Her black eye sockets were endless, skull ochre in the lantern light and the head wounds like shadows on her bone. It took all Gordon's control not to snatch the box and run. Instead he managed a nod and closed the lid, shutting Amy Dudley away. The warden seemed disappointed with his reaction and Gordon thinned his lips in what he hoped was a smile.

'You've done well, sir, very well indeed,' he said.

The warden nodded and looked pleased. Gordon took the bag and settled the strap across his chest, so it nestled comfortably on his hip. He shouldered his belongings and took up the lantern, managing to still his trembling fingers by sheer will, all the while aware the warden watched. Fumbling in a pocket he pulled some money free and gave it to the man, whose teeth flashed, gruesome in the light. Gordon tipped his hat and walked away, fearing a shout with every step, heading for the door to St Mary's Passage. Suddenly the warden was there, hand on the door latch, and a frown drew his eyebrows together. Gordon sped up.

'Thank you,' he said, and stepped outside.

'For the Watchers,' came the reply.

The door closed and Gordon hurried away.

CHAPTER FOURTEEN

Just under an hour later they left Oxford in the lightening of dawn. Fearing pursuit Gordon led a circuitous route, heading toward London on their newly purchased horses. He then swung back, to ride through woods and unknown countryside, using back-trails, a map and compass to ride toward Foxcombe Valley. McDougall seemed not to notice the strange route despite Gordon getting them lost more than once. The two men spoke little. McDougall rode with a studied focus that discouraged conversation. Gordon was too agitated for any discourse, for Amy Dudley rode with them. Her hidden presence made Gordon wary, gaze raking the trails and woods while he forced the pace to gain distance from Oxford. His thoughts tumbled from the harelipped man to the woman's skull and bones in his pack.

Someone wants Amy Dudley! Who are the Watchers? How are they still involved? The harelipped man must be a Watcher.

Nothing made sense, except now he understood why the harelipped man wanted him. Not for him. For what he knew, what he held on Amy Dudley. The same round of thoughts hammered on and on. They overwhelmed him, making his head hurt, and then, worse:

How long until they discover I have Amy Dudley?

THEY ALREADY KEN. COMING FOR YOU. THIEF. MURDERER.

Several times he caught McDougall frowning as they rode. He wanted to tell the lawyer everything but didn't. Couldn't.

McDougall will send her back.

THEY'LL FIND YOU SOON. YOU'LL BOTH BE AS DEID AS AMY DUDLEY.

Gordon pushed his horse to a ragged trot.

They were two hours out of Oxford when a black form dropped from the trees. Gordon cried out and McDougall cursed, reining in and flapping his hat. Quile paid no heed to either man's surprise and merely settled on Gordon's shoulder as if she had never left. Her presence comforted Gordon, amazed as he was at how the crow had found them so far from Edinburgh. Quile seemed none the worse for her journey, tucking into his neck quite happily and swaying in time to the ride. Gordon pushed them on through the grey day. Using the map and compass they finally emerged from a treeline to overlook Foxcombe Valley. Rolling iron-coloured clouds were massing to the east; the wind picked up, calling in the trees and making Gordon's horse fret. A drystone wall ran along the edge of the valley and it seemed to serve no purpose but to mark where a faint trail began at its right-hand end. Gordon studied it and thought it was built as if someone had grown tired having to constantly search for the way down. On closer inspection rusted marks showed signs that hitching rings had once been in the wall, allowing horses to be tied while their riders rested and admired the view. Gordon didn't rest. He checked his pack was secure, glanced at McDougall to make sure he followed and led the way down into the valley. Descending the narrow track, it was even clearer it had once been nurtured and well used. The way was packed with more stone that ensured a solid passage, draining any rain and preventing the path turning to mud. It started to drizzle, and Gordon hunched into his new Macintosh, pulling the collar up and his hat down. Quile tucked further in, obviously happy for the shelter. As the path ended, skeletal trees kept the worst of the rain off and Gordon reined in, patting his gelding's neck.

'This must be it,' he murmured.

McDougall peered about, his expression dubious.

'How can you possibly tell? It all looks the same to me.'

'Sam's notes tell of this trail and bloody encounters amongst trees at the bottom; it must be these woods. His account tells of the onward ride to Foxcombe Manor, heading south.'

He orientated and followed the compass through the trees, along scant paths. He glanced back once, up the trail that vanished in rain and mist, and saw no following shadow. It did little to quiet his bleak thoughts. The trees grew thicker in front and up the valley sides which gentled to sloping hills. But Gordon knew from his map that the hills became much steeper. They formed an unclimbable horseshoe shape at the other end of the valley cut through by more small tracks that led out to villages and towns. He estimated forty minutes had passed when the trees thinned to grow randomly in a grass clearing. Gordon reined in, gaze following the unnatural lines of old brick walls that furrowed the glade. He stared at a chimney, still standing nearly six feet tall and then spotted others in various prone positions, red bricks dappled with moss and grass. He slumped in the saddle, air hard to come by, barely noticing McDougall reining in alongside.

'Christ fend us!' McDougall's voice seemed too loud. 'Would you look at that? It's a house!'

The lawyer clapped him on the shoulder, causing Quile to flap. They dismounted and followed the manor's footprint until Gordon knelt at the chimney still standing, touching the pitted brickwork. He lowered his head and closed his eyes, feeling both weak and strong, giddy and motionless at the same time.

Sam did this. Touched here.

You're touched. Insane. Saving Amy Dudley will never work.

But I've already saved her, once.

He looked back at his horse, grazing placidly, pack strapped securely in place.

With Sam and Doctor Bennett's help, I can save her soul and myself. I can continue my work.

Above him, on the chimney, Quile watched the sky where other crows wheeled. She shifted her claws, opening and closing her wings and muttering to herself. McDougall walked the line of the brickwork.

'It was a big place,' the lawyer called. 'Bigger than I expected. I'm surprised it's been abandoned for so long.'

Gordon rose, gaze sweeping the treeline, trying to pierce the shadows. He turned and watched McDougall continuing to pace the ruins and wondered if anyone else knew of Foxcombe Manor.

Just after three o'clock Gordon set the coffee pot to heat over their cooking fire. On the other side of the pit McDougall stirred the beans, adding bacon to a sizzling pan. The lawyer cut thick slices of bread, spreading them liberally with butter. They ate, sitting outside the conical tent in the chill afternoon, gazing at the remains of Foxcombe Manor. Gordon fed Quile the bacon fat, watching her fastidiousness with amusement. The rain had given everything a glistening, fresh feel. Although the grey skies lingered the wind had dropped, making everything still and quiet. Even Iona was silent. It seemed to Gordon that somehow his bones had taken root in the soil and bricks of the old house. He felt that, should he lie down, the earth would cover him, and he would happily be part of this place forever.

After eating, Gordon took out his notebook and turned to his copying of the manor plans. It was an effort to get up and start work, but once they had the first room pegged out the excitement of reconstructing the manor took over. The two men spent the rest of the afternoon and evening mapping Foxcombe's foundations, lighting their work with fitful torches and lanterns. By full dark they had outlined every room with wooden pegs and string. Gordon took immense satisfaction in raising Sam's home from the grave. He noticed McDougall's pleased expression when the lawyer surveyed their hard work. They prepared and ate supper, speaking little, but the silence was companionable. Gordon's body ached but he felt light and awake. McDougall passed him a tin mug and Gordon, smelling whisky, smiled. He took a sip, nodding his thanks and felt a deluge of gratitude toward the lawyer. He took a deep breath and turned his face to the star-filled sky.

'Sam lived here,' he said.

'There's no doubt on it, your sheriff was as real as you and I.'

'Aye, he was,' Gordon breathed.

Iona muttered something, but he ignored her. He stroked Quile's head and stared into the darkness where he knew Foxcombe Manor lay mapped out.

Gordon woke at dawn with a feeling of urgency. Rekindling the fire, he fed and watered the horses accompanied by McDougall's snoring. Gordon set porridge and coffee to heat and sat once more outside the tent, wrapped in Macintosh and woollens against the cold. He watched the strings they had laid, wet with dew and shimmering in the early light. He imagined the walls and windows, stretching up from those twines, the roof and chimneys given form and shape in the early light. Before his eyes it seemed Foxcombe Manor came to life. He took out his notebook and turned to the plans. He traced the oblong that denoted the library and peered across the glade to where the room had stood, containing the lone standing chimney. He was disappointed that pegging out the room had revealed no deviation from the plan, no obvious addition. On their journey he hadn't spoken of the cipher to McDougall nor of his suspicions, fearing they would find nothing of Sam or Foxcombe Manor. Now they had, he still hadn't said anything. Amy Dudley's presence and fear of the Watchers held his tongue. Worry gnawed like a hunger.

What if the addition were a book, an object, a safe passage? Something long gone, sold, turned to dust, mouldering in an unknown library or collection.

His anxiety spiralled, making his chest tight and breathing rough. He gripped the notebook, knuckles tightly yellow, and stared at the ruins. He willed them to help him, but they remained glistening strands in the dawn, yielding nothing.

Did I miss something from the original?

THERE'S NAUGHT THERE. YOU'RE PATHETIC. THIS IS PATHETIC.

'Just shut up,' he hissed.

Gordon rose and moved stealthily into the tent. McDougall's guttering snores continued unabated and he retrieved the tome without waking the lawyer. He hated the idea of getting the old paper out in the elements, but such was his need to verify his copying, he felt he must. He managed to slip out the plans without disturbing anything else. Using his bundled Macintosh as a dry surface he studied Sam's originals and they were identical to his notebook copies. He dropped his head to his chest, the coffee tasting sour on his tongue, and his breath wheezed through his front teeth like split bellows. After a moment and with an effort he re-folded Sam's diagrams. He kept gazing at them, unable to stop following the lines of the plans, seeking answers he knew weren't there. Out of habit he paired them up, so the square indicating the well on the old plan matched up with its impression on the new, ensuring the folds remained exact. Opening the tome, he turned to the secret pocket and lifted the plans, frail and almost transparent in the morning light. He stopped, staring at the drawings. With shaking fingers, he flattened them out again, keeping one atop the other, and lifted them to the daylight. He peered at them. The well impression, visible within the walls of the library on the new plan, didn't seem a precise match to the old plan. With the daylight behind it, the one on the newer plan seemed slightly elongated into a rectangle. There was a symbol now visible, something he had taken for paper age, on the edge of the rectangle.

Lowering the plans, Gordon silently cursed for lack of a magnifying glass. Abruptly he tucked the drawings into the secret pocket and went into the tent. McDougall's snores had turned to heavy breathing and the man was on his side, his back to Gordon. Peering in the dim light, Gordon crept forward and nearing the cot he spied what he wanted. Scooping up the lawyer's glasses case, he retreated outside.

Putting them on, the spectacles slipped down his nose but stayed if he tilted his head and so, by squinting and keeping his head tipped back, Gordon could see the symbol in more detail. It seemed to have been painted on with an incredibly fine brush. Perhaps it had once been red, but now its russet hue matched the sepia paper and darker age spots. Still he was able to discern an eye, snout, long body and tail of a dragon. His heart tripped and excitement prickled his skin. Gordon pencilled the rectangle onto his notebook copy and drew the symbol much enlarged. The sun was coming up when he removed the glasses. He packed everything away, knowing he wouldn't share his discovery. Alert for any change, he crept inside the tent and replaced the glasses case and tome. Back outside he poured more coffee and pondered his reasons for not involving McDougall.

Like is no the same as trust. The lawyer would send Amy Dudley back to the church.

BACK TO THE HARELIPPED MAN. SEND YOU BACK TO YOUR DEATH OR TO BEDLAM. YOU SHOULD LET HIM. TELL HIM EVERYTHING.

He ignored her and tried to imagine telling McDougall about the new discovery.

Would he even care? But then, what if it leads to questions, arguments, and he discovers Amy Dudley?

HE'D THINK YOU STOLE HER. HE'D DESPISE YOU, WANT YOU DEID FOR SUCH HERESY. SERVE YOU RIGHT.

Gordon shivered and knew he wasn't going to involve McDougall. The exploration of the library must be his secret. It wasn't worth the risk of losing Amy Dudley, of losing McDougall's support or having to turn back.

The harelipped man is back there, somewhere. I can only go forward to escape him.

YOU COULD STAY HERE. WAIT FOR HIM. DIE AND BE COVERED BY THE EARTH HERE.

I wouldnae mind being buried here, but I'm no ready to die yet.

COWARD.

He sighed and wondered about the vagaries of fate and decisions. He sipped coffee and watched the sunlight wake the ruins and woods. From the tent McDougall's snores spluttered and renewed while Gordon thought through their plans now the ruins had been pegged out. His was the task to sketch and make records of the work. They then planned to leave two days hence, riding from the other end of Foxcombe Valley to Whitecross, then onto the village of Dorchester where they could sell the horses and camping equipment. From Dorchester they could take the stagecoach to Reading and thence the newly running train to London. He pondered how to gain enough time to investigate the ruined library without McDougall knowing. Behind him snores stalled and the sounds of the lawyer stirring gave an idea substance.

Gordon waited until breakfast was nearly finished before implementing his plan.

'I've been thinking about our onward journey,' he said, keeping his tone light.

'Oh aye, what about it?'

Gordon retrieved the map and spread it out.

'We're roughly here, I believe.' He pointed to a spot. 'We need to continue south as planned to reach Whitecross and then on to Dorchester and Reading.'

'I'm looking forward to the train journey to London. I've no travelled on such a steam engine before.'

'As am I, but I worry about the ride from here to Whitecross. There's no definitive track on the map, do you see? So, while I'm sketching the ruins today do you think you could ride out and find the way? Else I fear we could waste a day finding it and am loath to lose such time.'

McDougall eyed him with a sympathetic look.

'Is it the harelipped man you're still afeared of?'

It was, but not the main reason Gordon wished the lawyer away for a day.

'Aye. I know you must think me a fool, but—'

'No need to fash yourself, Doctor. It's a fair idea and

one I'm happy to undertake. Exploring rather than sitting watching you sketch suits me fine.'

An hour later McDougall, using the compass and map, rode into the woods to find the way to Whitecross. Gordon waited until McDougall's horse vanished into the trees, then moved quickly, taking out his notebook and pacing the ruins. The library had been a huge, oblong room, about fifteen feet wide and twenty-five feet long. Something the plan did little justice to. Three walls were entirely gone, leaving only scattered bricks and foundation lines in the grass that his strings faithfully followed. The fourth wall was fairly intact by comparison. It had broken brick teeth, a riot of grass and a huge gap, wide enough for four men to stand side by side. The collapse of this outside wall had been a slow leaning and the bricks were heaped in front of the gap. The standing chimney made up part of the still-standing wall. Quile picked along the bricks, eyes bright and intent for scurrying life. Every now and then she would cock her head and look to Gordon. Sometimes she would pause, staring up to the trees and sky at any crows that perched or flew. Gordon, watching her, wondered if she would finally leave him, and pushed away the desolation that closed his throat. He swallowed and consulted his notebook; rolling up his shirt sleeves, he moved bricks and cut the sod with a knife to loosen it. Then, using his spade, he turned the grass and soil.

The heavy work made him sweat even in the cool March air. He was digging in his undershirt when abruptly the spade met something solid. Gordon knelt and put his fingers to the hole, expecting a channel, or pipe for the well. His touch met something wooden, not clay or metal. It took nearly an hour of frantic work to determine the wood was a trapdoor. He sat back on his heels, breathing hard, and let out a strangled whoop. Quile, startled from the nearby chimney, flapped away. Moving more soil revealed a wooden trapdoor pitted by age and rotting in places. Yet it was still secured by iron bands, hinges and a round handle. Following the edge, he discerned hounds chasing dragons or vice versa had been carved into the wood. Wiping his face with a cloth, he couldn't think why there was a hound there, but the dragon carving was a mirror to that on the plan. Picking mud from it, following the dragon's graceful lines sparked a memory. Flicking back through his notebook he found and re-read the cipher message, focusing on a few lines.

> Be advised, in the event of change in our esteemed friend's silence, Foxcombe's addition will be used for us to gain Cymru. You should know, as no other will, that this route is all well.

Christ fend us! The dragon is a symbol for Cymru, for Wales. They were to escape to Wales.

Struck anew by Sam's wording, he tucked the notebook away. He rapped the shovel handle on the trapdoor and was immensely satisfied when it sounded hollow. Sitting back, a chill dimpled his skin and he glanced up to see the afternoon had shifted toward evening. He scanned the treeline, suddenly aware the lawyer could return at any moment. With quick movements he started scraping soil back across the trapdoor, keeping watch all the while. When McDougall finally returned the sun had dipped behind the woods. Gordon hailed him, sitting in his undershirt, drinking coffee and finishing off his sketches.

That night the moon rose lending an otherworldly sheen to the ruins of Foxcombe, a spell broken by McDougall's snores. Inside the tent, Gordon checked the man's colour and response and, satisfied the dose of laudanum had done its work, shouldered the spade and left.

Clearing away soil from the top and edges of the trapdoor he easily found the iron ring and hinges. He prised the door open, wood splinters falling into the hole it revealed. Gordon struck a match, letting it fall inside, and stared at brick steps that led into darkness. Swallowing his excitement, he hammered pegs into the ground and used them to secure rope. He dropped the rope end into the hole, listening as it hissed then smacked on what was surely a stone floor. He put several bricks atop the trapdoor, ensuring it stayed open. Then, lantern held high, he cautiously descended, watching his feet and his free hand looped about with the rope in case the stone steps disintegrated.

Naught but a cellar. No secret passage. The ceiling will fall on you. Death awaits.

Sam built this to escape his enemies. He will no let me die.

Keep on, fool. The earth will have you yet.

Worm food. Worthless murderer.

He shivered and pushed on, gaining the floor amidst cold air and the smell of dirt. Glancing up he saw the star-filled sky far above him through the open trapdoor. He tried to take comfort from it and lifted the lantern. Its light revealed intricate brickwork to his left and, letting go of the rope, he ran a reverent hand over the tight work. It was pitted with age but still looked solid. Raising the lantern higher he drew a breath at the graceful arch of the red brickwork that continued upward, making the ceiling. He turned a circle, the halo of lantern light revealing chamber walls on either side and behind him. Turning forward once more he found only cold air and saw the ceiling ended in a keystone archway that led into a black passage. The oblong stones holding up the tunnel entrance were different in size and material from the rest. He could see the large keystones were of yellow stone and suffering from age. Cracks wound their way hither and thither across the golden surfaces, some bigger than others. He didn't like it, not at all, but the empty passageway called to him. Patting his pockets Gordon found and broke his emergency candle in half. He trimmed and lit one half of it, using the flame to soften and drip wax from the other half onto the bottom step. Then he stuck the lit candle there, making sure he could see the light from the tunnel entrance. He put the other half candle in his pocket, in case the lantern went out or smashed. Squaring his shoulders, and with a silent wish for safety, went into the tunnel.

With each step the darkness felt like a living thing, trying to get past his light, but he pressed on. From all around the cold intensified and he tried to count his steps but gave up at fifty. Glancing back there was only blackness, the candlelight had vanished, and he realised the passage curved to the right, away from the manor ruins. Something brushed the hat from his head, and he yelped, backing away. Breathing hard he swung the light to reveal tree roots like stiff hair had pushed through the bricks. He retrieved his hat, put the lantern on the floor and, leaning on the wall, regained his breath. Checking his pocket watch he was surprised to find nearly an hour had passed since he'd left the tent. Time had been suspended by the dark tunnel.

Such a long time. What if the harelipped man has come. Found the lawyer sleeping? Stolen Amy Dudley? Waiting for you?

His fingers dug into the bricks, hating Iona's words, but terrified she could be right.

He'll follow you wherever you go. Steal Amy Dudley. Kill you. You should just wait here for him.

Standing, with the dark pressing in, limbs trembling, his

thoughts fled to Reading, then on to London and whatever came next. He imagined trying to keep Amy Dudley safe and secret from McDougall. From the harelipped man and the unknown Watchers.

I dinnae ken how to keep her safe.

BECAUSE YOU'RE PATHETIC. YOU DESERVE TO DIE. YOU CAN NO SAVE AMY DUDLEY. YOU WILL NEVER SAVE YOURSELF. NEVER WORK AGAIN.

His fingers hurt on the bricks and he turned, resting his head on the wall, trying to think past her words. Suddenly he raised his head, letting the darkness fill his eyes.

I can leave her here. Hidden. Safe. Until I'm ready.

He picked up the lantern and hurried back the way he had come.

Half an hour later he counted one hundred and fifty steps back along the passageway and stopped. Using his hands, he dug out a space in the dirt and roots behind the wall. Wiping his palms on his trousers, he opened the lead-lined box and gazed into Amy Dudley's endless eyes.

'You'll be safe down here,' he said. 'I'll come back for you, I promise.'

He turned her, studying the ragged holes in Amy Dudley's skull, before shutting her away. Rising, he slipped the box into its canvas bag and then into the hole, replacing the bricks. He packed dirt into the crevices between the bricks as best he could and kicked the remaining soil about the tunnel. Employing his knife, he marked one with a crude X and then he left, stopping every ten paces to score a line in a brick. He emerged from the trapdoor to find the night cool and clear, the grass of Foxcombe Manor overlaid with a heavy dew. Once back in the tent Gordon stripped off his grimy clothes, rinsed his hands using water from a canteen and wiped a damp towel over his skin. Shivering, he changed into his nightshirt and pulled on thick woollen socks, climbing into his sleep sack. He put the lantern out and, listening to McDougall's laudanum-filled snores, tried to sleep.

The next morning McDougall expounded on the benefits of fresh air for sound sleep and Gordon tried not to smile. Once they had packed, Gordon mounted his horse, Quile settling on his shoulder, and McDougall took the lead. Gordon paused, looking over the ruins with a deep sense of loss and sadness, wishing he could stay. He silently bade Foxcombe and Amy Dudley farewell, promising to return, then heeled his horse and followed McDougall into the trees.

Part Two

Chapter Fifteen

London 1840

Arthur Standish unlocked the rear door to the Park Street premises and stepped into the sparsely lit hallway. Seeing no one else, he made his way into his allocated flat and locked the door behind him. He immediately unfastened his smallest valise, taking out the clothes he had been obliged to wear in Edinburgh. From a cupboard he selected a burlap sack, stuffed the clothes inside and wrote 'burn' on a label, attaching it to the coarse bag. In the kitchen he placed the sack on the dumb waiter and sent it down. Taking all his luggage into the bedroom, Arthur unpacked, carefully removing the wigs, theatrical grease paint, glue and wax treatments. He picked out the wax harelip and turned it to the gas light, so it glistened, lifelike. For a moment he regretted the need to warm it back to a malleable lump, then placed it on the dresser for his later attention. He retrieved a handwritten business card from his pocket and traced the name, details and village, Balerno. He studied Angus McCraken's writing, confident he could replicate the whorls and loops. A bell tone called him to the kitchen and the return of the dumb waiter. Raising the hatch, he removed the sealed envelope there, opened and read it.

'Oh dear, Oriole,' he murmured.

He smiled and tore the note to pieces, trying to ignore his quickened pulse. He scattered the paper in the bedroom fireplace and put a match to it. Watching it burn, he poured a glass of port and sipped. Then opened his wardrobe to survey all his frock coats, shirts, waistcoats and trousers.

'Formal and officious or audacious and creative?'

He settled on dark blue frock coat and trousers, threaded with gold. He offset the seriousness with a cream shirt, plus turquoise and gold waistcoat. The cravat he held in place by means of an enamel pin depicting a burnished bird in flight. He surveyed himself in the mirror, touching the two scratch marks on his cheek with a slight frown. From a drawer, Arthur removed a black mask and slipped it on. It covered the top part of his face, the eye holes enough to see by, while leaving his mouth and chin bare. Arthur left the apartment, humming as he walked, enjoying the thought of what was to come.

Reaching the ground floor, he entered the long dining room. As usual, day or night, all the curtains were closed. Two fires warmed the large space and the room glittered in lit chandeliers that chased any shadows away. The table, big enough to seat twenty, was set for six. Five on one side and one, centred, on the opposite side. Arthur knew that through the centuries the Watchers' numbers had swelled and shrunk according to need. The members at this time were few, just the six, but their resources were vast. He took a moment's pleasure in the oil paintings and gilt mouldings then moved to read the place cards.

'Oriole, Hawk, Nightjar, Jay and Linnet.'

He settled at his own 'Nightjar' just as the door opened and admitted his fellow Watchers. Each wore an identical black mask and a pin depicting their particular bird type. No one spoke. When they had all settled, only the single space on the other side of the table remained. Arthur had counted to one hundred when a tall, greying figure entered from the opposite end of the dining room. The unmasked man stopped; the assembly rose as one and gave short bows. A faint smile creased the other's face and was gone. The man strode to the empty place opposite Arthur and a servant materialised from a curtained alcove to pull out the man's chair. The grey man studied the masked gathering with an air of quiet amusement.

'Be seated,' he said, and did so himself.

His voice was gravelly, like pebbles underfoot. Everyone obeyed.

'Edinburgh was a success,' the grey man said. 'Nightjar, tell us.'

Arthur stood and addressed them all.

'I pushed the doctor to the brink of madness, as instructed, to ensure he wouldn't pursue his investigation into Amy Dudley. I searched his home more than once, but to no avail. The correspondence intercepted between McCraken and Bennett, while alerting us to their plans for Amy Dudley, was inconclusive concerning what artefact each man holds. There was no mention of the locket, but that means little at this point.'

'Quite so,' the grey man interrupted. 'It only means we have yet to discover it. All our information indicates that it's highly probable one of these men has the locket. We will continue to bend all our efforts to its discovery and retrieval.'

Arthur inclined his head.

'I spent a few days in McCraken's boyhood village. I discovered information about the man and his family that may prove useful. Unfortunately, we cannot apply pressure to his more noble kin, the Kilbrides, as the current lord, McCraken's cousin, is living in America. However, McCraken and his lawyer have travelled to London these past few days, and I believe they can be more easily manipulated here.'

He bowed to the grey man and resumed his seat.

'Thank you, Nightjar. And thus, with your favourable outcome, so, we will eat.'

Servants appeared, ladling soup, passing bread and pouring wine. The meal was eaten in silence. Behind his mask Arthur surreptitiously watched his companions. One, two diners from his right, raised a spoon and for a moment it trembled at their lips. Arthur returned to his own soup, eating with relish. When the grey man had finished, wiping his mouth with a napkin, he waited until everyone was done. At his gesture servants poured claret for all. The grey man took a sip and nodded appreciatively.

'I would hear of Oxford,' he said. 'Oriole, tell us.'

Arthur sipped wine to hide his smile and moisten his mouth. The diner he'd noted earlier rose and he took a calming breath; the slender fingers teased a wine stem and then were still.

'St Mary's restoration gave us an opportunity like no other. Thus, I arranged for Amy Dudley's skull to be substituted as instructed.' The light voice was steady. 'I sent a man to retrieve the real one from Oxford. However, there was a problem.'

The grey man's gaze never left the standing figure.

'Indeed? Do enlighten us, Oriole.'

'It seems that someone else took Amy Dudley's skull, before my man arrived.'

'Just so. Do we know who removed Amy Dudley from our care?'

'No, but I have a description. The man was Scottish, tall, clean shaven and red haired. I'll know more when my man gets to London.'

'Not so. I'm afraid, Oriole, your man knows no more

than you. Even when questioned under extreme duress. No matter, for he's dead, as is the church warden you involved. And thus, with your unfavourable outcome, so we administer chastisement.'

The grey man motioned to the servant, who pulled a tasselled cord. This drew the curtains behind the grey man back from an alcove where windows should be. It revealed a brick wall and an upright wooden post, about six foot high and driven through the parquet, into the stone floor. Two looped straps were attached to the top and hung down to the middle of the post. The leather, Arthur knew, was as soft as a kitten. The grey man rose, and everyone followed suit. An oblong case was produced, unlocked and opened. From inside the grey man removed the cat o'nine tails. The silvery ends, sharpened to points, glinted in the light and its black leather shone from hours of polish. The grey man gestured to Oriole, who unbuttoned her bodice. Two servants stepped forward and removed it, leaving her naked from the waist up. Her skin was pearly white and small breasts goose bumped, nipples hardening on exposure to the cooler air. She walked to the post, resting her forehead against it and slipping her hands into the straps. Her back to the room was crossed with silvery scars. The grey man eyed her position and nodded.

'Nightjar.'

Arthur felt breathless, but walked carefully, keeping his steps measured. The whip handle was warm, and he relished its solid feel. He bowed to the grey man, who inclined his head.

'Three should suffice, Nightjar,' he said. 'Dependent, of course, on Oriole remaining silent while hanging thus. Any sound will double the chastisement. Proceed.'

He stepped back. Arthur moved into position, examining Oriole's back, determining where to let the lash fall. In some ways, he noted, this part was the best, savouring the moment, anticipating the pain. He felt himself grow hard and prayed Oriole would cry out. To help break her silence he decided to slice the base of her neck with a strand or two. He lifted her hair out the way, exposing the soft neck and almost groaned at the virgin skin. Controlling himself, he stepped back, raised the whip and snapped it, whacking down. She stiffened, the lashes ripping her skin to red welts, causing blood to run and drip. He hissed with pleasure, the sound lost in the whir of the cat. Arthur drew the whip lengths into his hand, enjoying the warmth of Oriole's blood on his palms. He lashed again, this time cutting her neck. She jerked about but remained silent. His third strike was the hardest, determined to cause some outcry. She convulsed, arching her back, breasts upturned silken mounds and mouth stretched in anguish. But still Oriole made no sound. He fought the urge to hit her again, to straddle her front and force himself inside her. He stepped away and held out the cat o'nine tails, letting a servant take it. He bowed to the grey man and returned to stand at his seat. They all sat, and dinner resumed.

For the next two hours Oriole remained silent, hanging and half naked. Arthur enjoyed watching her as he ate. Especially when she twisted on the straps, showing her breasts and then the blood running and drying down her back. At the end of the meal the Watchers rose, and the grey man dismissed them with a word. Arthur made to leave but stopped at a raised finger.

'Nightjar, remain.'

Everyone else silently filed out, and despite the masks, Arthur imagined some cast him curious or envious looks. The grey man waited until the door closed on the final Watcher.

'Oriole, you may leave.'

The young woman slipped her hands from the strap loops. She collapsed against the post, resting for a moment and then pulled herself upright. A servant appeared and held out her bodice. Oriole, shivering despite the warmth, took it and carefully put it on. Her gold and diamond bird pin glittered in the light. She managed a bow, and walked stiffly out, chin raised with her mask still in place.

'Come,' the grey man said.

He led the way in the opposite direction, out of the dining room at the far end. Arthur followed him out and down a thickly carpeted hallway where the grey man unlocked a door and went inside, Arthur close behind. A fire burnt in the grate, bringing the oak panelled walls into soft relief. The room was tastefully decorated with priceless paintings and sculpture. Against one wall a bookcase housed rare and first editions. When told to, Arthur settled into one of the leather armchairs while the grey man sat behind his desk and scowled.

'Take off that stupid mask. Bloody things.'

Arthur complied and then rose at the other's gesture to pour wine for them both. The grey man accepted his with a nod at Arthur.

'What happened to your cheek?'

'McCraken has a goddamn crow living with him. The beast took a dislike to me when I searched the house. I wanted to wring its neck but couldn't catch it.'

The grey man smiled and sipped wine.

'Possibly for the best. A strangled crow might've been too obvious, even to a man going out of his mind.'

Arthur grunted and resettled in the chair.

'By the sound of things, it would've been the least of our worries. Oxford couldn't have gone worse.'

The grey man's expression darkened.

'Yes, well, your sister has ever been too hasty in her

judgement of men. That dotard she employed to collect Amy Dudley hadn't the wit God gave sheep. The church warden was no better.'

'They brought their deaths on themselves then,' Arthur said. 'We're sure it was McCraken who took Amy Dudley?'

'Unfortunately.' The grey man's gaze narrowed. 'You had no indication he was going to Oxford.'

'None. As I detailed in my report, once I discovered he and lawyer were on the way to London, I searched the house again. Still there was nothing and no mention of Oxford. The lawyer's wife merely said that her husband had business here in the city. I had no reason to follow them.' Arthur sipped his wine, letting it warm on his tongue, enjoying the feel. 'So, I went to that godforsaken village, Balerno, where he was bred from. His family are a real treat, nasty as the small minded can be. The whole lot will turn their hands to anything to make money, carpentry, iron work, breeding animals, buying and selling whatever they can. Prise a penny from a dead man's hand, if they found one. Once I'd wrung all the information I could from them, I came straight here.'

'Well, an initial search of McCraken's lodgings yesterday was interrupted and achieved little. But we'll try again, even if we must rip the floorboards up. Once we have the skull, we can safeguard it for eternity. Hawk reports that McCraken may carry the artefacts and skull with him. The doctor and his fat friend are still rooting around in the new records office.'

'They'll not find the report, you're certain?'

'Arthur, you know as well as I that through the centuries Watchers have exhaustively searched for the coroner's report. If we haven't found it after this long, it no longer exists. Let them search, it gives us time.'

The grey man rose to pace, patting his pockets and

retrieving a pipe. He packed it with tobacco and lit it with hefty puffs, before perching on the edge of his desk, gaze calculating.

'We must find the locket. After all the centuries of search, we have to be the ones to discover it. Our members, under my leadership, will be the ones to fulfil the Watchers' age-old duty and our rewards will be spectacular.'

Knowing nothing more was required, Arthur nodded, hoping his father wouldn't take too long over the familiar ranting. The grey man blew a smoke ring, watching it lift and drift with a thoughtful expression.

'McCraken is the key, I'm certain,' he said. 'The man must be brought under our control. Yet I worry the lawyer, this McDougall, is being a stabilising influence.'

'Indeed. But with your permission, Father, I've a notion how to separate them, permanently.'

'Good. Be sure it's done before they make any approach to the Bennetts, as afterward it will be harder to accomplish. Especially if McCraken persists with his plans for Amy Dudley and the Royal College of Physicians, because the restrictions concerning the Bennett family remain in place, for now.'

Arthur sipped his wine, schooling his face to blankness.

'For how long?'

'Until the youngest Bennett is safely married to Lady Fielding's son. After the wedding, the secrets the other Bennetts carry may be used against them to secure the artefacts.'

'Searching their house yielded little?'

His father frowned, chewing the end of his pipe.

'Hawk and Linnet have been through it twice and found nothing. But the artefacts must be there. One of these men must have the locket. We *will* find it and the glory *will* be ours.'

'We could just kill McCraken. Now, we know the locket's not in the Edinburgh house or likely his lodgings. Once he's dead we can find it and retrieve the skull, if he has them on him.'

'And what if he's hidden them somewhere we don't know of, or given the locket to someone? We could lose it or risk others finding it. I'll not have this chance jeopardised.'

'Fine,' Arthur grudgingly conceded. 'But are you sure we can't apply any pressure to the Bennetts until after the wedding?'

His father puffed aggressively, smoke layering the room.

'You know Lady Fielding is too close to the queen. Any scandal before her son is married to the Bennett woman will reflect on her ladyship and the entire Fielding family. More, we cannot risk Lady Fielding approaching Her Majesty to intervene if a scandal ensues before they're wed. If it weren't a love match it would be a simple matter to break the marriage contract and proceed against the Bennetts. But George Fielding will not be denied that woman. It's sickening.'

Arthur agreed.

'And after they're wed? What of scandal then?'

'It won't matter. The youngest Bennett will officially be a Fielding and safe from any shame of her birth family. Lady Fielding will disown the other Bennetts quicker than you can say knife. Thankfully we know the bride to be, at least, has no vices nor hidden life.'

'Doctor Bennett?'

'All went well. No one suspected. Your sister at least accomplished that with no difficulty.'

Arthur rose, breath catching at the memory of Oriole, helpless and bleeding.

'I should retire, it's been a long few days.'

His father's expression grew sly and then he chuckled. 'Go then,' he said. 'But don't forget about dinner tomorrow evening and remind your sister. Your mother has invited the Foreign Secretary and the bloody Prime Minister; she's insisting you both be there.'

Arthur bowed, replaced his mask and slipped out. He walked swiftly, humming under his breath until he reached Oriole's apartment. He knocked the usual two, three beat and waited while his sister unlocked the door. She opened it, naked but for her mask and holding a riding crop. He grinned and didn't bother locking the door behind him.

CHAPTER SIXTEEN

Gordon and McDougall left the Southwark boarding house and made their way through mustard-coloured smog. Even this early the street was noisy with stallholders and hawkers. Cart drivers hissed and swore at each other, steering ponies and donkeys through the press. A butcher carved a pig carcass while calling out his wares, striving to be heard over the raucous parrots and songbirds at the next stall. Buyers haggled over flower baskets and smooth-eyed fish that swayed on lines. All around were stalls festooned with hanging rabbits, pig shanks and heads, pheasants and nets full of larks and sparrows. Nearby a big-hipped woman sold noise-makers, drums and whistles. Next to her was an old man who wheezed a tune on an accordion while his yellow-faced monkey danced and begged, hat in paws. Running children screamed and laughed, dodging through the crowds. At the end of the street four well-dressed men erected a cock-fighting ring. Dotted about their feet were screeching, caged fowl. Above all was the relentless noise of the Thames traffic and gulls. The worst thing for Gordon was the stench: excrement, human and animal; rotting vegetables and rubbish, along with the overflowing sewers, were a constant miasma and worry to the health.

The two men negotiated the crowds and refuse to enter

the lime-washed tavern on Ewer Street. The interior was thick with river stench, coffee and grease. Oil lamps swung from the ceiling and bronzed the interior. They found a table and McDougall beckoned a serving girl, ordering two coffees, kippers and bread. Gordon settled, took out and read his notes. He knew McDougall was unhappy and waited as the lawyer glanced at him, stirring his coffee.

'It's been four days,' McDougall finally said. 'We've yet to find the coroner's report. I truly think going to Doctor Bennett would serve us better.'

Gordon agreed, but found he couldn't say so.

Four days. Near three weeks since leaving Edinburgh. Why has there been no word from Doctor Bennett?

HE HATES YOU. HE'S AFRAID OF YOU. MURDERER.

Gordon's shoulders were tight. He swigged some coffee, trying to ignore images that pressed against his eyes; rejection from Doctor Bennett, Bedlam and condemnation.

MISTER LAWYER IS AGAINST YOU. GAVE HIS WIFE THE WRONG ADDRESS OR NO ADDRESS FOR LETTERS. WANTS YOU TO FAIL. WANTS YOU DEID.

Gordon looked at the lawyer. The other's belly was folded on the table edge and the man was entirely focused on eating his kippers. Gordon couldn't help but smile and didn't believe his dead wife. Over their time together Gordon had come to enjoy McDougall's company and to like the man immensely. The other's dry wit and unwavering optimism had made the frustrating search for the coroner's report bearable. Now the issue of Doctor Bennett's silence had been broached, Gordon knew he had to make a decision.

'Two more days,' he said. 'If we've no found it by then we'll go to Doctor Bennett, by invitation or no.'

McDougall raised an eyebrow.

'What's wrong with going to the man today?'

'It's just that…' Gordon's throat closed and words stuck there. He swallowed more coffee, his knuckles straining on the cup. 'The coroner's report is more proof, better proof. I dinnae want Doctor Bennett to have any reason to…'

McDougall gripped his shoulder.

'Aye, well, I understand. But it's a thankless task. I've a mind to think your Doctor Bennett would be happy enough to see you laddie, even without it. Still, another two days can be managed.'

He grinned and continued to eat his fish. Gordon stared at his own breakfast, unable to calm his thoughts.

'What of Margaret?'

'Lady Drummond?' McDougall stopped eating and looked serious. 'Och, there's no real deceit, no as yet. I've written that our meet with the eminent doctor has been postponed and you're filling the time with some research. Your sister-in-law has been most understanding.'

The tight knot beneath Gordon's ribs eased and he felt able to eat his breakfast.

Four hours later and it seemed to Gordon the world contained only frustration and dust. The rustling and hushed voices of the archivists, at first soothing, now crawled across his skin and scalp. He gripped the shelves, resting his forehead on the wood and tried very hard not to scream. A touch startled him. Turning he saw McDougall, waistcoat creased and grime colouring the lines on his face. Dust specked his glasses and made the man's beard more salt than pepper.

'I found some more,' he said.

Gordon nodded and moved to a table laden with heavy parchment rolls. He fingered one, noting the date of November, 1560. Rubbing a hand over his face he grimaced at his gritty skin. McDougall sat opposite at an angle and removed the top parchment. Using two wooden staves he unrolled it across the table. The lawyer peered at the tight, sepia script, standing to do so properly. Gordon lifted the next parchment and mimicked McDougall. He squinted at the old lettering and translated the Latin towns, names of criminals and victims long dead. For a moment it all swam together. He looked about seeking refuge in the vaulted ceiling. A figure appeared from between the shelves. A man whose grey eyes bulged insect-like and roamed continuously from behind thick spectacles.

'Here you are, Mister McDougall, Mister McCraken!'

Gordon still felt odd being called Mister, but it had seemed a better fit for their purpose here.

'Mister Green.'

Gordon greeted the Deputy Keeper. Stretching out a begrimed hand, he thought better of it and contented himself with a nod. Mister Green returned the nod with an understanding smile that included McDougall, and gestured for them to sit, doing so himself.

'Gentlemen, I've good news. I've made inquiries and checked our reports. I believe all the inquisitions post mortem and coroners' reports are housed here.' He looked about, taking in the seemingly endless stacked rolls. 'So, at least you're in the right place.'

Gordon managed a smile and McDougall sighed with relief.

'Thank you, Mister Green,' he said. 'It's been a worry that for all my hard work we would turn up naught here and have to move on.'

'Not in the least sir. I can say with conviction all the post mortems gathered since King Henry the Seventh are here.' He looked at McDougall, clearly noting the grime and tiredness. 'Still, I don't envy you your search. It would be so much easier if your academic endeavours could wait until all the cataloguing and storing are finished.'

'Aye, you're right there,' McDougall replied. 'It was a foolish notion of mine to think that as the Public Record Office Act was passed two years ago, most of the cataloguing work would be done by now.'

Gordon doubted McDougall feigned his look of weariness and disbelief.

'Pshaw,' Mister Green exclaimed. 'The wheels of government grind ever slowly, sir, ever slowly.' He fumbled in his pockets. 'There is something that may be of interest, if I could only find where I had written it down. Ah, here it is.' He produced a slip of paper, passing it to Gordon. 'There's other documents, just a few mind, that are not on rolls, but are post mortem parchments. Most are catalogued individually. You'll find them on the back wall, although I fear many are of a later year than the one you seek.'

'Your help has been invaluable, sir,' McDougall said. 'And I cannae thank you enough.' He gazed around, his expression resigned. 'Publishing my findings relies upon the documents I seek and we must press on if we're ever to find them.'

Mister Green stood, taking the hint, and glanced at Gordon.

'At least you've Mister McCraken here as an assistant to help with your endeavours. Good day and happy hunting, gentlemen.'

He bowed and took his leave. Gordon waited until he was certain the man had truly gone and shook his head.

'I still find it astounding that he believes we're researching a point of law for you to publish an article.'

McDougall bent back to the roll, his gaze intent, expression sour.

'Bribing him with the page from the Da Vinci tome helped immeasurably,' he said.

'Bribe is a harsh word,' Gordon said. 'You donated the

drawing in a fine gesture. Although I admit, without such a generous gift we'd no be allowed to look for our own documents. M'be inducement is the proper term?'

McDougall mumbled over the parchment and Gordon caught the words 'defaced' and 'disgrace'. He pressed his lips together and bent to his own roll, examining each line for a hint of Amy Dudley.

CHAPTER SEVENTEEN

That evening Arthur sat, huddled in a coat that smelt of piss and old food, at the mouth of Carey Street. He'd been there most of the day, watching and waiting. He pulled his cap further down, warmed his dirty fingers with a breath and eased his stiff legs. A familiar figure came out of the building opposite and Arthur rose. He bent over the walking stick, hobbling along, and followed McDougall to a tobacco shop. Arthur gauged the outside, choosing a darkened entrance next door and waited. McDougall re-emerged after a few minutes and Arthur doddered out, colliding with him.

'Oh goodness, excuse an old man his clumsiness.'

'Nay problem. Are you all right, sir?'

Arthur leant heavily on McDougall's arm, letting his breath wheeze.

'I'm fine, but could use a little help to the tavern, if you've a mind? I've a few shillings for a pie and jar of ale somewhere here.'

He made a show of patting himself, nearly falling, and McDougall's portly frame took his weight easily. He imagined slipping the knife into the fatty skin and skewering lawyer's heart. He curbed his impulse and reached into the man's pockets, then tottered back. McDougall steadied him and readily agreed to help him reach the tavern. Arthur took his time, wittering on and lurching as if on ancient bones until they gained the pub entrance. McDougall doffed his hat, pressed a few coins into Arthur's hand and headed back to the records building. Arthur grinned and pocketed the coins. He counted to twenty and followed the lawyer. At the mouth of Carey Street, he fingered his knife, watching McDougall re-enter the building, and settled once more to wait.

CHAPTER EIGHTEEN

Gordon stretched, raising hands high so his shoulder blades cracked. The ceiling was lost in darkness and shadows pooled around the shelves. Lamplight from other, unseen tables created halos and more shadows against the walls. He glanced at the empty seat and wondered how much longer McDougall would take to buy tobacco.

HE'S NO COMING BACK.

Of course he is.

WHY WOULD HE? THIS IS A FUTILE PURSUIT WITH A WORTHLESS MURDERER.

Gordon shook his head. Abruptly the shadows seemed blacker, crowding and trying to reach him.

HE'S MEETING THE HARELIPPED MAN. THEY'RE COMING FOR YOU. CREEPING THROUGH THE SHADOWS. FORCE YOU BACK TO AMY DUDLEY'S BONES.

NO! McDougall disnae ken I had her. No one does.

ARE YOU SURE? WHERE'S THE LAWYER THEN? HE'S BEEN GONE TOO LONG.

Picking up a lamp, Gordon moved away from their table, trying not to mind the shadows. He sought refuge in company. Anyone's company. He moved toward a halo of light and emerged only to find the workbench unoccupied.

ALONE. ALL ALONE. THEY'LL FIND YOU. SKIN YOU OF KNOWLEDGE, THEN KILL YOU. OR THROW YOU IN BEDLAM.

The lamp shook violently and Gordon put it down, fearing he might otherwise drop it.

Leave me be!

He thrust clenched fists into his pockets, muttering facts about Amy Dudley, desperate to banish Iona's insidious whispers. Still she continued, and he dug fingernails into his palms, using the pain as diversion, until eventually she quietened. He took out and unfurled his hands, inspecting palms now sporting blood-specked half-moons and a slip of paper stuck to his bloodied skin. He peeled it off, recognising the notations from Mister Green.

He's in on it. Left the doors open. Let them in. The harelipped man and the lawyer. Here they come!

Gordon spun, peering at the shadows while Iona laughed.

Shut up!

He smoothed the paper, read and re-read it. Suddenly he turned, staring at the shelf above the workbench, noting the record number.

These documents will be here, somewhere.

Aye waste more time. By all means look. Look. With your back to the doors. The shadows creeping up.

Gordon gripped the workbench, concentrating on the numbered boxes to drown her out. He found the right one and pulled it down. Sitting at the bench he thumbed through the contents, groaning when all were dated 1561.

Pathetic. You're a failure. Murderer. Friendless. Meant to die.

He pulled a document out, unfolding and reading the script, seeking to push Iona's whispering away with words. Gordon read the Latin script; it was a coroner's report dated August 1561. Desperate to keep Iona quiet, he deciphered the Latin describing a jury convened for a stabbing and at the inquest the verdict of murder had been passed. The victim's body had been recovered from the Thames at a place called Bablock and no one had been found for the crime. He glanced at the coroner's signature and his heart seemed to falter: Pudsey, and the man had dated it September 1560. Gordon reeled back, the document shaking in his grip, and closed his eyes. After a moment he calmed enough to re-read the report and carefully discerned every word, taking in the victim's details: Daniel Fleet.

The messenger from Sam's notes. The one that died taking Amy Dudley's final note. Watch for the Watchers. It's proof.

Gordon stared at the parchment and then at the box. His brow creased, trying to understand the oddity of dates. He refolded the document with care, placing it on the table, and went to the next, his mouth dry and fingers clumsy. He read four more reports before he found it. Neck cramped and eyes gritty, he translated the line three times to convince himself it was real. *Super visum corporis domine Amee Dudley, nuper uxoris Roberti Dudley*. There was no doubt. The line read, 'On inspection of the body of Lady Amy Dudley, late wife of Robert Dudley.'

'It's here. It's really here. I found it.'

Tears pricked his eyes and he blinked rapidly, swiping them away, breaths hiccoughing. When he calmed enough, he greedily read the rest of the coroner's report. Translating the names and dates at Cumnor, he realised what must have happened. Each document in the box was dated August 1561, yet the coroner signatures were dated individually and for the previous autumn. The assizes, he surmised, must have heard all the cases at once in the August of 1561. In doing so, those hearing the cases had recorded them all on this single date and so the coroner's reports were filed there. He sat back, suddenly feeling wide awake and letting out a breath he drummed his fingers across the bench in a merry tattoo. Gathering the reports into Amy Dudley and Daniel Fleet, he returned them to the box. Gordon hooked the lantern over his arm and carried the box back to their table.

McDougall was still nowhere to be seen, but the lawyer's frock coat now lay on the chair, testimony to his return. Putting the box down, Gordon gave dancing steps and moved about, seeking McDougall amidst the dark shelves, but to no avail. He returned to the table, humming and still doing his jig. Gordon hoisted the lawyer's coat up and waltzed it about. His face ached on a smile while the pockets of the frock coat banged his thighs as if in time to music. Abruptly something fell from the pocket, clattering to the floor where it skittered under the table. Placing his dancing partner over his arm, Gordon bent and retrieved McDougall's pipe. He slipped it back into the pocket where his fingers encountered thin paper. Withdrawing the letter, Gordon gave a throaty laugh.

It must be from Doctor Bennett! What a day, what a day!

He took the pages from the envelope and stopped at the familiar handwriting. He stumbled to sit heavily in the chair, blinking rapidly, his surging guts turning to water. He read the letter and swallowed against rising nausea.

How can this be?

Hates you. Going to kill you. Send you to Bedlam.

Gordon stifled a cry at a hand on his shoulder and McDougall's pear belly was warm at his elbow.

'What have you got there?' the lawyer asked.

Gordon shrugged off the hand and stood, towering over the other man.

'As if you dinnae ken! How long have you been in league with my father?'

McDougall backed away, looking blank.

'What do you mean?'

Gordon thrust the letter at him.

'This. This is clearly the last in a long line. Where are the others? Is that why you've been gone so long, sending the latest reply?'

'Of course not. There was an old man outside the tobacco shop, he needed help.'

'Dinnae take me for a fool! Is the harelipped man in the pay of my family? Are you? Oh my God, you are! Waiting for me to fail so you can send me to Bedlam.' He was shouting now, drowning out McDougall's protests. 'I'll no let you! Get out, get away from me.'

Gordon pushed past the lawyer, running from the building and out into a frigid night, tears chilling on his beardless face.

Gordon awoke in his room, clutching a half full whisky bottle. The sun through the shutters told of noon and he squinted in its light. He half rose, half fell out of bed, kicking an empty bottle, only to sink back, head in hands. Suddenly the memory of the previous night gripped him and he groaned, recalling McDougall's betrayal and his flight from the building. After that it was a haze of walking, drinking and fighting.

Fighting who?

He stared at his right hand, the knuckles were red and split, inexpertly wrapped in a ripped shirt tail. They stung and felt hot to touch, but he didn't care. More memories surfaced; McDougall's room, the lawyer hatless, coatless and bleeding. The man tottering away and of giving chase, roaring like a bull.

Shite.

BEDLAM FOR A CERTAINTY. OR PRISON. DEATH WOULD SAVE YOU.

What have I done?

He betrayed you. Conspired with the devil to let you fail. Should have let them kill you in Edinburgh. It would've been quicker.

Gordon stumbled to the corridor and banged on McDougall's door, but there was no reply. From the stairs, a squinty-eyed woman appeared, mop in hand.

'Where is he, the man who bides in here?'

'I'm sure I don't know.'

Gordon tried to smile and shuffled toward the woman, who looked alarmed.

'All right, no need to get nasty,' she said. 'He's gone, I know that much. Left this morning.'

Gordon's head felt fit to bust. He made it down the stairs to the landlady's apartment, tucking his shirt in and hiding his raw hand behind his back. The mealy-faced woman opened the door to his knock.

'Wotch you want?'

'Where's Mister McDougall?'

'As far from you as he could manage, I'd say. He left you these. Mind, I've taken the next two weeks' rent out like he said to.'

She thrust a money pouch and an envelope out. He took both, his thoughts tatty with questions. The door slammed shut.

Back in his room, Gordon read McDougall's note, trying not to notice the blood specking the page.

> I'm called back to Edinburgh. My daughter is ailing. I promise to return as soon as I'm able. I implore you to seek out Doctor Bennett. Your sincere friend, Iain McDougall.

Liar. He's gone for the harelipped man and your father.

Gordon gasped as if winded and the room blurred.

Lost. I'm lost.

He stared about, seeking some respite from the pain and betrayal, but there was only Quile, watching bright eyed from her new wooden cage. His thoughts tumbled like wind-thrown leaves and he retched, heaving until his insides felt battered and only spittle remained.

Pathetic failure. Without the lawyer's presence, you cannae retrieve the coroner's report. No proof. No Doctor Bennett. No redemption.

Never work again. Truly lost. Child killer.

Gordon folded onto the sickly floor, sobbing amidst Iona's laughter.

Chapter Nineteen

Reading

Later that same evening, in a hotel restaurant, Arthur Standish seemed wholly absorbed in his supper. At a nearby table McDougall ate sparingly, with no enjoyment, and kept touching his split lip. The lawyer's morose expression made it seem as if it, and the whole world, worried him. Arthur, sitting in full view of his quarry, had no concern at being recognised. The persona of Yorkshire wool merchant was meticulous. The use of black wig, beard and moustache along with the perfect accent was wholly different from the old London chap outside the tobacco shop. He surreptitiously watched as the lawyer hardly touched his beef and potatoes. Abruptly McDougall rose with a preoccupied air and left the dining room. Arthur finished his dinner, enjoying a glass of claret before retiring to his own room for the night.

At four in the morning, Arthur got up and applied greasepaint, a thin, pencil moustache and false eyebrows. He dressed in the hotel uniform he'd stolen earlier and, trusting the disguise, left his room. The reception desk, as he knew it would be, was silent and unmanned at such an hour. It took Arthur moments to pick the manager's door lock. A quick search of the office revealed no key cupboard and on instinct he picked the lock on the desk drawer. Inside he found the five master keys to the hotel. Taking one, he re-locked the drawer and office door, returning to his room.

Inside, Arthur removed the disguise, but kept the uniform on. He fastened his black cloak around his shoulders, putting on a cap and mask to hide the brightness of his face and hair. Silent as cat paws, Arthur opened the French doors and slipped onto his balcony. The cold night was lit by a half moon and he blended into the shadows it cast. From his leather satchel, he pulled a thick, silken cord ending in a blackened grapnel. He attached it to the ivy-swathed building, using it to help his ascent. He passed the first balcony above his own without pause and alighted at the second, where he crouched, listening. Assured by snores from within, Arthur opened his satchel. Parting a dressing robe, he removed a near empty bottle and a glass from its padding. Pouring a tiny amount of whisky into the tumbler, he arranged bottle and glass on the balcony table. He coiled the cord, replacing it and the grapnel in the satchel, tucking them beneath the robe to deaden any noise. Satisfied, Arthur picked the lock on the French doors and crept inside.

McDougall's room smelt of sweat and worry. Arthur stood at the end of the bed and watched the snoring lawyer. He imagined gutting McDougall, muffling any screams with his fist. He knew what it would feel like to drag out the man's slippery entrails and squeeze the faltering heart. He could almost taste the lawyer's blood and had to turn away. Going to the bedroom door, he took out the master key and slowly rotated it until the door unlocked. Turning back, he moved silently about the room, rifling the man's belongings. There was no locket. He fought the urge to slap the man awake and carve skin to bone for answers. Taking a steadying breath, Arthur found and removed the forgeries, the letter from Gordon's father and the one from McDougall's wife. Then, glancing at the still sleeping lawyer, he opened the satchel and removed the dressing robe. He took off cloak, hat and mask, putting them inside the bag. He then tucked the satchel out of sight beneath the chest of drawers. He hung his robe underneath McDougall's on the back of the door. Surveying the room, Arthur took another long breath and smoothed the uniform front. He lifted a lamp, turning the light up slightly before approaching the bed.

'Sir,' he whispered, shaking the sleeping man's shoulder.

The lawyer grunted and woke, blinking in the light. Arthur drew back, letting shadows fall on him.

'It's your six o'clock wake-up call,' he lied.

'What? Oh. Aye, of course.' He looked annoyed. 'Most just bang on the door, you ken?'

'I tried, sir. But I must be quiet for the other guests and you never replied. I'm not allowed to leave without a reply, or it'll be my job.'

'All right, all right.'

'Please sir, most other guests are sleeping. Could you possibly keep your voice down, or it'll be my job.'

McDougall sat up, bulbous tummy like a cushion in his nightgown.

'I'll be down for breakfast presently,' he murmured. 'Be sure there's eggs, poached, will you, laddie? I'm in a hurry to catch the seven o'clock coach.'

'Sorry sir, there's no breakfast served till seven in the dining room,' Arthur whispered. 'But the maid's put coffee on your balcony sir, so they can do turn-down in here. I can bring a breakfast up to you.'

The lawyer stared and shook his head.

'Ridiculous,' he muttered.

The man heaved himself up and out of the bed, shuffling into slippers and putting his glasses on. Arthur put the lamp down and held McDougall's robe so he could put it on.

'Let me get the door, sir.'

Stepping outside McDougall gasped at the cold air. Arthur, right behind him, blocked the way back in. In the semi-darkness McDougall half turned to him.

'Forget turn-down, laddie. Bring the coffee inside, it's bally freezing out here.'

Arthur tensed, weight shifting, preparing to strike. Yet the lawyer hesitated, frowned and turned, approaching the balcony table. His robe flapped in the breeze, revealing white legs.

'What's this, whisky?'

'Oh sir, the maid must've made a mistake.'

He moved alongside, between McDougall and the balcony rail, causing the lawyer to look at him. Arthur felt he could see everything, despite the dark, and revelled in the knowledge of what was to come. He glanced over the rail and down.

'Oh my God!'

'What?'

Arthur moved so McDougall could look.

'Down there, is that a body?'

The lawyer craned over the rail, peering into the fading dark.

'I cannae see anything,' he said.

With a practiced move Arthur bent, grasping McDougall by the robe back and white leg.

'Stop! What are you doing?'

Arthur grunted with effort but, using the man's weight, heaved him over the balcony. He watched McDougall flail and fall, screaming and screaming to a pounding silence. Grinning, he raced back into the room, retrieved his satchel and threw on his dressing robe. Stepping calmly into the corridor, he locked the door behind him with the master key. Amidst the first murmurings and horrified shrieks, he returned unnoticed to his own room.

Arthur breakfasted at eight o'clock. He and the other guests had been confined to their rooms while the situation was dealt with. But Arthur had used the hubbub to return the master key to the manager's office, as if it had never been missing. Now, the dining room was full and all a-twitter with the death. Some people, it seemed, had stood on their balconies and watched the grisly deed of prising the corpse from the spiked railing surrounding the hotel. Arthur recalled the gruesome scenes with immense enjoyment. While he tucked into his poached eggs, he listened to the gossip.

'Poor man,' a waitress remarked to a female guest. 'Drunk as a lord, he was, fell to his death.'

The woman shook her head.

'In drink, at five o'clock in the morning? What a disgrace!'

'Well, I heard he was a Scotsman.'

Arthur heard the same variation tattled across the dining room. Smiling, remembering McDougall smashing onto the railings, he ordered a fresh pot of coffee.

CHAPTER TWENTY

Southwark, London

Five hours before McDougall's murder, Gordon woke in darkness, too sober. His groping fingers found bottles that proved distressingly empty. Something clinked and he grabbed at it. Broken glass ripped his left palm open; he cursed at the searing pain as blood ran to the floor, hot and coppery. He sat, back against the bed, knees drawn up, and sobbed, calling for his wife and friend. He wept, desperate for things to be different and was wretched, knowing they never would be. Someone banged on the wall. Mortified, he hiccoughed, trying to stifle his sobs. His throat felt raw with old whisky and snot. Wiping his face, he found his hand pooled with blood, now smeared on his face. Gordon dragged his medical bag to him, found a whisky bottle with drips left and shook them over his cut. Clenching his teeth on the pain, he clumsily bandaged the wound. Abruptly exhausted, he stared at the floor, mind blank and skin heavy. His foot nudged something, and he peered down, hoping for whisky but instead found the purse McDougall had left. Somewhere a clock chimed midnight.

He's only been gone hours.

It felt like days. Gordon suddenly remembered visiting the nearest grog shop, buying whisky and gin; now all gone.

All gone. Everyone's gone.

NO, THE HARELIPPED MAN. HE'LL NEVER LEAVE YOU ALONE. NO UNTIL YOU'RE DEID.

Gordon struggled to his feet, clutching the purse.

'HERE I AM, YOU BASTARD!'

He staggered, almost falling while roaring for the harelipped man.

'CUT MY THROAT! KILL ME DEID!'

The door thundered and then flung open, revealing the landlady.

'Out. Get out of my house, Doctor McCraken!'

He swayed, staring and then spat to the floor.

'Youse old bitch, I'm paid up!'

The woman's mouth pursed, disappearing entirely, and she stepped aside. A man filled the doorway, hefting a cudgel.

'Me mum says you're to leave. I'll wait as you get your things together.'

Gordon wobbled, sniggering and gestured to the landlady.

'How did youse come oot of that?'

'Do you need help, man? I'll do it quick and painful, like.'

Gordon blearily eyed the cudgel and some small part of him managed caution. Kicking bottles aside, he packed his things, emptying Quile from her cage. The crow flapped onto his shoulder and he stumbled, fumbling his bags. The man helped Gordon down the stairs none too gently. He was then pushed outside, and the door slammed behind him, bolts ramming home.

'Fuck youse too!'

A bolt rattled. Gordon hurried away, swaying and slipping on wet brick and mud. At the mouth of New Street there came laughter and a grog shop lit the night. He made for it like a drowning man for shore.

Furnished with a fresh bottle of whisky, Gordon took no heed of his direction. He wandered, sobbing and berating the world and a couple of night soil men he nearly fell over. At Maid Lane, he staggered to sit in the lee of a statue. Quile flapped darkly to perch on the stone, feathers glistening with rain as she searched for insects. Gordon swigged, rocking back and forth. He cursed McDougall, his father and the harelipped man then:

'Iona! Iona! I've no one and nothing left!'

THE RIVER WOULD WELCOME YOU. DROWNING IS EASY.

He grunted, swallowed more whisky, and stuffed the bottle into a bag. He managed to rise, grappling his belongings, ignoring the pain from his hands, and headed for the Thames, Quile a following shadow. He weaved down Love Lane with tiredness and sorrow clinging to him then faltered, thinking of Amy Dudley. Her soul glowed like a ghost behind his eyes but he imagined the days and nights to come and hurt all over. He took a long breath, tasting the river, and straightened; gripping his bags he moved steadily onward.

CHAPTER TWENTY-ONE

On Bankside Gordon stopped, staring at fires illuminating the river shore. Music and laughter drew him and so patches of darkness became tents. Open flaps revealed coloured insides and raucous pleasures. Figures emerged, some dancing, others playing instruments; all were clapping and calling encouragement. Gordon moved among the Romanies, his chest tight and warmed by the welcoming smiles. His heart beat with the drums and blood sang with the pipes. All around a heavy opiate sweetness drifted and merged with the smoking fires. He stared, fascinated by the strangers' faces that yawned to alien lengths. Suddenly a monkey jumped to his shoulder; Gordon screamed then laughed. The musicians joined in, urging him on. Gordon capered, swinging his bags, and stumbled, nearly falling. He straightened, breathing hard and stood, loose limbed while the dancers swirled.

A woman, made of air and light, broke from the revellers. Bathed in an orpiment glow, her steps were elegant and ancient. Gordon, entranced, watched Amy Dudley turn in figures of eight, her skirts and ruff catching the light. Another woman joined her, colours flaring sapphire and emerald. The familiar smile and waltzing steps thickened Gordon's throat. Iona's cornflower eyes were bright on his.

She curtsied, before being swept back into the dance and he ached to follow her, but Amy Dudley still turned and turned about. She transfixed him, shimmering, insubstantial as flames on snow and then a spectral man came forward. Tall and powerful, Samuel Banks held silver fire at his fingertips and spun Amy Dudley, faster and faster while his smoky gaze never left Gordon.

All around them the opioid smoke grew intense, coating Gordon's throat with honeyed thickness. Suddenly flames leapt, dazzling, forcing him away and the figures of light vanished. Shaking, he turned to find the Romany dancers manic. A giant reached for him, bending on stiff, impossible legs and Gordon shrieked. The gypsy laughed and lurched away on stilts. From above, Quile landed, cawing on a tent, beak shining, dagger sharp. He bowed to her, hailing the goddess of night and fury, then danced on. And on. Until his head wanted to float and meet the stars. Finally, he stopped, lest he fall from quivering legs, and watched the pageant spin by. But his joy coursed away with it, and abruptly he tasted sour and empty. Head throbbing, he doubled over, stomach clawing to get out. At his feet, stones broke like scabs, blood surging across the shore. Gordon tried to run, but his legs failed, tipping him toward the Thames. He choked a scream, splashing into the water until it slapped his knees, numbing his legs.

A WEE BIT FURTHER AND ALL WILL BE WELL.

The current tugged at him and he raised shaking arms, holding his bags clear, horrified when the scarlet leached toward him. Gordon struggled deeper, slipping and nearly going in and the red-washed river reached his thighs, dragging at him. His deadened legs wanted to crumble and let the Thames take him.

DROWNING WOULD BE SIMPLE. BETTER THAN YOU DESERVE. ARE YOU NO TIRED?

So tired.

He shook, the cold was lulling, and the bloody river seemed to sing, calling him. A sudden shadow fell, became Quile, knocking his hat off, cawing and grappling his hair. Gordon flailed, almost falling.

'Hie! The river spawned a god!'

He raised heavy eyes to the shore and a woman stood there. She waved and shimmered, golden against the fires and dancers.

Amy Dudley?

NO! THE RIVER WANTS YOU. LET IT TAKE YOU.

Others broke from the dance and joined in, calling to the river god. Men waded out, laughing and beckoning, leading him back to the gleaming bank.

Once ashore Gordon was led inside a tent by a brown-skinned woman. She patted his arm while saying things he hardly understood. In the dimness she took his bags; when he protested, she tutted, and pushed him to sit. Against feeble objections his wet trousers were removed and he was wrapped in a blanket, given mutton to eat and strange tea. The woman cooed about sleep and safety and left. Gordon wondered if he should feel alarmed, but everything seemed muffled in wool. He was comforted by his bags, heavy against his legs, and Quile, perched on his shoulder. Eventually, he lay down and let the darkness in.

In his dream he waltzed with his wife in a sunlit garden party. All around, couples did the same, while more talked on the fringes. Lavender wreathed the air and Iona felt warm against him.

BUT YOU KILLED ME.

Abruptly she turned to blood in his arms, drenching him, the dancers and bystanders. Gordon screamed and everyone laughed, pointing and pushing. They turned grotesque, condemning him. He fell, weeping; silence and blackness crashed in. Loneliness, a lumpen lead, dragged his chest. The darkness inside and out hurt as if he were skinned alive. Abruptly a speck of light, amber and rose, drew his gaze. Amy Dudley pulsed with a flickering heart that mirrored his own. Then blackness took him.

Shouts woke Gordon and he struggled against a blanket. The tent flap opened, letting in pre-dawn light and the brown-skinned woman carrying an oil lamp.

'Awake is it?'

In the light the tent transformed with colourful scarves that draped and hung from poles and hooks. Perched amongst them Quile watched him. The woman's sable hair escaped from a headscarf and she was layered with skirts that jingled with coins and bells. She gripped his chin and peered into his face, her hazel eyes filled with mirth.

'Ha! River God is sober and fearful! Don't fret Godling, none stole yon coins or belongings with Martha watching over.' She held out some material. 'Yon dry now, yes?'

Mortified, Gordon recognised his trousers and he took them, pulling them on under cover of the blanket.

'Foolish immortal child.' Martha chortled. 'I've seen more than yon hairiness in my years!' She cackled, head cocked, and clucked to Quile, who flapped down to her shoulder. 'This girl now, she protect yon last night and always. Good harbinger. And I'd not let them devils out there hurt Godling, nor steal from him.'

'You shouldnae talk like that. I'm no a god.'

'Yon don't say?' Martha winked. 'Why then, did yon try and walk on Old Man Thames last night?'

'The river?' It rushed red and viscous back to him. 'I've no idea why I did that.'

'Ah, now then, there's no needing to think on it. Them

devils put too much powder in the fire for those not used to it. Pay no mind to the thoughts yon had. Confuse an angel they would.'

Martha offered up bread smeared with honey and bitter-scented coffee which Gordon ate and drank gratefully. Afterwards, searching his bags for the purse, he took out the whisky. Martha held the bottle up to the light, swinging the liquid back and forth, making gold patterns.

'This will make yon deader than old skin. Better feeding it to the river and never seeing the like again.'

Gordon held out some coins.

'With my thanks,' he managed.

Martha swept them up, disappearing them into her skirts and handing the bottle back. Quile hopped from Martha's shoulder to Gordon's and set about picking his hair.

'Godling will never be alone with that one about,' she nodded at the crow. 'No matter how much the other makes yon wish it.'

'I dinnae understand what you mean,' Gordon said.

'No, Godling, that's as clear to me as my own sight. Now, we're packing up.' She grinned. 'Yon to walk on Old Man Thames again or like an earthly man, along the streets and fields?'

Gordon somehow smiled back and put the bottle away.

'Streets and a safer crossing of the Old Man, Mistress Martha.'

She clapped him on the shoulder, sending Quile flapping to the scarves.

'Then with sureness, next time stay and dance longer and with happier imaginings. Ha! God of the river, in my tent! Blessings be on me!'

She laughed and bustled about, packing things. Gordon finishing his coffee, watched, and felt strangely quiet inside.

Chapter Twenty-Two

Just after eight that same morning, when Arthur was ordering poached eggs in Reading, Gordon arrived in Russell Square Park. He had changed his shirt, re-dressed his hands and managed a shave before leaving Martha's tent. He felt a semblance of respectability despite the loss of his hat and the constant pain in his palm and knuckles. Crossing the Thames had been unsettling. The other paddle steamer passengers had watched and whispered, avoiding him. Now, finally at the park, he nearly turned away, back to the river. But, hidden in the morning mist and with nowhere else to go, he studied the houses, trying to pick out Doctor Bennett's. All around the haze turned white and gold making Gordon's head light and eyes sting.

What do I say?

Nothing. Run away. Leave. Now. Back and let the river take you.

He returned to the path and glanced to the gate, imagining leaving. Suddenly a woman, skirts swinging, came in walking a cocker spaniel. Gordon waited, and to his surprise no one joined her. Seemingly unperturbed to walk alone, she closed the gate and unclipped the dog, who pottered away, sniffing the trees.

'Topaz, come, un po madre.'

The woman turned and walked along the path where

Gordon stood. She hesitated on seeing him, but then raised her chin and came on. Her olive skin became slightly flushed and her jaw set, dark curls bobbed beneath her fringed cap. She moved as far across the path as possible, without stepping on the grass, and with a nod strode past. Topaz had no such qualms. Stubby tail wagging, she approached with honeyed eyes and happy nose to sniff his fingers. It seemed to Gordon, head afloat, that meeting the golden dog emerging from the burnished air was an ethereal moment.

Quile dropped from the trees to his arm, head cocked at the dog. The crow made an odd sound and strutted to Gordon's shoulder, breaking the spell. He straightened to find the woman watching.

'What is that bird – crow?'

He wondered at her accent.

'Aye. She's my friend.'

ONLY FRIEND. ALONE. ABANDONED. MURDERER.

'How do you teach her to stay?'

'Quile does as she pleases and she refuses to go.'

The woman glanced at Topaz sitting at his feet. Gordon could see she was older than he'd first thought, maybe in her forties. She stepped closer, eyes intent on Quile.

'In my language it is la penna – this quill. A feather.'

'In my old tongue, quile means coal, for the black, do you see?'

She eyed him, taking in the bags and his hatless head.

'You sleep here?'

'No! I'm visiting someone who lives on the square.'

She raised her eyebrows, gaze travelling to his damp-edged trousers.

'I see. Well, we'll not keep you.'

The woman's gaze lingered on Quile as she called the dog and then turned away. Gordon felt stung and heat rose in his cheeks.

'I'm a physician, from Edinburgh, here to visit a Doctor Bennett. I lost my hat to the Thames and my patience in the early morn, madam!'

She swung back, frowning.

'Ah a medico! What is this man's address?'

He hesitated and she sucked her teeth, clicking her fingers at Topaz. Gordon recited the address and the woman smiled.

'Buona. You come with me, we visit together, or Topaz may become your next friend who refuses to go. How are you called?'

She swept past him, heading for the gate, and bemused he followed.

'Doctor Gordon McCraken. And you?'

'Signora Scarletta.'

At the gate she bent and clipped Topaz to her lead. Gordon watched the assured movements and felt the other's sideways gaze.

'Do you often walk in the park alone?'

The woman straightened, her expression closed, and gestured to the spaniel.

'I'm not alone,' she said. 'And in the mornings the park it is quiet and there are no judging looks or tutting old ladies.'

He opened the gate for her and felt anxious, eyeing the houses.

'Are you familiar with Doctor Bennett?'

'But of course! For many years now. He is a fine man, a good doctor.'

'Why then did you ask his address?'

Signora Scarletta rolled her eyes.

'If you had answered wrongly how could you be here to visit with the man, ah? Come.'

She left the park and Gordon followed, helpless in the Signora's wake.

CHAPTER TWENTY-THREE

Along the row of tall, grey and white town houses they stopped at one. Gordon tugged at his frock coat sleeves, and wished he had a hat. Signora Scarletta mounted the steps and suddenly the door was open. He was ushered into a hall where the wallpaper rampaged with birds, animals and plants. Amidst the jungle hallway were four doors with a further, smaller one under a staircase. Wrought iron stands festooned with plants added to the tropical muddle. Underfoot, black and white tiles stretched to an end door. Behind him the front door shut and sunshine from the fanlight above it stippled the walls. Gordon coughed, queasy on gas lamps, unidentifiable chemicals and baking bread. Topaz pawed at a door, which Signora Scarletta opened, letting the dog through. Gordon frowned, looking about.

'Is this your house?'

'Si, I live here.'

'But I thought you were taking me to Doctor Bennett?'

'And so I have.'

Gordon desperately wanted a whisky and was certain he could feel the bottle through the sealskin bag. To his right, the Signora indicated he should follow Topaz through the door. Gordon did so, but halted at the threshold, staring. Daylight saturated the library and bookcases covered every wall, kissing the ceiling. Rugs dotted the polished floorboards and four wing-backed chairs completed the haven. Topaz was sprawled in her bed by the fire and her stubby tail wriggled on seeing Gordon. He acquiesced to removal of coat, wanting whisky, an hour and a lifetime, just to sit in the room. Settling in one of the chairs he put his belongings on the floor, still staring around. Signora Scarletta paused at the door.

'Do you want some coffee or tea? Lemonade, perhaps?'

'No, thank you. Signora, I dinnae understand what's happening here. I only want to visit with Doctor Bennett, at his house.'

'Ah, but this is Doctor Bennett's house! Did you not notice the number? No? I am the housekeeper of the Bennetts. I will fetch you the doctor, it is no problem. For that, I will make the coffee. The man is a bear without the coffee.'

She left, closing the door. Gordon heard her move away and, listening, heard nothing more. Arrested by the quiet room he turned his gaze to the books. Amidst the many titles he noted, Hegel's *Phenomenology of Spirit,* Scott's *The Lady of the Lake* and Hoffmann's *The Devil's Elixirs*. On a high shelf, a book bore the words, *Queen Elizabeth*. He stood, with little effort positioned a pair of wooden, wheeled steps and climbed to the book. *The Speeches of Queen Elizabeth*. He pulled it and a light clipped voice spoke.

'By all means, Doctor McCraken, make yourself comfortable.'

The book slipped back. He glanced down to see a striking woman in her late twenties. Her black hair was stylishly draped in loops around her ears and pulled into a bun at the back. Square, capable hands held the ladder. Her navy gown enhanced a tiny waist while a paisley shawl, clasped with a cameo, was draped around her shoulders. There was no weakness in her jaw or chin. Her wide mouth neither frowned nor smiled at him.

'I'm sorry,' Gordon said. 'I was just…'

She stepped aside and he gained the ground, unsure of himself.

Too close. She's too close.

WAIT UNTIL SHE KENS WHO YOU ARE. MURDERER.

SHE'LL RUN THEN.

'My apologies,' he said. 'Your servant said I could wait here for Doctor Bennett.'

'Sofia isn't exactly a servant.' A lace-gloved hand extended. 'I'm Miss Liberty Bennett. I thought to keep you company. I certainly didn't expect you to be scouring our shelves for reading matter.'

Doctor Bennett's eldest child.

Her fierce grip was thankfully brief. She waved him to sit and arranged herself in another chair, unfazed by their solitude. Topaz heaved herself up and ambled to Liberty, nosing for fuss.

'Are you from Scotland?'

'Aye.'

Gordon looked at the door.

How much longer can Doctor Bennett be?

HE'S DECIDING HOW TO EXPEL YOU. DERIDE YOU. CHILD KILLER.

'Doctor McCraken?'

'Aye?'

'I asked if you hailed from Edinburgh or Glasgow.'

Liberty stroked the spaniel's silky ears, watching him. Gordon exhaled slowly and posed relaxation.

'I apologise, Miss Bennett. I'm a medical doctor, practicing in Edinburgh.'

LIAR. YOU'RE NAUGHT BUT A DRUNKART MAGGOT.

SHE'LL KEN SOON ENOUGH.

'Why are you visiting London?'

He took a breath and the rehearsed words came easily.

'I've been in correspondence with Doctor Bennett. He mentioned I might visit regarding an advocacy he's making for me.'

Liberty frowned; her gaze, briefly alarmed, became speculative.

Why will she no just leave me to wait?

He touched his cravat, then forced himself to stillness, wondering how to get rid of her. A smiling Sofia entered with a tray laden with coffee pot and crockery, bringing the earthy smell of fresh grounds. Gordon rose and helped, glad of movement and distraction despite it hurting his hand. He had agreed to a cup, watching a silent Liberty pour when a brawny young man strode in, black hair swept from a broad forehead. He was faultlessly attired in a charcoal frock coat and embroidered waistcoat.

'Doctor McCraken?'

The newcomer's rugged face echoed Liberty Bennett's finer features.

'I'm Tiberius Bennett. Forgive me. It's been a difficult few weeks. I don't recall our correspondence. What were we to talk about?'

'You're no. I mean, it's no you. Where's your father?' Gordon asked.

Deid!

The word atrophied his mind and will.

'My father had a weak heart. It was very sudden.'

Like Father John!

THE HARELIPPED MAN IS CLOSING IN. COMING FOR YOU!

Gordon stared around, drowning in Tiberius's meaningless prattle.

Did the harelipped man see me come here? Doctor Bennett's deid!

Tiberius puttered, petered out, frowning at him. Gordon opened his mouth, tried to form words, but nothing happened. He rose and swayed, so the bookcases threatened to fall. Tiberius seized his shoulders and Liberty reached for him. Gordon cringed back from her and nearly fell.

'Doctor McCraken, you must lie down,' Liberty said. 'If you cannot walk, Tiberius will carry you. Nod if you understand.'

Gordon focused and contrived the scarcest of nods.

Gordon didn't want to wake but the pain from his hands was sharp, forcing him out of darkness. He opened his eyes to a small bedroom with daylight stripping through shutters. The stringency of mothballs reminded him forcefully of his mother. He struggled to sit, head awhirl, teeth numb and a syrupy tongue, too big. His swollen palm burnt and knuckles on his other hand throbbed, all under fresh bandages. He inspected the wraps, unsettled that someone had tended him without his knowledge. Spying his belongings Gordon fumbled his satchel from the floor and retrieved the leather tome. Clutching it to his chest, he flopped back onto the pillow.

I have to leave.

RUN. IT WILL DO NO GOOD.

He rose on unsure legs, repacked the tome and slipped the satchel strap over his shoulder, picking up his sealskin bags. Outside the bedroom, the hushed hallway was unlit by window or lamp. He reached the stairs as quietly as he could and hesitated, wondering who was down there. The front door was visible at the bottom of the stairs, tantalisingly close.

I could just walk out. They wouldnae care. But what of Amy Dudley? All that Doctor Bennett knew, had, must still be here.

THEY KEN YOUR NAME. THEY'LL FIND OUT WHO YOU ARE. THE HARELIPPED MAN IS WATCHING, WAITING FOR YOU.

Doctor Bennett's deid.

He sank to the top stair, heat flushing his body, and put his face to his palms. Sweat, rubbing alcohol and coffee fused nauseously and the new bandages roughed his cheek. He imagined Tiberius dressing his wounds, remarking on pitiful Doctor McCraken while Liberty, cool and detestable, nodded agreement. Gordon rocked.

'I'm so sorry,' he whispered. 'It didnae work. He's deid. I've no idea what to do.'

GET UP. RUN. RUN INTO THE HARELIPPED MAN.

Gordon wiped his face, gathered his belongings and managed the stairs. He reached the bottom, to stand in the sunshine from the fanlight. Turning, the mosaic hall seemed to swell before him, patterned with pregnancy, threatening his balance.

LEAVE. THE RIVER AWAITS. THE HARELIPPED MAN WILL END YOU.

Gordon closed his eyes, and in that darkness Amy Dudley danced.

I'll find the Signora. She'll help.

He moved down the hall and a foul odour caught his nostrils, prickling his throat, coming from the door under the stairs. He took a step toward it and the chemical taint grew, became familiar.

'Acid something. Something acid,' he muttered.

A whine sounded from below.

'Topaz?'

IT'S A TRAP. THEY WANT TO BURY YOU DOWN THERE.

Go down there.

The dog's trapped down there, with that chemical.

He dropped his sealskin bags and opened the door on buttery hinges. The steps down were unlit and an acrid reek drenched him.

Shite, it's butyric acid!

The whine came, louder, pitiful and he wrestled a plant stand to keep the door open, ignoring the watery mud that showered him.

I need light. A mask.

The whining intensified, grating his teeth and wrenching his heart.

I'm coming. I'm coming. Hold on little one.

He took a breath and groped his handkerchief over his nose and mouth. Ignoring his painful palm, he gripped the rail and descended the shadowed steps. He reached the bottom, eyes half shut and stinging with his hand on fire.

'Doctor McCraken, how nice that you're up,' Liberty called.

A laboratory filled the cellar. Gas lamps glowed from shelves and on four long wooden tables where apparatus gleamed. Cupboards and bookshelves ran along every wall. A blackboard and sink darkened a corner. The only window, long and rectangular, opened to daylight and damp grass that was level with the windowsill. Liberty Bennett stood at one of the tables. A stiff leather apron covered her blue gown and she held tongs in gauntleted hands. A strip of material was tied over her lower face and she stood next to a tripod, burner and a noxiously fuming pot. Putting the tongs down, she turned off the burner and a small fan whined as she turned its handle.

'There now, I've finished. The smell will dissipate.'

With a free hand she removed her mask. Gordon lowered his handkerchief, struggling to take everything in.

Liberty stopped turning the fan and picked up the tongs, carefully putting them into a beaker. She removed the leather gloves and apron, keeping her gaze on her work. Gordon stared about, eyes streaming.

'What is this place?' he croaked.

'My father converted it from the cellar, for his experiments and to practice his lectures. My brother uses it now. I've always assisted them with their work.' She gazed around. 'But lately, it just makes me sad.'

You're trapped. They want to steal your book.

Take Amy Dudley. Bring the harelipped man.

Gordon focused on the open window, imagining he was back at university. In a lecture room, somewhere that led outside.

'Are you all right?' Liberty asked.

'I heard your dog whining.'

Liberty looked surprised.

'She's in the garden, with my sister. Neither I nor my brother would allow Topaz in here, Doctor McCraken. The fumes alone would be enough to cause the poor girl discomfort, if not harm, especially as she's pregnant. Can I ask what you've been doing?'

He followed her gaze to the filthy water that covered his hands, waist and frockcoat.

'I thought you'd trapped your dog down here.'

Her gaze narrowed.

'I see.'

There will be no help here. I need to return to Amy Dudley. To Foxcombe Manor.

'Miss Bennett, while your hospitality has been welcome, I'll be taking my leave.'

'Of course, but we should tend to your hands again, else infection could set in.'

She gestured. He glanced down, seeing the bandages

dirty and wet, with blood seeping through from his palm. The pain was suddenly intense and nausea gripped him, but he shook his head, unable to bear the thought of her touching him.

'Thank you. But I've no need of a woman to lecture me on the dangers of wound infection.'

Liberty flushed and her mouth twisted.

'If you wish to die of stupidity then, Doctor McCraken, don't let me presume to stop you!'

Liberty moved away without meeting his startled gaze, depositing the beaker and tongs in the sink. She forcefully poured liquid from a large jug, so water sloshed the sides, splashing her bodice. Liberty put the jug down with exaggerated care and her sharp intakes of breath were loud. Beneath the wet bandage his palm felt hot and sticky. Gordon moved to Liberty and held out his hand.

CHAPTER TWENTY-FOUR

Gordon sat near the sink, next to a bookcase and winced.

'Hold still,' Liberty murmured.

She rinsed his knuckles with water and changed the bandages. Although the knuckles ached, the discomfort was mercifully small. She turned her attention to his palm and picked at the stuck linen where the grimy bandage crabbed into the gouges. He clenched his jaw against the pain while blood bloomed, and the cuts wept. Liberty turned his hand to examine it and her muskiness combined with the strong acidic taint made a sweet rotting. Gordon closed his eyes and the gas glow turned his eyelids pinkly white. The bandage lifted, peeling away and making him gasp.

'Roll up your shirt sleeve,' Liberty ordered. She seemed to notice the state of his dress anew. 'And if you're not in a hurry, we should have your clothes brushed and dried before you go.'

He removed his frock coat and resettled on the stool but kept his satchel in reach. His naked forearm goose-bumped in the cool air. She positioned a stool in front of him and sat sideways, placing a towel and bowl on her lap. With no hesitation or asking she picked up his hand, putting it in the bowl. He grunted as she gently opened his fingers to inspect his palm.

'Hold it here. I need to wash the dirt off.'

When she picked up the jug, Gordon tensed. Liberty glanced at him, nodded and then tepid water poured. His hand jerked spasmodically. Pain spiked and his palm stung as if beset with wasps.

'You learnt nursing from your father?' he asked through gritted teeth, seeking diversion.

To keep from hissing and gasping, he studied the bookcases while Liberty dabbed his palm.

'Yes,' she murmured. 'Since I was a child. My father thought it would be good for me.'

Her voice was indistinct, and she patted harder, so his palm turned savage.

'Why was it good for you?' he managed.

'Father wanted me to understand his work. I also had to look after my younger brother and sister, after our mother died. He felt such teaching would help me learn responsibility and how others, such as the sick and crippled, were less fortunate than us.'

'I'm sorry you lost your mother.'

She glanced at him.

'Thank you.'

He hated speaking of Doctor Bennett, it made him hollow and wasted, but he could think of nothing else to say to distract from the pain.

'And your father's teaching helped you as he wished?'

His hand was afire again, deep rooted as if burning to bone. Liberty turned it.

'I believe so. But in the end, it was all he knew to try and help me grow up. Now he's gone too.' She took a long breath. 'Please hush and let me tend to this.'

Desperately trying to ignore the pain Gordon took a book, balancing it on his lap. He flicked open the slim volume, but, one handed, it kept slipping away.

'I can't see properly,' Liberty muttered. 'Let's go over

to the window.' She glanced at him. 'Doctor McCraken, you're forever stealing our books. Is my company so bland?'

'I'm interested in,' he looked at the spine, 'Lord Robert Dudley, Earl of Leicester.'

She smiled and rescued the book from him, moving to the window. He followed, palm throbbing and weeping. She gestured and he sat on a stool in a patch of sunlight while she placed the book nearby. He watched it. Through the open window someone laughed. The table was warm under his arm, but his palm still throbbed while his fingers twitched uncontrollably. Liberty took a large, blue bottle from the cupboard and placed it on the table, moving the book to do so.

'Lord Robert Dudley,' she said returning to the cupboard. 'He was my father's passion. Well, not just Dudley, but everything about him. The man's wife, his friendship with Queen Elizabeth, his career.' She took some rolled-up lint and wadded cloth and carried them over. 'What about you, why do you like Lord Dudley?'

'I didnae say I liked him. I said I was interested in him. Frankly, I think the man was a profiteer who found his equal in Elizabeth. He used the queen to get what he wanted. She used him for the same reason. They were well suited.'

The words spilt before he could bite them off. Liberty's eyebrows rose and she arranged a towel and bowl on the table.

'Put your hand in the bowl. I won't lie, this is going to hurt.'

He did as she bid, trying not to tense his arm. The wounds on his palm gaped scarlet and pulpy, throbbing like a malicious heartbeat. Liberty soaked the cloth; iodine and alcohol were pungent. She glanced at him and Gordon nodded. Liberty took a breath and applied the cloth. The pain echoed to his teeth and he sucked air in to stop from screaming. She picked up his good hand and rested it atop the cloth.

'Hold it there. Keep the pressure applied.'

'I ken what to do.'

'Yes, of course. My apologies.' Liberty unwound linen bandages. 'So, you think Lord Dudley was a scoundrel then?'

He shifted on the stool; the pain had lessened, but not much. He focused on Dudley.

'I think Robert Dudley was obsessed with success. Without it he would've perished, so the queen's friendship and royal favour were everything to him. Robert Dudley knew precisely what to do to keep Elizabeth's goodwill and he did it well. He learnt from his father.'

'My father believed the rumours that the two were more than mere friends.'

'I think Dudley believed they could be. Once.'

Liberty lifted the padding and inspected his wound.

'Let the skin dry for a moment,' she said. 'You think Lord Dudley believed he was going to marry Elizabeth, after the death of his wife, Amy Dudley?'

The name, said out loud, shocked him. He turned his hand and the bloodied wounds, now stained brown from the iodine, caught the sun's faint warmth. He gathered his thoughts, trying to keep his voice steady.

'I imagine Lord Dudley believed so, after his wife was murdered.'

'You sound just like my father, he thought Amy Dudley was murdered too. I can hear him now, down here, lecturing us.' She glanced about, her expression sad. 'I even think I see him sometimes. Just a flash. A slight motion, but of course, he's never there when I look.' She began expertly wrapping his hand, casting him sideways looks. 'Earlier, you mentioned Doctor Bennett was going to advocate something for you. You meant my father, not my brother.'

Sorrow gagged him and he pecked a nod. Liberty continued to bandage.

'Can I ask what my father was helping you with?'

SHE WANTS TO STEAL YOUR BOOK AND WATCH YOU DIE.

TELL HER.

He shook his head. Liberty was silent, her expression inscrutable as she worked. Gordon couldn't speak, he felt as if he were rotting inside.

'There, you're all better now,' Liberty said.

Gordon's bandaged hand showed no blood and his palm ached dully.

'Thank you,' he said.

Liberty smiled, picked up the Dudley book and replaced it on the shelf. Her eyes were distant, expression clouded.

'I still talk to him, my father.' She blinked and flushed. 'I'm sorry, that sounded ridiculous.'

Gordon tensed, sweat dimpled his back.

'I wouldnae say so.' He swallowed. 'I think talking to someone who has gone is… important.'

Liberty nodded and began tidying, pouring the water away and discarding the bloodied cleaning rags. Gordon rose, not looking at her, and tried to brush dirt from his frockcoat. Liberty glanced at him

'I think we should go up,' she said. 'We can see to getting your clothes cleaned.'

CHAPTER TWENTY-FIVE

Outside, the garden was chilly in delicate sunlight and the house cast shadows over the lawn. Four mildewed lawn chairs dotted the grass. A wooden table held a pitcher of lemonade, glasses and nearby a bowl of water rested on the grass. A young woman of eighteen or nineteen played with Topaz, rolling a ball for the ambling dog. In one of the chairs, Sofia crocheted, and, with a sigh, Liberty settled in another.

'Good morning once again, Doctor McCraken,' Sofia said. 'Are you quite recovered?'

'Aye, thank you, Signora Scarletta.'

Despite the keen air Gordon accepted a glass of lemonade.

'I'm afraid Verity is spoiling that dog,' Sofia continued. 'She feeds her scraps from the kitchen and lets her sleep on the beds. Topaz will be birthing on sleeping feet.'

As if conjuring her, the golden dog came over and drank from the bowl before greeting Gordon.

'Hello little one.'

Gordon petted her, enjoying the silky fur. Verity joined them and Gordon could tell by her colouring and features she was sister to Liberty and Tiberius. Yet, on Verity, the slanted cheekbones and upturned nose were finer and more exquisite. She tugged her linen cap, from which black hair was escaping its plaited bonds. She then shook her skirts, spilling grass, and he noted the dirt-stained hem.

'Hello,' she said. 'I'm Verity. You're Doctor McCraken. Liberty has told me everything.'

She stuck out her gloved hand and Gordon solemnly shook it. Her wide Bennett mouth smiled prettily, and she dropped into a chair.

'Please, excuse my sister,' Liberty said. 'She's an absolute bohemian. How she ever persuaded the lovely Doctor Fielding to marry her is a mystery. But since she became betrothed, she's thrown all decorum away.'

'Societal politeness,' countered Verity, 'is all very well in society. But Liberty darling, why should I bother in my own house?'

Sofia's hands stilled.

'Because child,' she said, 'if your exploits become too well known outside of your own house, such absence of politeness and decorum might decide Doctor Fielding to sever your engagement.'

'George would never break our engagement. He loves me. Doctor McCraken, you won't tell anyone, will you?' She smiled at him, her gaze travelling over his clothes. 'I must say, you're quite crumpled. Whatever has Liberty been doing to you?'

'Verity!' Liberty scowled at her sister. 'Doctor McCraken had an unfortunate encounter with one of your plant stands and that frock coat and waistcoat are now being cleaned.'

Gordon plucked at his lapel.

'I'm afraid these came from my bags with no hint of pressing.'

'Oh, such a prosaic explanation, I am disappointed. Liberty said you were here for Father. I'm sorry you had a wasted journey.'

'I'm sorry for your loss,' Gordon replied colourlessly.

'Can Tiberius help you?' Verity asked. 'He's taken over Father's practice and students. He's…'

'Tiberius can't help,' Liberty said, 'his workload being what it is now Father has gone.'

Verity looked to the house, fingers twisting in her lap. Gordon studied Liberty, wondering if she were lying.

Could Tiberius be my support and shelter, replacing his father?

'Doctor McCraken shares Father's interest in Robert and Amy Dudley,' Liberty said suddenly.

'Oh,' Verity brightened. 'Perhaps you should see the pocket watch then?'

Sofia abruptly stood, putting her crocheting into a bag.

'Verity, we should go indoors. It's not as warm out here as I imagined. You don't want the chill before your wedding.'

'Certainly not, Sofia. I'd better go and sit cosily by a fire and read something utterly appropriate.'

Verity smiled at Gordon, called Topaz and followed Sofia from the garden. Liberty watched her sister go.

'Doctor McCraken, I hope you won't let Verity's waywardness put you off our family entirely. It would be remiss if we couldn't entertain a friend of Father's. Lunch will be served soon, could you stay and dine? It will only be us ladies, I'm afraid. My brother will be teaching most of the day and then going to his club.'

THEY'LL FIND OUT WHAT YOU DID. WHO YOU ARE. STEAL THE BOOK AND CAST YOU OUT. RUN. THE HARELIPPED MAN WILL FIND YOU. THE LAWYER KNOWS EVERYTHING AND WILL BRING YOUR FATHER TO FORCE YOU TO BIDE WITH THE WITLESS. BETTER OFF DEID THAN IN BEDLAM!

Suddenly the lemonade tasted bitter and his palm

throbbed anew. A black shadow abruptly swung across the lawn. Liberty gasped as Quile landed on Gordon's chair cawing and hopped up his arm.

'All right,' he murmured. 'I'm all right. Happy to see you too.'

He stroked her head and down her back, gentling the rustling wings.

'Well,' said Liberty in a shaky voice. 'You are full of surprises.'

'I apologise. This is a friend of mine, Quile. She's quite tame to me but can be a wee bit cantankerous with strangers. Would it be too much to ask that she be allowed in the house, if I'm to stay for lunch? She'll be pleased of any sort of makeshift nest, perhaps a box of sorts?'

Liberty watched Quile, who had settled on Gordon's shoulder in her usual place. He could feel Quile's head was turned and knew the black eyes returned the woman's scrutiny.

'I think we can find somewhere for her,' Liberty said. 'But we should avoid letting Verity know, else I fear your friend might be pestered to ill temper.'

'That's kind, thank you, as I would like to stay for lunch.' He turned his gaze on the grass. 'Your father did mention showing me the pocket watch,' he lied. 'Would it possible to see it?'

He glanced at her. Liberty smiled slightly, gazing at the house, her expression unreadable.

SHE KENS YOU'RE A FILTHY, LYING MAGGOT.

'Of course, you can still see it as Father was willing to show it to you. I imagine you would be interested, as it belonged to Lord Dudley.'

'So Doctor Bennett mentioned, in one of his letters,' Gordon fleshed out the lie.

'My father bought it in Norfolk. He also purchased a list,

detailing goods and belongings transferred from Cumnor Place. I'm sure you know that's where Lord Dudley's wife died. The list is a receipt of sorts, to Lord Dudley accepting his wife's chattels after her death. There's even a description of the watch.'

When I am destitute and dying in some squalid place, I'll remember this.

It will no be long now. Remember well.

Liberty was looking at him, her expression serious.

'I'll show it to you, as Father wanted. But only if you promise not to steal it or murder us in our beds for it.'

She didn't smile.

Chapter Twenty-Six

They returned to the house and Liberty bade Gordon wait in the hall while she went into the library. She returned after a few moments carrying a cigar box and led the way into the laboratory. Down in the converted cellar they found an old wooden crate for Quile and Liberty lined it with odd ends of rags – most, Gordon noted, were ruined aprons. The crow settled quickly, tucking her head in so her neck vanished, and she closed her eyes. Gordon murmured to her, wondering how long Quile had kept watch for him, and felt guilty for having left her alone for so long. He stroked her black head with a fingertip, down her neck and along her wings. She half opened her eyes and clicked her beak with pleasure.

'We can prop the window open,' Liberty said. 'As it's at a level with the grass your friend can come and go as she pleases while you're at lunch. Does she need something to eat?'

'Thank you for the nest and, aye, if you've something to spare. Chicken skin, bacon fat or the like, if possible. She enjoys fish too.'

'Sofia can find something suitable, I'm sure.'

He turned and abruptly the laboratory seemed dark, folding in. Iona's muttering was constant, and Gordon closed his eyes, trying to block her out. Liberty seemed not to notice his discomfort.

'Could I ask that you keep your back to me, Doctor McCraken, until I say it's all right to turn? Father was very careful about hiding his objects. I feel obliged to maintain his secrecy.'

Gordon nodded and turned, remaining still and facing away from Liberty. He could hear her moving about and he itched to turn to see what was happening.

Why didnae Doctor Bennett trust me? What other things was he keeping from me?

HE ALWAYS HATED THE BONES OF YOU. HE UNDERSTOOD THE KIND OF CREATURE YOU ARE.

A table scraped, hinges squeaked and he fought the urge to turn. Glancing up, he saw his reflection, unwieldy in the cellar window, but beyond his, Liberty's likeness was clearer. He became taut and squinted to see. Liberty knelt, extracting objects from what seemed to be a hole in the floor. She turned, placing the items on a table, then bent and lifted a heavy door so that it thunked back, sealing the hole. Reaching down she turned and retrieved a large key from the door, slipping it into the cigar box. She straightened, smoothing her gown, and he dropped his gaze from the window, lest she notice his spying.

'You may come over now, Doctor McCraken.'

He turned, thrusting his hands into his trouser pockets to hide the shaking. He approached, trying surreptitiously to see where the safe lay. But then all his attention became riveted to two wrapped bundles and a leather folder that lay on the table. Liberty didn't seem to notice his intent stare. She unwrapped one of the bundles revealing a large, ornate pocket watch.

'This belonged to Robert Dudley. As I said earlier, it came to him as part of his wife's estate when she died.'

Gordon bent over the watch, captivated by the

workmanship and details.

'May I touch it?'

Liberty nodded.

Gordon stroked the ivory rim.

Amy Dudley held this.

Liberty watched, a crease marring her forehead.

YOU SHOULD NO BE HERE. SHE KENS THAT. LIAR. KILLER.

He lifted the watch, finding it heavy. Its body was as deep as four of his fingers and it covered his hand, fingers and all. Sprouting from the top, the lever and spindle nestled along and out of his middle finger, like an extra digit. On the left of the body he felt a caked hinge and thumbnail-sized lid. He rubbed a nail over them, flaking dirt like old skin. Yet despite the layer of grime the watch was utterly captivating, its beauty undiminished. Twelve numbers were etched on the ivory rim in carmine red, mirroring the inner rosewood body's hue. Carved into that body were ivory and brass rosettes and at the heart of the watch face a small, chased brass door opened to expose a mother of pearl sundial compass. The gold-chased back was engraved with reflections of the rosettes in minute detail. With gentle persuasion he pried open the side lid on stiff hinges. The opening revealed a blackened, funnel-shaped hole that bored into the watch's interior. From the hole he inhaled ancient tannin, charcoal and sulphur.

'It's a powder flask,' he murmured.

'How do you know that?' Liberty sounded surprised.

'My uncle would show me diagrams of old powder flasks from his archives. This one's beautiful.'

He didn't want to put it down, turning it to the light and studying each detail. His fingers ached for a cleaning cloth and oil. Abruptly Liberty plucked the watch from him, placing it on the table, and with an effort he swallowed his protests. She opened the leather folder, displaying an aged parchment page, written in old English. Thanks to his time with Sam's notes and amongst the mortuary records, he was able to decipher the document fairly easily. It detailed the chattels delivered to Lord Dudley's estate upon Amy Dudley's death. Dated the twenty-fifth of September, in the year of our Lord fifteen sixty at Cumnor Place, the list held fifteen items and at number seven the watch was described perfectly. At the bottom were two signatures and thumbprints in wax. One signature whorled and looped luxuriantly: Lord Robert Dudley's. Around the edges the wax had deteriorated, but the thumbprint was still there. Robert Dudley was still there.

These things can help me. More links, more evidence. They've been waiting for me. Amy Dudley's been here, waiting for me.

He longed to touch the parchment, run his finger across the signature and feel the wax.

'Please don't,' Liberty said. 'You may find some of the language difficult to interpret, but I assure you the document is authentic.'

His hand closed a hair's breadth from the page, and he tried not to scowl.

'You can read it?'

'Father taught me Latin and old English so I could help him with his work and studies.'

Liberty snapped the folder shut and he felt bereft; the whorls and loops engraved in his mind.

BITCH. HATES YOU. TEASES YOU. WAIT TILL SHE FINDS OUT WHAT TYPE OF BEASTIE YOU REALLY ARE.

He ground his jaw, forcing Iona's words away, and focused entirely on Liberty who was unfolding an oilskin wrap. She peeled back the last layer and inside was a large wooden candlestick with an ornate silver base. He gripped the edge of the table, breath shallow and head awhirl.

Distantly Liberty's voice came.

'Doctor McCraken, what's wrong?'

His knees bowed, muscles watery, and he groped for the stool, but it rocked beneath his hands, pulling him sideways. He teetered on limbs suddenly numb and fell into blackness.

Chapter Twenty-Seven

On the same day, Arthur entered the Southwark lodging house. His rough clothes made him inconspicuous and he pulled the broad-brimmed hat low over his eyes, gaze cutting everywhere. No one challenged him or paid him any attention. He reached McCraken's vacated room and the lock yielded easily. Inside was dim, the shutters closed, and it smelt of stale alcohol. That Gordon was at the Bennetts' Arthur knew. Yet he couldn't help but wonder if the locket had been hidden, forgotten or lost in the doctor's haze of drink and despair. The need for the jewel was a continual, high-pitched whine, a constant buzzing in his mind as if a bee battered behind his eyes. It drove in, stinging his jellied nerves at every failure. Arthur searched methodically and found nothing. He tested the floorboards, easing his feet, searching for one that could be loose or uneven. A board moved under his heel. Arthur slipped a flat metal tool, like a sharpened shoehorn, in-between the wood. Conscious of noise, he eased pressure on, and inched it up. Lifting the board clear, he peered into the hole, but the dark space seemed empty. He felt inside, seeking a pouch, a bag, anything. His fingers found nothing, and he imagined bleeding McCraken, slowly. Abruptly the door creaked, making him look up to see a large man standing on the threshold, staring.

'Who the hell are you?' the man asked.

Arthur rose, hiding the tool in his coat and smiling, gauging the chap, wondering where to cut first.

'I was told there were rats under these boards,' Arthur said. 'Just trying to lay traps and poison.'

The man moved forward in response to the quiet tone. The door swung closed and he peered into the hole, then his gaze narrowed.

'Me Mum never said—'

Arthur's hand lashed out, fingers stiff, catching the man's throat and he fell, gasping. Arthur reversed the metal tool, fingers digging under the man's chin, lifting to expose the throat. The dark veins beckoned. Abruptly the man's meaty hand grabbed his arm, yanking him down. Arthur went with it, to one knee, driving the tool into the man's thigh. Trousers and skin split, blood burst, causing a strangled cry. He twisted the metal, relishing the feel of severing muscles. The door creaked again, and someone shrieked.

Arthur leapt up and pushed past the woman in the doorway. Her mop caught his legs and nearly felled him. He stumbled and clattered down the stairs, out into Southwark busyness, to be quickly lost in the crowd.

CHAPTER TWENTY-EIGHT

In hell there was only high-pitched agony. Gordon groaned and forced his lids, weighted and gritty, open. Bright light, like stinging needles, stabbed into his sight. He cried out, snapping his eyes shut. Hot and heavy, the needling diminished and the whirling light behind his lids dimmed to become dark again. He flinched, causing more pain, at the abrupt dampness on his brow. The wet cloth relieved nothing. His body ached and his soul seemed high and filled with white. A soft mattress under him was a contrast to his grating bones and skin. When he tried to turn his head, it felt like a hammer blow on his temples.

'Doctor McCraken?'

Iona? Liberty. I cannae move. I hurt.

'Try to be calm, Doctor McCraken. You hit your head.'

Tiberius's low voice, blurred, too far from his fragile consciousness to register words. Next to him Liberty rustled, then her warmth disappeared as she stood.

'I'll stay,' she murmured.

A door opened and closed, and the chair creaked when she sat at his side again. The damp cloth returned, and the white pain subsided. A cool, dark note spread, bringing relief, and he fled into the blackness.

Gordon woke in darkness with no knowledge of how much time had passed. He took a breath, feeling in his bones and skin that the pain had retreated to an all-encompassing ache. He squinted at the thin slivers of moonlight that creased the shutters, revealing the familiar, mothball-scented bedroom at the Bennetts'. A coppery shade shimmered across the floor and Gordon gasped when a wet nose quested, pushing his hand. He gathered the dog.

'Topaz.'

She licked his cheek and stretched out along his body in a warm column. Stroking her soft fur, the aching tightness inside him collapsed and between one thought and the next, he slept.

When next he opened his eyes, the moon had vanished from the shutters leaving only night. A hard rhythm pulsed in his head and the darkness shivered his arms. He gingerly felt the lump on his temple, tender and painful. Topaz was a snoring puddle at his side. Reminded of McDougall, he shifted her to the other side of the bed. The dog snorted, settling quietly, and he stared into the dark, thinking of the items he had seen downstairs. His breath caught at the remembered candlestick, his thoughts circling it. Knowing sleep had fled, he raised himself on one arm, and found a candle in a holder and matches on the bedside table. He lit the candle and in the flickering light he put on his frock coat. He pulled his satchel open, checking its contents and then the sealskin bags; all seemed untouched. Standing, he swayed and sat abruptly on the bed, the darkness tilting behind his eyes. He felt Topaz stir and roll over to lie next to him, head on his thigh.

He slowed his breathing and smoothed the dog's head, counting the movements. By the time he reached twenty the darkness had stilled, so he opened his eyes and rose on steady legs. Topaz yawned, teeth white in the gloom, and heaved herself onto the floor. She sat, looking up at him, plum eyes lit by the candle flame. He shouldered his belongings and glanced at her.

I want the candlestick. I want them all.

THIEF? WHY NOT, YOU'RE ALREADY A LIAR. A WASTREL. A KILLER.

He shook his head.

It's no stealing. It's redemption and salvation. For Amy Dudley. For me. For my work.

PATHETIC.

In the unlit hall, the wavering candlelight hurt his eyes. Topaz, a golden shade, went waddling ahead and all about him the silent house was unnerving. His head felt light as if filled with air and wool and he stopped at the top stair. His blurred senses imagined the steps bent and bucking as if in a strong wind while Topaz, descending, was a swaying accomplice. Up and down the walls the printed birds and animals danced queasily. He swallowed a burst of saliva, closing his eyes. Opening them he used his free hand to grip the banister, raising the candle so the light swept down as far as possible. With many pauses for dizziness and nausea, he managed the steps carefully, one at a time. It helped to focus on Topaz's solid shape, waiting at the bottom. He gained the hall and transferred the candleholder to a small table before sitting on the last stair. Above the door only blackness showed through the fanlight. He rested his pounding forehead against the newel post, reassured his bags were resting behind him and the satchel on his left; all were still slung on his shoulders. Topaz sighed and lay down, head a solace on his foot.

He awoke cold, in the gloom of the hall, the candle having gone out. Topaz was the only warmth, now tucked into his right thigh. His fingers automatically found her head. He wondered if Quile had flown out of the laboratory and debated going down to find her. A notion of muted voices lingered in his mind like an odd dream. From somewhere upstairs a clock chimed three, the sound muffled. His head felt clearer and the image of the candleholder, dark and silver, hovered in his mind. Gordon's legs were stiff; he shifted Topaz, who stretched and ambled away toward the library. He fumbled for matches, putting flame to wick, and lifted the light. The front door was bolted top and bottom, brass keyhole empty. He fingered the hole and knew there would be no leaving now, even if he managed to steal the items. He sighed, and rested his head against the wood door, feeling exhausted. But still the candleholder remained, like a talisman, like a promise.

I could take it. Take them all and leave in the morning, civilly. No one would know. At least they would no find out for a while. Long enough.

AYE. STEAL THEM AND RUN. OUT, INTO THE ARMS OF THE HARELIPPED MAN AND DEATH.

That Iona approved helped not at all, but still the pull of the items was like a tide on his soul, drawing him onward. He went to the library, seeking the cigar box that held the safe key.

Half an hour later tiredness weighed his body and stupefied his mind. There was no box, anywhere. He had, however, found a drinks cabinet. Slumped in a chair, his bags at his feet, Gordon swallowed whisky, sighing as the burning spread. He fell into it, drifting and let his eyes close to hang in that void between wakefulness and sleep. He listened to the house, his heartbeat and the indistinct voices carrying in the dark. He blinked.

Iona?

'Iona?'

But his dead wife didn't reply. He picked up the candle, the flame reflecting Topaz's coat where the dog lay in her bed. Her stump wagged and she heaved herself up, padding from the library, and he followed her into the hall. Her plumped form sniffed at the laboratory door, head turning to look at him. He bent to her, fingers trailing in her soft fur and from beyond the door, faint syllables rose and fell. Topaz whined and put a paw to the door, dark eyes seeking entrance. He frowned and lifted her easily, and careful of her pregnant belly, carried the dog to her bed. He settled her with whispered words and a firm stay. Topaz huffed and curled, nose to tail, closing her eyes. Gordon swallowed some more whisky and returned to the hall. Putting an ear to the door he heard vocal ebbs and flows. Carefully, slowly, he opened the door, letting muted light out. From below a clipped tone offered odd phrases; *stir slowly*, *use tongs* and *Boyle's law*.

Liberty?

Another lower voice, fell and rose.

Tiberius? What's going on here?

Sudden light-headedness made the door sway and he steadied himself, listening to the voices. Then, with a breath and firmer tread, Gordon slipped inside and hunkered down. Below, the laboratory's far corner was brightly lit, casting the rest of the room and steps in deep shade. He shrank further, pressing to the wall, putting himself as much in the shadows as possible and studied the scene. Liberty was standing in front of the blackboard, which was now covered with diagrams and, it seemed to him, a lesson plan. Tiberius sat at one of the long benches, frowning over paper and pencil, taking notes. Chalk squealed as Liberty's light voice explained a medical procedure in detail, tapping the board with the chalk for emphasis. Gordon frowned and crept downward until he hunched on the last step, still hidden in the shadows.

'Goddamn it!' Tiberius swore. 'I can't do this.'

Papers flew to the floor.

'You can,' Liberty soothed. 'You're doing so well.'

'Don't patronise me!'

His panicked voice was sharp and stung at Gordon, so he wished he had brought the whisky with him. Liberty's dress sighed and boots creaked as she walked to put an arm around her brother.

'You'll be fine,' she said. 'You're almost there. The practical will be easier to learn after the method, I promise. Come on, Tiberius, don't be defeatist. What would Father say?'

In his craven darkness, Gordon frowned and settled to listen.

CHAPTER TWENTY-NINE

An hour later, in the library, Gordon reclined in a leather chair, easing his feet toward the fire he had built and lit. In his hand Robert Dudley's pocket watch weighed like a secret. Ownership rolled through him, causing him giddiness as if drinking strong wine. He glanced down at his satchel, where now resided the precious candlestick holder and receipt. Opposite him, Liberty shifted in her chair, white face half hidden in shadows.

'Miss Bennett, there's no need to be so angry,' Gordon said. 'It's a simple trade.'

Liberty's expression was masked, but he could feel her fury. All around shadows stretched from the bookcases, as if the ink from the books spewed across the floor.

'Forgive me, Doctor McCraken, but the loss of my father's prized possessions is not easy to bear, especially for silence from a disgusting blackmailer.'

Gordon shrugged and kept his features schooled to stone. Liberty bent to look at the other chair, seeking support. Yet unsurprisingly, Tiberius was long abed. His agreement to the deal had been a mumble, his face ashen and infused in turn, before he had quickly retired. She sat back, fingers digging into the leather and shoulders tense. Gordon turned the watch in his hand, feeling it warm as if part of him.

'Out of curiosity, how long do you intend to make your brother continue the charade?'

Liberty's fingers dug deeper into the chair, then dropped either side, her mouth a shadowed twist. From her bed, Topaz's head, flame gold in the firelight, rose and she went to Liberty, who fondled the soft ears.

'At least until Verity's safely married, and then, only if I'm certain Tiberius can manage his patients and lectures without me.'

The smell of books and the comfort of the library belied Liberty's tension and restless intensity. Gordon sipped his whisky, studying her and wondering at her motives and frustration.

'Forgive me,' he said. 'Your plan is seriously flawed. Judging by what I witnessed, your brother will never be able to manage in a professional doctor's capacity on his own. He has neither the wit nor the inclination.'

'He's not stupid!'

Gordon raised his eyebrows.

'Perhaps no entirely. But Tiberius is far from being a capable doctor or teacher of medicine in his own right. I can only imagine he passed his exams with your help in some form. Dear me, cheating is such an easy way to become disgraced and discredited. Did you no worry about discovery?' Liberty looked away and Gordon smiled. 'Och, of course you did. But then that didnae matter, did it, until your father died.'

Liberty's eyes narrowed, bitterness making her ugly.

'It should've been *me*,' she said. 'I'm the one Father taught! Tiberius would be happier being a banker or some such nonsense. But, being a mere woman, I'm only meant for embroidery, charitable works and marriage.' Her mouth warped as if the words tasted foul. 'Or a *governess*, if I must have a profession to play at! Play at!'

Her breathing was harsh in the quiet. He put the whisky down, cradling the watch in both hands, letting the firelight catch the rosewood and gold inlay.

'And exactly when does Verity get married?'

Liberty inhaled, controlling herself with an obvious effort.

'Two weeks' time.' She pleated her skirt, eyes downcast. 'Then Verity's reputation will be safe, removed from any disgrace our family invites. Surely you can understand, I just want her to be safe. Please, keep your promise to silence, we've paid what you asked.'

Gordon rubbed the watch, his gaze sliding to the satchel.

'Indeed, but I thought Verity's marriage was for love? Surely the good doctor she's to wed would no care if she came from a ruined family?'

'True, George wouldn't give a fig if Verity were in rags and homeless. But some of Doctor Fielding's family, his mother in particular, would use such a scandal to forbid the marriage. George's grandfather was the royal physician and his mother sees no reason why George can't reach the same footing. But if our family situation is laid bare, then that woman would move heaven and earth to separate George and Verity. I've no doubt she would succeed, given her close relationship with the queen. But if they're already wed and scandal comes to us, Verity will be safe from it.'

'I see. Let us put it plainly then: if Tiberius's reputation and standing in the medical community are exposed, with you no more than a mere woman pulling her brother's strings like a puppet, any friends or credit, monetary or otherwise, will be lost and your family, livelihood and reputation will be ruined. Equally, your sister's happiness and future with Doctor Fielding will be destroyed, along with any alternative, future prospects for her to decently wed. Does that about cover your situation?'

Liberty turned away, her mouth pulled down.

'You really are unpleasant aren't you?' she muttered, then looked at him. 'If I hadn't seen the letter, I would never have believed my father was in contact with one such as you. What would he think of you, blackmailing his family?'

Gordon's fingers tightened on the watch and he remained impassive only by pure will.

I dinnae want to think about it.

HE WOULD HATE YOU FOR THE MONSTER YOU ARE.

Liberty rose, face stark in the firelight.

'I don't believe you care about anything. What sort of man destroys people's lives like this? You're despicable.'

Her disgust was palpable, and he pocketed the watch afraid she might lunge for it. Liberty moved to stand before him, arms folded and expression defiant.

'What exactly was my father to you?'

'Doctor Bennett was more to me than you could ever understand, but that's irrelevant to your current predicament.' Anger caught him, anger at this blunt, beautiful woman, and at her father, for dying. 'Since I stepped into your house you've lied and deceived me about your family. Much like you're doing to your father's colleagues and friends, as well as the medical establishment. Does your sister ken your scheme? Does the Signora? How many will you drag down and disgrace to gain some bitter satisfaction over a society that deems you unworthy to practice medicine? By chance I realised you were hiding something. I wanted to ken what it was. Now I do. This is no one's fault but your own. Think carefully how you wish to proceed, Miss Bennett.'

The library seemed to darken. Liberty paced and then perched on the edge of her seat, her voice resigned.

'Doctor McCraken, our fate is in your hands. Verity's happiness is held at your whim. Please, why should I trust you to keep your word, now you've got what you want?'

Gordon's fingers trailed to his satchel, his anger dissipated, and he felt sudden surprise at how much he wanted to reassure her.

'I'm no longer a good man, I'll own that. My word, for what it's worth, is all I've left to offer. Unfortunately, you've no choice but to agree.' He paused. 'And perhaps I haven't got everything I want. Yet.'

Liberty's eyes narrowed, the planes of her handsome face tightened to sharpness. He knew then what a part she had played to gain his sympathy, to spare all she held dear. He smiled at her stony expression.

'If you hurt my family,' she said, 'I guarantee your destitution. I'll ruin *your* reputation, drag you down with me. And if you touch me, I'll scream.'

Gordon grunted a laugh.

'Miss Bennett, I assure you, I've currently no desire to hurt you or your family. And there are more willing whores.' She gasped and sank back into her chair. He continued, 'However, there are things I need to do, work to complete. If I dinnae accomplish what I mean to, my life will have no meaning. In this, I think, we're very similar.'

'We most certainly are *not* similar, in any way!'

'You, madam, are deluded. You practice the same unpleasant, underhand deceit you accuse me of. Yet you practice it to an entire professional body, your friends and your sister.'

'I do it *for* my family. You do it for your own selfish gain, uncaring of who you hurt.'

Gordon steepled his fingers, stopping their tremors.

'By performing your wholesale deceit,' he said, 'you practice and teach medicine, through your brother. Because it's something you would no be permitted to do for your own sake. Is that no for selfish gain? As for your intentions concerning your family… you've said Tiberius would be better suited to banking. By your own admission, Verity's to be married into a noble, influential family and you *could* be a governess. But you love medicine. So, you force your wee brother to play doctor for your thwarted ambitions. Now tell me, how are we different in our selfish gains?'

She stared with narrowed eyes, hating him, and he didn't care.

'I don't hurt people,' she said.

'Neither do I. But I have to gain the redemption I need, bring about change with my work. If anyone, such as yourself, poses an obstacle, I cannae let it stop me.'

'How can you redeem yourself when you stoop to vile blackmail?'

'I'll no deny my path to salvation is complex, as are my sins. Yet, it's hardly as if my crime of blackmail is against an innocent, now is it?'

Liberty seemed carved from stone. Her eyes were dark holes, then she turned away, white face golden in the firelight.

'It seems you've thought of everything,' she said. 'Understand though, I don't agree with your summary of my motivation, but I cannot ignore your threat, for my family's sake. So, let us put an end to this. What more do you want from me for your silence?'

He inclined his head, trembling too much for any other movement, catching and holding her gaze.

'Be assured it's something that could help you and your family.' He bent forward, seeking to persuade rather than force. 'Your father and I sought to change the face of medicine and it's still possible. If you and I continue, and succeed, Tiberius would be hailed as a pioneer in the medical profession, and your family would be forever beyond criticism.'

Liberty frowned, the whites of her eyes glinting in the firelight while she thought.

'It seems too good to be true,' she said, 'and so it must be. Yet, I need to know, will it end, once I help you? Will you leave us alone and keep quiet?'

Gordon nodded. Liberty straightened, smoothing her skirts, her expression empty.

'Well then, as you so gleefully told me, I have little choice. What is it you want my help with?'

'A murder.'

Liberty's hands stilled, her gaze rose, eyes wide and dark in the firelight.

'You're mad. My father would never have helped in such a venture. Our conversation is done. You should go, now. Take what you have and leave us in peace, please.'

She glanced at the door.

Wondering if she can reach it, before I reach her.

SHE KENS YOUR ILK. EVIL. MURDERER.

He bent and picked up his satchel. Liberty looked startled and then relieved, clearly thinking he meant to leave. Gordon withdrew Sam's notes, watching her. Liberty frowned and eyed the old silk package.

'What's that?'

'This is something your father was desperate to see. We were working together, despite the distance between us, to bring about a change to medicine. There was also a common interest that bound us, and this is at the heart of it.'

'Why should I believe you?'

Her gaze followed his fingers, caressing the silk.

'I can show you,' he said.

Liberty sniffed.

'About a murder? I think not.'

'A murder, that if proved, will bring everything you desire. It's a murder that intrigued your father and began our friendship. A murder we've already spoken of, one that you already understand much about.'

She frowned, her expression confused then incredulous.

'You're talking about Amy Dudley?'

'Indeed.'

'You and my father wanted to prove Amy Dudley was murdered? How on earth, and why would you want to do such a thing? What would be the point?'

'I can show you,' he repeated, fingers spread across Sam's notes.

She stared at him.

THINKS YOU'RE MAD. YOU'LL BE OFF TO BEDLAM AS SOON AS YOU'RE SLEEPING. OR DEID. THE HARELIPPED MAN WILL COME IN, CREEP IN.

Liberty held her hand out for the silken package and he shook his head.

'I'll no allow it in another's hands so easily. I'll only show you what's in here.'

Her eyes narrowed and she rose, arranging two small tables side by side in front of the fire. Her expression was closed, full lips a tight line and features shadowed. Gordon dragged their chairs to face the tables, settling himself back into one. Uncertainty made his movements thick and clumsy. Liberty glanced at him, then sat in the other chair, pressed as far away from him as possible.

SENSIBLE. WHO WOULD WANT TO BE NEAR YOU?

Gordon rested the package on the table and unwrapped it. He took out the first of Sam's notes, placing it on the table in front of her.

'What is it?'

'Evidence of Amy Dudley's murder,' Gordon said. 'And thanks to you and your father, I can now prove it.'

They talked for a further half an hour, with Liberty asking insightful questions about her father, Sam and Amy

Dudley's murder. Despite himself Gordon was impressed. Then just after the muffled clock had struck six, Liberty rose. She manoeuvred slowly round the table to stare at the dwindling fire, rubbing her temple.

'This is much more than I imagined. More than I…'

Her voice was rough, skirts suddenly swaying in the firelight, and she sat on the chair arm as if too tired to stand. Gordon rose then, limbs heavy, and stifled a yawn.

'It seems, Miss Bennett, that the long night has taken its toll on me. I'm away to my bed and suggest you do the same. We'll finish our discussions later today.'

Liberty looked at him, her gaze weary but still sharp.

'I need more time.'

'For what?'

She glanced at the silk wrappings.

'To read Sam's notes and understand as much as I can, before I can talk further. Will you grant me that?'

His head felt light, yet his limbs ached anew, dragging at him. His eyes were full of grit and firelight.

'Aye, but no for long, you ken?'

She nodded and reached for Sam's notes, but his hand was quicker.

'You can read these only in my presence.'

He put them away and, leaving her to bank the fire, returned to his bed.

CHAPTER THIRTY

Later that same day Arthur studied the Romany camp, watching the sable-haired woman. From Hawk's description he knew it was Martha. He got up from the grass, straightened his ragged but serviceable coat and pushed his hat back. He skirted the camp, pitched near Regent's Canal, wondering if the woman had stolen the locket or if McCraken had hidden it here. The thought of the doctor pained Arthur, like glass in his guts, and he decided it would take the man a long time to die. He reached his donkey and cart, untethered the beast and led it toward the camp. If the gypsy bitch had anything, information or the locket, he would find it. He got hard thinking of flaying her, skin peeling like a grape and shredding her bleeding muscles beneath. The wagon rattled as they went, filled as it was with his tinker's wares and tools. He whistled while walking and called out his services, hallooing and hollering. The children came first, calling excitedly with dogs barking in their wake. Their mothers came more slowly but carrying copper pots and pans for re-tinning and knives for repair. He knew the Romany menfolk would come later, to chat and pick through his goods. No money would be seen. Instead Arthur prepared to barter for food and exchange news and information for his work.

He chatted and smiled his way through easy repairs

for nearly half an hour with little but information on tides and old news for pay. Then Martha appeared and handed him three knives. They were worn and thin from use, their handles and blades nearly parted. He pursed his lips, lifting the knives and inspecting them.

'Ah Mistress, yon used these well.'

'They be good knives. I want them for many a year yet. What be the cost?'

'Repair of handles to blades be easy enough and cost no more than news of good fishing hereabouts. Sharpening is likely to break yon blades though as they be thin as old Nick's patience.'

Martha laughed, but it didn't reach her eyes and her gaze remained fastened on him. He showed her other knives he had, but she shook her head.

'Yon won't last near as long as mine. I'll be wanting my own at the heart of any new.'

'Crucible it must be then. Cost be a warm meal, of decent meat, mind. Don't be passing off no rat on me.'

'Cheeky bugger! Rat has no place at my hearth. Be fish stew and there's potatoes too, if yon does good work.'

He nodded and prepared the crucible, setting it to heat high enough to melt the ore, reminding him of smouldering bones and skin. While it was heating, he fused the blades to the handles, ensuring they were solid. Lifting a scarf to cover his mouth, he donned leather gauntlets and softened the ore. He then used tongs and a small hammer to repair the blades then left them cooling and dealt with other repair tasks. Then, as a final job, he sharpened Martha's knives to almost new. The Romany men came then, and he had to wait, making more barters for various items. Alone at last, he packed up the cart and led the donkey through the camp asking for Martha, as if he didn't know where she was pitched. Darkness was falling, the wind picking up when he reached Martha's tent. He secured his wares and tools and unhitched the donkey. He led the animal to the makeshift paddock and let it loose amongst the gypsies' ponies and goats. His coat flapping in the gusts, Arthur walked to Martha's tent, seeing her cooking fire curling and jumping in the wind. The need to find the locket was a throbbing in his temples, a pressure behind his eyes. He stared at the woman, willing her to give him a reason, a suspicion of a reason, to cause pain. Martha stirred a pot which hung from a spit-pole stretched across the fire.

''Tis a miserly eve,' she called. 'Yon finished with them knives?'

He handed them over, thinking how easily they would slice skin and muscle to bone. She tested each blade, smiling and nodding. Martha ladled out two bowls, handing him one, and pulled potatoes from some embers. One went into his bowl, the other into hers. Rain smarted on the wind.

'Yon can eat in the tent, if yon be of a mind.'

She didn't wait for an answer but doused the fire and went inside, leaving Arthur to follow. Two lamps lit the interior while myriad scarves hung from above and trembled with the force of the wind outside. Martha gestured and he settled on cushions. She smiled and lowered herself into an oddly fashioned rocking chair swathed in blankets. It was shorter in the back than normal, but with a wide seat and arms. She handed him a spoon and rocked while she ate her own supper. Arthur savoured the stew, finding it light and delicate, the fish cooked to perfection and the baked potato buttery. He watched Martha while he spoke of his tinker travels. She seemed not to notice his scrutiny, but merely listened, occasionally sharing thoughts on their commonly visited places. All the while gusts drummed the tent and Arthur's shoulders were soon taut with the sound. Martha passed him a heel of bread to mop the stew juice and he set to it gladly. The meal finished, she lit a pipe and sweet smoke drifted.

'If yon's a taste for it, there's a cup of goat milk I can spare.'

Arthur declined, getting to his feet.

'I've a way to go yet, Mistress, and can't let the weather hold me here.'

She rose, standing near the tent flap. Arthur clenched his fist and moved alongside, as if to leave. In a fluid motion he punched, seeking her neck. But she was quicker, ducking away from his fist and flowing to one side. He stared and swayed. Martha winked.

'Yon best sit, afore yon fall.'

She pushed and he staggered back, collapsing onto the cushions. Martha settled in her chair, puffing the pipe with an odd, sad smile.

'I sees yon with my sight and more. Blackened inside, tinker who's no tinker. Yon won't find what yon seek here; neither Godling nor jewelled answers, but surely lessons. The first be, I never thieve. The second, I honour the River God and the protection he left.'

From her sable hair she pulled a crow feather and twirled it. He tried to speak, but no words came. His sluggish mind wanted him to move, but his legs wouldn't, couldn't respond. The tent flap opened showing night, and a man entered staring impassively at Arthur; beyond him were three more. Martha nodded, rose and left. The men lifted Arthur and carried him outside to where a crowd stood watching, holding lanterns that lit the darkness. Arthur's gaze widened at the emptiness; everything was gone. Only Martha's tent stood amidst the packed-up wagons and caravans. All the ponies were in harness, ready to leave, with goats tied to the rear of the vehicles. The wind bore down, tugging Arthur's coat and whipping his hat away.

He still couldn't move. They took him to a dark shape that became his cart with the donkey picketed nearby. With a quick movement they hoisted him in the back amongst the wares. Beyond the tailboard he could see Martha's tent being dismantled and packed away. His limbs were numb, and tiredness swamped him. A shadow blocked his view and sweet pipe smoke lingered over his face.

'Yon shouldn't have eaten the bread, tinker who's no tinker,' Martha said. 'Wetted with a little poppy juice and more, to make yon still and sleepy.' She snapped her fingers in his face, focusing his gaze on hers. 'Listen good, yon's dark to us now. Meaning yon and any like yon won't ever find us again, not even if we was under yon fingers and in front of yon eyes.' She gripped his hand, pinching hard enough to break through his stifled mind. 'Tis a lonely road yon's walking and will only end in darkness. A warning given that yon won't heed, I know.'

Arthur tried to speak, but sudden blackness stole him. He next woke in the pearly beginnings of dawn with nothing to show which way the Romanies had gone.

CHAPTER THIRTY-ONE

Two days later shadows chased across the Bennetts' garden casting light and shade through the laboratory window. Inside, under a gas lamp, Gordon lightly pressed on the small wooden picker, meticulously lifting and discarding dirt from Lord Dudley's pocket watch. From above, somewhere in the house, Verity's muffled laugh rang out. Gordon scowled and his fingers tightened round the rosewood body. Two days effectively trapped in the Bennetts' house had shredded his nerves. The constant wedding plans and insipid small talk barely masked the tensions between him and the older Bennetts. His only solace was that Verity rarely entered the laboratory, so it had become his refuge. Quile now had a nest in his bedroom as well as her apron-lined box in the laboratory. Each day the crow had flown from his window to the garden and thence the laboratory. Gordon took immense comfort from Quile's presence, making sure she was never away from him for too long. He took great pains to ensure Quile remained secret from the youngest Bennett, certain the girl would, however kind heartedly, torment the crow to cantankerous and wounding behaviour. Thankfully it seemed Liberty and Sofia were of the same mind. They all ensured the crow remained a stealthy presence whether in his room or in the laboratory tucked into her shadowy nest. Equally, the laboratory was an ideal place to study his new belongings while watching Liberty read Sam's notes.

He had meticulously measured and recorded the candlestick's weight, its every inch and surface, in his notebook. Using all the new details he had re-plotted the weapon's impact on Amy Dudley, revising his sketches, pleased with the accuracy he had achieved. Yet he constantly, keenly felt the lack of the skull. Real, the wound holes undeniable, it would prove his findings beyond any and all doubt. Whenever he worked on the candlestick, headaches plagued him. Whether from the blow to his temple or frustration, he couldn't be sure. A tincture of belladonna helped, but never entirely relieved the pain. He found cleaning the watch soothing, alleviating the tension that seemed forever throbbing behind his eyes. Whenever Tiberius and Liberty used the room for experiments or teaching, he generally retreated to a corner. Sometimes they were too loud and intrusive so he would have to go to the library and try to ignore Verity's excitement. The muted laugh came again, making his head hurt.

How does the seamstress manage? I pity her bridegroom.

PITY YOURSELF. LOATHSOME FOOL. YOU EVEN FAILED AT BLACKMAIL.

Hardly failed. I've nearly got everything I want.

SHE'LL NO AGREE TO HELP. AND YOU DINNAE HAVE THE WIT OR THE COURAGE TO EXPOSE THE FAMILY. PATHETIC. NO MATTER. THE HARELIPPED MAN WILL FIND YOU.

He sighed, trying not to mind the shadows or look at the window.

He disnae ken where I am. I'm safe here.

WHENEVER YOU LEAVE, HE'LL FIND YOU. NO ESCAPE. NO REDEMPTION. NO WORKING AGAIN. ONLY DEATH.

He squinted and tapped the timepiece to remove the

stubborn flakes. Glancing at Liberty, he noted her mannish fingers all over Sam's notes and turned away, the urge to take the pages from her nearly overwhelming him.

How much longer can her study go on?

'It's amazing that he survived all that intrigue and deception,' she murmured.

'Sam was exceptional,' he said. 'So I find the man's durability scarce surprising.'

Liberty continued fingering her way through the pages and seemed not to hear him.

'And why did he draw this, do you think?' she asked.

She smoothed a sketch Gordon loved of a blue perfume vial. He couldn't bear to speak to her and longed to grab her hands to stop them fondling the drawing.

It's no a bloody cat.

'Why are there two plans of Foxcombe Manor?' she asked.

Gordon ached on tight muscles and he rolled his shoulders trying to ease them. Liberty was watching, waiting for a reply. He strove to keep his voice level.

'In 1561 Sam must've built an extra wing on the manor. The plans are before and after, I assume for nothing more important than posterity or reference.'

'Why include them with his notes on Amy Dudley, then? And why do all his notes finish so abruptly in December the year she died?'

Gordon blew on the watch, scattering dirt flecks.

'I've been unable to find a satisfactory answer to your second query. As to the first, I have no idea,' he lied.

Liberty's eyes narrowed for a moment and then returned to studying the parchments.

'Do you know anything else about Sam – when did he die, for instance?'

'I did find a reference to a Samuel Banks in some

records. He died in 1578 and was buried with his wife in Oxford. I cannae tell if it's the same man and there's no record of what cemetery he's buried in. It's something I intend to find out when I can.'

Liberty studied the parchment while her foot, large in its buttoned boot, swung slowly, back and forth.

'All this is incredibly interesting,' she said. 'You have, as I asked, given me time to think about all you said concerning my father and Amy Dudley, and allowed me the leisure to read through Sam's notes.' She gave him an assessing look. 'Yet it makes no difference to how I feel, Doctor McCraken. To be blunt, I neither like nor trust you, not that I've made it secret. However, I'm in no doubt that to deny you is to ruin my family. So, I've done all you asked, you have the items from my father, and I've read everything. Now is the time for frankness. Explain what more you want from me, from Tiberius, for your silence?'

His breath fluttered the dirt flecks away like minute insects on the wind.

'For you and your brother it's a simple thing. I'm certain it would please your father for you to help me.'

'You're jesting, surely? Blackmail is a despicable way to engineer help. Please don't presume my father would ever condone what you're doing to us!'

Spots of high colour had sprung to her cheeks and her voice was loud. He eyed her, wondering at her passion.

'Perhaps if you had more integrity, blackmail would be unnecessary?'

She drew a breath, eyes flashing, and he held up a hand.

'Let's stop this, it's getting us nowhere. Now listen, your father believed in my idea for a new medical field. One we could use to prove Lady Amy Dudley was murdered.'

'So, you've said,' her tone was acerbic, impatient, and his dislike intensified.

'Miss Bennett, my doctorate is from Edinburgh and so I can no practice in London. My only hope is to introduce a new field to the Royal College of Physicians. One that is viable and proven beyond a shadow of a doubt. Then I can teach it and perhaps earn the right to practice. Use it to save others and continue my work.'

Her expression became incredulous and then hardened.

'I see. What you want is to peddle my family's name and my father's reputation. You want Tiberius to support you at the Royal College of Physicians. All in pursuit of a 300-year old murder? Do I look touched to you? Does this seem like a place for the insane? Doing as you ask is as much a death knell to my family as telling the truth about my brother would be.'

He swallowed, his head light at her choice of words. Iona gibbered about Bedlam.

'It's no insane. I'm no mad,' he said. 'The field I propose is already practiced in Germany and is getting noticed in Scotland and Europe. In fact, one or two lectures have been given in London.'

'All right, what is this mysterious field?'

'Forensic medicine.'

She laughed tightly, looking relieved.

'Doctor McCraken, do you take me for a fool? This is certainly not a new field. I've heard of this forensic medicine and I believe my father attended one of those lectures. Regardless of what you might think, it seems to me a useless field to promote. Moreover, I fail to see how its advocacy to the Royal College can provide your redemption or help solve anything, least of all Amy Dudley's death.'

'I'll use Sam's notes as reference, and I'll prove his existence to add validity.'

Her expression became pitying.

'That's hardly enough. Sam's notes are all in the

world that mention Lady Dudley's head wounds. Hers is still a controversial death, one that rumours bandy equally between suicide, accident or murder. History only remarks on a broken neck.' She smoothed her skirt. 'Surely, even such as you can see your proposal for the Royal College is pathetic. Forensic medicine has no value and cannot help in what you seek.' She rose, her whole bearing quietly jubilant. 'You have my father's items. I suggest you take them and leave. Surely you must know that I have to deny you help in a such lost cause.'

She looked at him then, her eyes heavy with triumph and mouth a tight line of expectation, clearly thinking she had taken all his leverage. Gordon let her believe for a moment and then:

'It gives me great pleasure, Miss Bennett, to say that you're wrong. I propose to take measurements from the candlestick that so recently belonged to your father. Its previous owners I believe to be Lord and Lady Dudley. For while I dinnae believe it's the one the murder was committed with, I do contend it's that weapon's mate. As such the dimensions will serve the purpose.' Liberty rolled her eyes and tutted. He smiled, knowing it infuriated her and continued, 'Using the new science of forensic medicine, I will map Amy Dudley's wounds and their pattern against the dimensions of the candlestick. This will confirm the puir woman was hit on the head, as well as her neck broken. There will be no doubt of murder. The science will prove her broken skull could no be caused by accident or self-harm.'

Liberty looked unconvinced and wary, sensing a trap.

'But Doctor McCraken, you've nothing to support Sam's writings or give you the state of the body. The coroner's report is gone. Lost, destroyed, and the dimensions of a random candlestick will convince no one.

Most importantly, for what you're describing, surely you would need Amy Dudley's skull?'

For the first time in days, Gordon smiled properly.

'Let us say, for hypothesis's sake, that I could use the coroner's report and Amy Dudley's skull, what then?'

She stared at him, as if expecting some qualifying statement. He returned her gaze steadily, so she frowned, looking away.

'I can indulge in supposition, if I must,' she said slowly. 'If it were possible to apply this forensic medicine to skull and candlestick to prove murder, and, if by some miracle, the coroner's report still existed, and it supported Sam's notes on the head wounds.' He inclined his head at her questioning look. 'Then, in theory,' she continued, 'I could see all of it together proving the field's viability and make a case for Royal College.'

'Indeed. So, would championing such a field successfully put Tiberius beyond all criticism and query? Allowing you, through him, to specialise in any field you chose?'

She frowned, her gaze narrow, but her eyes were alight.

'I can see that it would, yes.'

'Then will you agree to my terms for help?'

'Are you saying you can lay your hands on both items? Skull and report?'

'I can.'

'You're lying.'

He shrugged and resumed picking at the pocket watch. After a moment he glanced up to find her careful gaze on him.

'Let's say I believe you. Where are they? Here in the house?'

'I'm no daft, woman, they're certainly no in this house! I'll no say where they are, until I must. But you've yet to answer my question: will you agree to my terms?'

She paced while casting darting glances at him.

'I have some conditions of my own.'

'I kenned you would. It's a natural thing for a woman with no options to bargain with some.'

She stopped and put her mannish hands on the table, looking him full in the face.

'We must prove the murder first, with forensic medicine. Using candlestick and skull, as well as having the coroner's report, *before* taking the advocacy to the Royal College.'

Her stance was belligerent, waiting for his argument.

'Agreed.'

'Oh…' She sat on a stool and their gazes flickered at each other. 'And Verity must never know what we're doing.'

'Agreed; och, no quarrel there.'

She spread her hands, gaze down while rubbing her thumbs over her index fingers.

'And we won't do anything until after Verity is wed. Two weeks from now.'

He had expected it, dreaded it and welcomed it. Two weeks, caught in the Bennett house, seemed little better than his time in prison. Yet with two weeks he could find a way to retrieve the coroner's report. Then, after the wedding, go to Oxford for Amy Dudley. Equally, in the purpose-built laboratory, he could certainly prove murder. Still, he hesitated, letting the tension build before nodding.

'Agreed.'

Liberty gave a tight smile and held out her hand. He put down the picker, and they shook, briefly, with hard movements. As they parted Verity's laugh came again, closer, louder, from the hallway. He turned back to the pocket watch, wondering how he would manage.

CHAPTER THIRTY-TWO

Over the next four days Gordon struggled in the Bennetts' company. Every day he was assailed by wedding plans that engineered a constant undercurrent of excitement through the house. The heightened joy fed into the tension surrounding himself and Liberty, making his nerves taut and unpredictable. His surroundings didn't help with their chaotic decor and cluttered rooms darkening his spirit. More and more his only relief was the laboratory where he retreated for most of every day, cleaning the watch and studying the candlestick. At night, in his room, he took solace in Quile, whisky and books filched from the library. But he couldn't stay isolated all the time and dinner held particular anxiety.

All meals were held in the vermilion dining room and as a guest he was expected to attend. Any unexplained absence would have caused Verity to ask uncomfortable questions. But each time he entered the room, the vivid colour recalled nightmares and caused Iona to start spitting abuse, round and round in his skull. Completely unaware of his discomfort the family continued with their usual routine, bending the task of eating to a social event. Inviting friends and Tiberius's colleagues to dine, ensuring an added layer to Gordon's particular hell. Tonight, Gordon knew, held no respite. Descending the stairs, he could hear rumbling men's voices amidst Liberty and Verity's higher tones, and braced himself.

Entering the dining room his senses were rendered toxic at the colouring, Iona's constant whispering rose to a babble. He smiled through clenched teeth at the men he didn't know.

'Doctor McCraken.' Liberty's smile was brittle. 'Let me introduce you to our dinner guests. This is Doctor Travis.'

His hand was caught in a clammy grip and a scrawny man nodded at him before turning to Tiberius with a jocular air. The two other guests were talking with Verity. She had one, the dark-haired man wearing a pince-nez, by the arm. Smiling, she waved Gordon over.

'This is my fiancé, Doctor Fielding. George, meet Doctor McCraken, a friend of my father's, who is staying with us for a little while. He and Tiberius are working on something together.'

George Fielding was everything Gordon imagined a second son of a wealthy English family to be, strong boned, with hefty shoulders and a slim waist, impeccably dressed and presented. Yet his dark eyes twinkled with a friendly expression and he shook Gordon's hand, covering it with both of his own and smiling broadly.

'Doctor McCraken? How lovely to meet you, Verity has spoken of your visit. I'd be very interested to hear your thoughts on our fair city but let me introduce you to an old friend of mine.' He gestured to the other guest, a blonde-haired man with startling blue eyes. 'Lord Arthur Standish.'

'Pleased to meet you, Doctor McCraken.'

Gordon took the proffered hand, finding a warm, firm grip and an interested gaze. Dinner was called and he made his way to his seat, pleased to have timed his entrance to avoid pre-dinner chit-chat. He was seated next to Liberty and across from Lord Standish, who appeared to be fascinated by Verity's wedding. The man listened intently on the trivial details, asking about flowers, catering and arrangements and Gordon was grateful to him. The wedding conversation dominated the table; it was all about things he had already been subjected to, and therefore required no involvement from him. The talk ebbed and flowed, letting Gordon float in its midst, eating his cod with the occasional murmur of appreciation and agreement. A lull occurred and Lord Standish caught his gaze.

'So, Doctor McCraken, what brings you to London?'

'I'm working on an enterprise with Doctor Bennett.'

'How interesting. What sort of enterprise?'

Lord Standish looked between Gordon and Tiberius.

'Ah, well,' mumbled Tiberius.

Liberty had gone still. Gordon swallowed some potato and smiled.

'We're in an early period, my lord, and we're no really ready to discuss it, just yet. I'm sure you can respect that.'

'Of course, I understand. Although, the medical field is not something I'm overly familiar with, I can appreciate the need for secrecy.'

'How true,' said Verity. 'You see, Doctor McCraken, Lord Standish's family breeds horses. They train and race them all over the country which is clearly something that's shrouded in secrecy and vagueness.'

She smiled impishly and Lord Standish laughed.

'You may tease, good lady, but as a breeder and trainer I have to be far more secretive than you'd think. For the competition is fierce and owners and trainers will go to great lengths to find out what others are doing with their animals.'

Tiberius and Liberty nodded, smiling. Gordon continued eating, hoping the conversation would drift from him again. Verity inclined her head.

'How interesting,' she said, mischievously. 'What lengths exactly?'

George shook his head with a smile and engaged Doctor Travis in a low conversation about patient treatment. Lord Standish seemed not to mind the question, his expression serene.

'Ah, the unscrupulous will send men to spy on horses' training and bribe stable-hands for information. Some will even attempt to harm or enhance a horse's chance at races, with powders and such like.'

'And, of course, you're not one of the unscrupulous, are you my lord?'

'Verity!' Liberty said.

Lord Standish chuckled.

'No matter, Miss Bennett, it's a fair question.' He dabbed his mouth with a napkin, his gaze roguish. 'I'm only as shameless as I can get away with. Anything else and my father would disown me. It is, after all, his reputation and horses.'

Doctor Fielding chuckled and the others laughed, Doctor Travis nearly choking on his wine in doing so. Gordon frowned.

'Do excuse them, Doctor McCraken,' Lord Standish said. 'They know that my father has fewer scruples than most thieves and blackmailers.'

Liberty stopped laughing, drawing a quick breath, and sipped wine. Lord Standish seemed not to notice, his gaze on Gordon, who shifted in his chair, easing rigid fingers around the cutlery.

'I see,' he said. 'If it's no impertinent to ask, who is your father?'

Lord Standish's eyes crinkled, and his mouth lifted slightly, showing white teeth.

'If I tell you, you must promise not to judge me too

harshly? I feel that judgement of a person's actions or family should never be based on hearsay.'

Unable to speak, Gordon inclined his head. Lord Standish flourished a napkin as if performing a trick.

'My father is the esteemed Duke of Exeter.'

Gordon stared at the blonde man sitting so diffidently across from him. The name was well known to him; Exeter was a legendary rake as well as a genius at breeding and racing horses. Moreover, the man was a peer of the realm and close to the royal family.

'So, you see, with my father's reputation to uphold, I must conduct myself with all due deference.'

Doctor Fielding coughed, breaking the odd tension.

'Arthur, where are you racing next?'

'We're to Liverpool in the week and then Newbury in a fortnight. Doctor McCraken, do tell of any racing you've seen in Scotland. My father has ventured up there more than once, but never had a winner. Have you attended a race, perhaps this year or last?'

Their expectant faces turned to him; sweat prickled his spine and he swallowed.

'I had little time for such,' he managed.

Too busy killing. Murdering.

'Ah, what a shame. There's nothing like the roar and thunder of the racecourse. Perhaps you could join me as a guest sometime.'

They'll find out who you are. What you are.

Run, now.

His lordship turned to Doctor Travis, asking about his practice, and Gordon's shoulders sagged. Liberty refilled his wine without asking and he sipped, trying to drown his fear. Thankfully, talk continued to meander across a variety of subjects that needed little input from him. The fish course slipped to the meat, and thence to the pudding with no more than his occasional involvement. The conversation then turned to the royal wedding, held the previous month.

'Did you attend, Lord Standish?' Liberty asked.

'I had that honour, Miss Bennett.'

'I imagine it was wonderful,' Verity sighed. 'To actually be there. Were your family very close to the front?'

'Somewhat near, yes. My cousin the Duke of Northumberland and his wife were the only family members closer. It was indeed a stupendous affair, utterly enchanting. Her Majesty is the epitome of regal.'

Tiberius, flushed with drink, raised a glass and toasted Queen Victoria and Prince Albert. Everyone joined in and the mood lightened. Verity told a supposedly hilarious story about her seamstress who seemed of Hungarian or Polish descent, garrulous and ill tempered, but a genius with fabric. Gordon thought longingly of the laboratory and Amy Dudley. Then, into a sudden hush he lifted his head to see Verity nodding and holding everyone's attention.

'It's true, Sofia told me so. The man took an antique clock, hundreds of years old apparently, and worth a fortune, along with some jewellery. Poor Mister Bainbridge is distraught. We've been warned to keep all windows and doors locked. You know, Mister Bainbridge only lives on the other side of the square. It's unnerving.'

George Fielding tutted, his expression concerned.

'Between this spate of thieving and those Chartist riots in January, I fear London is becoming very dangerous.'

Lord Standish looked at his wine, moving it gently in the glass.

'How do you know this thief was a single man?' he asked. 'Perhaps it was a gang of ruffians?'

'A man was seen in the square, the same time as the robbery, running away. He had a very strange face, unmistakable, Sofia said. So it must've been him.'

Gordon couldn't move; his head felt iron heavy and his limbs entirely numb.

'What do you mean, a strange face?' Doctor Travis asked.

'It was disfigured.' Verity lowered her voice. 'His upper lip lifted and grotesquely twisted, apparently.'

Gordon wanted very badly to be sick. Iona's laughter drowned all else. He swayed and the white tablecloth, along with the bloodied walls, swung back and forth.

'Are you dizzy?' Liberty asked. 'Your head could still be troublesome.'

'Aye, Miss Bennett, I might excuse myself.'

Somehow, he stood, and managed to leave the room, hearing Liberty's excuses for him. Knowing he would never climb the stairs he stumbled into the library, dropping into a chair, head in hands.

YOU'RE A DEID MAN BREATHING. HARELIPPED MAN KENS WHERE YOU ARE.

I have to leave. But where, how?

His thoughts scattered like grass seed. Abrupt images of candlestick and skull came to him, yellow and silver, winking and circling.

I'm so close. It's so unfair. What does he want of me!

AMY DUDLEY. YOUR DEATH. A LIFE FOR A LIFE, YOU KEN? YOU KILLED TWO OF US. WIFE AND BAIRN. 'TIS ONLY RIGHT THAT TWICE IS PAID FOR.

'No!'

'Doctor McCraken, are you well?'

He looked to find Lord Standish stood in the doorway, his expression concerned. Gordon sat back, trying to keep his voice steady.

'I'm sorry, my lord, I suffered a minor head wound a few days ago. It appears to be troubling me a wee bit. It's naught to worry about.'

Lord Standish frowned and moved toward Gordon.

'Oh dear, head wounds are a nasty business. I've known a few riders who took tumbles. They seemed fine for a few days then abruptly died from minor head wounds. You should have one of the doctors look at it.'

He turned as if meaning to summon someone.

'Please my lord, I just need to be quiet for a moment.' Gordon's head throbbed. 'Let's no disturb the dining any more than I have done.'

Lord Standish studied him, then nodded.

'All right, if that's what you feel is needed. But I'll stay with you a moment longer.'

Gordon made to speak, to send him away.

'To satisfy myself you're not about to expire,' his lordship continued. 'We can't have such a scandalous event as an honoured guest dying touch this good, honest family, now can we? Especially not when young Miss Bennett is so close to marrying so well. It would cause a tragedy of gossip-mongering for all involved.'

Gordon stared at the man, suddenly uneasy. Standish settled in the opposite chair, sitting back so he was entirely in shadow. There was a scraping sound and then a cigar lit, its puffed smoke curling so the smell crept about the room. Lord Standish's disembodied face was ghoulishly lit by the tobacco glow and his eyes became black pits of nothing. Gordon stared at the apparition and felt a coldness at his core.

COME TO TAKE YOU TO THE HARELIPPED MAN. HUNTING YOU. KNOWS WHERE YOU ARE. WATCHER, WATCHING.

That's no true! Please!

The cigar moved, revealing a hole from which words emerged.

'Doctor McCraken, you look awfully queer. Are you certain I can't fetch someone?'

Gordon rose, glancing at the door and back to the shade. 'I need to lie down.'

His lordship didn't move, just watched with endlessly black eyes. Gordon stumbled around the chair, making for the door on disobedient legs.

'Somebody needs to watch you.'

He gripped the door to stop from folding to the floor and managed to turn. The figure in the chair seemed to have grown, risen and enlarged, although it remained still, lit solely by the cigar end.

'I dinnae believe that to be necessary,' Gordon managed.

Lord Standish abruptly stood, still in shadow thanks to the fire behind him, and approached. Gordon's nails hurt on the door, breath raking his dry throat. His lordship stopped a mere hand's breadth away, his hair oil sickening in Gordon's nostrils and throat. So close, his blue eyes were like ice-chips.

'You would know, I suppose, being a doctor.' Lord Standish said. 'But still, I would be loath to have an innocent death on my conscience. That does terrible things to a soul, so I've heard.'

The lips lifted in a parody of a smile and then he was gone. Gordon sagged, head against the door, struggling to understand what had happened. He yelped at a soft touch and Liberty was there with Doctor Fielding just behind. Together they helped him start up the stairs. Gordon heard Tiberius and Verity bidding Doctor Travis a good night below, the hall crowding with movement. Yet Gordon's gaze was filled with Lord Standish, lounging in the dining room doorway, watching his slow upward progress.

CHAPTER THIRTY-THREE

Gordon woke early the next morning, feeling clearer headed. It seemed the fear of the night before had coalesced his thoughts and determination. He knew now what he had to do and that he must do it quickly. In the thin morning sunlight, he thought about the previous night's events.

Lord Standish can no be involved. The man is a peer of the realm, at least his family are. It was the head wound and hearing of the robbery, I'm sure.

YOU NEED TO BE WATCHED. HE SAID SO.

Concern, it was merely concern.

Even so he shivered and shied away from the image of the shadowy figure with its blank eyes.

HARELIPPED MAN ROBBED ACROSS THE SQUARE. CLOSER AND CLOSER. COMING FOR YOU AND AMY DUDLEY.

Gordon rose and quickly dressed, determined to speak to Liberty.

He found her in the laboratory, skirts the hue of fresh grass and inspecting the contents of two ornate boxes. A third box, which he recognised as holding the safe key, sat nearby on the table. Liberty looked up as he approached.

'Oh, you're awake.'

She glanced at where the safe hole was hidden, then away. He kept his attention on the middle distance and sat opposite her.

'My apologies, Miss Bennett, but I need to speak with you urgently and privately.'

She inclined her head and sat on a stool, skirts rustling. 'How dramatic. Please continue.'

'We must leave as soon as possible. I realise that supplies need to be purchased, but— '

'Wait, what are you talking about?'

He took a breath, trying to calm his bounding heart and arrange his thoughts.

'Things have changed. Firstly, we need to buy camping equipment. I'll make a list and you can send Tiberius to make the purchases. We should be ready to travel to Oxford in a couple of days.'

'Oxford?'

'Aye, it's where I've hidden Amy Dudley's skull. We have to retrieve it as quickly as we can.'

'You can't be serious? Verity's wedding is only ten days away, I can't just leave, and Tiberius has his patients and students.' She touched one of the boxes, her expression carefully blank. 'You could go alone.'

He barked a short laugh.

'I dinnae think so, Miss Bennett. I dinnae trust either of you once my back is turned.'

THEIR PRESENCE WILL NO KEEP YOU SAFE FROM THE HARELIPPED MAN. MURDER YOU ALL.

Liberty's eyebrows rose.

'And you think I trust you? It worries me enough that you'll be here on your own for most of the wedding day. Who knows what you'll pry in to.'

He looked away, his thoughts battering, trying to find a solution.

'We'll go the day after Verity's wedding then,' he said. 'That must be enough time for Tiberius to make purchases and arrangements for his students and patients? We'll train to Reading and then Oxford by stagecoach. There's plenty of places in Oxford we can get horses.'

He stared, willing her to agree. Liberty returned his gaze in a gauging fashion, as if trying to measure his determination. He felt sweat break on his brow and wondered what he must look like. Footsteps on the stairs made him turn. Sofia stopped at the sight of them and then, smiling, advanced.

'Good morning, Doctor,' she said. 'I'm hoping your head is feeling better, no?'

'Good morning, Sofia, aye, it is. Thank you.'

Liberty placed one ornate box atop the other and pushed them toward Sofia.

'Put them in Verity's room, please,' she said. 'We can go through them after breakfast and make a decision. Thank you, Sofia. We'll be up soon.'

Balancing the boxes, the Signora turned and stumbled back, causing the top box to slide and the lid lift. Gordon caught Sofia's elbow, and steadied the box with his other hand. She thanked him with a smile and left. When he turned back, Liberty was studying him with narrowed eyes.

'All right, Doctor, we'll go to Oxford the day after the wedding.'

'Thank you.'

'I'm not doing it for you. I want this whole business over with as quickly as possible. But be aware, I'm not travelling on an evening or night coach, they're too dangerous. If you insist on us coming, I'll write to a hotel in Reading for rooms and we can get a coach to Oxford the following morning. And Verity will have to be told we're going.'

'Why?'

'Where would you have me secrete the supplies and equipment you're suggesting we need? Verity even comes down here occasionally. Perhaps I should fit a lock and bar my sister from rooms within her own home, then face the questions she'll certainly ask? What of Sofia, should I lie to her as well? Or ask her to lie to Verity?'

Lord Standish will find out. Tell the harelipped man. Watching. Waiting.

Standish can no be involved.

You dinnae believe that. Murder for a murderer.

'Fine, but if you must tell her, then make up some reason for the trip and don't tell her it's Oxford. I dinnae want her gossiping to all and sundry.'

'My, what a high opinion you have of us.'

'No more than you have of me, Miss Bennett.'

Her expression tightened and, picking up the safe key box, Liberty went up the steps. He followed her out and into the hall. She didn't go to the library as he expected but continued to the second floor. On impulse he followed her. At the top of the stairs she went down the corridor to her bedroom. Once inside his own room, Gordon sat on the bed and made plans.

That night Gordon drowned in the bloody Thames. It smacked his skin, splattering his eyes into stinging. Someone else was there, swimming, powerful, and Gordon was afraid. The shore was a grey, distant line and he tried to swim there, flailing at the great scarlet washes, sinking. He struggled on, swallowing blood and clawing the viscous surface. He somehow managed to stay afloat and kicked for the shore. Suddenly Iona appeared there, as near as the moon to the sun, and she shouted and waved to him. Unthinking he cried out and thick blood rushed in, choking him, then the red abruptly drained away. It left him lying face up, on a muddy bank, gasping and sweating while standing around him were the Bennetts. Staring at them, their white faces smeared and bled into each other.

He woke, spluttering and crying. Topaz put her front paws on the bed, whiskery face worried, and he helped her climb up. He held her, rocking and silently weeping while Quile watched him from her rag nest and dawn slipped under the closed shutter. All the while the nightmare remained, imprinted behind his eyes.

CHAPTER THIRTY-FOUR

Just after 10.30 that morning a hansom cab halted in the mouth of Carey Street which spilled out onto Chancery Lane. Omnibuses, carts and horse-riders clattered, drivers hollered and swore. Gordon alighted amidst bankers, printers, clerks and black-cloaked lawyers. He tried not to notice them, instead focusing on the stone pillars of the Law Society. He turned and helped Liberty out onto the crowded pavement. She fussed with her dress and bag, making sure they fell right. Finally, they moved off and he held Liberty's elbow by necessity, lightly. He was glad she seemed unperturbed by the press of men and that she let him guide her with no fuss or scene. Although her charcoal dress, large purse and discreet bonnet blended into the crowd she still occasioned mild curiosity.

WHICH CLOAK IS HIDING THE HARELIPPED MAN? WILL HE NO CREEP UP BEHIND YOU, YOU SCUNNER?

He's no here. Leave me be, woman.

He glanced back, trying to check the moving crowds, and increased their pace. They crossed the uneven road, avoiding a dray cart and an omnibus's black smoke that wreathed the passengers and passers-by. Frock coats seemed to form a wall, black hats swaying. Gordon's shoulders grew taut at the approaching men and Liberty glanced at his tightened grip. He huffed a breath of relief when he escorted Liberty left, under familiar arches, away from the crowds. They passed into a sun-pocked courtyard, thankfully deserted, and Gordon opened a painted door, ushering Liberty through it.

Inside, the high-vaulted ceiling and mosaic floor were the same, but he was different. His insides hollowed at the thought of McDougall and he banished the thought, quickly, but not painlessly. At his side, Liberty gasped, staring, and he followed her gaze to the mullioned windows letting the spring sunshine fall on the mosaic tiles. He sighed, recalling his own initial joy, then moved through the splendour, with Liberty staring and following. Gordon knocked at a carved oak door and a voice called from the room beyond, bidding them enter. Inside the room was cluttered and Mister Green was seated at his desk, surrounded by bundles of paper, rolls and boxes of documents. He rose and smiled, shaking Gordon's hand, inclining his head at Liberty's introduction.

'Mister McCraken,' he said. 'I'm pleased to see you. I was beginning to wonder if you'd received my note.'

Gordon frowned and his prepared speech stalled; instead he merely nodded, unsure what to say. Mister Green ushered them out.

'Come along then and see how the donation looks.'

They followed Mister Green across the hall, under a stone arch and into a long, sun-striped room. Shelves lined the walls, bundled with papers and documents. Cases of shelving stood in regimented lines dissecting the room with a few desks scattered amongst them. Mister Green turned, beckoning them inside, and gestured to the wall.

'There, Mister McCraken, and a more fitting place for such a wonderful document, I wouldn't know.'

Gordon followed his indication and found the Leonardo da Vinci sketch in a prominent position. Anyone leaving or entering the room couldn't fail to see it. The ochre parchment had been mounted on white background and placed in a large gilt frame. Beneath it was a small brass plate bearing McDougall's name, grateful wording and the date. Liberty frowned, not looking at the sketch, but rather at Gordon.

'It looks perfect,' Gordon said. 'Thank you.'

'Not at all. It's a real honour to have it here. We're immensely grateful and I'm sorry Mister McDougall isn't with you. Will he be coming back soon?'

Gordon avoided Liberty's curious gaze and shook his head.

'Ah, unfortunately no. He's away to Edinburgh. His daughter's been taken sick. So, I'm here in his stead.'

A young man sauntered in, his dress enough to stop any conversation; navy frock coat shiny with expensive mohair and matching checked trousers. His waistcoat was extravagantly embroidered with peacocks. A gold-embroidered cravat, midnight gloves and hat completed his attire. He looked solemn, carrying a heavy square case and tripod with reverence. His gaze alighted on Mister Green and he bowed perfunctorily.

'I'm ready to situate the equipment for your portrait,' he said.

Mister Green appeared flustered and glanced at Gordon, his expression clearing.

'Ah, yes. Splendid, Mister Sidney, thank you. Now then, Mister McCraken, would you join me in a portrait with the wonderful donation? It will be something to repay Mister McDougall's generosity. Something you can take back to Edinburgh for him.'

'Portrait?' Gordon asked.

'A daguerreotype. Mister Sidney has brought the camera and all the necessary equipment from Majestic Studio. It's all proper and licensed, I assure you, and shouldn't take too long, I've been told.'

Mister Sidney nodded, eyeing Gordon and then the windows full of sunlight.

'Half an hour to set the equipment, less to take you and your friend in such a nice light room.'

Gordon looked to refuse, the words ready, when Liberty stepped forward, clasping his arm.

'Why, Gordon,' she gushed. 'How perfectly lovely. While they're getting ready you can show me the fascinating works Mister McDougall spoke of. The reasons he donated such a beautiful parchment in honour of these ancient documents, if Mister Green won't mind?'

Gordon stared at her and then her hand on his sleeve, his throat closed in shock. Liberty continued, smiling devastatingly at the other man.

'That will be all right, won't it, Mister Green?'

'Well, it's most unusual.' He glanced at the Leonardo da Vinci parchment and then back to Liberty. 'But I believe it will do no harm.'

'Oh thank you, Mister Green.' She swung round, including the dandy in her charm. 'Mister Sidney, we'll be sure to return in half an hour. Come along, Gordon, I'm longing to see where you and Mister McDougall worked.'

Liberty turned on her booted heel and walked deeper into the building, giving Gordon no choice but to move with her.

In the hallway between rooms, Liberty dropped his arm as if burnt and rounded on him.

'What's going on?' she demanded.

'You called me Gordon!'

'Oh, have I offended you, Doctor McCraken? Perhaps you should've thought of that before you mutilated that beautiful book you don't deserve to own. And who is

Mister McDougall?'

By unspoken agreement their voices were hushed, even as the words were nails.

'It disnae matter about McDougall. The man is gone, aye, and no returning. All you need to ken is how important it is they accept me here. The donation helped with that.'

Liberty bristled.

'I care not at all for you, nor your manipulations. Why did you bring me here?'

'And I dinnae care for you at all, but you're necessary here. You'll curb your tongue if you want me to keep to our pact. Now then, you'll have to listen as we go, for thanks to you, we've no much time.'

Gordon moved down the corridor making sure Liberty followed and ignored her truculent expression.

'This building has only been open two years,' he said. 'The government has gathered documents from many places such as the Tower of London and Westminster Abbey.'

He ushered Liberty into a second, windowless hallway, lit by gas lamps and peppered with doors. Gordon increased his pace, forcing Liberty to trot alongside, holding her skirts with one hand.

'To what purpose?' she asked.

'Supposedly to allow everyone the chance to view and use historic papers.'

'But there don't appear to be many people here, except lawyers and clerks. And us.'

Gordon opened the door into the tower and up the stone spiral stair into the top chamber. Thankfully no archivist appeared and the desks in sight were empty. He lowered his voice.

'They charge lawyers and doctors a fee to use certain documents, which they must find amongst the rolls and ancient texts. A subterfuge was necessary to allow my search and the wee donation drew extra help from Mister Green and his ilk. There was no harm done.'

'Except to the book!'

'Och you're talking as if I tore the parchment up and cast it to the winds. It's in a prized place, woman, and will be well looked after.'

He walked to the familiar desk, now clear of documents and touched the wood, his eyes clouded. He glanced at Liberty, who wandered, reading the handwritten cards on the shelves and running fingers across parchment and rolls.

'But why did you come here in the first place?' she asked. 'And, again, why am I here, now?'

Gordon moved through the shelves, his heart a galloping horse and sweat stippling his brow. He reached the workbench and studied the shelves above.

It has to be here.

THE HARELIPPED MAN HAS TAKEN IT. BURNT IT. YOU'LL NEVER FIND REDEMPTION. YOUR WORK WILL BE UNDONE. MURDERER.

Liberty followed him, reading the cards attached to the boxes.

'Court of the King's Bench. 1561 to November, 1562.'

Gordon turned so quickly he almost fell over his feet. He tugged the box down, fumbling and nearly dropping it on Liberty.

'Don't mind me, Doctor,' she said.

Putting it on the workbench he rifled through the box but reached the end empty handed. His head dropped, stomach clenched, and he drew a deep breath. Then, with more careful fingers he took each document out, studying it and making a neat stack. Liberty watched for a while but when her questions went unanswered she drifted away. Gordon's search took over half the documents out before finally with shaking fingers and stinging eyes, he found the coroner's report. Clutching it to his chest he breathed silent thanks and, laying it down, read it twice to make sure it was correct. Each word felt like a hearty meal to his starving soul. After refolding it he searched for Liberty, finding her wandering through nearby shelves.

'We're leaving,' he said.

'Did you find what you wanted?'

Aye.' He glanced about seeing no-one and lowered his voice. 'It's the coroner's report into Amy Dudley's death. I'm going to steal it, and you're going to help me.'

He expected protest and refusal, but after a moment's shocked silence, Liberty laughed.

'Oh my goodness,' she gasped.

Gordon stared at her merriment and then glanced around, alarmed.

'For love of Mary will you no compose yourself,' Gordon said. 'We need to hurry.'

Liberty smoothed her dress, shaking her head, but a smile remained.

'Doctor McCraken, in the first instance, I'm not sure I believe that it is the report. Secondly, even if it is, I'm not going to help you steal it or anything else. I find it vastly amusing that you think I would, or for that matter, that you want to steal it. What good can it do for the reputation you intend to build? Or should we add thievery to your attributes for the Royal College of Physicians?'

'Dinnae be foolish. It needs to come with us for translation and to check for any mention of Amy Dudley's head wounds. You dinnae understand, but these walls are no safe for me. My continued study here would be impossible without, well, being alone. More, I will no risk it being moved or found by others. We can announce the finding when we present the case to the College. None will bother how we came by it then.'

From his satchel, he produced a hand-sized leather case. Opening it, he showed her knitting patterns he'd borrowed from Sofia's wool bag that morning. He placed the coroner's report inside the pattern book, closed the case and held it out.

'Put it in your oversized purse.'

Liberty clasped her bag, her gaze defiant.

'Why not just take it yourself?'

He stepped toward her, watching her expression grow alarmed.

'Listen, I've been here too often. If anyone is going to suspect a thief, they'll look to me. I can be searched. As a woman and of no particular account, you'll be less likely suspected or searched, you ken?'

She backed away, her mouth a thin line.

'And if I *am* searched?'

'Och, for the love of… You merely open the front and they'll see naught but the knitting patterns.'

'You're mad to think I'd be a part of this. I refuse.'

'Suit yourself,' he said, making a pretence of removing the document. 'It's a shame for Verity's wedding, though.'

Liberty's eyes narrowed while her expression hardened, full of loathing. Stepping forward, she opened her purse.

Twenty minutes later, he shifted on a hard chair. He desperately wanted to stand, to see where Liberty was, but couldn't, knowing it would only cause questions he had no good answers for. Mister Sidney, he realised despairingly, was a fiddler. The wiry man tweaked and twiddled the camera apparel, seemingly never satisfied.

'Exposure will only take a few seconds in this excellent light,' Mister Sidney said again. 'But please, when I tell you, both remain perfectly still for the duration.'

Behind him, Mister Green's breath was garlicky, and

Gordon continually fought the urge to get up, get away. Liberty hadn't helped; after initially watching the tableau taking shape she had wandered away, out of sight. The worry of it gnawed at him, but he couldn't move, could think of no excuse not to just sit and watch the camera's covered eye that stared and stared.

'We're ready,' said Mister Sidney. 'Now remember, you must remain still at all costs, else the process will be ruined and need repeating.'

The lens cap was removed, its black Cyclops gaze pinioning Gordon. He clenched his muscles, forcing himself to stillness. Finally, it was over, but the tedium continued. Mister Green insisted they sign registration books and have a formal receipt for the donated sketch.

'Can't have your Mister McDougall changing his mind now, can we?'

Mister Green smiling in a strained way, ushered Gordon into his office. Glancing back Gordon glimpsed Liberty, a grey spectre standing under the arch, and then the door closed. He hurried through the signings and formalities, trying to hold his impatience at bay. He only managed to extract himself after nearly half an hour had passed with promises of McDougall returning in the near future. He emerged from the office, worry chasing him like a terrier, to find Liberty gone. He looked for her, moving quickly but trying not to appear hurried.

GONE FOR THE CONSTABLES. GONE FOR THE HARELIPPED MAN. GONE. LIKE MCDOUGALL. LIKE DOCTOR BENNETT. ALL GONE. ALL ALONE.

He couldn't imagine her risking the streets by herself, but with each passing moment his doubts grew. He searched, silently cursing the shelving that hampered his view and increased his speed, sighting down each corridor between the cases. He paused at the last, squinting at shadows that might be charcoal dresses. Suddenly he spied her, a shade amidst the cases.

'Where have you been?' he demanded.

'Here. Why?'

She returned his scrutiny with a challenging look and he lowered his voice.

'Do you still have it?'

'Yes.'

She looked guileless and it worried him, but with no other choice, he caught her elbow and walked toward the exit. Keeping his movements smooth across the mosaic floor and gaze fixed on the way out took an effort of will. He longed to look back, and round, to check for anyone watching, following, suspecting. Finally, he pushed the door open and they emerged into daylight and none challenged them. Still, Gordon didn't feel as if he breathed properly until they were back at the Bennetts' and the front door was locked behind them.

CHAPTER THIRTY-FIVE

That same day Arthur made his way through the Park Street building. Reaching his father's door, he peeled off fingerless gloves, stuffing them into a pocket. After a cursory effort at rubbing dirt from his face, he gave up, knocked and entered. His father gestured him to sit without really looking up. Arthur settled in an armchair, his bones seeming to sink into its depths, and he fought to keep his eyes open.

'Report.'

Startled, Arthur bent forward, blinking.

'There's not much to say.' He yawned. 'I traced them to the docks and believe they may have taken a boat to France or Italy. I came back to collect some things and then I can follow.'

'No. You're to leave the Romanies. They've slipped you for too long and know you now.'

Arthur stared at his nails, holding himself very still.

'What of the woman, Martha? I have plans for her.'

'Not any more. I'll send Linnet after them. It's doubtful the gypsy woman has the locket, but we must be sure and you're no longer useful there. You're the best placed to deal with the Bennetts, and I need you to help shadow McCraken. Things have moved on.'

Arthur resisted the urge to argue, knowing it would be

useless. Instead he rose and poured wine for them both, handing a glass to his father.

'Why, what's happened with McCraken?'

'He returned to Chancery Lane this morning and took Liberty Bennett with him.'

'Why would he do that?'

'It seems Mister Green arranged a photography studio to immortalise the gift that McDougall donated. McCraken attended in his place.'

Arthur frowned, sipping his wine.

'That seems a shade odd.'

'Yes, it was unexpected. Thankfully, I've kept Jay embedded there, since McCraken started his little research endeavour. Jay watched as the photograph was duly taken. It seems the two men retired to Green's office where receipts were signed for the gift. McCraken and Liberty Bennett did return briefly to the room where the McCraken and the lawyer had worked. Jay had to remain a goodly distance from them for fear of being too obvious. Still, he observed that they used no rolls nor took any from the room. Equally, they would've been unable to remove any such cumbersome things from the building, if they had found something, without someone raising the alarm.'

'Well, then it seems nothing more than a jaunt of some kind. Perhaps McCraken merely wanted to impress Liberty Bennett?'

'Perhaps. Did you speak to your man?'

'I did and George is adamant. Liberty Bennett has the only key, hidden somewhere. Verity has told him that Liberty is the only one in the family who knows where the safe is. It seems Doctor Bennett was well aware of his son's little gambling problem and didn't trust him. Equally, he shielded his youngest from any sort of responsibility.'

His father's expression twisted in exasperation.

'That house has been searched from cellar to attic and no sign of any blasted safe! Where the deuce can it be?'

Arthur shrugged, finished his wine and wished the old man would shut up whining. He wanted a bath and some food, perhaps to see if his sister were in residence. He poured another glass of wine and stared at the claret, rocking it gently, imagining the liquid to be blood.

'I could torture Tiberius Bennett, to see if he knows anything. Buy out his gambling debts to lure him in, it wouldn't be hard. Or go directly to the source, Liberty Bennett. I could make her scream until she told all. I did well at the Bennetts' yesterday without really trying; McCraken was terrified.'

The silence made Arthur glance at his father, who looked away and shuffled some papers.

'I doubt torturing will be necessary,' the grey man said. 'We'll manage with guile until after the wedding. When are you dining with George Fielding again?'

'Now I'm no longer following the gypsies I can call on him at the club later today.' He settled back in the chair. 'The man is a mine of information and loves nothing more than talking about his annoying fiancée.'

'Good. Orchestrate as many dinners at the Bennetts' and outings with them as possible, will you? See if any of the women mention the locket, or jewellery of any kind. They probably store it all together in that bloody safe.'

'What of McCraken? The man is starting to annoy my sensibilities.'

'We'll continue to watch him, for now. But this jaunt of his and Liberty Bennett's bothers me. I would rather they stayed at odds with one another than became friends or, God forbid, something more. We should devise a way to unbalance McCraken and ensure that Liberty Bennett is unsettled about him.'

'Oh, there's something I brought back from Edinburgh that should work. I just need the right moment to deliver it.'

'All right, but no violence, not as yet. I've set Oriole to watch the house and intercept any correspondence, but restrictions on what we can do to the Bennetts remain. Unfortunately, that includes McCraken just now. So, you must unbalance the man with care. Additionally, the doctor's a wily bugger and I don't want him unnerved so much that he slips away with any artefacts, especially not the locket. Remember, you're the way inside and as such you must remain unsuspected by the Bennetts.' The grey man gave him a calculating look. 'By the by, how much did you get for that clock you stole from the Bainbridge chap?'

Arthur drained his glass and rose.

'Nothing. I threw it in the river. Can I go now? I've barely had anything to eat today.'

His father stared at him and merely nodded. Arthur bowed and took his leave. Walking to his rooms he decided to send a message to his favourite restaurant for lunch. He hated it when no table was available for him and he really wanted a bath before dining.

CHAPTER THIRTY-SIX

At the time Arthur took his bath, sunlight was streaming through the Bennetts' laboratory window. It made Liberty's charcoal dress dash with mauve hints and her black hair shine like Quile's feathers. Her handsome face was flushed, eyes bright and expression jubilant and Gordon had never despised her more.

'You did *what?*'

His tone was menacing in its softness. She faltered, eyes darting to the stairs, then her chin raised and her gaze fixed on him.

'Don't get riled. I did say I wouldn't steal. I put the report back in the right box, but slipped inside another document, so it's not obvious.'

'You stupid, idiotic—'

'Doctor!'

'You've no idea what you've done! Everything, ruined!'

Speech left him and he sat heavily on a stool, head in hands. She rustled toward him and he gritted his teeth, lifting his head. She stepped back at his expression, raising her purse.

'If you'd let me finish,' she said. 'I recognise the need for the report, if that's what it really is. So, while you were in with Mister Green, I persuaded that Mister Sidney to photograph it and sell me the plates.'

She put the purse on the table, pushing it toward him. He noted it bulged squarely when laid flat.

'You owe me some money, Doctor McCraken.'

He stared at the bag, then at Liberty.

'I dinnae ken what…'

Abrupt clattering on the stairs revealed Verity, breathless and white faced.

'Topaz is ill. Please, you have to come. Now.'

The cocker spaniel was lying prone in her library bed. Her sides heaved and she whimpered with each breath. Her golden coat held a starkness and she didn't raise her head when they knelt to her.

'How long has she been like this?' Gordon asked.

'I'm not sure,' Verity replied. 'Twenty minutes, maybe more. I was in the garden, I didn't know. Is it her puppies?'

Gordon made soothing noises and felt the dog's tummy, gently moving the small bodies inside. Topaz's lip curled and she made a growling huff. He felt the blankets under her, finding them wet, and was relieved when his fingers came away clear.

'Her waters have broken, but no puppies are coming.' He sat on his heels and looked at the sisters. 'I've seen this before. We need to put her on dry blankets, or she'll risk a chill. Find some clean linen to wrap the puppies in and bring me some oil – olive, vegetable or some such. Clean, mind, nothing that's been used for cooking yet. I need water and soap to wash my hands.'

They stared at him, and then at the whimpering dog.

'Ladies, there's no time to send for a veterinarian. Topaz and her puppies will die unless you do as I say. Move, now.'

They scattered. A few minutes later Sofia bustled in with a bowl of hot water, soap and a towel. She was quickly followed by Verity carrying two blankets topped by a folded sheet and Liberty, bearing a ceramic jug. Together they lifted Topaz and changed the blankets, resettling the dog with the minimal of movements. Gordon stripped to his shirt and rolled up his sleeves.

'Tear or cut the sheet into strips about a foot wide and two feet long,' he instructed.While Liberty and Sofia saw to the sheet, he washed his hands, watching Topaz's struggles. Verity knelt next to the dog, her expression worried, but murmuring soothing words.

'Where's the oil?' he asked.

Liberty pointed to the jug on the floor, her questioning gaze matching Verity's. Gordon knelt by Topaz and pulled the jug to him.

'I suspect one of the puppies is breached,' he said. 'Turned on its side and cannae be born, preventing the others from coming. I need to find out and turn the breach, if I can.'

'You've done this before?' Liberty sounded worried.

'I grew up in a village, surrounded by sheep farms, Miss Bennett. We had no veterinarian in easy distance. I learnt from a very young age how to help in difficult births. Now, hush while I work.'

He dipped his first two fingers into the oil and gently felt inside Topaz. Almost instantly he encountered a long, smooth shape he recognised as a puppy's back. He grunted with satisfaction and with small, deft movements turned the head into the birth canal, removing his slick fingers. Topaz whimpered and her belly rippled, but this time with a soft sound the puppy slipped from her. Gordon quickly lifted it to Sofia who rubbed the little body expertly in a strip of linen. The warmed puppy whimpered, its small paws flailing and head moving.

'Thank God,' said Liberty, smiling at him.

Verity, her eyes bright with tears, stroked Topaz, still

whispering to her. Gordon nodded and then Topaz held all his attention. He didn't stop helping her until four more puppies were born. All were warmed and put to her silky belly, crawling and whimpering. But Topaz wasn't finished and gave birth to a sixth and final puppy, tinier than the rest. It lay unmoving in Sofia's hands, despite having been rubbed and warmed. Verity was crying, stroking the little one's wet fur and murmuring to it. Liberty's face was drawn in lines of sadness and she swallowed.

'It's so small,' she said. 'It had no real chance.'

She put her hand on her sister's arm. Gordon rose, took the puppy from Sofia and quickly left. The women followed, tried to get his attention, but he ignored them. Reaching the kitchen, he found, as hoped, the baking oven warm and popped the puppy inside. Verity screamed, staggered back, collapsing on the floor and Sofia looked shocked, silently mouthing. Liberty, her knuckles strained white against her skirt, moved toward him.

'Take it out! You bloody beast!'

Verity wept on the floor while Sofia comforted her, throwing him savage looks. Gordon shook his head, trying to focus. Liberty lunged but he caught her wrist and pulled her round, shielding the oven with his body.

'Count with me,' he hissed. 'Twenty, twenty-one. Do it!'

White lipped, she tried to free herself.

'Twenty-three,' he said, tightening his grip.

She grimaced.

'Twenty-four,' she managed.

He nodded and together they counted, his grip vice-like and her voice taut as steel cable. On a hundred he released her and stepped away. She staggered, threw the oven door open and took the puppy out, cradling it to her breast.

'You twisted bastard,' she said.

Under her fingers the linen stirred; Liberty looked

down and gasped. Beneath the covering the puppy mewed.

'They do it for lambs,' Gordon said. 'I thought it might work, but there was no time to explain. It should be all right now but keep it warm and make sure it gets fed.'

They stared at him in stunned silence. He shrugged and went to check on Topaz.

CHAPTER THIRTY-SEVEN

Later that afternoon the Bennetts' laboratory had been darkened. Yellow paper covered the window. The gas lamps were unlit, and the door firmly shut. Gordon gripped the stool and watched Liberty; his brow creased. On the table, the spirit lamp's glow illuminated Liberty's face and hands as she placed it under the cast iron fuming box. The black inverted pyramid became chased with shadows from the small flame.

'You're certain of this process?' Gordon asked.

'Yes, once again, yes. It's not exactly difficult nor secret. In fact, Doctor McCraken, I find it strange that you seem woefully ignorant of it. When the process was published last year, my father was one of the many who embraced the daguerreotype. I'm surprised you didn't.'

'I was busy.'

She looked unconvinced.

'I see. Well, Father decided the licence for the actual daguerreotype was neither feasible nor profitable. He merely wished to experiment with the practice and so didn't purchase the camera. However, we kept the processing equipment and chemicals and occasionally he indulged with the odd surplus exposed plates provided by a family friend.'

She rustled away in the gloom.

Busy. Murdering wife and child. Held in prison.

You disgust me.

Suddenly the room seemed too dark. On his shoulder Quile cawed softly, her beak shining in the odd light and he took solace from her solid, warm body. Liberty returned and slid a flat, metal case, about the size of his hand, face down into the slot in the top of the fuming box.

'It's such a wee thing. How will I read the letters?' Gordon murmured.

'It's very simple. I had the man from the Majestic take three exposures of the document, top, middle and bottom. A magnifying glass will be sufficient.'

She's lying. She'll ruin it, deliberately.

Gordon studied Liberty's face, bent in concentration.

'Tell me again, what you did with the coroner's report?'

'I returned it exactly where it came from, but I slipped it inside another document so it wouldn't be obvious.' She returned his gaze with a curious one. 'Although why you're worried about others finding it is odd. After all, who would look?'

Dropping his gaze, he stroked Quile.

'That it survives is a miracle,' he said. 'It took me so long to find it, I'd hate for it to be lost again or mishandled in some way.'

'Hmmm. Well, I won't pretend to understand, but rest assured it's as safe as it can be.'

He longed to go back and check. Liberty struck a match and lit a taper, her gaze on him.

'Take this and tell Sofia I'd like some tea in the library, please. I should be finished with the exposure in about half an hour.'

She's going to destroy it. She kens who you are.

Monster.

He briefly closed his eyes, but the whispering remained.

'What of Verity?' he asked.

'What of her?'

'She might come down again. I would hate for anything to happen to this process or for her to be asking questions, to discover things that jeopardise our arrangement and her future.'

Liberty became still, her face a white stain against the dark.

'Is that a threat, Doctor McCraken?'

'An observation, you might say.'

'I've told Verity we're conducting a delicate experiment and she's not to disturb us. Besides, she's too taken up with Topaz and her puppies at the moment. So, there's no reason anything should damage the process or that Verity might discover our arrangement, is there?'

'I see no reason for either thing to happen.'

Hating her stubborn look, he took the taper and climbed the stairs, listening to Liberty muttering to herself.

'And keep the door shut,' she called.

His jaw clenched on a retort and, wishing he could stay, Gordon left, closing the door. Head down, his thoughts unruly, he almost ran into Verity heading for the library. She smiled, then her eyes widened, and her expression became amazed.

'Is that a crow?'

He silently cursed his preoccupation and stepped back from the younger woman.

'Aye. Her name's Quile and she's a friend of mine.'

Verity moved, stopping mere inches away to peer at the bird.

'Goodness me! May I stroke her? What does she eat? Has she been living in the laboratory all this time?'

Gordon strove not turn away and just leave her standing there. On his shoulder Quile stirred and hopped down his arm.

'Have a care, she's no used to being petted,' he lied. 'She can be a wee bit temperamental, it's best to leave her be.'

Verity seemed not to hear and extended her hand to the bird. Quile stared at it and cocked her head, obsidian eyes intent. Then, to Gordon's amazement, the bird hopped onto Verity's wrist, causing a surprised gasp. The crow stayed there even as she was raised level with the girl's curious gaze.

'She's beautiful.'

'Aye.'

'Has she met Topaz? Will they fight do you think? I'm sure they won't. Topaz is really gentle. Quile wouldn't hurt the puppies, would she?' Verity gazed at the bird. 'No, of course you wouldn't, would you?'

Before Gordon could speak Verity and Quile had disappeared into the library. He hurried in to find the girl knelt at Topaz's basket where the spaniel lay with her wriggling puppies. Quile hopped onto the floor and cawed, shifting toward the bed. Topaz heaved herself up, scattering puppies and snarled, low and guttural. Gordon knelt next to Verity and tried to coax Quile to his shoulder. The crow flapped her wings and pranced a little, out of reach, ever toward the basket and helpless puppies. Topaz stood squarely over her children, growling and utterly focused on the crow. Suddenly Quile raised her head and gave a mighty croak, throat throbbing on the call, its soft under-feathers totally exposed to the dog. When Quile shuddered to silence, the two animals stared at each other. Abruptly Topaz gave a chuff and resettled herself, nosing the puppies back to her warmth. Quile strutted over and climbed on the bed, ignoring the puppies. She hopped across the dog and tucked in behind Topaz's rump, resting her beak on the golden flank.

'Well, that's settled that,' Verity said.

'I would no have believed it, if I hadnae seen it. It was an awful risk you took.'

Verity looked at him.

'Where's the fun if you always avoid a little risk, Doctor?'

He met her frank gaze and wondered at how innocent she really was.

'Still, Quile's no a pet,' he said. 'She might've gone for the puppies.' He eyed the crow. 'She still might.'

'Nonsense. Quile's far too intelligent. She knows Topaz will kill her if she tries anything. Besides, I think they like each other.'

Gordon wasn't convinced, but despite repeated attempts, Quile refused to move. She even snapped at him when he tried to pick her up. Topaz seemed unperturbed by the crow's presence and in the end, Gordon admitted defeat. He retreated to a chair however, to keep watch on the crow and let Verity organise the tea.

An hour later in the laboratory, Gordon tilted the daguerreotype to the light, admiring the small, but perfect image. Despite its size the script was legible and translatable under the magnifying glass. Framed against the window, Liberty watched him.

'I'd prefer the original,' he said. 'But I'll manage with this.'

She turned slightly, looking at the grass, expression inscrutable.

'Well, as long as you can manage.'

He stared, but she didn't turn. Gordon pulled the picture toward him and bent to translating the report.

Chapter Thirty-Eight

That evening Gordon stood on the stairs listening to the silence and breathed deeply, as a man coming up for air. He entered the dining room, to see only Liberty and another place set, opposite. He briefly closed his eyes against the scarlet walls and settled at the empty place. They exchanged stilted greetings and he steeled himself for an uncomfortable meal. Liberty gestured to the table.

'Tiberius is dining at his club. Verity has gone to a late supper and the theatre with Doctor Fielding. So, it's just us, won't that be pleasant.'

He managed a smile and inwardly groaned. They ate in silence, but for a few words of thanks to Sofia as she served. Despite wanting to get through the meal as quickly as possible, he noticed Liberty's gaze kept darting to her lap. He frowned and she looked up, catching his gaze, and reddened. Putting down her soup spoon, Liberty took a book from beneath the table and placed it next to her bowl.

'I apologise, Doctor McCraken.'

'No need. What are you reading?'

'My notes, actually. I'm trying to teach Tiberius about a fracture case and it's proving problematic.'

'Oh aye, surely no problem can be too much for one such as yourself?'

She flushed at his tone.

'A woman died of heart failure, but at first a suspicion of murder was conceived,' Liberty said. 'And at the autopsy the surgeon noted a broken wrist. But the fracture occurred over six weeks before the death, so it should've healed. I'm trying to decipher why, so that Tiberius can demonstrate it to his students. Satisfied?'

'How old was the woman who died?'

Liberty looked surprised, but opened her book, turning the pages.

'Thirty-six.'

'Apart from her heart, was the woman in good health?'

'So it seems. She was a portly woman who worked as a housemaid and the surgeon noted no other organ problems nor medical issues.'

'Did he note any skin discolourations that were unusual?'

Liberty scanned the pages, turning them, soup forgotten.

'Only redness over the knee joints. Probably caused by her job.'

Gordon wiped his mouth and nodded to her journal.

'May I?'

Liberty passed the book over, her expression neutral. Gordon nodded his thanks and easily read her copying of the autopsy report, the strong handwriting meticulous in its detail. Her own comments were neat and insightful yet lacking in places. He glanced at her and she seemed intent on her soup.

'It would be the gout,' he said.

He handed the notebook back and she took it, expression startled, then puzzled.

'What do you mean?'

'The redness over the knee joints is surely a sign of gout. Such things can hamper the uniting of bones.'

Liberty flicked through the pages, searching her notes.

'But she never complained of gout. There's no doctor visit or medicine and no one she worked with mentioned it.'

'Would she have told them if she wanted to keep her job? No, it's gout that slowed the bones uniting in the wrist. Possibly strained her heart as well. That and her hard job; there's little surprise she collapsed of it all, there was no poison involved. Did she no have any family? For in my experience she would've told them of the gout.'

From the folds of her dress, Liberty produced a pencil and began writing, asking questions as she did so. He was surprised to find himself answering readily. The rest of the meal was eaten as they spoke of other cases and Gordon was taken aback at Liberty's questions. Each went to the core of the problems and skilfully plucked the knowledge she lacked from him. Gordon felt light as they spoke. Leaning forward to better express a certain point, he realised with a pang that he was enjoying himself. Liberty abruptly rose.

'I've left the rest of my teaching notes in the laboratory. I won't be a moment.'

She left and he sat back, toying with his fork, throat tight.

How dare you. Murderer. You no deserve such pleasure.

I ken that. I'm sorry.

No sorry enough.

He rubbed his face, trying to blot Iona out, but the tirade continued. He rose, needing to leave. To retreat from her, from Liberty, from himself.

'Doctor McCraken?'

Liberty stood in the doorway, holding a book and a newspaper.

'I'm sorry, Miss Bennett, I'm no feeling too well.'

She put the book and paper on the table and peered at him.

'Is it your head, still?'

'Aye.'

He looked away; the newspaper caught his eye and he picked it up.

'Where have you got this from?'

'Oh, it was on the mat by the front door. I thought it was yours as it's a Scottish paper, did you drop it?'

He stared at the old copy of *The Herald*, unable to move. The room seemed to contract, making breathing hard.

'Are you all right, Doctor, you've gone white. Perhaps you should sit down.'

Liberty took the paper from his unresisting fingers and glanced at it.

'How strange,' she said. 'It's got my name written on it and the number three.'

He sat, his mind an empty space. There was only the rustle of paper, the turning of pages, then silence as she read. Then the paper was slid along the table, open at page three showing his trial and all the details.

Now she kens. Monster in their midst. Run! Run!

He turned his head away, unable to bear it. Liberty, footsteps overly loud, walked to her chair and settled there.

'Is it true, you were in prison for murder?'

'Aye.'

'But you were acquitted?'

'That's what they tell me.'

He glanced at her. She was watching him with a thoughtful expression.

'You sound as if you don't agree with the verdict?'

Murderer. Child killer.

He stared at his hands, then back to her.

'I should've saved them,' he managed.

He tensed for condemnation but saw only sadness in her expression. He swallowed.

'Are you no shocked by all this?'

Liberty sighed and ran a hand over her face. She looked at him, as if weighing what she knew against how she should speak.

'No, not shocked,' she said slowly. 'Surprised, perhaps. Yet I knew something had to be amiss. I'd like to think that no sane or trouble-free soul behaves the way you have.' She leant forward and tapped the paper. 'Now I know why you're so driven to prove your forensic medicine with Amy Dudley.'

'You do?'

She pulled the newspaper across the table, carefully folding it.

'It's clear to me from this account and your actions that you're guilt ridden, Doctor. Running from a place no one wants you. You're escaping what you believe was a failure to save your wife and child. In doing so, you're trying to rebuild your career on the back of my family. Using my father's legacy and my secret shame to ease your blackened soul for your own ends.'

He abruptly rose, making the chair rock.

'You understand nothing about it!'

'Then tell me!'

NEVER BELIEVE YOU. DESPISES YOU. RUN! RUN! RUN!

Gordon's whole body shook, and he gripped the table, swallowing bile on a gulp of wine. 'It disnae matter,' he mumbled.

'It matters to me! You're living in my house. We're involved in, this, this pact, together. You owe me an explanation.'

He stared at her, abrupt anger like fire on oil.

'Owe you? I owe you *nothing* and I'm giving you everything!'

'Everything? Oh Doctor, my idea of everything is clearly far different to yours.'

Liberty advanced, gripping the newspaper. He shrank back, but she thrust it on him.

'Tell me, or our deal's over. I'll know the truth or be damned!'

Her gaze was hard, and his anger drained. He sank to the chair, holding the paper to his chest while Liberty remained rigid next to him. He breathed deeply trying to find the words, a way to explain, then frowned, lifting the newspaper to his face.

'Where did you say you found this paper?'

She stared at him, defiant and baffled. He rose, hands trembling on the pages.

'Where did you get this?'

'I told you, it was on the mat by the front door. I didn't find it by prying, if that's what you're insinuating!'

'Tell me everything you ken of Lord Standish.'

'What! Why?'

'Because I think he's trying to kill me.'

She gave a short laugh.

'Don't be ridiculous. Don't try and change the subject with foolish statements.'

'Smell this.'

He shoved the paper at her, and she batted it away.

'No! Where are you going?'

Gordon stopped at the front door and waited for her. He pointed to the left, where the mat lay beneath the letterbox.

'There, you found it there?'

'Yes. I thought you must've dropped it when we got home and no one else noticed.'

'It's no mine you, daft woman! Someone posted it

through the box, deliberately, wanting you to find out about me. My money's on Lord Standish.'

'You're being ridiculous. Why would his lordship care about who you are?'

'It's no about me. It's about Amy Dudley.'

She looked from him to the paper, and back again.

'That sounds absurd, but if you want our agreement to continue, you need to tell me everything. Because I've had enough of your half-truths and risible suppositions.'

Liberty turned on her heel and walked into the library. After a moment he heard the sound of glass clinking and drinks pouring. Clutching the newspaper, he went inside, accepted a glass of whisky and settled in the chair next to Topaz's bed. Liberty sat in the chair opposite, turning her glass of sloe gin and watching him. Gordon stared at the fire, unwilling to look at her.

'What do you want me to say?'

From the corner of his eye, he knew she studied him over the tumbler rim.

'Tell me about your wife.'

CHAPTER THIRTY-NINE

Much later Gordon barely heard the upstairs clock, but thought it struck ten. He felt drained and strangely light. The fire popped, drawing his attention, gaze following the dancing flames. He heard Liberty stir but didn't want to look, didn't want to break the stillness. She rose and refilled his whisky, then her own sloe gin, before returning to her seat. He finally looked.

'Now you ken everything,' he said.

She sighed, misting the inside of her glass, her gaze on the vanishing fog.

'Why do you think Lord Standish is involved? You only met him once.'

Gordon picked up *The Herald,* holding it out.

'It smells of Macassar oil.'

She rose and took it, sniffing delicately, before handing it back.

'All right, it does. But Macassar is a very popular hair oil. Why must it be Lord Standish?'

Gordon folded the paper, recalling the man's menacing presence.

'He stank of it the other night and said I needed watching.'

'Needed watching for your head wound, surely?'

He pressed his lips together and bent forward.

'It was no like that. Tell me about him.'

She shrugged and stared at the fire.

'Lord Standish is one of the most eligible bachelors in the country, but you must know that? Despite his father's womanising the family are well regarded and highly placed at court.'

'I thought they bred and raced horses?'

'They do. But they also oversee the Heralds' College.'

'What's that?'

'From what I gather, the College decide who gets coats of arms according to lineage. They also investigate established families to determine if they're as blue blooded as they claim, especially if said family decide to purchase land, houses or turn their hand to business. To remain in favour, none must sully the nobility of the realm or embarrass the royal household. It's rather brutal the way Lord Standish tells it. Do you honestly believe a man so highly thought of could be trying to kill you?'

'What if he's part of the Watchers? They obviously still exist. I heard them mentioned when I acquired Amy Dudley's skull.'

'You're asking me to believe that Lord Standish is working with your harelipped man – to murder you as part of some ancient plot over Amy Dudley's death. It's a bit far fetched.'

'No more so than in Sam's time. Lord Dudley was involved and was the most highly placed noble in the country. What if whatever secret Amy Dudley's death holds continues to threaten the monarchy?'

'How?'

'I've no idea and will waste no time caring about it. All I want is to prove she was murdered and validate forensic medicine, to continue my work.'

'Maybe that's it, by proving Amy Dudley was murdered,

it somehow threatens the queen.'

He thought about it, turning over the connotations in his mind.

'I cannae see how. It makes more sense if we follow Sam's idea that whatever Amy Dudley held was the threat. But all I have of hers are the watch and the candlestick. Both were in her chambers at her death and then went to Lord Dudley, so are no threat. More, they were both here when I was in Edinburgh – and why do the Watchers want Amy Dudley's skull?'

He rubbed his face and then swigged whisky, trying to think. Liberty stirred and he looked over at her.

'Perhaps these Watchers just wanted to stop you from getting Amy Dudley exhumed,' she said. 'Without her bones, where would your proposal be? You would have to rely on current cases, which no doctor or professional would work with you on. Especially not the victim's families, given your history and fall from grace. Taking the skull would stop any investigation into Amy Dudley's death. There would be no chance of anyone reinvestigating, perhaps finding the thing she held, or stirring up others to do so.'

'Aye, it's a possibility,' he conceded.

'Yet you still believe Lord Standish is involved somehow?'

'There's no denying the smell on the newspaper.'

'Again, that hair oil is very popular. If he's that dangerous, then why not just murder you when you were alone together in here, and make it look like an accident or something?'

'Too risky. He even insinuated as much. That having someone die in your respectable house would be a scandal too far, especially for the Fieldings. I'm safe here, I think.'

She seemed about to reply when the front door opening

arrested them. Verity's laugh came and the rustle of coats being removed. A moment later the youngest Bennett entered the library.

'Oh, hello. We thought we'd get a nightcap,' she said.

Behind her were Doctor Fielding and Lord Standish. Gordon tucked the newspaper into his jacket and rose, glancing at Liberty. She was already on her feet and moving toward the guests with a pasted-on smile. Amidst the flurry of greetings, Gordon grazed Lord Standish's hand rather than shake it, hating the man's knowing look as he did so. Verity sauntered past to the drinks cabinet and began preparing gin slings. She chatted about the people at the restaurant and the play they had been to. Gordon retreated to his chair, whole body trembling, and wondered when he could politely leave. Verity turned to Liberty.

'Oh, you'll never believe the cake I had at supper, it was delicious. I suppose it's too late to change the one for the wedding?'

Liberty laughed and they began talking about the upcoming nuptials. Suddenly Lord Standish was in front of him, smiling down.

'So, Doctor McCraken, how's your head?'

'Fine, thank you.'

'It must be a comfort to be staying where the talented Doctor Bennett can look after you. And of course his lovely sisters.'

'Indeed.'

Lord Standish stepped away, settling in Liberty's vacated seat, watching. Doctor Fielding, warming himself at the fire, accepted a drink.

'Are you still enjoying London, Doctor McCraken?'

'Aye, it's a splendid city.'

Lord Standish bent forward, smiling though his eyes were cold.

'It must be difficult living so very far from your family,' he said. 'Do you hear news from home regularly?'

The room seemed to grow dark and Gordon's hands hurt round the glass. Liberty stopped speaking. The quiet stretched, smothering them all, then an abrupt croak broke the silence. Lord Standish frowned, peering into the shadows, and exchanged a puzzled look with Doctor Fielding. Then he got on his knees to find Topaz and her puppies in their bed.

'What do we have here?'

Verity moved toward him.

'Oh yes, aren't they darling?'

Lord Standish reached forward. Quile exploded from the bed, beak stabbing. Standish cried out and fell back, clutching his hand. Topaz rose, her teeth showing, guarding her puppies. Quile continued to flap in front of the bed, cawing harshly. Gordon noted Standish's look of fury then the man scrambled back and up. Verity and Doctor Fielding rushed to his aid, taking him to the kitchen for nursing. Quile hopped after them a little way, before turning back muttering to herself. She wiped her beak clean on the rug and fluttered to Gordon's offered shoulder. He looked from Topaz to the library door, recalling the murderous rage on Standish's face.

'I think,' he said, 'I'll take Quile and retire to my room, if that's all right?'

He met Liberty's gaze, noting her stark face and tight lips. She nodded.

'Certainly.'

He made to leave, but suddenly Liberty's hand was on his arm and he looked at it, then her.

'Doctor, do you think you could help me move Topaz and her puppies up to my room?' She glanced at the library door. 'I feel the need of their company tonight.'

'Aye, of course.'

When they knelt to her bed Topaz wagged her tail and was happy to be coaxed out. Liberty scooped all the puppies onto her lap, forming a makeshift pouch from her skirt and rose with Gordon's help. He picked up the bed and, with Topaz close behind, followed Liberty up the stairs.

'Should you no make our excuses?' he said.

Liberty paused, then continued upward as if she hadn't heard.

CHAPTER FORTY

In the following days, Gordon didn't leave the house for fear Lord Standish and the harelipped man were watching, waiting. His bloody nightmares continued unabated and he felt sick from Iona's constant mutterings. He kept Quile close and pressed on with translating the daguerreotype. When this proved too intense, he cleaned Lord Dudley's pocket watch.

Preparations for Verity's wedding gained momentum, engulfing the house and dinner conversations until he felt it had always been thus. Whenever Lord Standish was due to guest at dinner, which wasn't often now, Liberty quietly arranged for Gordon to eat in the laboratory. He envied Tiberius's escape; teaching, patients and late evenings at his club. Liberty, with Sofia's help, seemed to immerse herself in her sister's plans, barely coming up for air. Yet, late nights she still spent with Tiberius in the laboratory, teaching and trying to impart knowledge. Gordon endured some afternoons with the two older Bennetts, while they practiced experiments, to maintain the illusion of collaboration. Gordon tried to plan, but Standish and the harelipped man corroded his thoughts, making sleep erratic and engineering slow-feeling days.

The day before the wedding was busier than he could have believed. The constant noise and strangers invading the house fragmented Gordon's concentration. He retreated to the laboratory as soon as breakfast was over and, with the door shut, the noise blessedly lessened. Quile was in her raggedy nest worrying at pork rinds and the atmosphere was a calm haven compared to the rest of the house. He went to the window, opening it and breathing in spring air and new grass. Quile hopped to his shoulder and thence outside, cawing and flapping away. He knew the crow would find her way through his bedroom window and somehow to Topaz and her puppies. They had tried to keep Quile away from the dog, but somehow she still got into Liberty's room. He shut the window and went to his preferred work table, peering at the daguerreotype, but his mind felt too fraught. Instead, he picked up the pocket watch, turning it in the light. He rubbed the bevelled edge, now free of dirt and debris, feeling it pleasingly deep and even. Taking up the small wooden pick, Gordon started cleaning the chased silver hinge. He eased out dirt, the falling flakes dotting his hand, and he wiped them with a wetted cloth marking the material like bloodstains. His thoughts flitted to Lord Standish, thence to Oxford and Foxcombe; he hadn't told Liberty where Amy Dudley's skull was actually hidden nor about the cipher. The need to retrieve her was like an itch under his skin, a constant burr that he couldn't reach. He glanced at the camping equipment piled in the corner.

Only two days now.

It felt like eternity.

Harelipped man will be waiting. Watching.

Follow you. Kill you all.

Gordon gripped the watch, digging the cloth into the hinge crevice. From above laughter came, floorboards creaked, and he scowled, fingertips hurting on the silver hinge. Abruptly something gave and the watch opened, exposing the powder flask. The smell of ancient tannin came strongly, embedded with sulphur. Gordon stared.

Nestled inside the flask was a soft, leather pouch, worn and faded, but whole.

It must be old gunpowder.

He used the picker to help ease the pouch out. Something solid inside made it a stiff job, and he wondered if the gunpowder had hardened. He teased the leather open, peering in, and extracted a tightly folded parchment. It felt heavy, the paper wrapped around something, and with trembling fingers he peeled it away. At the heart lay an oval gold locket, engraved with whorls and flourishes, studded with chips of emeralds and diamonds. He stared at it, skin tingling, and ran his fingers over the face. Feeling the back, he turned it to see a boar's head etched in detail. He stilled his trembling fingers and using the picker he eased minuscule rust and dirt particles from the locket's edge. He used the wooden stick to press the alcohol cloth into the clogged gold hinge. Gordon lost all notion of time, uncaring now of noises from above, painstakingly working. Slowly the locket's wings yielded. Abrupt footsteps hurried down the steps. He glanced up, seeing Liberty, her bell-like skirts swaying. She came over and noted the watch, touching the inside of the powder flask.

'You managed to get it open.'

'Aye. This was inside.'

He didn't dare release the pressure on the locket and barely breathing he inched the wings apart. She bent, looking at the winking diamonds and emeralds.

'It's beautiful. Imagine it being in the watch all these years.'

'It was well looked after, wrapped in that parchment and inside the leather pouch there.'

Liberty touched the pouch and picked up the parchment. She unfolded the yellow page, turning it over and looking at it.

'Doctor.'

Her voice, taut with excitement, made him pause in his work.

'What is it?'

'I think it's a letter to Amy Dudley, from her husband.'

Gordon put down the locket and took the parchment. The old English was legible and there, beneath the writing was a faded thumbprint and Lord Dudley's signature. Liberty proffered the magnifying glass and he studied the letter.

'Is it genuine?' she asked.

'It must be, hidden in the watch all this time.'

'What does it say?'

Heart too fast, he studied the words, trying to get an idea of the meaning.

'It seems to be about a meeting. I'm certain this part,' he pointed, 'concerns the Sunday she died. I need time to properly decipher it.'

'It must have been important for Amy Dudley to have hidden it, and the locket. It's a wonder Lord Dudley didn't find them.'

'I doubt he knew they were in there.' He touched the watch with a trembling finger. 'It's a beautiful piece but cumbersome. I dinnae imagine Robert Dudley would have need of a powder flask from his dead wife. No being the queen's favourite.'

Liberty moved closer and peered at the letter.

'Are you sure it's really from Lord Dudley and not a forgery? Remember Sam's notes.'

'Aye, I do recall. There's no way to ken it's from her husband and no some scunner arranging the puir woman's murder.'

Liberty moved away, pulling on cloth oversleeves, opening a cupboard. Gordon continued to study the letter.

Reaching inside his satchel he retrieved the folder and from it the chattels list that had accompanied the watch. He overlapped the receipt and newly found letter, signatures side by side, and used the magnifying glass. The loops and whirls of each writing were distinct, the slope of letters identical.

'The signatures look the same,' he said. 'But it's a shame the thumbprint on the letter is so degraded.'

From the cupboard Liberty heaved out a large, bell-shaped, glass jar, the kind that split in the middle. She put it on the table, her expression preoccupied.

'What difference does the state of the print make?'

'Aye, I forget you've no formal training. About fifty years ago a Doctor Mayer wrote a book on anatomy. I have… *had* a copy. Mayer suggests that no two people have the same fingerprint, although some are very similar. If the thumb mark was in better condition, I could compare it to the one on this chattel receipt, which is undoubtedly Robert Dudley's.'

Liberty frowned and removed the fist-sized glass stopper from the jar neck, giving it a wipe with a cloth. With a deft movement she removed the jar's top half and set about cleaning both sections.

'Do you believe this Doctor Mayer, about fingerprints?'

'It's no a commonly held theory, but I think it has merits.'

A heavy scraping came from above followed by laughter, making Gordon grimace. Liberty glanced up.

'Verity is being very particular about her wedding party,' Liberty said. 'We're clearing the parlour in readiness for tomorrow.'

'So I understand.'

'Oh, don't be so sour.' She gestured to the camping gear. 'Two days and we'll be on the way to your precious

Oxford and soon after all this will be over. You need never see us again.'

'We can only hope.'

She gave a sardonic look and returned to cleaning the jar.

'Tiberius has a lecture this afternoon, so he won't be here,' she said. 'But this experiment seems to be causing him difficulties and so we're going over it one last time before he has to demonstrate it. I can't understand the problem,' she mused. 'I wish he would focus more and spend less time carousing at his club.'

'He probably would, if you stopped forcing him to be a doctor.'

Liberty's gaze narrowed. He shrugged, returning his attention to the letter. Quick steps clattered and a bleary-eyed Tiberius appeared. He greeted Gordon perfunctorily and then fell into muted conversation with Liberty. After a few minutes glass clanked, irritating Gordon enough to look up. The jar had been put back together and now contained a silvery substance amidst darker, grey crystals.

'Do I need to go upstairs?' he asked, hating the idea.

Liberty didn't even look at him.

'No,' she said. 'You're quite safe, the experiment will be contained in the jar.'

'Are you sure? What is it, exactly?'

'Extraction methodology of iodine fumes,' she said. 'It's to show the students the versatility and—'

'I ken what it's for, Miss Bennett.'

'In which case, you should also *ken,* that even if they weren't contained in the jar, the fumes, harsh though they are, won't harm your precious parchments.'

She returned to her brother, pointing and explaining, while he took notes. Gordon scowled and bent over the parchments with the magnifying glass. The thumbprint on the chattels receipt was strong in the wax with Dudley's ridges and whorls finely picked out. He shifted the glass, peering at the letter's faded thumbprint which was only a few waxy, sepia lines. Something rocked the table and he frowned, glancing up to see Tiberius tipped forward on his stool, intent on the jar. Abruptly the stool legs slipped, and the man's windmilling hand caught the glass stopper, sending it crashing from the jar, shattering on the floor. Out of the jar neck crept the iodine's thick, purple fumes.

'For pity's sake, Tiberius!'

Liberty grabbed the top of the jar but Tiberius, still unbalanced, reared back, violently rocking the workbench. The bottom of the jar slid, making the top slip from Liberty's grasp to clonk on the table and acrid, violet fumes poured out. Gordon leapt away, stool crashing to the floor as bitter fumes rolled across the table engulfing everything. Gordon coughed, eyes streaming, grabbed his satchel and followed Tiberius up the stairs with Liberty close behind.

After half an hour Gordon ventured back into the laboratory and found the acrid air just bearable. The fumes had dissipated, but still hung like a thistledown mist. At the table he stopped, staring. The documents lay where he had left them but were now peppered with deep yellow and orange finger marks. Some were grainy, a few darker and smudged, but they were definite fingerprints. Moving to the table he saw that the degraded print on the letter from inside the watch now showed clear. He grabbed the magnifying glass, bending over the documents, and wasn't even aware of Liberty until she was at his elbow.

'I'll get the fan. Goodness, where did all the marks come from?'

Gordon wiped his stinging eyes.

'It must have been the chemicals. I'd need to experiment

and find out more. But meanwhile, look here.'

Liberty took the magnifying glass and moved from one thumbprint to the other.

'The Robert Dudley prints are different,' she said.

'Indeed,' he coughed and continued, 'and if Mayer is to be believed, then one of these is no Lord Dudley's. It would make more sense that the letter to Amy Dudley is a forgery, rather than the receipt for her death goods.'

Liberty shook her head, coughing.

'I can't think,' she managed. 'The fumes are too much.'

Gordon, eyes streaming, agreed and gathered the documents, carefully holding them at the edges. Retreating to the library he laid the parchments out and Liberty peered at them.

'The marks are fading!'

Even as they watched the prints slowly vanished.

An hour later and the laboratory was largely clear of fumes, thanks to the hand-wound fan, open window and door. Gordon, having examined his documents and other artefacts, emerged into the hallway which now held a chemical taint. Abruptly Verity swept from the library, her hair awry and face furious.

'And you!' She pointed at him. 'You're the absolute worst of them!'

She burst into tears and, gripping her skirts, ran upstairs. He gaped after her, turning to find Liberty in the library doorway.

'What did I do?' he asked.

She gestured to the laboratory.

'That. I'm afraid we've managed to upset Verity with all the disruption.'

'Oh aye, can you no calm her down?'

She stared at him.

'Honestly, Doctor McCraken, my sister's getting married tomorrow. I think she's entitled to be a little overwrought today.'

'I ken that, but I'd like to develop a safe way of re-creating what happened with the iodine. If Verity's all riled, her nerves will ruin my concentration, I cannae abide the outbursts.'

Liberty stiffened and then moved to within inches of him.

'Enough,' she said. 'Threaten me if you will, but we will not ruin Verity's wedding, and that includes today. Until she's wed, no more experiments. No more poking about down there, like some miserable shade. Stay in your room, sit in the library or kitchen; I don't care. But do not upset my sister again, or as God is my witness, I will turn you out of this house and damn the consequences.'

She walked away, calling for Sofia to take tea to Verity. He watched her go and, with a sigh, closed the laboratory door.

Close to midnight, Gordon sat in the fire-lit library and nursed a whisky. His thoughts, full of Amy Dudley, fingerprints and documents, made sleep impossible. A shadow appeared in the doorway, fleshed out when Liberty came in. She paused on seeing him, nodded a greeting and made her way to the drink's cabinet. The clink of glasses and sweet smell of sloe gin accompanied the sound of pouring. He hoped she would take the drink upstairs, but instead Liberty sat opposite him, looking tired and drawn. Her glass reflected the firelight, turning her drink indigo and gold.

'I wanted to say thank you,' she said.

He stared at her in surprise. She looked into her glass and took a sip.

'You could've forced the laboratory issue earlier, but you didn't. I know you don't care, but everything with Verity went smoothly after the mishap. It took a lot of promises on my part and thankfully you, unknowingly, kept some of them today. So, I'm grateful.'

He didn't know what to say and tipped his glass toward her in acknowledgement. She smiled. They drank, both staring at the flames, and the occasional slither of wood to ash was all that disturbed the silence. After a few minutes Liberty looked at him.

'The difference in the fingerprints, what do you think it means?'

'Och, I've thought of no much else all day. If Lord Dudley didnae write that message to his wife, then I'm thinking Sam's theory is right.'

'That Amy Dudley's murder was a plot by these Watchers to undermine her husband, even get him hanged for her death?'

'Aye, and that it was a cover to steal whatever the puir woman held, to use against Queen Elizabeth.'

'But what could Amy Dudley have had that might threaten the queen?'

'I dinnae ken and I've thought about it till my head hurts.'

'That sounds unpleasant. Do you have any painless thoughts of who might've have murdered her?'

Gordon sat forward, cradling his glass in both hands. The flames were dwindling, making the library darker and colder.

'I wondered about the queen.'

'Queen Elizabeth? Why on earth would she have had Amy Dudley killed?'

'The woman was a law unto herself, you ken? Brilliant, aye, but a wee bit damaged by her father.'

'I see what you mean, because her father cut her mother's head off.'

'And the amount of times the man married and terrorised his wives.'

'All right, but what's that got to do with you thinking Elizabeth somehow concerned herself with murdering Amy Dudley? She was in love with Robert Dudley – having his wife die in mysterious circumstances could do nothing but harm the man.'

'Aye and there it is, Elizabeth made it plain that she would marry no one. Even told Parliament so, but she loved Robert Dudley, he was her weakness. By Amy Dudley dying as she did, the man was forever tainted with murder no matter what any jury said. Elizabeth could never marry him and keep the throne, you ken?'

'So, you're saying Elizabeth plotted Amy Dudley's death to implicate Robert Dudley and thereby give her an unassailable reason never to marry him? What of the Watchers? Why charge Sam to investigate if she knew what had happened and that Dudley wasn't to blame?'

'Investigating to discover Dudley's involvement or no was the reason the queen gave Sam; it didnae have to be the truth of it.'

Liberty looked unconvinced and Gordon knew it seemed outlandish given everything they and Sam had uncovered, but still it nagged at him. Using a poker, Liberty rustled the dying fire to more life.

'Surely there must be something or someone else more likely?'

'Aye, well, now we ken Lord Dudley wasnae to blame, there's enough enemies of the man and the English crown to choose from. I spent today looking at a list Sam made of those he suspected of manipulating the murder. I've been seeking those he listed in your father's books.' He gestured to the volumes, taken from the library shelves, stacked next to his chair, his notebook atop them. 'I hoped to find something that occurred after 1560 that might give a clue as to who orchestrated the murdering of Amy Dudley.'

'Did you find anything?'

'Mary, Queen of Scots was highest on the list, being Elizabeth's natural successor and Catholic.'

'Yes, I can see why Mary of Scots as master plotter would make sense to Sam at the time, but on Elizabeth's death, Mary's son James became king of England as well as Scotland. So, if the item could be used against Elizabeth in favour of Mary, why would the Watchers still be searching for it, now, hundreds of years later?'

'There's the nub of it. Elizabeth and Mary's common descendant sits on the throne still, in the body of Queen Victoria. Mary of Scots may have plotted for Elizabeth's throne in 1560 and definitely throughout her life, but there'd be no need for the Watchers to continue searching. No once James was on the throne, least of all through until today.'

'Anyone else on Sam's list make sense?'

'M'be. Have you heard of Katherine Grey?'

'Do you mean Jane Grey, queen for nine days?'

'Katherine was Jane's younger sister.'

'I didn't know she had one. Is Katherine on Sam's list?'

'Aye, her and her husband, Edward Seymour, Earl of Hertford. Katherine, like Jane, had close claim to the English throne through their grandmother, Mary Tudor. She was Henry the Eighth's sister and Elizabeth's aunt. Katherine was even considered heir apparent when Elizabeth's sister, Mary, was on the throne according to what I read today.'

'There are far too many Marys for such a late hour. Why the name was constantly reused for such close family members, I'll never know.' Liberty sipped her drink. 'For ease and sense, let's agree to differentiate them, please. I know Mary was Elizabeth's older sister and queen of England before her – let's use her nickname, Bloody Mary. Mary Tudor, what did you say she was, Elizabeth's aunt?' Gordon nodded and she continued, 'And Mary, Queen of Scots, was Elizabeth's cousin, that's right, isn't it?'

'Aye, she was. Granddaughter of Henry the Eighth's other sister, Margaret.'

Liberty's expression turned thoughtful, her lips moving as she sorted out the lineages. Gordon had no such problem having meticulously researched and drawn into his notebook all the Tudor family trees that afternoon. Liberty, eyes on the embers, spoke slowly.

'So, as Jane and Katherine Grey were granddaughters of Mary Tudor, they too were Elizabeth's cousins. Meaning they had just as much right to the throne as Mary, Queen of Scots.' She shook her head and looked at him. 'Goodness, what a tangle. All right, while Bloody Mary was on the throne, did she really loathe Elizabeth, her own sister, so much that she put Katherine as heir in her stead?'

Liberty rose to put more wood on the fire, poking it to a fierce heat. Gordon closed his eyes enjoying the warmth, thinking about her question and everything he had read and recorded earlier.

'Aye, she did. Bloody Mary hated the bones of Elizabeth, for her mother's woes, you ken? She longed for rumours of Elizabeth's illegitimacy to be real. Such hatred made it easy for the woman to supplant Elizabeth and make Katherine successor to the throne. More, once Elizabeth was crowned the rumours over her legitimacy, founded by her own father, would've made Katherine a ripe prospect for any rebel.' He opened his eyes to find Liberty re-seated and watching him. He sat straighter, feeling strangely vulnerable under her steady gaze. 'They would only need some political leverage to take to Rome, for the pope to lend his support, and fire some Catholic rebellion. The Church was forever wanting England back in the Catholic fold.'

'So, you're saying that using Katherine Grey as a figurehead, religious rebels could've created the Watchers. Used them to steal this political threat to Elizabeth from Amy Dudley, killing the woman in the process, to damage or even get Robert Dudley hanged as murderer. I understand wanting to take the throne for herself, but what reason had Katherine to want Lord Dudley ruined or dead?'

'He killed her sister, Jane Grey.'

'No, he didn't. Jane Grey was crowned queen of England as part of some failed rebellion. That's why she died, executed for her part in the rebellion.'

'Aye, executed by Bloody Mary when she quashed the rebellion and took the throne from the Greys. But do you ken who Jane Grey was wed to, two months before her fatal coronation? No? It was Robert Dudley's younger brother, Guildford. Do you know who orchestrated the rebellion and crowned puir Jane Grey? Robert Dudley's father, John.'

'Well, the Dudley's were an ambitious family, weren't they?'

'Aye, but an ill-fated one. All the men perished in the tower by Bloody Mary's order, but for Robert and two of his brothers. By the time Elizabeth was crowned, a mere four years after wee Jane was executed, only Robert and his brother Ambrose remained of the entire Dudley family. And Robert looking to marry Elizabeth to make himself king of England is something I think Katherine Grey would no be pleased about.'

'Goodness, that makes sense I suppose. But what of now? Why are the Watchers still searching? Katherine

Grey is long dead.'

'The woman had a tempestuous relationship with Elizabeth while she was alive, mind. But Katherine Grey's line didnae die out with her, nor did any successor ascend the throne like Mary, Queen of Scots' son did. I think whatever Amy Dudley held is still a threat to the monarchy, maybe enough to put Katherine Grey's descendant on the throne, if found by these Watchers.'

'Who is her descendant?'

'The Duke of Northumberland.'

'Where have I heard that name recently?'

'Lord Standish mentioned him at dinner the other night. They're cousins, I believe.'

Liberty became still, one side of her face golden in the firelight, the other shadowed. Flames danced across her glass as she raised it, gulping the contents. She lowered her drink, much reduced, and didn't look at him.

'Everything we find out, seems to include that man,' she said.

'Aye, it's no comforting, is it?'

'No. Although I'm still not sure he's involved in any dastardly plot with these Watchers.'

Gordon grunted and finished his drink, suddenly glad the day was over.

'Thanks to you and your sister,' he said. 'I needed some distraction today. Yet all this conjecture on your English crown means no much to my plans. All I care about is proving Amy Dudley's murder and pioneering forensic medicine. So, I'm to bed, as tomorrow promises to be long.'

'He's coming you know, Lord Standish, to the wedding. And afterward, here.'

'Then I'll be well and out the way, be sure of that.'

She nodded, her gaze on him. He picked up his notebook and stood, swaying slightly, tiredness like lead in his bones.

'Goodnight, Doctor McCraken.'

He inclined his head and left, but stopped at the door, looking back. She was outlined against the firelight, golden and dark, like some ancient goddess.

'Miss Bennett?' She turned her leonine head to him. 'I hope everything goes well tomorrow.'

'So, do I, Doctor McCraken.'

Liberty raised her drink and downed the contents. He went upstairs hearing the clink of glass and pouring of more sloe gin.

CHAPTER FORTY-ONE

Gordon awoke with the dawn, worrying about the journey to Foxcombe the next day. It would be gruelling dealing with Liberty and Tiberius, and he wasn't looking forward to it. He went through the arrangements, fretting about the hotel in Reading.

EASY IN THE NIGHT TO FIND YOU. KILL YOU IN YOUR BED. M'BE FOLLOW YOU TO AMY DUDLEY.

He had no answer, no reassurance to banish Iona with. Pushing the covers back he rose and dressed, trying not to think. He hesitated at the door, wondering what he might find at breakfast on this, Verity's wedding day. Steeling his nerves, he found a smile and went down to face whatever the morning would bring.

Thankfully, Lady Fielding had insisted her son be married in their family church in Belgravia. This necessitated the bridal party leaving for a hotel at midday to prepare and dress. After everyone else had left, the house settled as if after a great storm, creaking and grumbling to silence. Gordon put his forehead on the front door and breathed easily for the first time since waking. After a blessed moment of peace, he sighed, knowing time was not his friend, and went on the hunt.

Liberty's bedroom was white, from the curtains to

the painted iron bed frame. White and ivory. Something about its purity rocked him. It was church-like, a bridal boudoir with no bridegroom. Topaz rose from her bed, tail wagging, and he ruffled her ears. The puppies were nearly old enough to see and rolled about, squeaking at each other. Quile, a black shadow in the bed, supervised them. Their presence reassured him, and he began to search, aware of minutes ticking away. After some searching, he found the familiar safe key box beneath the dressing table, empty, and cursed the woman, hoping she hadn't taken the key with her. After a further frustrating half an hour, he ran his hands along the iron bed frame and around the bed head. There, looped on a piece of ribbon and tied snug to the iron post was the safe key.

From Liberty's bedroom he went to the far end of the hallway, where he hesitated, resting fingertips on a door. Every part of him weighed down, even the air in his lungs was a burden. But he knew of nowhere else to get what he needed, undetected.

How far have I fallen?

NO FAR ENOUGH. HELL AWAITS.

He gritted his teeth and opened the door, entering Doctor Bennett's bedroom. The silk patterned wallpaper was dark with leaves and lilies while a chest of drawers sported a carriage clock, papers, books, ornaments and scientific instruments. Three coloured rugs scattered over the floorboards and a rosewood bed was moored like a ship amidst the multi-hued sea. He stood, smelling old tobacco and stale air, before moving to the chest of drawers. He picked up papers, reading ideas for experiments, lectures and correspondence. He handled the instruments, revelling in touching where Doctor Bennett had.

This room was the first thing he saw every morning.

HE'D DESPISE YOU. MONSTER IN THEIR MIDST.

He smoothed the bedding with reverent fingers. The carriage clock chimed, reminding him of time slipping away. He pulled open the drawers, wondering if he could use the wood, but found them full of clothes and mothballs. He peered under the bed and spied a heavy, square piece of wood propping up the middle slats; around it books and boxes were haphazardly stacked. Lying flat he pulled out the bed prop and two boxes. Opening the boxes, he found the first empty and the second was filled with his own letters. He stirred the papers.

USELESS, DRIED UP WORDS FROM A MURDERER.

He shook the pages out and shuffled them back under the bed. Rising, he gathered the boxes and the thick bed prop. After a final look at his friend's room, he closed the door and went to the laboratory to start work.

An hour later, he held up the duplicate back of the safe he had made from one of the boxes, satisfied it looked right. Putting the wood down, he picked up his satchel, clutching it to his chest. Through the leather he could feel the Leonardo da Vinci tome. He breathed easier, knowing all the documents and Sam's notes were secure in the hidden pocket. Nestled along with the tome, were the pocket watch, with the locket closed inside, the daguerreotype plates wrapped in wool, the candlestick holder and his notebook. He hated leaving everything behind, even for such a short time, but Lord Standish and the harelipped man were sinister shadows, waiting. Watching. He knew this was the only way to protect everything, himself, Amy Dudley and his hopes of redemption. He placed the precious satchel into the back of the safe, carefully wedging it in and fitted the cut-down wooden square over it. The dark wood blended in perfectly. Unless someone deliberately pulled the wood, it would seem like the back of the safe, hiding his belongings behind it. Gordon picked up and examined the key. It was a long, iron instrument with four teeth. Rifling the camping equipment for more tools, he set about reproducing the key onto the wooden bed support.

Just over three hours had passed and he carefully inspected his work. The thick wood haft of his duplicate key was spiky and chafed his palm. He put Liberty's leather gauntlets on and sat next to the hole with the safe door yawning open to his left. Twisting, he managed to insert the key in the sideways door lock. Taking a breath, he exerted pressure and released it, testing the wood. It seemed strong enough. He clenched and unclenched his fingers, tensed and turned the key. Something clicked. Gordon paused, afraid the wood would snap.

It only has to work a few times.

He nodded to himself, exerted pressure again, and this time the mechanism slipped as wooden teeth caught the cylinders. The safe's locking latch slid out and he smiled. It took a further half an hour to file the original iron safe key. He shaved off just enough from each tooth to stop it working. Any more and Liberty might notice. He tried the mutilated key in the lock, pleased when the mechanism wouldn't move. Even if Liberty tried to open the safe before they left for Oxford tomorrow, she'd have no time to get another key made. He opened the two boxes he'd removed from the safe, the same ornate ones he'd seen Liberty give Sofia. Diamonds and sapphires glinted from amidst gold chains and rings. He wondered what Verity had chosen to wear for her wedding. Closing the boxes, he returned them to the hole, nestled against the false back. He rose, heaved the door shut and locked it with his duplicate key.

All safe until we get back from Oxford.

Lord Standish will find it. Prise it open. Give it

ALL TO THE HARELIPPED MAN.

No. It's hidden, protected until I return.

NEVER COMING BACK.

The wedding party returned just after six that evening, and Gordon was obliged to join them in the cleared parlour. Even though he watched, tense and afraid, for Lord Standish, Gordon found milling through the guests bearable, knowing all he had achieved that day. Finally, he came to the glowing bride and her new husband, resplendent in silks and taffeta.

'Congratulations,' he said, shaking Doctor Fielding's hand.

Verity offered her fingers and he kissed the back of her hand.

'You look beautiful,' he said.

A diamond and pearl necklace set off her green and cream gown, while a tiara winked from her ringleted black hair. She inclined her head.

'You're too kind. And don't you look dashing!'

He bowed and held out the frock coat so she could see the dark blue lining, contrasting with the silvery front.

'Madam Olarf did a splendid job,' he said. 'I can see why you found her invaluable for your gown and bridesmaids.' He bent forward. 'Even if she does talk for queen and country.'

Verity laughed and gripped her husband's arm. A stir in the guests caused Gordon to turn to see Sofia, carrying a salver with hired servers following, likewise burdened.

'Supper is served,' she called.

An hour was taken up with eating and mingling. Gordon was pleased to discover Lord Standish had left after the wedding. His mood was so lightened that he stayed for the dancing, whirling Verity through a waltz and

Liberty through a foxtrot, before retiring to bed. The party noises continued until he knew not when for he finally fell asleep to the muted music and thudding below, to dream of Foxcombe.

CHAPTER FORTY-TWO

The following evening Gordon and the Bennetts reached their hotel in Reading. Despite the cool air Gordon felt overly warm and his head ached. He had wanted to arrive much earlier, but between the late night and Liberty's fussy preparations, everything had been delayed. In his hotel room he sank onto the bed, head in hands, trying to think past his throbbing skull. He knew it wasn't just the company he had suffered. His relief that Lord Standish had not stayed at the wedding celebrations had turned to fear.

Why did he leave? Where is he?

FOLLOWING. FOLLOWING. BRINGING THE HARELIPPED MAN.

I'd have noticed. I havnae stopped looking all day.

SAFE BREAKING. NO ONE'S AT HOME IN LONDON.

STEALING SAM, THEN COMING FOR YOU.

Sofia's there. Everything's guarded and hidden.

He rose, not bothering to unpack, and went downstairs. At the bar he ordered a whisky. He glanced at his pocket watch, noting there was only half an hour before he was due to dine with the Bennetts. When the whisky arrived, he downed it, then ordered another.

He was the first at their table and ordered a third drink. Liberty bustled to her seat, followed by Tiberius. He endured small talk as they perused the choices and ordered wine. Raising his menu, he was shielded from them and took a long breath. A sudden presence made him look up. Lord Standish smiled wolfishly, before politely greeting them all. Liberty's expression fell, but she managed a smile.

'What brings you to Reading, my lord?'

'I'm here to see a horse breeder. And you? I'm surprised to see you travelling so soon after the wedding.'

Liberty glanced at Gordon and made to speak, but Tiberius was quicker.

'We're to Oxford tomorrow,' he said. 'There's some texts in the Bodleian that can help with our collaboration.'

He smiled, pleased with himself, and didn't notice the shocked looks from his dining companions. Lord Standish's expression remained politely interested, but Gordon noted his eyes narrowed briefly at the mention of Oxford.

'And you, Miss Bennett? Are you just going along to see the fair city of Oxford?'

'Indeed.'

The silence pressed and Gordon hoped it would send the man away. He shifted, insides painful as if pinched by unseen fingers. Tiberius glanced from Gordon to his sister.

'Would you care to join us?' he asked.

Gordon exchanged a panicked look with Liberty.

'Why thank you, Doctor Bennett,' said Lord Standish. 'I'd like that *very* much.'

In a few short moments another chair and place setting had materialised. Lord Standish settled comfortably, sipping wine.

'It's so fortuitous running into you all,' he said. 'I was feeling a touch lonely. Tell me, did the wedding continue well after I'd left?'

Thankfully Tiberius picked up the thread and the two

chatted about Verity's celebrations until the first course arrived. Lord Standish raised a glass and they all followed suit. His gaze held Gordon's.

'May you always dine with friends, or at least without enemies,' he said.

They sipped in silence, even Tiberius aware of the brittle atmosphere. His lordship gestured to the soup.

'I hear the food here is excellent.'

'Have you stayed here before?' Tiberius asked.

Lord Standish sampled his soup.

'Oh no, but an acquaintance of mine did a few weeks ago and recommended it. Although if wasn't for his recommendation, I wouldn't have stayed here.'

'Oh, why's that?'

'Nothing to do with the hotel per se, but there was a terrible accident when he stayed. A man died.'

'How dreadful.'

'Yes, very unfortunate. The poor soul fell from a balcony, drunk, in the early hours of the morning.'

'Goodness,' said Liberty, 'that's truly awful.'

'Yes, it was, and a frightful shock for everyone staying here. I found out afterward the chap was a lawyer, from Scotland.' His gaze was nailed to Gordon. 'Name of McDougall, I believe.'

Everything stopped. Sound, movement, even his own heart. A blackness descended and then, roaring, Gordon leapt. The table overturned. He closed on Lord Standish, throwing him back, chair and all. They slammed to the ground, grunting and thrashing. Gordon found the man's throat and squeezed. The white face strained, turned puce, struggled and contorted. Abruptly Gordon let go, reeled back, let hands lift him and ran. Ran, shaking and trembling to his room, to collapse, sobbing on the bed.

Eternity passed. Or hours. Or minutes. The knocking wouldn't stop, forcing Gordon to rise and open the door. Liberty pushed in without speaking. He stumbled to the bed and lay prone, uncaring she was there. He heard her move and sit on the bedside chair but didn't look.

'McDougall, he was the man you knew?'

Tears crept down the side of his face, gathering unpleasantly on his ears, in his sideburns. He closed his eyes, made it worse and started when something brushed his hand. Then, lifting the handkerchief, he wiped his face and, sitting up, blew his nose. Liberty's expression was sorrowful and kind, which he hated. Her handkerchief balled in his hand and his knuckles strained.

'He was my friend.'

'I'm so sorry.'

Gordon shook his head, unable to speak, and they sat in silence for a few minutes. Liberty bent forward, fingers playing with her sleeve.

'Do you think Lord Standish… I mean, do you believe he might've had something to do with it? Your friend? Here.'

He drew a breath and felt old enough to be dust.

'More than that, I think Standish is the harelipped man.'

She stared at him, her expression puzzled then horrified.

'Why, why would you say that?'

'His face, when we were fighting. It screwed up and looked like, like the other one. The harelipped man.'

Gordon shuddered. Liberty looked stunned; her hands trembled and she clasped them together.

'But that means he broke into that house in our square and maybe yours in Edinburgh. Oh my God, he killed that priest as well as your friend. He's a…'

'Watcher. Lord Standish is a Watcher.'

A knock on the door froze Gordon, but Liberty rose

without hesitation and admitted Tiberius. He carried a bottle of whisky and one of sloe gin as well as glasses. He arranged them on the chest of drawers.

'Lord Standish has retired to his room. A local doctor saw to him and there's no real harm done. His throat is bruised is all. A maid took him some soup, apparently.' He glanced at Gordon. 'Don't worry, his lordship's happy to leave it alone, says you were overwrought or some such. I've arranged for a late supper to be brought up here. I thought it best under the circumstances. Strangely enough the manager was most eager for us not to eat downstairs.' The younger man poured drinks, handing them out, eyeing Gordon speculatively. 'Don't you think you should tell me exactly what's going on?'

Liberty looked at Gordon and he read entreaty in her expression.

'Fine, you do it,' he said.

For the next twenty minutes or so Gordon was alone, despite being in the Bennetts' company. Liberty talked and Tiberius listened while he sat wrapped in misery and memories, drinking steadily. When Liberty had finished, Tiberius, white and shaking, drained what was left of his whisky and poured another. Gordon roused himself.

'We need to stay in here, together, tonight.'

Liberty frowned.

'Why?'

'We're too vulnerable alone.'

'He knows we're going to Oxford,' she said. 'We should go home.'

Gordon imagined it, the train, returning to Russell Square and then what? Trying to prove the murder without the skull? Returning secretively to Oxford and thence Foxcombe? Giving it all up? Abruptly Tiberius rose, his jaw set.

'No,' he said. 'We stay here and go on as planned.'

'That's ludicrous,' Liberty said. 'It puts us all in danger.'

'It's no worse than going home,' her brother replied. 'Lord Standish or these Watchers will follow us wherever we go and try to stop us, even harm us or Doctor McCraken.' He gripped Liberty's arm. 'Don't you understand? We'll only be truly safe if we get the skull and prove the murder with forensic medicine. Then it's over. It'll show we're no threat to these... Watcher people and they'll leave us alone.'

Liberty broke away from him.

'I can't believe you would put us all in such danger, for this! If we stop, now, it all ends. It's the safest way.'

Tiberius shook his head.

'I want this Liberty. Forensic medicine is my way out of teaching things I don't fully understand. To stop treating patients in ways I'm not sure of. Doctor McCraken can tutor both of us in any and all the intricacies of this new field. None will question me once we prove it with Amy Dudley. Don't you see, it will be the making of me, of us. We need never fear exposure again.'

She stared at her brother and slowly sat, as if her legs couldn't hold her up any more.

'You mean it, don't you?'

'Yes, I really do. Doctor McCraken agrees, I'm sure.'

Gordon looked at them, one eager and suddenly steadfast, the other frightened.

'It's no going to be easy,' he said. 'Even if we reach Amy Dudley's hiding place, there's no certainty that we can evade Lord Standish. Your sister's right, it's going to be very dangerous. Are you sure about this?'

The younger man nodded, his expression determined. Gordon looked at Liberty.

'You could go home,' he said. 'We can continue alone. I trust you to keep our pact, especially now.'

Liberty's gaze raked her brother and her expression tightened.

'No. Lord Standish might not care for you, Doctor McCraken, and even at an extreme, consider harming Tiberius to get his own ends. But he'd think more than twice about hurting me, a woman and utterly defenceless. I can keep you both safer by going with you than by going home.'

Gordon wasn't sure he agreed but knew there was little he could do to stop her. He rose and rummaged through his pack, pulling out his revolver.

'No one is to be alone, agreed?' They nodded, gazes on the gun. 'So, we all go, together, and get your belongings and the hotel bedding and we'll stay in here tonight. Doctor Bennett, did you bring any sort of weapon?'

'Nothing, except a knife.'

'You know how to shoot?'

'A little.'

'All right, that'll have to do. Hopefully Standish will no expect us to figure him out or that you'll be helping me. It'll give us some advantage and— '

A knock sounded, startling them all. They stared at each other in consternation. Liberty moved to the door.

'Who is it?'

'Your supper madam,' a woman said.

Tiberius sagged. Gordon hid the gun under the bedding, holding it there, and motioned to Liberty to open the door. A young maid wheeled a cart in and fussed with cutlery and crockery. Gordon left the gun and gestured the Bennetts aside, speaking quietly.

'We'll leave before dawn and get the mail coach to Oxford.' He looked at Liberty. 'It won't be very comfortable or as safe as the stage.'

The maid was abruptly at his elbow.

'Will there be anything else, sirs, madam?'

Irritation coloured Tiberius's tone as he dismissed her with a coin. Liberty waited until the door closed and then faced Gordon.

'If we take the mail coach, will you have your gun readily available?'

'All the way to Oxford, Miss Bennett.'

'Then I will gladly forgo comfort to put distance between us and Lord Standish.' Her expression softened. 'I think we can dispense with the formalities. I'm Liberty.'

They looked at each other. Liberty put her hand out and he shook it.

'I'm Gordon.'

Tiberius joined in. For a moment there was a lightness in Gordon. He retrieved the gun and showed Tiberius how to load and unload it while Liberty set the places for dinner.

CHAPTER FORTY-THREE

Arthur opened the door at her knock, and she slipped inside. Pulling her to him, he kissed her deeply, letting his fingers run through her hair, dislodging her cap. The young maid wriggled free and reset her uniform.

'Now, sir, you shouldn't be doing that.'

He put on a hurt expression.

'You know I can't help myself.'

She giggled and let him kiss her again. Arthur released her, noting her flushed cheeks and breathlessness with regret.

'Now tell me, have you seen the other buyer we spoke of? Did you find out anything of his intentions, or his companions?'

'Well, I set up a late supper for them in the buyer's room. They were all in there and I heard him say they're leaving at first light for Oxford, on the mail coach of all things.'

'That cad! He's determined to play me for a fool and delay me.'

'Is that why he attacked you?'

Arthur touched his bruised throat, thinking of all the things he planned to do to McCraken.

'Yes, but thanks to you I can turn the tables.' He kissed her again. 'Can you come back later?'

She shook her head.

'No, for I must be away to ma's after my shift which leaves barely an hour to finish my work.'

'It'll be quite late by then,' he said. 'Do you have far to go?'

She pinked at his concern.

'Oh no, just a short way, down along the river to Lower Caversham and I know it well.'

'That sounds all right then. But remember, my darling, you must keep all we've spoken of to yourself if I'm to succeed.'

'Of course.' She sounded indignant, then her voice lowered. 'You will come back, won't you?'

'Naturally. Have I ever let you down?'

He pressed some coins into her hand, kissing her chapped fingers, and she took her leave.

Arthur wasted little time in making his preparations. He hurried downstairs and approached the front desk.

'Good evening, Lord Standish. How may I help you?'

'I've a meeting in town early tomorrow and then I'll probably be catching the train back to London around lunchtime. I'll settle up now, rather than waste time in the morning. If that's convenient?'

'Certainly, my lord.'

Arthur duly signed the register and paid his bill, knowing if anyone asked, they would be told he was leaving Reading in the afternoon for London. Back in his room he applied the dense, false beard and moustache of the Yorkshire wool merchant, fixing the dark wig over his blonde hair. Using the warmth of his fingers he moulded a small amount of wax and altered the shape of his nose. With greasepaint and make-up his complexion became florid. The final flourish of spectacles completed his transformation. He packed his belongings, shouldered the bag and left via the window, climbing down the hotel and trusting to the thick ivy to hide him.

It took only ten minutes to arrive at the stabling where Hawk had left his mount. Oriole's information, gleaned from Liberty's correspondence with the Reading hotel, had enabled the Watchers to remain this far ahead. However, McCraken's onward destination of Oxford had needed confirmation, which Tiberius and the maid had now unwittingly provided. Arthur, having successfully sent himself as Lord Standish back to London tomorrow afternoon, could now travel unnoticed as the Yorkshire merchant. He presented himself at the yard and roused the stable boy from the hayloft.

'I've come for my horse. My man left him here two days ago.'

The lad dutifully took his details and his eyes brightened, all tiredness leaving his face.

'Oh sir, he's as lovely an animal as I've ever seen! Bit of a handful, but good as gold.'

Arthur agreed and waited while the stallion was tacked up and led out. Blackstone emerged, the lantern light gleaming on his ebony hide. The horse pranced, tossing his head and clattering his bit with his teeth, but there was no malice, only mischief in his bright eyes. Which was just as well because at seventeen hands he was big enough to cause any man trouble, never mind a stable boy. Arthur ran his hands down the stallion's legs, finding him in perfect condition. With the horse deep chested and powerfully built, Arthur knew Blackstone could run and run, and would need to tonight.

Leaving the stables, Arthur nudged Blackstone to a walk and then a fast trot, realising the night was stealing away.

Reaching a crossroads, he drew rein to get his bearings from the fingerpost. The Thames was roughing the banks ahead and to his right. He turned the stallion that way, peering about the roadside until he found a small stand of trees. He rode in and dismounted, looping the reins over a branch, placing a hand over Blackstone's nose to indicate the horse should be silent, and settled down to wait. The cold didn't bother him, but the thought of McCraken was a hard knot in his mind. He longed to ride back and slip into the man's room, bring him screaming awake with blades and fists. His imaginings kept him warm and it seemed no time had passed before a church bell tolled nine. Arthur moved to the edge of the treeline and crouched down. Some ten more minutes passed before his patience was rewarded. He saw the lantern first, bobbing along, before the figure carrying it emerged from the gloom. He tensed, breathing shallowly to minimise any mist from his mouth. The figure passed and he stepped out. Moving swiftly and silently behind her, he grabbed her head and with a brutal twist snapped the young maid's neck. She dropped like a sack of old sod and the lantern rolled in the mud. He pulled her body into the trees and retrieved the lantern. He stared at the corpse and it distorted, becoming bigger and wider. He imagined it to be McCraken. Taking his knife Arthur sliced the face to dribbling ribbons, delighting in the feel and look of the tatty skin. Afterwards, he used her coat to wipe his hands clear of blood.

Minutes later he rode from the trees with her body draped in front of him. It took mere moments to reach the river and let her slip into it, to be borne away. Arthur rode back to the crossroads and headed for the Oxford road. He spared a thought for the maid, hoping her body wouldn't be found for a goodly time. At least she wouldn't be able to talk to anyone about his interest in McCraken. In essence, he decided, it was her own fault. She should never have trusted a stranger. Reaching the Oxford road, he urged Blackstone to a mile-eating canter and left any thought of the maid behind.

He reached Oxford's principal coaching inn on the High Street just after midnight. He ascertained the mail coach from Reading was due at 8.30 the following morning and took a room. He woke the inn's stable boy and made sure Blackstone was warmed down after his hard ride, paying extra for bran mash. Consequently, he didn't get to bed until nearly one o'clock, asleep almost as soon as he lay down; he awoke refreshed at 7.30. Arthur ate a hearty breakfast in the inn's public bar while sitting reading a paper and watching the High Street from the window.

CHAPTER FORTY-FOUR

The same morning had barely greyed when Gordon and the Bennetts left the hotel in Reading. The mail coach horses stamped and tossed their heads, harnesses jingling. The lanterns on either side of the coach gave an illusion of safety. Other than the driver and mail boy, no one else was apparent in the darkness. Gordon watched their luggage being stowed amidst the post-bags and parcels. He kept turning and studying the shadows, eyeing the unlit hotel, grey and black in the dawn.

Will I see him, when he comes for me?

NO. HE'LL BE HIDDEN. QUICK AND TOO MERCIFUL FOR THE LIKES OF YOU.

I cannae let him stop me.

YOU DINNAE HAVE A CHOICE. HE'S BETTER THAN YOU.

'Gordon?'

He turned to see Liberty and Tiberius, crammed between luggage and post-bags. He climbed in and settled, legs resting on a sack of letters. The inside smelt of leather and cold. Unbidden, the memories of McDougall rose, his comforting presence and unwavering friendship. He swallowed and closed his eyes, misery tightening his throat. The lanterns were extinguished, the coach lurched, and hooves beat a tattoo as the horses put their weight to the harnesses. They moved off into the pre-dawn darkness.

Gordon fell into a waking slumber where memories were made real and painful. He relived conversations with McDougall, travelled with Iona and laughed with them both. He couldn't seem to wake properly. Each time he tried, a heaviness took his thoughts and he sank back to those gone. The shadowy Bennetts took on fearful aspects in his half-wakeful state.

THEY'RE IN LEAGUE WITH STANDISH.

I cannae believe that.

YOU DO. TIBERIUS WAS ALONE WITH HIM, AFTER YOU FOUGHT AT THE HOTEL. THEY MADE PLANS.

What plans?

TO STEAL AMY DUDLEY FOR THEMSELVES.

How do they ken where she is?

STANDISH COULD'VE FOUND FOXCOMBE.

Then why do they need me?

LURE YOU THERE. KILL YOU THERE. LEAVE YOUR BODY TO ROT THERE.

His muddled thoughts conjured Foxcombe and the soft earth would welcome him, he knew.

THEY'RE GOING TO LET STANDISH INTO THE SAFE. DESTROY SAM. DESTROY YOU AND YOUR WORK. YOU KNOW TOO MUCH OF THE WATCHERS.

He was abruptly awake, the coach rattling and bouncing like a cork in water. Liberty and Tiberius were talking and stopped to look at him.

'You've been asleep nearly an hour,' Liberty said.

Her feet were braced on a large box and Tiberius was wedged between sacks. They looked uncomfortable and tired. Liberty offered him one of the buttered rolls and a piece of lamb saved from dinner last night. They hadn't ordered breakfast, not wanting to alert anyone they were leaving before checking out. Gordon ate and swigged the food down with whisky. He felt a little better and watched the daylight under the window covering.

'We were just wondering,' Liberty said, 'how long our journey will be once we leave Oxford?'

'About an hour, maybe more,' Gordon replied.

'It'd be nice to know where we're going.'

TELL THEM. THEY'LL GET A MESSAGE BACK TO

STANDISH. FOLLOW YOU. KILL YOU.

'Now we're all facing this together,' Liberty continued. 'And trust each other.'

Despite the dim interior he knew they were watching him.

'It's no a question of trust.'

AYE, IT IS.

'Isn't it?' Liberty asked.

He took a breath and tried to think past Iona, past the fears dragging his thoughts.

'It's just that I've been afraid of the Watchers for months. I thought I was losing my mind. Now I find out they're real and so influential.' He thought of McDougall and swallowed. 'That they'll no stop to get what they want. Standish is ruthless and he cannae be the only Watcher. What if they get hold of you? Then what? They force you to talk, find Amy Dudley and it's all for naught. I cannae take the risk, I'm sorry.'

Tiberius shifted forward.

'What if they get hold of *you?* Then we'll never be able to find Amy Dudley.'

Gordon recognised the truth of this.

TELL THEM. LET THE WATCHER FIND YOU. MURDERER.

They're no helping Standish. They're helping me.

Iona sniggered. Gordon felt nauseous, whisky and lamb tasting unpleasant in his throat. He swigged more whisky and reached a decision, peppered with doubt, but knowing his options were scarce.

'All right, I'll tell you where we're going, but no exactly where I hid Amy Dudley, will that suffice?'

Brother and sister exchanged looks and Tiberius nodded. Liberty shrugged and gestured for Gordon to continue.

'We're travelling west from Oxford, to Foxcombe Manor,' he said. 'It's where Sam used to live. I've hidden Amy Dudley in the ruins of the house.'

'Open to the elements?' Tiberius sounded shocked.

'She's safe, trust me.'

'As you trust us?' Liberty's tone was mild, but he knew she was annoyed.

Hates you. Wants you deid like you deserve.

The siblings sat back as one, their faces blank in the darkness, and Gordon returned to his memories. The shades of his wife and friend seemed more substantial with every mile and he shut his eyes, wanting them close.

The mail coach reached Oxford just over two hours later. When they disembarked, they found the city awake, the streets thronged with early morning shoppers, stall holders and hawkers. Gordon stared at everyone, trying to see Standish.

In the shadows. Watching. Waiting.

He must be behind us by at least three hours.

The Watchers have been following, following.

M'be already riding to Foxcombe to wait and kill you. Murder for a murderer.

Gordon stared up at the sky wishing it would fall on him, but it remained stubbornly blue and cloud strewn, high above. He felt the Bennetts watching and moved off, down the High Street, stopping at a random stall to purchase provisions. He noted several places to hire horses, but shied away, thinking them too close to the coaching inn. If

Standish were following let him waste time searching for where they had hired from. Hefting his bags and with the Bennetts following, he walked to Turl Street. Amidst the shops and houses, Gordon found a small stable yard that hired horses and went inside.

The proprietor was a squat figure who provided them with a bay mare each for Liberty and Tiberius and a grey gelding for Gordon. They paid and completed the paperwork, all three putting the Russell Square house as their home. The proprietor squinted at the address and eyed their camping equipment.

'London folk, here for a little jaunt, are we? Boating is a good way to spend a day, if you're interested.'

Gordon stared, his mind full of Amy Dudley and Standish, unable to think of a reasonable answer. Liberty stepped forward with a smile.

'I'm here to paint watercolours, actually,' she said. 'I believe there's some wonderful scenes to be had near Godstow?'

'That there is indeed and down near Iffley too. Are the gentlemen to paint as well?'

'No, not at all, but they do love to fish. So, the camping outdoors will suit us all.'

Once they had strapped their bags to the horses, reached the High Street and mounted, Gordon reined in.

'What was that about painting and fishing?'

'Before we left London, I familiarised myself with Oxford and its surroundings,' Liberty said. 'If I'm not mistaken, Godstow is somewhat north of the city. Now, if Standish wants to follow us, he'll get no help from our conversation back there.'

'That's clever,' he admitted.

'Why thank you and there's no reason to be surprised; all indications are that I'm fairly intelligent, for a woman.'

Tiberius chuckled. Gordon felt his cheeks flush and urged his horse onto the bustling thoroughfare. They rode down St Aldates, out of Oxford, and then turned west toward Foxcombe Valley.

CHAPTER FORTY-FIVE

Arthur watched the mail coach arrive and unhurriedly folded his paper, tucking it under his arm. He rose and made his way to the doorway, loitering as if trying to light his cigar. He watched Gordon and the Bennetts disembark, dishevelled and wary. McCraken stared up and down the roadway and at passers-by. Arthur smirked, knowing he would never be recognised disguised as he was, or even seen in the gloomy doorway. The three gathered their luggage and moved off. Arthur followed, lost amongst the busy thoroughfare. He noted the camping equipment and wondered where the hunt would take him.

Arthur shadowed the three travellers down crowded Turl Street until they entered the stable yard. Discarding his paper, he hastened back to the coaching inn, settled the bill and collected Blackstone. Leading the big stallion, he crossed the High Street now thronging with carriages, riders and carts. Reaching Alfred Lane, opposite Turl Street, he halted in the lee of a building. There, even Blackstone was unobtrusive, hidden by passing foot traffic and road users. McCraken and the Bennetts emerged, mounted and stopped briefly, before turning right toward Carfax. Getting a leg up from an obliging passer-by, Arthur mounted. Turning Blackstone, he followed the three riders, finding it easy enough despite the bustling road. At Carfax they turned left down St Aldates and Arthur surmised they'd be leaving Oxford. He continued after them, closing the distance, knowing even if noticed, none of the trio would recognise him. Outside Oxford the crowds lessened, allowing McCraken and the Bennetts to push their mounts to a trot. Arthur urged Blackstone to follow and had to hold the stallion in, his stride so much longer than the hired horses. Abruptly, the three ahead slowed and swung right, out into the deserted countryside. Arthur grimaced and reined in. He bent down, as if fiddling with the stirrup leather all the while watching his quarry vanish into woodland where, even in disguise, he'd be too obvious a follower.

CHAPTER FORTY-SIX

Gordon took a circuitous route through the woods, as he had with McDougall. After a few miles he changed his mind and doubled back. The need to reach Foxcombe and retrieve Amy Dudley was an urgency driving him to push his horse and take the most direct route. Yet he felt the woods were too dense, hiding Watchers in every shadow, and to use the tracks would be too obvious for someone following. With shattered nerves he led the Bennetts on an odd journey, one that saw them skirt well-used tracks and stay on the edge of treelines. The wind rose, soughing the trees, and with it came the fresh feeling of impeding rain. High grey clouds obscured the blue sky more and more. They spoke less and less as they rode. Gordon could see the others were tired and anxious, especially Liberty, but he pushed on – the sense of urgency growing like a canker under his skin and behind his eyes. After what felt like hours, they reached the woods above Foxcombe Valley. Despite the nagging urgency Gordon drew rein and dismounted on unsteady legs. The others followed suit. Liberty looked around, holding her mare's reins with a puzzled expression.

'I can't see any ruins, is this it?'

'We're nearly there. I just wanted to stop for a moment.'

AND LISTEN. FOR FOLLOWING, FOLLOWING WATCHERS.

Darker clouds were colouring between the trees and rain spotted his face. Birdsong became muted and the wind seemed too loud. Tiberius peered into the trees, shifting position to see better. Liberty sat on a fallen log and seemed to be listening, playing with the reins. He strained to hear, trying to sense if anyone moved or rode through the woods, coming closer, closer. Minutes passed with only the restless wind and, reassured, he remounted. The Bennetts joined him and they rode to the valley edge. Out of the sheltering trees, the air felt colder. Turning the collar on his Macintosh up, he looked back, studying the treeline. Then he led the way, past the drystone wall, to the steep path and down into Foxcombe Valley.

In the valley the woods were misted with drizzle and the wind picked up, making the ride unpleasant. He glanced back, seeing Liberty swaying in her saddle with tiredness. Tiberius was white faced and taut, as if held up by pure will. Gordon pushed on, until he could just discern the red brick chimney like a finger beckoning. He avoided his previous campsite and halted a goodly distance from the ruins, to camp amidst sheltering trees. It seemed to take a long time to set everything up, fingers slick with rain and weariness making them slow. They picketed the horses and lit a fire to lunch quickly on bacon and sausage with large chunks of bread and sweet tea. Gordon chafed at the delay but knew even he was too tired and hungry to continue without this respite.

Even if Standish follows us to Oxford, he cannae know where we are. The journey back will most likely be the danger.

WATCHERS WILL FIND YOU.

He ate quickly, determined to get to Amy Dudley and away as soon as possible, wondering how to persuade the others to travel through the unfamiliar countryside that night. While they ate wind drummed on the canvas, making a dull companion to the meal. When he finished eating Gordon shrugged back into his Macintosh and picked up a spade, rope and lanterns. Settling his hat, he set off for the hidden entrance, uncaring if the Bennetts followed or not. He was uncovering turf over the trapdoor when they reached him. Tiberius set his spade where indicated while Liberty piled the turf to the side and together they made short work of the task. When the trapdoor was finally exposed, Gordon straightened and studied the surrounding woods. Rain pattered his hat and next to him Tiberius's breathing was loud. Nothing stirred amidst the greenery and he let himself hope.

'What's down there?' Liberty asked.

'A tunnel. It goes off into the woods. Sam had it built as an escape route.'

'Is it safe?'

'It seemed to be the last time I was here.'

He bent and prised back the bolt, heaving the door open. The outrush of air was damp and fresh. He peered into the darkness, making out the walls and stairs; all seemed as he had left it. They tied a rope and dropped it down, to hold on to for safety's sake in case the steps crumbled. Gordon placed turf atop the door, holding it open.

'One of us should stay out here,' he said.

They looked at each other.

'I'll do it,' Tiberius said. 'If anything happens, I can pull you up.' He glanced at the trees. 'I'll be more use up here, should anyone happen to come.'

Gordon took the revolver from his pocket. He showed Tiberius the mechanism, the way it moved and how to fire. The younger man seemed fascinated by the gun, taking the instruction easily, handling the weapon comfortably.

'If you see Standish,' Gordon said, 'shoot him. Dinnae

talk, nor let him get near you. Just shoot him.'

Liberty looked horrified.

'You can't do that, that's murder!'

'And what do you think he'll do to us?'

She stared at him.

'I'll not let you make a killer out of my brother.'

Tiberius lifted the gun, sighting down the barrel.

'I'll aim for his legs. Man can't get far or do much damage if he's shot in the leg.'

'What if he dies anyway? Blood loss, haemorrhage or infection.'

'There's three doctors here,' Gordon said. Tiberius grunted. 'All right, two and half. We've got medical supplies, fresh food and not many options. If Standish comes and gets shot, he'd get no better care anywhere else. No that he deserves it.' He noted her tense jaw and set expression. 'We'll call it an accident if it makes you feel better, three against one.'

Liberty's hands clenched and unclenched. Rain had plastered black hair to her forehead, contrasting starkly with her white face. Gordon sensed her measure Tiberius's determination and his own impatience.

'Fine,' she said. 'Just don't kill anyone.'

Her brother grinned. Gordon lit a lantern and, taking hold of the rope, led Liberty down into the earth.

At the bottom of the steps they had to pick their way over stones and mud. Gordon lifted the lantern and the light threw the chaos into greater detail. With a sick feeling he recognised two of the six keystones, fallen from the arch leading into the tunnel to lie in the entrance surrounded by debris. His heart twisted when he shone the light up, picking out three other cracked and loose keystones, either side of the central gap.

'That doesn't look safe,' Liberty said. 'Must we go in to retrieve Amy Dudley?'

For a moment he couldn't speak such was his heaviness.

'Aye. But you're right, it's no safe.'

He lifted the lantern higher, gauging the weight of earth against the condition of the supporting arch.

'We need to prop up those left, else if it comes down, we'll be trapped. Damn it all to hell!'

The lantern swung in his grip, making crazy patterns.

'Wait,' Liberty said. 'If it's an escape route, there must be another way out, or in.'

He drew a deep breath, striving to calm his thoughts.

'Aye, but who knows what other cave-ins there are, or even if the other entrance is still useable. It could be under a tree by now.' He glared at the keystones. 'We must shore it up.'

He eased his grip on the lantern, silently cursing, and ushered Liberty to the steps.

CHAPTER FORTY-SEVEN

Arthur had been lost for nearly three hours when he reached the edge of Foxcombe Valley. From the road out of Oxford, he had managed to track the riders for nearly forty-five minutes but missed where Gordon had doubled back. Muttering promises of bloody torture he had finally turned back and picked up the trail. Now, tired and frustrated, he dismounted, unknowingly close to where the others had descended into the valley. He patted Blackstone's neck, uncaring of the mud and wetness. The stallion tossed his head and nudged Arthur, endurance undiminished. Arthur sat on the drystone wall that marked the valley edge and noticed a narrow track descending the steep side. Thinking about McCraken engineered a pinching behind his eyes and he clenched his fists, imagining squeezing the doctor's throat. Uncurling his fingers, he touched his tender neck, the longed-for death of the man still grisly in his mind. Arthur suddenly sighed, wondering if he should eat, and stared across the misted woodlands below. He stiffened, gaze drawn down into the valley and watched what seemed to be mist spiralling up from the woods in a fitful stream. He peered at it and smiled, studying the smoke patterns, gauging how far away his quarry was. With quick, practiced movements he removed his false beard and wig. When he found them, he wanted them under no illusion who he was.

CHAPTER FORTY-EIGHT

It had taken Gordon and Tiberius nearly two hours to measure and cut posts suitable to secure the arch. Slender yet tough silver birch provided the wood and while prudence suggested four posts, the circumstances decided them on two. Liberty had provided a constant stream of coffee, prepared over their small cookfire and, at Gordon's insistence, kept a tense watch on the treeline. Now, the two men knocked the posts into place while Liberty waited above. She had been given instructions on how to fire the gun if anyone approached, not to hurt, but to alert those below. In an agony of impatience and anxiety Gordon hammered the second post into place, straining to hear anything from above.

What if Standish has managed to find where we went? What if he reaches her before she can fire?

HE'LL KILL YOU ALL. TAKE AMY DUDLEY.

Tiberius eyed the supports.

'I think they'll hold for what we need.' He peered into the tunnel. 'How far in is Amy Dudley?'

Gordon looked at the younger man. Sweat had run dark rivulets down Tiberius's face and his shirt was drenched and filthy.

'One hundred and fifty steps. Then, on the left, I've scored marks to find her resting place.'

Tiberius looked startled at his precise answer, then smiled.

'Thank you for telling me.'

Gordon returned the smile and gave the wood a final tap. As prearranged, Tiberius returned to the surface and Liberty made her way down. Gordon waited, wiping his face and glancing up at the cloud-strewn sky through the trapdoor. When Liberty began her descent, he checked the lantern was filled with oil and placed it next his sealskin bag just inside the tunnel entrance. She approached, her own light swinging in the dimness and studied the posts, eyeing the keystones they supported.

'Are you sure…'

'Doctor McCraken!'

The shout echoed from above and they froze, staring at each other.

'Standish,' whispered Liberty.

'I have Doctor Bennett. I think you should come out. We don't want anything to happen to him, do we?'

'He's got the gun!'

'Shut up, Bennett. Out you come, McCraken, Miss Bennett.'

'He daren't hurt us,' whispered Liberty.

Gordon grimaced, unconvinced. She moved, heading for the steps, and he caught her wrist, shaking his head.

'He's a killer. Your social standing means naught to him, nor the fact you're a woman.'

'You don't know that!'

'He murdered a priest!'

'He's got my brother!'

She wrenched from him and started upward.

'You seem reluctant,' Standish called. 'Let me be clear.'

A shot thundered, echoing off the walls and Tiberius screamed. Liberty cried out and hurled herself upward, disappearing over the edge. Gordon raced after her, but never made it out. Liberty blocked the way, collapsed just outside the hole. She sobbed on the mud, hand outstretched to her brother. He could just see Tiberius on the ground, clutching his bloody shin, teeth gritted against the pain. Standish stood over the younger man, holding the gun to Tiberius's head and staring at Gordon.

'Ah, Doctor McCraken, how nice to see you again. Do come out and join us.' The cold gaze flicked to Liberty. 'Miss Bennett, do stop snivelling and come and tend to your brother. You're quite up to the task of doctoring, I believe.'

Her head snapped up and Standish smiled.

'Oh yes, I know lots of filthy secrets. Come along.'

She scrambled to Tiberius, murmuring words Gordon couldn't hear. Standish gestured him out with the gun, but he stayed where he was. Liberty prised Tiberius's fingers away and ripped his trousers. A ragged bullet wound wept blood.

'It's gone right through,' she said. 'I need to get him to the tent and our medical supplies. Please.'

Standish glanced down at them.

'I think not,' he said, and shot Tiberius in the head.

His body fell back and Liberty screamed, reeling away. Standish caught her arm, lifting her as if she were no more than flotsam. He half dragged her to the hole, forcing Gordon downward as he came, pushing Liberty in. She collapsed on the first steps, grey and shaking, mouthing silently, her eyes huge. Standish loomed above her.

'Don't waste your sorrow, woman. He was a dolt. Now move.'

He forced them down the steps to the tunnel entrance. Liberty seemed only vaguely aware of what was happening. Gordon tried to think, his gaze casting about for a weapon.

Do it. He'll shoot you before you reach a stone.

I dinnae care about me!

Steal Amy Dudley.

He's going to take her and kill us anyway.

'Where is Amy Dudley?' Standish said.

'I've no clue what you're talking about.'

'Oh dear. Let's see how this will play out, Gordon. May I call you Gordon? It seems fitting after all we've been through. Now, you've already been accused of murdering your wife and child. Finally, fully unhinged, you've murdered the good Doctor Bennett and his sister, committing suicide afterward. Unless you give me what I want, that is how this little scenario will be remembered.'

Gordon glanced up to the patch of daylight.

Run. He'll shoot you as you go.

Framed beneath the arch Standish pointed the gun. Gordon took a step back into the tunnel and felt the void behind him.

Nowhere to hide.

Try and run, see how far you can get before you die.

He glanced at Liberty, bleached and mindless. Standish cocked the revolver.

'Tell me where Amy Dudley is, and the locket. What have you done with that?'

'Locket?'

'This is getting tiresome.'

Standish grabbed Liberty's arm.

'If you don't tell me, I'll kill her, just like her stupid brother.'

Liberty's eyes widened in the lamplight; she half turned.

'He's not stupid.'

Standish laughed. Suddenly Liberty slapped him, striking again and again. They rocked back, thudding into a birch support, arms windmilling. The gun retort was deafening, the bullet ricocheted off the arch and Gordon cried out. With a loud crack the stones shifted, coming apart, there was a rumble and beyond the tunnel entrance, darkness fell. Abruptly the arch toppled; like water, dirt and stones poured down. Something hit Gordon's head and legs and he staggered back, coughing, engulfed by dust and dirt. Falling, everything went black.

He opened gritty eyes to darkness and the smell of soil. Everything hurt. He managed to get on all fours, choking and crawling forward. Dirt and small stones still showered down and he stopped, gasping in the clogged air and waited. When everything stopped moving, he saw daylight, sprinkled across where the arch had been. Beyond, there was a wall of soil and stone where the whole chamber had crumpled inward. Poking from the rubble Standish's head and torso were visible, crushed beneath keystones. In his fist was a clump of black hair, still attached to Liberty's scalp. Their blood splattered the stones and earth that sealed Gordon inside.

Chapter Forty-Nine

Gordon didn't know how long he sat there, sobbing and rocking in the light-specked tomb. Eventually he became numb inside but hurt all over. He felt light headed and was sick, spitting the bile out and dry retching. Gasping he held his head and pain shot through him. Touching his hair hurt and inquiring fingers met dried blood. He knew more blood welled and was trickling down his leg. He crawled to the tunnel wall and slumped there, closing his eyes, and his fingers touched something. He jerked back, gasping, fearful it was clothing or worse and his mind conjured Liberty, hand outstretched trying to reach him. He sobbed a breath, gaze catching Standish's head in the middle of the rubble. He frowned, hurting his face and tentatively touched the unknown object. Sealskin. His bag.

He tugged, grunting with effort and pain, and managed to free it, covered in soil but whole. Beneath it lay the lantern and he felt the oil that had leaked out. Opening the bag, his fingers found his Macintosh, whisky, clean shirt, matches, lantern wicks and oil. Gordon inspected the lantern with trembling fingers, finding cracks in the glass and the frame dented. The oil stopper was gone. He refilled the lantern and wedged his handkerchief into the oil hole. He stopped, panting, and tried to stay focused, then after some minutes he contrived to put a lit match to the wick and blinked in the sudden light.

Gordon ripped his trousers more to examine the cut on his calf, which proved to be deep and oozing blood. He tore his clean shirt into strips, soaking one in whisky, and rinsed the wound, hissing with pain before binding the cut with more strips. Slumped against the tunnel he swigged whisky, trying not to look at the bodies. His head pounded and he dabbed at his scalp with another soaked strip. It stung and throbbed with a harshness that made him stop. He closed his eyes, aching and pained all over, and hoped not to wake.

When he woke the only light came from his lantern. The pinpricks of daylight were gone. His head still hurt but not as much and he drank some whisky, hoping to ease it more. Lifting the lantern, he inspected his leg wound, finding the strips bloodied but dried. The light showed, beneath the dirt, the cuts and bruises peppering his arms and hands. He stared into the dark tunnel that yawned away to his left.

There must be another way out. Liberty said so. Sam built it to escape.

ARE YOU NO TIRED? YOU DESERVE THIS. DYING IN THE DARK.

He glanced at the black mass of rubble, Standish's head a smudge in its centre. Using the wall as support he managed to stand and put on the Macintosh. He shouldered his bag, picked up the lantern and, leaning against the brickwork, shuffled into the tunnel.

Minutes passed or hours. It seemed as if he had never been anywhere else.

How far have I come?

STOP. LIE DOWN HERE. DEATH WILL COME FOR YOU.

His hand hurt on the wall and his leg was burning. His

throbbing head made the lantern light beat like a golden heart and he stumbled on, nausea cramping his stomach. Abruptly he retched, whisky and bile burning his throat. He put the lantern down and wiped his mouth. Turning, he rested his head on the cool wall, holding on to the bricks with both hands. Beneath his fingers he felt scratches, score marks he knew, and stared at his hands.

Amy Dudley.

WHO CARES?

Is she safe?

WATCHERS WILL COME. SEARCHING. FIND YOUR BONES HERE.

The Watchers want her bones, no mine.

He pulled at the brick, resting his whole body against the wall as support.

AYE, AND THE LOCKET.

Safe inside the watch.

WATCH FOR THE WATCHERS.

He stopped, resting his poor, pounding head on the brickwork. He knew this was important and desperately tried to focus his woollen thoughts.

She meant the pocket watch. Watch. They were looking for the locket inside the watch. But why?

His arm ached but finally the brick came loose. Putting his fingers into the hole he touched the canvas bag, feeling the solid box where the skull rested.

Still there. Safe.

He managed to put the brick back and stumbled on.

Eternity passed. He tripped and staggered, making the lamplight swing fitfully. He lowered the lantern to see bricks scattered on the floor and upward to view the ceiling, thankfully intact. Yet onward, more stone beset the passage. Gordon picked his way through and then like a tide the bricks swelled away from him, grew massive to a mountain, barring the way. He floundered to the bottom and looked up at the hole the cave-in had made. The blackness above was pricked with stars, criss-crossed with branches, and cool air touched his skin. The tumbled mass was too high; he knew he would never be able to climb out. He sank to his knees and turned and sat, breath harsh and face wet with tears. A shadow dropped and Quile landed at his side. He gulped, hiccoughing on snot, and his fingers trailed over her sleek head. Quile croaked and hopped up his arm, settling on his shoulder, nestled into his neck. His thoughts were light, cobwebbed and downy. His leg no longer hurt, and his head seemed clear. He closed his eyes.

'Am I to die here, all alone, but for a crow?'

'You're no completely alone,' Iona said.

Gordon smiled and opened his eyes.

'True,' he replied. 'I'm never that.'

When dawn lit through the cave-in hole, Quile hopped away from Gordon's lifeless body. She half flew, half hopped up the bricks and emerged into Foxcombe Woods. She tipped her head, peering up, and then took off to fly low through the trees until they thinned and became the ruins of Foxcombe Manor. Quile flapped down and perched on the newly fallen chimney. She hopped onto the ground and then went beneath the red brick stack. Her black gaze became pinned on a shiny shirt button and she pulled at it, but Tiberius's tailor had been too good. Muttering, she crossed his soil and brick covered body and found an earthen square, free of grass and alive with insects. A worm wriggled and she stabbed it, gulping it down. Next to the square, Quile strutted onto the wood trapdoor, now hidden like Tiberius' body, in the long grass and beneath the downed chimney. She wiped her beak on its frame and took off to alight back on the freshly fallen stack, surveying the ruins and surrounding woods. Dotted amongst the trees were the shapes of other crows, cawing and shuffling in the early light. Four took off, performing acrobatics in the chill air. Quile croaked, launching up, spiralling on the wind and joined them.

EPILOGUE

May 1840

First extract from The Times.

Yesterday, what is believed to be the deserted campsite of Doctor Tiberius Bennett and his sister, Miss Liberty Bennett, was found. The siblings were last seen three weeks ago, leaving Oxford in the company of the notorious Doctor Gordon McCraken. Doctor McCraken, formerly of Edinburgh, spent time in prison last year accused of murdering his wife and unborn child. On release from prison he travelled to London against medical advice. It is believed that Doctor McCraken, having befriended the Bennett family, lured Doctor Bennett and his older sister to Oxford for a social and research trip. All three were last seen leaving the city on hired horses with the supposed intention of camping in nearby Godstow or Iffley. However, a search began when two of their horses were found wandering outside the city a few days later. It is understood that Doctor McCraken is suffering from lunacy and should not be approached by the public. Any information or sightings should be reported directly to the Oxford or London constabulary. The campsite, some ten miles or more from Oxford, reportedly shows all three horses broke their pickets and weren't stolen. One horse is still unaccounted for, although there have been sightings of the missing mare freely roaming the area with an unknown black stallion. The campsite was intact with no signs of foul play, which has led investigators to believe Doctor McCraken kidnapped the Bennett siblings for reasons as yet unclear. A reward for news leading to the safe recovery of Doctor Tiberius Bennett and Miss Liberty Bennett has been offered by Doctor Henry Fielding on behalf of his wife, Missus Verity Fielding, née Bennett.

Second extract from The Times.

The memorial service of Lord Arthur Randolph Montgomery Standish was held today at Exeter Cathedral. His father, the Duke of Exeter, revealed sorrow that his son's tragic death means that his body is unlikely to ever be recovered. Family members who saw Lord Standish fall into the sea desperately tried to save him, but he was swept away and lost. It is thought that Lord Standish joined the family pleasure cruise after unexpectedly returning home to Devon from a trip to Reading. He is survived by his brother, James, now heir to the Dukedom, and a younger sister, Ophelia.

Here ends Book Two in The Watchers trilogy.

Visit www.miaemilie.com to find out more about The Watchers trilogy and the author.

ACKNOWLEDGEMENTS

I would like thank my friends, Gilly Banfield, Ian Whitmill and Gill May for giving me their unfailing encouragement, time and invaluable help in completing this novel.

My thanks also to my friend, Christine Hammacott of The Art of Communication, whose talents have wrought another wonderful cover for my novel and whose ongoing support and advice is immeasurable.

My editor, Andrew Chapman, has, as ever, my heartfelt thanks for his keen insights, in-depth knowledge and unflagging patience.

I would also like to thank my proof-reader, Helen Kavanagh, for keeping my narrative under control. Very special thanks to my husband, parents, family and friends - without them none of this would be possible.